AFTER MY FASHION

JOHN COWPER POWYS

After My Fashion

Foreword by Francis Powys

faber and faber

This edition first published in 2008
by Faber and Faber Ltd
3 Queen Square, London WC1N 3AU

Printed by CPI Antony Rowe, Eastbourne

A CIP record for this book is available from the British Library

ISBN 978-0-571-24211-5

Foreword
by Francis Powys

John Cowper Powys had already written *Wood and Stone* and *Rodmoor* which were published by Arnold Shaw of New York. The reviews of both these early books were encouraging but the sales were infinitesimal. 1916 was no time to issue a novel in America. J.C.P. however was already thinking of a third book, one which had Sussex for a background, with nature obtruding itself less, a quieter novel, free from the influence or suggestion of any other writer – Thomas Hardy, for instance, to whom he had dedicated *Wood and Stone* and who was indeed a good friend.

During this period J.C.P. met Isadora Duncan and he speaks of her in a letter to one of his sisters.

Do you know Isadora sent me a telegram once from San Francisco to New York which said 'I am thinking of you as I dance here tonight – love Isadora.' And she danced the Marseillaise for me once in New York. That was one day when I found her reading Nietzsche's *Birthday Tragedy*. I first met her in Marian's [another sister's] shop in Washington Square. Marian told her fortune and in her mischievous way kept saying 'Why don't you two go to Spain?' She is the only one who ever gave your eldest brother – the veteran Chatangua lecturer – hundreds and hundreds of red roses, so that my little room in 12th Street was flooded with them.

There can be no doubt but that Isadora Duncan is the model from which Elise the dancer in *After my Fashion* was drawn, though she herself was born in San Francisco while Elise was born in New York.

The novel begins with the return of Richard Storm (in many ways a projection of J.C.P. himself) from Paris where he has left his mistress Elise. He has had some poetical success in the French magazines but now wishes to assess his thoughts over Elise and also visit his grandparents' grave in the village of Littlegate. He stops at the ancient town of Selshurst and walks over to Littlegate nearby. While there he meets the vicar's daughter, a beautiful girl, and also her fiancé, a war hero and painter with curious manners. Returning to Selshurst Richard finds that the girl, Nelly, has made a deep impression on him. He cannot believe that she is really in love with the painter; indeed he finds out later that she is marrying him chiefly to help her father, a naturalist, who has neglected his parish and is about to be retired by the bishop.

Intermingled with the story of Richard Storm, the dancer Elise, Nelly, her father, Robert Canyot the painter and others are many beautiful descriptions, not only of the country town of Selshurst, the village of Littlegate, the lanes, fields and downs, so reminiscent of his homes in Sussex near Lewes and at Burpham, but also the streets and buildings of New York and especially Greenwich Village where J.C.P. himself lived for so many years.

It is doubtful if any publisher's reader even looked at *After My Fashion* in those difficult days, let alone gave it his serious consideration. J.C.P. rarely re-offered a book after it had been turned down and *After My Fashion* seems no exception. His *Keats*, a critical work, he refused to alter even slightly and when sent back it was put aside and eventually lost.

J.C.P. had no real wish to become a writer. His ideal future he wrote in one of his letters was to be a famous actor living with Nelly (his favourite sister) for he says: 'She and I were alike exactly in our mental life, our aesthetic or artistic life, our emotional and our erotis life.' But it was not to be, as she died of peritonitis at the early age of thirteen. In spite of chronic ill-health he started his tours, becoming no ordinary lecturer but one who was able to enter the minds, the bodies almost, of those on whom he was speaking. He actually seemed to become his subject. His only difficulty, he himself said, was his inability to stop. 'I used to try to stop and even begin my peroration, but something, some delicate nuance, some metaphysical nicety would come sliding into my brain and I would go whirling on.'

This is what Maurice Browne the theatrical impresario had to say of him: 'Once I heard him talk on Hardy for over two hours to an audience of two thousand in a huge auditorium in the heart of Chicago's slums. Throughout those one hundred and thirty minutes there was not a sound from his listeners save an occasional roar of applause or laughter. And when he had finished speaking we rose like one person demanding more. The man was a great actor.'

The books that he had written between 'mean jumps', as his manager Arnold Shaw called his journeys from coast to coast and into Canada, were already published and when ill-health forced him to retire he went to live in Hillsdale. *A Glastonbury Romance*, probably his greatest work, *Weymouth Sands* and the *Autobiography* were among the masterpieces written during this period.

In 1934 J.C.P. returned to England, settling first in Dorset and later in North Wales where he turned out novels and philosophical works in rapid succession. Great though he undoubtedly was he remained a neglected author. Maybe, at last, through the efforts of some discerning publishers he will come into his own. He is of the same mould as Hardy, perhaps even greater; only time will tell.

Chapter 1

By the time he left the train at Selshurst, and bag and stick in hand started resolutely upon his five mile walk to the village of Littlegate where his family associations lay, Richard had succeeded in thrusting Elise Angel into temporary oblivion. He concentrated his mind, as he followed the little by-street towards the centre of the cathedral city, upon those aspects of his life which were independent of the beautiful dancer.

He had not seen England for some twenty years and the last four out of that twenty had held him captive in a small French town doing unheroic but necessary work at a certain military base. His war record, as he looked back on it now, had been neither especially noble nor especially mean. He had paid the penalty of his lack of heroic impulse by his lack of any particularly dramatic memories.

What he felt now, in regard to so many of his French friends, who were lying dead in their crowded graves, was a deep desire to justify the accident of his own escape by some really adequate contribution to the bitter-sweet cup of the world's hard-wrung wisdom.

Such a contribution in his case could only be in the form wherein he was already a tolerable adept and with a fair reputation. It must in fact be some species of what we call Literature, and his prayer to the gods was that it might prove to be poetry – poetry different altogether, and far more human and original, than the easy charming verses, with a faint fragrance of morbidity, which had so far contented him.

Such reputation as he had already won was rather of the critical than of the creative order and was mostly due to his 'appreciations' of the more modern poets of France; among whom he still numbered the only intimate friends he had, and in whose society he had almost continuously lived through a vividly crowded youth.

Though he had seen comparatively little of its real horror, the war had profoundly affected him; and one of its most noticeable effects was a sudden strange restlessness and a curious dissatisfaction with his Paris life and with his poet-friends.

They had behaved heroically in the deadly struggle, much more heroically than he had himself. And yet, now the thing was over and he was free, he found himself, for some deep reason he could only very crudely analyse, out of touch with them and out of sympathy with them. He had changed, he had most drastically changed; and they – those of them who were left alive – seemed to have become more violently, more dogmatically than ever, their old, fierce, hard, fantastic, hedonistic selves.

What he, Richard Storm, was really 'after' now, what he was in search of, what he actually wanted to express, in this new poetry he intended to write, he himself could hardly have said. But whatever it was, it was something that, even in its cloudy and embryonic fumblings after a living identity, was strong enough to break up and shatter to bits his contentment with his previous existence.

The hard, clear-cut, artificial fragilities of his French friends seemed only to fret and tease him now. A certain craving for air, for space, for large and flowing movements, for unbounded horizons, had suddenly come upon him and had ruined the peace of his days as he returned to his old haunts. He found himself weary of his old critical subtleties. Some queer unexpected stirring in his soul seemed driving him forth into a world larger and more onward-looking, if less clear cut and complete, than the one he had dwelt in contentedly for so long.

He found himself trying to visualize Russia and the exciting world-shaking experiments there; and it was as if he were gazing into some turbulent cosmic workshop where the world-gods, in heat and sweat and dust and smoke, were hammering out a new groove for the great wheel.

Elise had certainly upset his old life – the war and Elise! Those two together had taken him by the hair of his head and pulled him up by the very roots out of his old pastures.

He had run away from Paris without a single day of farewells. Never before in his life had he fled from an adventure. Well! he must not think of that any more; not any more; lest he curse himself as a cowardly fool. Ah, those eyes, those hands, that unequalled woman's body! Was it really some actual Socratic demon that had snatched him away from her and hurled him into the train for Havre just when his chances with her were at their hopefullest?

As he made his way now through the leafy purlieus of Selshurst Cathedral that tantalizing figure hovered maddeningly before him. It mingled with the green moss and with the ancient ivy of the episcopal garden wall; and it interfered with his delight in those pleasant places and with the thrill of remembering that it was here that Keats must have composed his fragmentary 'Eve of St Mark'.

It was strange that he had not a living relative in England; nor any friend beyond mere acquaintanceship. All his emotional as well as all his professional entanglements had been associated with Paris; and Paris at this moment, with the weight of memories it contained, was reduced to the dimensions of one solitary figure, dancing on an empty stage against black curtains!

His own parents had been long dead; dead years before the war; and it was only the knowledge that his father's parents – the old Benjamin and the old Susanna – lay buried at Littlegate, that had induced him in his craving for some foothold in his native land, to make his way into these Sussex fields.

He did not enter the cathedral, though he saw one of. its cool cavernous doors wide open. He felt the need of rapid movement and the need of a completer solitude.

He hesitated for a moment between two rival tea shops which faced one another across the narrow street. But there were cheerful citizens of Selshurst drinking tea in both of them, and he continued on his way. Finally he obtained a glass of milk in a tiny dairy shop in the outskirts of the town, upon the polished counter of which stood an enormous china cow and a glass full of buttercups.

Directed by a voluble signpost at the first crossroads to the north of the little city, a signpost that seemed to have room for every village on the sea-side of the Downs, he found his road speedily narrowing into a most agreeable country lane between high hedges white with hawthorn.

For two miles he followed this lane, getting constant glimpses of light-foliaged woods in front of him, of upward-sloping parklands and, above these, of the naked crest of the Downs, mistily blue through the mid-May haze.

At last, a little tired and heated by rapid walking, he climbed over a gate into a small field shadowed by oaks and put up for hay and, sinking down among buttercups and clover, he set himself to take stock of his surroundings.

The spire of the cathedral rose nobly out of the pasture lands, the vaguely outlined roofs of the city beneath it mingling with trees and hedgerows so as almost to efface themselves. The broad meadows stretched away, flat and monotonous, in one unbroken level of living greenness until they reached the edge of the sea. Storm was not high enough up yet to get a glimpse of the water. The sea's edge from where he lay was dimly marked by a sudden arrest of that flowing stream of leafiness, an arrest which took place before the natural horizon could have been reached; the sea-banks being further indicated by the isolated look of individual objects, such as windmills, gates and solitary trees, presenting that peculiar suggestion of an unbounded expanse behind them which dwellers by that particular portion of the English Channel come to know so well.

As Storm stretched himself out on the cool grass, with the constant scent of the clover in his nostrils and the far-blown gusts of bitter-sweet fragrance from the May-bushes coming and going on the light wind, he felt a deep thrill of pure delight to be once more in the land of his own people.

He found himself instinctively offering up a votive prayer to the souls of the dead, and the souls of the maimed and blighted, who had thrown their breathing, vibrating, passionate youthful bodies between the cruel engines of the invader and this fair country.

As a philosopher he was well aware of the sinister ambiguities of most patriotic moods, but something subconscious and very deep in him drove philosophy away at that moment. Whatever might be the responsibilities of rulers and governments, he felt a thrill of plain gratitude in that hour to those who had suffered so incredibly that these fields might remain as they had remained since the waves of the sea receded from the face of the land.

Philosophy might whisper that it was not the tillers of these pastures who got the good of them or who gained most from this great escape; but into *that* matter our returned wanderer had no intention of entering on this pleasant afternoon. English labourers, English farmers, English squires, English shopkeepers, English tramps, he was prepared to rejoice with them all, that they could renew their private and particular controversies in profound peace! Might the fathomless Unknown be propitious, that those who had endured so much for the sake of the future should not be altogether forgotten and betrayed by those who lived on!

The sweetness of his mid-May afternoon in these incomparable fields sank so deeply into Storm's soul that he never afterwards quite forgot that walk to Littlegate.

It returned upon him with all its strangely mingled impressions, again and again in later days; and it always returned with a kind of symbolic value.

The remaining three miles of his road were taken more leisurely. He stopped frequently to listen to the birds. He lingered over the fast fading hedge plants of the earlier spring, such as celandines and cuckoo-flowers. He clambered down a steep bank to the margin of a slimy pond to touch with his fingers the cold wet roots of the water ranunculus. He waited long for the reappearance of two swift-winged butterflies, marvellous specimens of the Red Admiral species, who floated over the hedge making love to each other.

Advancing thus slowly it was after six o'clock when he arrived at the hamlet of Littlegate and made his way to the churchyard.

Littlegate church was one of those typical smaller Sussex churches, looking as if it had been made out of the fabric of some huge barn, with the little squat erection, half-tower, half-spire, like an extinguisher upon an extinguished candle, plumped down upon its. west end.

In place of yew trees there were two tall ilexes on each side of the graveyard; and, in the field adjoining it, stood four or five enormous sycamores which added as much perhaps to the monumental dignity of the scene as did the roof of the church. It was certainly the roof of the church, high-tilted and sweeping down almost to the ground, that gave the building its character. It was covered with brilliant orange lichen, and Richard thought he had never seen so imposing a roof except upon certain great barns in the north of France.

He was surprised at the smallness of the village and found himself regretting that he had not secured a room for the night in some Selshurst inn. There was evidently no inn of any kind in the hamlet of Littlegate. There was nothing that he could see from where he stood at the church porch except a rambling old farmhouse, a row of ancient cottages facing a still more ancient-looking pond, and a small, neat, nondescript dwelling, which he assumed to be the old parsonage of the place adapted to modern ideas of cleanliness and light.

He promptly made up his mind that it was in that particular house, behind the churchyard wall, that his father had been born and had spent his childhood.

It looked a charming place now but, for all Richard knew, it might have been altered out of all recognition. It might be a completely new vicarage. He found himself without rhyme or reason suddenly prejudiced against the present incumbent of his grandfather's living, and he gazed at the top of that wall, over which a spray of red roses was waving in the wind, with something bordering upon hostility.

He moved hastily around the church, surveying it from every quarter, and then began searching among the graves for Benjamin and Susanna.

He soon found the place. The old people's headstone was still legible enough after its fifty years of Sussex rains and frosts and Richard, mechanically removing his hat, as he had got into the habit of doing among the too crowded cemeteries of Catholic France, read without any cynical afterthought the unquestioning assurance of the pious epitaph. Over his head, as he bent above the grave, the long shadow of the little squat tower fell upon the uncut grass and upon the oblong mounds new and old. Above the tower rose the golden weathervane, pointing now towards the east; and above the weathercock darted the great swifts on their clean-cutting, sharply curved wings, as they had done since the day in King Stephen's reign when the place had been consecrated.

All at once Richard Storm became aware that he was not alone. His pious vigil was being shrewdly and shamelessly observed from a sunny nook under the mossy wall between two upright tombstones. Richard hastily put on his hat and shot an angry glance at the intruder.

A rubicund, quizzical eyed young man he appeared to be, the sleeve of his right arm hanging empty, his left hand holding a paint brush. By his side was a small easel; and on the grass at his feet a cup of water and a palette. He was evidently sketching the church.

Instead of looking away when Richard frowned at him, the young man laid down his brush, threw back his head till it rested upon the surface of the wall, gave a queer little jerk with his shoulder to the stump of his missing arm, and stared at the wayfarer with a fixed and rather supercilious smile.

Confound the fellow! thought Richard. *Why the devil can't he go on with his silly picture? Does he want me to go over there and admire it?* To indicate how little interest he took in this arrogant young man's proceedings he turned sharply on his heel and entered the church. When he had carefully closed the heavy door behind him, he obeyed an irresistible impulse and shot the gigantic iron bolt, barring himself in. The coolness of the interior was quite a shock after the hot sunshine; and for a moment the place seemed dark and tomb-like.

As with regard to the outside of the building the great sloping orange-coloured roof was the dominant feature, so with regard to the interior of it what held a stranger's attention, to the exclusion of all other interest, was the ponderous Norman arch dividing the small nave from the diminutive chancel.

Apart from this arch, huge, elaborately carved, weighty with historic secrets, the rest of the church seemed meaningless and without character. The arch dwarfed the pillars, took all dignity away from the windows, and seemed to be endeavouring to draw to itself the natural human piety that would pass it by and press forward towards the simply furnished altar.

The arch seemed to be upholding the barn-like roof above it with a kind of stolid confederacy, as if between these two half-heathen things there existed a dumb conspiracy to substitute some other, earlier worship, for the one that had raised that quiet silver cross and had set in order those unlit candles.

Richard Storm vaguely recalled the fact that out of all England the land of the South Saxons was the last to be converted to Christ.

Half-oblivious to what he did and under the influence of French customs he looked about for some small observance, some slight offering of respect, that remained to be paid to the quiet souls of his dead.

Half-atheist, half-superstitious as his mind had become, among those passionately pagan and passionately medieval friends of his, it seemed to him a bad omen to leave the place his father's father had served as priest without some act of filial devotion. To kneel, to pray – anyone might do that! He felt a desire for some more objective, more symbolic act. He hesitated for a moment, leaning against the great arch. Then with a glance backwards at the bolted door and a hurried genuflexion he advanced boldly up to the altar, and, striking a match, lit the two candles on either side of the cross.

It took a little time for the two small flames to burn upwards, clear and unflickering, above their pedestals of wax, but when they were well alight, he moved away down the aisle without any further obeisance and ensconced himself in a remote seat under the tower. A single bell-rope hung down above him through a hole in the roof and a long quivering shaft of sunlight, heavy with golden motes, fell upon the floor in front of him.

Between the candles on the altar and this heathen finger of the setting sun obtruded from beyond the planet's edge, the Norman arch in the centre of the church gathered darkness round it and became itself a thing of darkness.

Richard Storm stretched his legs out in front of him, clasped his hands behind his head and sat motionless, staring at the shaft of light and at the candles.

Suddenly the light faded. The darkness about the arch moved instantly to where he sat and embraced him. The candles on the altar were no longer little pyramids of palpable colour. They became flickering points of flame. The wanderer's thoughts concentrated themselves on the old dead people from the accident of whose remote encounter – Benjamin Storm with Susanna Talbot – his own appearance in the world at all, the son of his father who was the son of *his* father, so absolutely depended!

A strange sense came over him of the continuity of the generations and their fatal sequence; and under the power of that feeling he felt the unrolling of the long scroll of his days upon earth as he had never felt it before. Things that had been of primary importance to him, vivid passions, fierce infatuations, savage quarrels, seemed now to fade into complete insignificance, even as the sunset shaft had faded, and to leave him in the presence of deeper, older, more earth-rooted things.

A craving stirred within him to find expression, expression that he and others, bewildered and chance-driven as himself, might hold to and live by, for this mysterious undertone of the earth's gathered experience, moving through generation after generation of human subconsciousness and binding the ages together.

Those little flickering candle flames at which he stared seemed a signal to him that he in his turn had to wrestle with the Figure made of darkness and the shadow of death, until he or It cried 'hold, enough!' And what he felt most clearly just then was that the secret the clue, the sign – whatever it might be – of the thing which lay hidden under the phantasmagoria of life was something that was less involved, less connected, less fatally mixed up, with the evil and the good and the sweet and the bitter, than in the pell-mell of existence one was apt to hold.

What he felt at that moment was a profound craving to put into such magical words that nothing could destroy them the idea that there was some ultimate vision of things that could be reached by humanity, from the ground of which one was saved both from fear and remorse and from the fret and the fever of this perpetual choice and rejection.

He was startled out of his meditations by a sudden unexpected creaking of woodwork somewhere in the church. At first he fancied it was just that automatic relaxing of some old bench or board which one often may hear in a hollow-echoing place where the slightest sound is distinct. It ceased as suddenly as it had come. But a second afterwards it recommenced. This time he leapt to his feet and realized what it must be. It must be the secretive steps of some light-footed person trying to descend unnoticed from the organ loft. His entrance into the building had evidently surprised and caught some organ player who being reluctant to play to an unknown auditor was endeavouring to slip out of the church unobserved.

Richard moved hurriedly up the aisle, went to the altar and blew out the two candles. Then returning to the shelter of the great chancel arch he paused and waited, in as indifferent and negligent a pose as he could assume, for the emergence of this shy prisoner.

He could not help smiling to himself rather mischievously when he remembered the enormously stiff and heavy bolt he had drawn across the door. But perhaps this embarrassed organ-player possessed the key to some other exit. He seemed to have alarmed the invisible one into petrified stillness by his expectant attitude. Evidently the idea in the prisoner's mind was that this lighter of candles would leave the church at once now that his little ceremony was concluded. It gave Richard quite a quaint and pleasing sensation to think that he had bolted himself in with a mysterious unknown who was now too shy to appear. 'It must be a girl,' he said to himself.

The footsteps became suddenly impetuous and daring. The final stages of the descent were accomplished in something resembling a precipitous rush to escape; and a slender feminine figure emerged into view. With the quickest possible glance at Richard as he stood motionless under the arch, she slipped away down the aisle. *She'll never move that bar*, he thought, remembering the violent force with which he had run it through its rusty groove.

He was quite right. She was unable to make the thing stir an inch.

He recognized that it was incumbent upon him to open it for her and he moved down the aisle feeling as if he were going to let loose a bird or a butterfly that might hurt itself by its blind beatings against the obstacle.

She heard his steps behind her and turned round. 'Allow me to do it,' he said and moved to her side. But before he had touched the bolt there came a violent rattling and shaking of the door from the outside.

With an irresistible movement of contrariness he drew back, and the girl and he stared at one another in a sort of confederacy of hesitation. Then she smiled with the frank amusement of youth at the incongruity of the situation. 'Someone wants to get in,' remarked the girl. He looked into her eyes and realized how full of mischievous amusement she had become. It was clear too that she liked the look of her unwitting captor. She suddenly became grave and moved a few paces away from the bolted door. They stared at one another with renewed interest. Then, with a quick nervous little gesture she rested her bare hand on the edge of the font. 'I saw you light those candles,' she whispered. 'I wanted you to do something.' He now found his voice. He thought to himself, *If she had said nothing about the candles it would have been better. Why must women always say something about things like that?* But aloud he said, 'I thought I was quite alone. How did you know I wanted to *do* something?'

Then she smiled at him from under her broad-brimmed hat so sweetly and so sadly that he changed his mind in a moment and was glad she had spoken. 'I knew,' she murmured. 'I knew you were thinking of the war.' He hadn't of course been thinking of the war at all; and yet, in a very profound sense, he had been. The whole thing was 'the war' and the peace after 'the war' again! Like the shooting of a shuttle or like the darting of a fish his mind moved up and down all the vistas of confusion and misery that filled the world. Something in this girl's gravity as she looked at him brought vividly to his mind many things he had forgotten. 'The war can never really end,' he found himself muttering.

His companion frowned a little, in an obvious youthful effort to say something that did not sound silly.

'Well! This is beautiful weather anyhow,' she remarked, 'and on days like this one oughtn't to think too sadly of things. It seems an insult to the happiness that is left. I mean to the happy people that are left.' And she coloured a little as if aware that her remark lacked weight.

Richard's mind once more became critical of her. *Why do women mince their words so?* he thought; *and why are they so devilishly self-conscious?*

'You're a stranger to Littlegate?' she said. 'It really is a lovely village, quite worth seeing.'

She knows I thought her a little prig just now, Richard's critical demon whispered. *How sharp they are, the minxes!*

But the girl had caught sight of his travelling-bag covered with foreign labels. 'Have you far to go tonight?' she asked, speaking with a direct almost maternal concern and in a new tone.

'I really don't know,' he muttered rather awkwardly.

'Because,' she went on, 'you strike me as the kind of person who wants looking after.'

'Do I?' he answered quietly. 'Well, perhaps I do,' he added smiling at her; but his secret thoughts ransacked that remark of hers and combed it out. *They can only be natural when they are fussing over you or being fussed over – everything else is 'showing off'.*

They were standing opposite each other now, she waiting for him to say goodbye, and he scrutinizing her with an intent concentration. Suddenly an unaccountable wave of tenderness towards all these self-conscious, secretive, evasive, fragile, tenacious beings, who were so invariably 'up to some game' and yet were so inevitably betrayed by something or other – by Nature perhaps – that was 'up' to some still deeper game with them, took possession of him and disarmed him. The curious awkwardness and embarrassment which they both seemed aware of in the presence of that bolted door became a sort of palpable 'third presence' linking them together. At that moment the door was once more violently shaken from outside.

The girl instinctively drew away from him; and an odd sense of having been caught in some humorous predicament passed in a quick wave from one to the other.

Then she smiled mischievously and gaily. 'I've half a mind *not* to open it, she whispered.' 'How silly of him to make that noise!' Richard laid his hand on the bolt but did not draw it. 'Is it your brother?' he asked abruptly. The question seemed to change her in a moment from a discreet self-contained young woman into a naughty little girl.

Storm got a faint impression that she actually put out her tongue. She certainly suppressed an inclination to burst into peals of laughter.

'My brother? Good Heavens, no! It's Robert. It's Mr Canyot. He's so fussy and funny. He probably thinks you are murdering me in here. Oh, I would love to give him a tremendous fright! Do you think it would be *too* wicked if I were to scream or something?'

There was enough light left in the church for the violent protest on Richard's face at this suggestion to throw her into a fit of convulsive merriment. She shook with suppressed laughter and leaned against the font to recover her breath. She finally gasped, 'I'm not often as silly as this. It's so funny though. You don't know how funny it is. You don't know Mr Canyot!'

Richard under his breath gave Mr Canyot to the devil. 'But I think I do,' he said. 'Wasn't he sketching out there? He frightened me into the church. He didn't seem a very friendly youth.'

She had recovered herself now – 'Oh he's all right!' she said, 'with a slight annoyance in her tone at having revealed too much to a stranger. Open the door, will you, please.' And then before he could obey her she held out her hand. 'I am Nelly Moreton,' she explained gravely. 'My father's the vicar here.' Storm was pleased with her for this explanation and still more pleased by something trusting and confiding in the way she gave him her hand, the whole of her hand, not just the clammy tips of lethargic fingers. Indeed he was so pleased with this gesture of hers, and the frank look that accompanied it, that he found himself pushing back the bolt and opening the door before it occurred to him to return her courtesy by revealing to her *his* name. They were met on the threshold of the porch by the indignant Mr Canyot. 'It's too bad of you to give a person such shocks,' he began severely. Then he looked Richard up and down. 'Excuse me, sir,' he said, 'but how was I to know that you knew – ah! – the ropes, as one might say.' He paused again as if to emphasize his displeasure. 'I mean Miss Moreton,' he added sternly.

'Really Mr Canyot,' protested the lady, 'you mustn't mean me when you talk about "ropes". This gentleman hadn't till a moment ago the least notion who I was.' She glanced whimsically at Storm. 'I don't know *your* name yet – this is Mr Robert Canyot, our Sussex Painter.'

Richard muttered the syllable 'Storm' and bowed to the young man. 'I must be making my way back to Selshurst, I expect, if I am to find a room. I had a vague notion that there might be an inn here. That's why I brought this with me.' He indicated his bag.

'Oh I'm sure you'll find a room all right – in Selshurst,' Mr Canyot earnestly remarked. 'There's the White Hart and the Blue Pig and the King George and the George and Dragon. The one I'd try first, though, is the Richmond Arms. But it would be well to get in before eight, anyhow; or you might have difficulty about your dinner.' Saying this, Mr Canyot considerately pulled out his watch.

'What *is* the time?' inquired the vicar's daughter putting her hand on the artist's wrist and looking at the watch he had produced. 'Why it's twenty minutes to nine! Father must be awfully late or he'd have come to fetch me. I'm afraid we *must* say goodbye, Mr Storm. And you too, Robert, I'm sure it's past Mrs Winsome's suppertime.' She turned quickly to the wayfarer from France. 'Mr Canyot is stopping at the farm,' she said, 'but I'm afraid there is no inn in Littlegate. So do try the Richmond Arms; and be sure you *make* them give you something decent to eat.'

Again she tendered him that frank confiding handshake. 'If you stay longer you must come and call on my father. He can tell you everything there is to be told about this part of the country.'

'I don't quite know what I am going to do,' Richard replied cautiously. 'It depends upon – many things.' He nodded to Mr Canyot and turned slowly away, not however without receiving a look from the girl's eyes which a little startled him.

What was it? he thought as he made his way slowly back towards Selshurst through the long twilight, the evening sounds and scents stirring old memories in him that drifted away over the fields and were lost too quickly. *What was it that her look meant?*

He was too far-sunken in the faint sweetness of the place and the hour to laugh at himself – he, the runaway from the world-famed dancer – for his sentimental interest in this young person. Not one sardonic leer from the deadly critic within him rose to the surface to spoil his orgy of delicate dreams. He let his mind wander at large and as it pleased over the strangeness of the quick mysterious *rapport* which had risen between them.

What was it that that parting look meant? It seemed to have something in it of a definite appeal, of a definite call for help. But the girl's life appeared serene enough, all that he had seen of it. Was there something odd about the Reverend Moreton? Was that insolent young coxcomb of an artist teasing her, persecuting her – and the father, perhaps half-crazy or a drunkard, aiding and abetting him?

He leaned over a gate and stared at the thousands of sleeping buttercups and at the white hedge parsley. What absurd nonsense it was, to turn an accident like that, a mere chance encounter, into something worthy of serious analysis! What did it matter to him if the girl *was* unhappy? He had not escaped from Elise Angel to act the Don Quixote through the villages of Sussex. Let her play her organ to stray visitors! Let her marry the great Canyot!

He pursued his road at a quicker pace and before long came to a footpath which evidently led straight into the city. There were one or two town lights already visible; and with the deepening of the twilight the great meadows which surrounded the place were already covered by a filmy sea of thin whitish mist.

Drinking in, as he made his way through the wet grass, a hundred subtle fragrances, each one of which carried his mind back to the remote past, the wanderer felt that, however England might have changed, something essential in it, something that belonged both to the earth and the race, remained unchangeable and secure. The home of one's people! There must, he began to think, be some sort of intangible emanation proceeding from that which, more than any ritual, had the power to call one's mind back to its lost rhythm, to its broken balance. Too long, he decided, had he occupied himself with questions of technique, with problems of style. The work which he would do now, the poetry he would write, should primarily concern itself with some definite vision of things that should be left to evoke its own method of expression, its own music, in accordance with the intensity of its accumulative purpose. And to some such vision of things he began to feel himself distinctly led, as the warm May night poured its magic through him.

Yes! he must bury fathoms deep, the dangerous lure of that perfect skin, 'like cruel white satin' as one of his poet friends had written of her. He must bury 'deeper than did ever plummet sound' the memory of that entrancing figure 'as of a bassarid in the woods of Thessaly'.

One thing at least, he thought to himself, as he made his way along the edge of an ancient wall covered with a tangle of early yellow roses that brushed, cool and wet, against his face and showed ghost-white in the dusk, one thing Elise Angel had done for him; she had blotted out and obliterated all his earlier complications. How faint and dim she had made them – as dim as these shadowy roses – those Mathildes and Maries of his earlier Paris life!

He shuddered with fearful relief when he thought how nearly he had come to the point of actually *marrying* La Petite Charmille because Raymond de la Tailhede told him he had treated her badly! Well! he was clear of all that now, clear and free, and he had no intention of permitting the weakness of remorse to poison the good blood of his new intention.

The streets of Selshurst were all lit up when he finally stood before the entrance of the hostelry he fancied the most. It was neither the George and Dragon nor the Richmond Arms but a quiet and clean little place, in the city's main thoroughfare, laconically entitled the Crown.

It appeared he had chosen with a wise instinct. He was allotted a charming and beautifully neat room looking out upon a well-kept kitchen garden, the scent of whose aromatic herbs floated deliciously in as soon as he opened the window.

A filmy mist, wavering and undulating as it moved up from the sea-ward meadows, rolled, like some aerial phantom river, round the old walls and the high garden trees; and through the fluctuations of this mist Richard could discern as he leaned out of his window, hushed and still in the scented night, the shadowy bulk of the cathedral and its majestic spire.

The landlady of the Crown and her buxom barmaid seemed

prepared to contendwith each other in making their visitor comfort-able; and it was not long before he was seated in the private back parlour before an admirable supper heartened by as large a quan-tity of before-the-war wine as he cared to consume.

Wine immoderately imbibed may become, as Panurge informs us, a powerful sedative to the erotic madness. But wine moderately enjoyed – and Richard was habitually temperate in these things – has a different effect. Thus it turned out that in spite of his ascetic resolutions it was difficult, when once more at his open window he smoked cigarette after cigarette into the quiet night, to keep that fatal image 'like a Bacchanal on a Grecian urn' drowned in the oblivion he had laid upon her.

She rose out of the white mists of the aromatic garden beneath him. She stretched out her arms towards him. She came nearer and nearer to the window. With a face more haggard and much older than his face had been all that day, he struggled to bury her again and to recover the new purpose of his life; but the struggle was not an easy one; and he smiled grimly to himself, as stretched in bed he inhaled the garden smells and listened to the chiming of some near-by clock tower, to think what simple prayers, for his escape from the wiles of Satan, the old Benjamin and the old Susanna would have raised at that juncture.

After all, he thought, the more complicated pattern of our modern days has not liberated us from the old accursed duality. Will the balance, the rhythm, the lovely poise of things, *never* be obtained by luckless humanity, torn and divided between the two natures?

In his case, that May night, it was the hand of sleep, not of philosophy, that closed the debate; and though the soft eyes that followed him through his dreams were the eyes of Nelly Moreton, the form that drew him towards itself through the entangling ways of a land whose mountaintops were covered with meadow flowers was not the modest form of the daughter of the Vicar of Littlegate.

Chapter 2

As he sat at breakfast in the front room of the Crown, watching, between a great bowl of cowslips and a tall vase of bluebells, the pleasant sun-bathed traffic of the main Selshurst street, it presented itself rather forcibly to his mind that he had not made the remotest kind of plan for his future. He had just run away; and that summed the whole thing up. Had he, in the treacherous way the human mind works, secretly avoided making any plans, with a subconscious hope that no plans would be necessary; but that Satan, with the lure of that skin 'softer than sleep', would draw him back again?

Well! It shouldn't draw him back! He was resolved firmly upon that. The freshness of the morning, the vase of bluebells, with two ungainly stalks of pink-campion evidently thrust in by childish hands, the pleasant rustic voices of loiterers outside the door, and all the cheerful stir of the placid town, helped him to hold tight to his renewed purpose.

He would 'dig himself in' in English soil and write such poetry as would really satisfy the stern Arbiter whose hidden purpose, whatever it was, had kept him alive while so many better men had fallen.

He had not even left an address behind in France. The lean concierge from Auvergne who looked after the rooms in the Rue de Vaugirard had orders to retain his correspondence till he sent for it.

The question immediately to be decided, then, was where should he settle so to be sure of tolerably harmonious surroundings wherein to work?

It would be quite pleasant to remain precisely where he was, ensconced at the Crown Inn, Selshurst. And yet for some secret reason he didn't feel altogether satisfied with this project. Superficially he explained to himself this reluctance, to interview the landlady at once on the matter, on grounds quite remote from the real one which lay all the while hidden in the depths of his consciousness. He explained it to himself as a scruple of economic prudence, lest the woman should persuade him into some hasty agreement which second thoughts might wish to revoke; but, in reality, lurking in that remote portion of the mind where actual decisions are made, was a sort of shadowy signpost pointing to the hamlet of Littlegate.

Moved as much by an instinctive tendency to put off such decisions as long as possible as by a traveller's natural curiosity he
spent a leisurely golden morning wandering about the streets and
passages of the old town. He wandered in and out of the cathedral.
He loitered in the cloisters. He leaned against the mossy posts of the
old iron railings behind which the smooth-cut grass of the close
showed green as a velvet altar cloth, covering the ashes of a thousand years. He listened to the cawing of rooks in the dark tops of
immense elm trees. He surveyed with delight the impenetrable
quietude, exhaling an atmosphere of refined serenity comparable to
certain passages in the English Prayer Book, of the great red-brick
Georgian houses, with their polished door-knockers and high-
walled gardens, mellow and rare like the fragrance of old wine.

Fortunate people, he thought, those aged ecclesiastics who
brooded on choice Latinity and high divinity behind those rose-
tangled windows! Theirs was a life, he supposed, in which the
sting of mortal trouble was reduced to the minimum point,
consistent with the calamity of being alive at all on this harassed
earth!

Instead of returning to his inn he lunched luxuriously in a little tea
shop close to the cathedral gates; and here, as he drank cup after
cup of beautifully made tea, and watched the indolent unhurried
people chatting together in the sunshine and going in and out of the
trim shops, he felt that there was, after all, a certain genius for sheer
contentment in the race that had its place, say what one might, in
any wise scheme of existence.

For it was not that all this material well-being was a superficial
thing. It had endured, with its exclusive neatness and trimness and
cleanliness, many strange blows and shocks from the hand of fate –
this final 'great war' only the latest of such disasters – and had
endured them cheerfully. There was a look, especially in the eyes of
the elder women, even when they were lightly chatting to each
other, that suggested that this refmed-upon maturity, like time's
own polish upon very old and very solid furniture, was not a thing
obtained without sacrifice and cost.

He had noted and relished deeply the passionate feeling for intel-
lectualized beauty, for lucid and lovely organization, in his adopted
French home, but *that* could exist – he had found often to his

wondering surprise – side by side with curious lapses from instinctive daintiness and delicacy.

Here, in this English country-town there was a meticulous cleanliness and neatness showing itself in a thousand charming ways, from the aprons of the little girls to the wheels of the farmers wagons.

And it was all so deep-rooted and instinctive, so unconscious and taken-for-granted! It was not, it seemed to him, as he drank his fifth cup of tea and nibbled his fifth 'halfpenny' bun, any sort of conscious art-impulse that had produced it in those simple, self-centred, humorously wily men and those cheerful, secretive, patient women. It was a kind of immemorial moral code, touched here and there with a faint tincture of religious unction, like the half-mechanical performance of some very old ritual.

He went out into the street in extraordinarily good spirits. The shiny-faced young woman to whom he tendered payment had looked at him with that quick indescribable look, full of innocent subtleties, with which the simplest maiden can enchant and disarm a philosopher.

He stepped into one of those small tobacconist shops that display among their glossy pipes and smoking-materials such a vast assortment of dignified walking sticks as would supply all the elderly beaux of England with the insignia of retired leisure.

Emerging, still more well-pleased from this repository of epicurism, fortified with an immense number of cigarettes and a second entrancing smile, Richard seated himself upon a comfortable bench, just within the precincts, and gave himself up to meditation.

A queer mood of languid and drowsy indifference came upon him, as the hot sun warmed his limbs and the voices of children ebbed and flowed. It seemed to him as though nothing in the world greatly mattered so long as quiet harmless people could go about their affairs, undisturbed by official arrogance and unvexed by words of command.

The very secret of English life, a thing not of politics or economics, but of the obstinate right of every Englishman to meditate upon his own sensations in reserved isolation, took possession of him and gave to the brooding voices of the doves, hidden away among the trees of the dean's garden, a symbolic significance.

By slow degrees, as he sat there, the encroaching spell of sheer physical well-being, emanating from every object within sight, covered him with a kind of pleasant cloud of leafy vegetable contentment.

He smoked and nodded. He nodded and dreamed. And over his head the rooks went by and the elm trees faintly stirred in the warm wind and a hidden clock from somewhere, with a voice that might have been the voice of generations of dead bishops, chimed the slowly moving quarters.

His relaxed and drowsed nerves, freed from the feverish tension of his Paris life, responded to some profound atavistic appeal in that soil, that air, that sun-bathed masonry, those silent tree trunks.

He dimly regretted the fierce passion of his struggles to articulate and intellectualize his life. Why should he articulate anything, or analyse anything, when it was possible to let his soul sink peacefully into the being of these old calm eternal things, until it became a portion of them and lived their life, large-flowing, placid, deep-ruminating, unruffled, content?

In the process of these thoughts, Richard's eyes found themselves negligently fixed upon a remote untraversed grass-plot, surrounded by smaller houses, lying a little back of the main cathedral close. Little by little he became aware that the stream of his meditation was flowing over some hard, resistant and hostile object that disturbed its smooth current like a sharp rock.

At last there came to him the sudden jerking consciousness that he was looking at a familiar figure seated before an easel. Yes! even at that distance the empty sleeve was visible. But what brought his mind into a different focus with a yet more violent jerk was the sight of a slim flexible figure in a thin summer dress bending over the artist's shoulder and watching every stroke of his brush.

The observing demon in Richard's brain did not fail to prod him into recording the fact that the sight of his little new acquaintance completely destroyed the drowsy trance of the preceding hour.

He got up and began walking slowly, and with all the negligence he could assume, towards the pair.

As he moved, his heart beating a little more quickly than usual, and his head turned rather ostentatiously towards the cathedral, that same mocking demon in his brain kept whispering to him the sardonic comment that the only cure for the mania for one woman was another woman. 'You are making the most of this organ maid,' whispered the voice, 'because you know well that with all your fine resolutions your heart is still in the Théâtre des Arts.'

But even below this demon voice yet another interior commentator made itself audible. This second mental imp challenged the sincerity of the first one and protested that what Richard was really trying to evade was the shameful confession that he was just simply a fickle philanderer who, while more dangerous sport was renounced, made the best of safer pleasures.

Richard himself found it difficult enough as he rather nervously 'stalked', so to speak, the 'position' of his acquaintances to give an adequate answer to either of these voices. What he actually achieved, before he greeted her, was a rapid association of this friendly child with his vaguely outlined poetic impulse.

She seemed, in the quietness of her conscious reserve and the steadiness of her look, to be in some secret 'rapport' with the vision of things towards which he was groping.

There was an unpleasant moment of embarrassed approach across that secluded grass-plot while the girl hurriedly pointed him out to her artist companion. But she came with a quick eager step to meet him and he felt sure there was no dissimulation in her unconcealed friendliness.

Robert Canyot rose to his feet, removed his hat with his left hand and sat down again.

Nelly lifted her eyebrows with an imperceptible little grimace and a faint shrug of her shoulders, as though to indicate that the hopeless *naïveté* of men passed the limit of comprehension.

'Are you interested in painting?' she said, turning to Storm with an unmistakable appeal to him to be sensible and tactful.

'He won't be interested in *my* painting,' remarked Mr Canyot, 'if he's been long in France.'

There lurked in this speech a double implication; that the French in general were crazy fanatics and that Storm in particular was a priggish dilettante primed with the latest aesthetic pose.

Having thrown out this remark Mr Canyot went on applying colour to his canvas with the sort of self-satisfied indifference with which a competent builder might regard an amateur architect.

Richard longed to give the fellow's complacency some kind of a shock; but when he looked at the picture on the easel he was startled to observe that there were real signs there of a noticeable originality. The style of the thing appealed to him. He knew enough of the studios to know that this was not ordinary work. The man was clearly no fool at his job.

'I like the way you've gone straight to the atmosphere of the place,' he found himself saying. 'It isn't the cathedral or the trees or the houses; it's something much more important. It's the *happiness* of England that you're after.'

Nelly Moreton looked as if she could have kissed him for his words. Her face lightened up as though the flesh of it had become transparent. 'Yes! that's just what I've been telling him. Look at that branch against the buttress! They seem to melt into each other. And you can actually *see* the warm air flowing round them both, caressing them both!'

They contemplated Mr Canyot's quick decisive movements in silence for a while. Then the girl laid her hand on the artist's shoulder. 'We won't disturb you any more, Robert. I'll take Mr Storm to see Canon Ireton's garden. They're all away; but I'm allowed to take anyone. He'll be pleased with it. The peonies are wonderful.'

The artist lifted his head, laid down his brush, and placed his hat beside it on the grass. Richard received from him a long scrutinizing look and was rather pleased to note that his expression became perceptibly puzzled.

The conformation of Mr Canyot's skull, covered with thick tow-like bleached hair, struck him as remarkable; but the contours of the man's face were arrogant, his mouth morose, his eyes jeering.

'Certainly, by all means. But let's have tea fairly early, so that you won't have to rush back and tire yourself out.'

The girl patted his shoulder affectionately. 'All right,' she laughed, 'we'll be here in good time. I'm not going to kidnap Mr Storm.'

Her tone apparently gave satisfaction to the painter, for he bestowed upon them an amiable nod of dismissal and resumed his work.

Miss Moreton led her companion past the west door of the cathedral, down a little avenue of limes, between nursery-maids holding gargantuan infants, and aged nondescript philosophers, the smoke of whose placid pipes ascended to heaven.

On the further side of the close she led him down a narrow brick alley, over one wall of which hung wistaria and over the other white and blue clematis.

At last they came to a little brightly painted green door which she opened with a small key taken from her purse. 'Mrs Ireton was a friend of mother's,' she said, and they passed through. 'I can pick anything I like here, as long as Mr Tip doesn't see me. They're all terribly afraid of Mr Tip. He's the dean's man really; but he works for them all since the war.'

How much of England and its incurable charm lay, for Richard, at that moment, in that insignificant sentence! The obstinate importance of personal character, or personal peculiarity; the relaxed, easy-going, unofficial casualness of the old traditional methods which lent to Mr Tip – who doubtless tyrannized mercilessly over the dean – a more carefully respected authority than was vouchsafed to any chief of police, how profoundly national it all was!

Richard could see Mr Tip among his own private roses, in his own trim villa, reading *The Times* through his spectacles to his good lady who in her day had doubtless ruled over more difficult personages than deans.

'Well! what do you think of it?' sounded the youthful voice at his side. 'Isn't it a sweet place? Do you wonder I wanted you to see it?'

Richard was indeed so overcome by the beauty of it all, by the charm of Nelly herself, by the delicious symbolic figure of Mr Tip – who fortunately was elsewhere just then – that this wonderful garden seemed to him the last drop in the cup of mortal happiness.

It was the sort of garden that one cannot conceive of as existing outside England. It was not large, and the high walls that surrounded it – for the house against which it lifted its waves of fragrant fertility was itself, it seemed, no more than a great buttressed monastic wall with massive-mullioned windows – made it look smaller than it really was.

The lawn across which the girl led her new friend was so velvet-soft to the touch and so incredibly smooth that it seemed to reject as sacrilege the idea of any sportive usage except perhaps the ancient and venerable game of bowls.

Richard thought to himself that he would feel as indignant as Mr Tip if anyone suggested playing croquet or lawn tennis here. It was hieratic grass, suitable to be trodden by the most learned of all canons, as he read his Greek Testament before Matins. It was not grass from which tennis balls should be allowed to bounce.

'How many years has it taken, do you suppose,' he asked his little friend, 'to get this lawn as smooth as this?'

'That tree,' she pointed to a tremendous cedar of Lebanon, 'is supposed to have been planted by Henry the Third. And they always planted cedars on lawns; so I suppose it was there then.'

They stepped off the grass upon a long brick path, on both sides of which was a high herbaceous border from whose carefully weeded brown earth rose in luxuriant green profusion the promise of every sort of summer perennial. Many of the plants, canterbury bells, London pride, pinks and stocks and sweet william were scarcely in bud; but 'the wealth of the globèd peonies 'was in full glory and the delphinium flowers were already appearing, some purple, some light blue, like delicately poised butterflies, on their tapering stalks of pale fresh green.

The brick path ended in a terrace at both its northern and southern extremity, and each terrace was overhung with white and red and yellow roses. On one of these terraces, under the massive stonework of the old monastic house, Nelly and her companion sat down upon a wooden bench.

Richard removed his hat; and with a charming blush of girlish self-consciousness, for which this time no critical demon in him found a mocking jibe, the girl did the same. –

Moved by a simultaneous impulse they then proceeded quite openly and without shame to survey one another from head to foot, smiling happily as they did so as if well pleased with the result of their scrutiny.

They made indeed a charming contrast as they sat together, the man's grizzled hair, swarthy unbearded face, and hawk-like profile, pedestalled in the manner of some old imperial statue against a cluster of white roses, while a neighbouring spray of heavy damask ones, deep red as a wood-god's blood, overhung the girl's fair head, fair face, and bare slender neck. She might have been, but for her English dress, some early Forentine's conception of Psyche waiting for her invisible lover.

'We seem to be making friends extremely quickly,' Nelly shyly observed, withdrawing her eyes from his face and following the sweep of the great cedar's shadow as it turned the sun-warmed grass into cool velvety blackness.

There was a faint recrudescence of the imp of criticism in him at this. Was she, after all, just an ordinary little flirt? And then some other, subtler, deeper devil reminded him that all these pathetic, frail, wilful beings were driven by the eternal necessity of things to be something of that sort, if life was to proceed. How else could anything at all, in this chaotic world, *begin to happen*?

'It was certainly fate,' he remarked stupidly, his thoughts more occupied with the general situation than with anything he actually said, 'that brought us together like this.'

'I hope,' she responded quickly, 'not the fate whose name is also Sorrow.'

Richard felt slightly annoyed with her for this. He wanted her to be receptive, silent and dreamy. He didn't want her to indulge in neat quotations from authors which he might possibly have forgotten!

'It's odd,' she continued, 'how little we know of each other except that we are getting on so well. What was it that brought you back to England?'

One of his troublesome demons prompted him to answer quick as a shot, 'The white skin of Elise Angel,' but what he said was quite different. 'I'm a writer, you know – what I suppose you might call a professional critic. What I've done so far is to write about poetry, mostly about the French. Now what I want to do is to say something for myself, something that's come into my mind lately, something that can't be said in any other way except in the form of poetry.'

Nelly looked at him with deep interest. Her instinct made her aware that he was less certain of his 'line', less confident of his power, much more receptive to influence, than was Robert Canyot. The profound feminine passion for offering 'help', any sort of 'help', to an artist, a thinker, a person with ideas, thrilled her young blood with a thrill like the answer to a caress.

'And you came to England because you thought you could express your real self better here than in a foreign country?'

He loved the eager girlish tone with which she said this; but the too familiar expression 'your real self' made him jib like a touchy horse. He seemed to remember that every woman who had ever got him into her power had used the expression 'real self' when the sharp claws came out from below the velvet pads.

'Yes,' he replied, 'I felt I must hide away from everybody. And everybody for me means France nowadays. Why are you smiling? Was that a rude thing to say? Of course I couldn't know I should meet Miss Nelly Moreton?'

It was the twinge of anger at being discovered in something approaching a *faux pas* that made him give her that little stab; but she did not hold it against him.

'And Sussex?' she inquired. 'Why Sussex?'

'Oh, that's another story,' he responded, gratified to her for letting him off, 'that's a matter of duty. I wanted to see the graves of my people who're in your churchyard. My grandfather was the Vicar of Littlegate.'

The girl jumped to her feet at this, so pleased she was. To a well-brought-up young Englishwoman such clerical ancestry was a kind of hallmark of security. It meant a social equality between them which was a decided point to the good. She felt immensely reassured. *Now*, at any rate, no one could say she had acted in an unladylike manner in making friends with a stranger.

'How silly of me!' she cried in radiant spirits. 'Of course your name is *Storm*; and there's a monument in the church to the Reverend Benjamin Storm, D.D. I see it from my pew. I'd have shown it to you if I'd known. I *will* show it to you when you come out again!'

He also had risen to his feet and they stood surveying that unequalled garden with the peculiar thrill of inter-conscious pleasure which comes at the first stage of any *rapport* between the sexes and is never quite reproduced again. It is the discovery of the fact, which the solitary soul in us can hardly believe to be really true, that another person can feel, at the same moment and under the same influence, exactly what we feel. It is the stirring of the waters by the divine Eros, before the appearance of desire, jealousy, responsibility and suspicion mar and spoil it all.

The girl's 'I *will* show it to you when you come out again' had been accepted by them both as natural and inevitable. The mocking demon in Richard seemed to have been exorcized by the spirit of a garden seven centuries old.

With a movement that was tenderly possessive in its gentleness he handed her her broad-brimmed hat and watched her thrust the long hat-pin into her soft hair. He resumed his own hat and picked up his stick as soon as she was ready, and there swept over both of them a delicious sense of intimacy as they moved away; as if the bench beneath the red and white roses had been some sort of a shrine that had initiated them into a sacred conspiracy.

Their silence was at that moment more voluble than any words. Their silence moved at their side as they moved, and whispered to them things sweet and strange, things older than that ancient garden. Life however turns only too quickly its terrible hourglass. Before they had even crossed the lawn their hour was gone.

They were near the little green door into the lane when an odious discord rose from just behind it. A cruel rustic laugh was followed by a chorus of gross merriment and a rush of stampeding footsteps. Then there was the noise of a shower of stones and then a blood-curdling hush. This hush was immediately broken by a horrible cry which made them stand for a moment as if petrified. It was the cry like that of a hurt animal and yet it was sickeningly human. It had in it something weird and unnatural, something that seemed to proceed from a level of existence obscure, tragic, dark, different and alien.

The indestructible pain which like an underground stream of poison flows round the roots of all the roses in the world had burst its barriers once more. *The war was not over.*

They flung themselves together upon the little green gate, pulled it open and plunged into the alley.

They caught sight of a group of boys fleeing helterskelter round the corner, two hulking rapscallions among them, half-boys, half-men.

Squatting on the ground, his face streaming with blood, was a wretched hydrocephalic child beating on the earth with his clenched fists and uttering a horrible wailing cry. Even at that moment the callous observer in Richard's brain noted two facts. That in one of the boy's clenched fists was a stick of dust-covered sugar candy; and that the cry he uttered when they approached him was like the scream of a frightened plover.

Nelly Moreton was on her knees in a moment by the child's side, staunching the blood with her handkerchief and lifting up his hands to see if they were hurt.

It was this movement that made the child think that she intended to take away his candy and with blind fury he struck at her heart. 'That'll do! That'll do!' cried Richard, bending down from above them and lifting the boy upon his feet The child staggered against the wall, hiding the hand that held the candy behind his back. 'He didn't mean it. He didn't hurt me. They've driven him mad, the brutes! Give me your handkerchief will you? He'll be better soon' And she put her arm tenderly around him and pressed him tightly to her, kissing his tear-stained cheek.

The blood on the child's forehead was soon staunched. The skin was only slightly scratched; but there appeared a great bruise where a stone had struck him.

'I won't take your candy away. Nice candy! Give the lady a little taste.' The great abnormal head began to droop now against her neck and long quiet sobs took the place of his former anger.

Suddenly he became quite still, leaning against her, his face buried.

'He seems all right now,' said Richard; thinking in his heart – *shall I have to get this child to his home? Shall I have to call upon the police or some terrible society? Shall I have to take him to a sweet shop? Have I displayed sufficient sympathy?*

The girl did not speak. She seemed to derive a strange pleasure from hugging this idiot to her heart and feeling his head nestle down against her in some obscure baby-instinct.

The situation was – for Richard at least – relieved by the appearance of a red-faced panting female of about forty who, with many exclamations of 'Thank you Mum! He be the trouble of my life Mum! Much obliged to you Mum!' slapped the child severely, threw his squeezed-up piece of candy over the wall and dragged him off by the hand.

'The wretch!' cried Richard Storm when the two had gone a little way. But Nelly was watching them intently.

'She's not a cruel woman,' she remarked at last. 'She's probably fonder of that child than of all her other children. Look!'

And Richard saw to his surprise that the woman had picked the idiot up in her arms. 'Listen!' murmured the girl; and a strange crooning chant made itself audible. 'She's singing to him,' she said with a queer smile.

'But she slapped him,' remarked Richard staring after them, 'and she threw his candy away.'

'You all have to be slapped sometimes,' said Nelly Moreton. 'I wouldn't have let him eat that filthy thing!'

They made their way slowly back to where they had left Mr Canyot. The girl was silent and abstracted, as if she still felt against her breast the head of the idiot.

Richard in his heart was making plans for the future. 'Is there,' he asked at last, as they came out into the open space by the cathedral, 'any least chance of finding a room in Littlegate? I believe if I settled down there I really should be able to write.'

They were passing close to the open door of the cathedral as he made this inquiry. In the distance, just where they had left him, they could see the painter still absorbed in his work.

'Let's go in here for a minute,' said Nelly. 'I want to tell you something.'

Her tone was strained and tense. Richard was completely puzzled. Nothing, after all, had passed between them of sufficient seriousness to warrant her making confessions to him or elucidating difficult situations. She was a sweet creature, but he was by no means sure that he would ever be more than mildly attracted to her. He was still a little irritated by the flippant way she had said, 'You all have to be slapped sometimes.' That remark did not harmonize, he thought, with her mood in the garden. She ought to remember that, after all, he wasn't a lad of her own age. There was a certain respect due to his – well! not grey hairs, but experience of the world!

Nelly Moreton, as she looked about for a convenient place in the great dim building, had not the remotest idea of what was going on in his mind. One of the most touching forms that a young girl's innocence takes is her ignorance of the labyrinthine vanity of men. Respect for one's father, quite a childish feeling, made one very considerate with old men. But a man in the prime of life, like her new friend – she took it for granted that she could say things to him, anything that came into her head, as she would have hesitated to say them to a younger person.

She found a suitable place at last for their colloquy, in a little altar-less side chapel surrounded by monuments to extinct Sussex worthies.

Richard was still too puzzled and startled, too engaged in frantically wondering what on earth she was going to say to him, to take much notice of the noble pillars and beautiful carved mouldings of the spacious antiquity about him.

As he sat down by her side, however, his eyes fixed themselves upon the recumbent image of a dead crusader lying with his mailed feet upon a crouching dog and his sword pressed close against his thigh. The hands of the figure were clasped in an eternal gesture of prayer and his whole pose suggested such absolute quiescence of patient expectation that it seemed as if nothing short of the final catastrophe could ever disturb him.

The girl seemed unwilling to break the silence that fell between them then, a silence not like that which had whispered to them in the garden, but a sad human silence, through which the gulf that divided their ages seemed to tick out the moments like a clock in a drowned ship.

Thoughts, swift as bits of wreckage on an inrushing tide, whirled one after another through Richard's brain; and, as they came, the demon observer within him noted them one by one.

Queer – what thoughts *can* follow one another without conscious incongruity! Her phrase 'You all have to be slapped sometimes,' associating him, Richard Storm, with a hydrocephalic idiot, jostled in his mind with those eternally lifted marble hands of the silent crusader. Had some daring maiden *slapped*, in her time, those solemn and courtly cheeks? Well! with that cross-handled sword on his armoured hip, he seemed able to lie quiet enough now, without any blush of tingling memory.

But what was he, Richard Storm, doing – *that* was the next thought that drifted by – seated here with this young girl? Vanity whispered to him that he had already made an emotional impression on her – where would that impression lead them both to, if it deepened and increased? Where did he desire it to lead them to? Hurriedly he moved out of the track of this final thought! She was a sweet child; but what was she to him? His business was with something deeper, more serious, more worthy of his age, than flirtations with little girls.

He became suddenly aware that Nelly Moreton was speaking to him.

'What I wanted to ask you, Mr Storm,' her voice caught in her throat just then, with a queer little sound like the gurgle of a night-ingale in late summer; but she made a gallant effort and continued firmly; 'was whether you think it right for a person to go on being engaged to someone when you've come to the conclusion that you're really not suited? I know you have to be good and submit to your fate when you're married,' she went on, with another little gasp in her throat, this time more like the bursting of some dry seed-pod, 'but it doesn't seem as though being engaged were the same thing as being married – except that one ought to keep one's word, I suppose, else what does one give one's word for?'

She stopped dead at that and turned, quite unexpectedly, right full upon him, searching him with anxious candid-questioning eyes.

While she was speaking Richard's demons had kept up such a clamour of caustic commentary that when she had finished he was glad enough to be able to smile nervously and mutter, 'You must give me time to think.'

The trusting candour of the look she had given him left his thoughts hopelessly confused.

They came fast, the impish suggestions – such as, 'she is angling for you'; 'she is bored with her life at Littlegate'; 'she has been driven by her father to accept that ass Canyot'; 'she's trying to excite your pity'; 'she's betraying some honest fellow's affection to the first newcomer'; 'she's infatuated with the idea of one's literary reputation' – and with it all his mind became so wretchedly en-tangled, that the long stare he proceeded to give to the crusader's tomb brought him nothing but the most obvious and simple answer.

'My dear child,' he said, turning his gaze upon the grey gloves lying so quietly in her lap while with her firm sun-warmed fingers she hugged her knees, 'in these things you must follow your own instinct. Certainly it would be very wrong to plunge into marriage with someone you had ceased to love. No one can bind love down, or command it to remain fixed, when it wants to fly away. Much more harm is done in this world by marrying unsuitable people than by breaking promises.

'Promises are things that oughtn't to be brought into these matters at all. Promises ought to be confined to business and war and material affairs. You have no right to promise away the free-dom of your heart. It's like selling your soul. Your heart is not your own to promise here or there. Your heart belongs to the Great Spirit of life which gave it you. Engagement promises are only a sort of play-acting promises. If you are religious and have taken marriage vows it's quite a different matter. That's what engagements are for – to give girls like you, who've seen little of the world, a chance of changing their minds.'

The obviousness and even *naïveté* of his eloquence, considering his own sudden interest in her, seemed to him genuinely justified. If it *were* that arrogant young painter, with his bleached mop and jeering mouth, to whom the child had promised herself, the rebuff would do him good. Richard contemplated with pleasure his receiving it. It would be a shame to tie her up with a self-satisfied rascal like that, who was probably *persona grata* with half the petticoats of Bloomsbury.

He was a little surprised at the silence with which his words were received and at the unembarrassed way she fixed him with a pondering puzzled unconvinced look.

'But if breaking your word made a person very unhappy, perhaps spoilt their life?'

'Men's lives are not spoilt as easily as all that.'

'Don't you think all human lives are very easily spoilt?'

'By themselves – not by others.'

'Don't you think we ought – sometimes – to sacrifice our personal moods to larger, more important things, to things that will go on after we are dead?'

'I don't understand you. What things do you mean?'

The girl did, this time, look away from him, down the long vista of the receding pillars and arches.

'Things of art,' she said, and then,· with heightened colour, 'and of literature of course, too.' She paused and gave a little sigh. 'Things that do something,' she added wistfully, 'to help the struggle of the beaten ones.'

Richard's demons were abominably active at that moment. He permitted them to whisper terrible things. One of them accused the girl of sickening sentimentality, another of odious priggishness, a third of a pedantic arrogance that was unpardonable.

What does a chit of a thing like that think she can do for a man's serious work? Young women with what they call 'ideals' ought to marry carpenters or bricklayers!

His mind took a long fantastic leap. *Suppose I was fool enough to cut out this precious Canyot and carry her off. How should I like her sympathy? How should I like to feel her with her eye on me, helping me to be 'my real self'? How should I like to be reminded of 'humanity's struggle' when I was in my evil mood and loathed the whole farce? How should I like to have the 'beaten ones' called to my attention just when I was, for one lucky moment, able to forget that men had more nerves than animals?* Nom de Dieu! *she makes me feel as if my whole purpose, my great secret purpose, my* very poetry, *were some thin tender fragile thing that had to be pressed to a virgin's breast – that had to be* mothered! *Bah! Let her go. Let her marry her jeering Canyot!*

The accumulated howl of all his interior demons might have gone on still longer in this manner – for his fair-haired companion had fallen into a frowning disputation with herself – if his eyes had not chanced to be arrested once more by the lifted hands of the sleeping crusader.

It happened that a shaft of the bright afternoon sun, in its flickering passage across the aisles, had fallen upon these eternally praying hands, while it left the rest of the recumbent figure in shadow. It was the merest accident, the most casual chance; yet to Richard's superstitious mind it seemed one of those omens of ambiguous decision, one of those auguries of warning, which he found himself always looking for as his life advanced; just as if he really did possess some 'tutelary genius', whose only permitted intercourse with him was through the dubious medium of such things as these.

A cloud passed across some distant window, and the light faded away; but an immense shame flooded the man's whole being, and something awoke within him that made him look at her with a changed expression.

'It is harder for me than you can believe,' she began again, raising troubled eyes to his, as if conscious of his softening. 'I can't bear to make life more difficult for another person. It's like pushing a child into the nettles instead of moving them out of the way. And I know I'm much more able to stand things going wrong than most people are. I'm awfully detached from my body, I think. It's not any credit to me. I don't seem really to mind what happens in that way.'

The poignancy of this, from a young creature at the threshold of life's deepest revelation, struck Richard, in his new receptivity, as a heartbreaking thing.

The exquisite innocent! What did she know of the ache of mortal flesh? With a virginal body like hers, 'detachment' might indeed be easy! Between faint distaste for an intimacy she had no conception of and ideal respect for 'art' and 'artists' the struggle might very well be a light one.

Richard suddenly became conscious that there really were grave possibilities of tragedy here, such as, in his preoccupation with himself, he had not focused. Suppose she were to idealize *him* as she was evidently idealizing Canyot, would it be right for him – granting he cared for her more than just enormously – to carry her off and marry her?

The 'eternally praying hands' gave him no light upon this. He was left at the mercy of the now reawakening voices of the 'eternally denying' demons in his own heart: 'Girls have to find out what life is like just as anyone else has'; 'she gets her pleasure out of these self-sacrificing movements'; 'she likes offering herself up on an altar'.

As these voices subsided, and the more normal Richard thought his own thoughts again, the temporary conclusion he came to was that it all depended upon whether she was really 'in love' or not. If she were not, it was an outrage, unjustifiable by any sophistry. If she were – well! it became quite a different matter.

One obstinate demon in him insisted, however, upon having the final word; 'girls can mechanically become "in love" with the man they marry out of respect and admiration. The erotic automatism of the system of things drives them to that,'

'I'm afraid we must go now,' said Nelly Moreton, rising with a little shiver. She wanted at that moment to relieve both her muscles and her mind by a terrific stretch and yawn, but as respectable young women do not yawn and stretch in the aisles of cathedrals she could only give a jerk to her frock and a touch to the back of her head.

They took one last comprehensive glance round the great, cool, hushed place, in which they seemed at that moment isolated from all the world, and then emerged into outer sunshine.

Robert Canyot welcomed them with quite boisterous alacrity. He was tired of painting and anxious for tea and conversation.

He packed up his things and left them in the care of a friendly lodge-keeper at the gates of the close and together they wandered down the old narrow street enjoying the epicurean pleasure of a carefully considered discussion as to where they should have tea.

They passed by several attractive places as too crowded and decided at last upon a little modest confectioner's which offered them a table in a bow window right against the street. Here they proceeded to make themselves thoroughly comfortable. The first cup and the first taste of thin bread and butter put them all into excellent spirits. Nelly, either in reaction from her troubled soliloquy, or out of some deep-buried feminine discovery, was as radiant and gay as a child; nor did the latent hostility of her companions cloud their response to her cheerfulness. They laughed and chatted and ate and drank hungrily, the men demanding boiled eggs in addition to the bread and butter, and the girl insisting upon the famous local honey.

It was not till quite the close of the meal that the smouldering antagonism between the painter and the writer began to reassert itself.

'I suppose you get quite a lot of royalties from those books of yours? I seem to remember having seen them on bookstalls in town. They're all about absinthe drinkers and cognac fiends, aren't they – with illustrations of night life in the boulevards – the sort of thing Oscar Wilde used to tell us to read?'

'They're about the literature of France,' answered Richard, keeping his temper with difficulty, 'and my Life of Verlaine is certainly illustrated; but not *all* my authors have the weaknesses you speak of. Two very interesting ones are priests.'

'They may be nuns, for all I should know,' threw out Mr Canyot. 'I daresay nuns, in France, compose literature like the rest. What puzzles me is how a sensible Englishman like yourself can waste time over such affected frippery. Come now – between ourselves – when it isn't a matter of *selling*, don't you think all this modern stuff – *vers litre* and so forth – is just tommy-rot?'

Richard was certain that he caught a direct appeal from Nelly that he should behave well under this attack. On the strength of an understanding with her he felt ready to be quite magnanimous. 'I'm not prepared to defend anything *en masse*,' he said calmly. 'But I think we're bound to take a critical interest in every new experiment.'

'Rats!' responded the other, his great corrugated youthful countenance getting red with anger as he caught a sympathetic look pass between Richard and Nelly. 'Rats! you know perfectly well that any genuine production is the result of three factors – skill, insight and inspiration. These people just flop and wallow around, and call their damned impertinence "genius". We're not by any means bound to take a critical interest in things which we know, by the smell, before we touch them, are thoroughly worthless!'

Nelly burst out laughing at this. 'Mr Storm doesn't judge literature by the smell,' she said. 'Everyone hasn't got such terrible second-sight as you have, Robert. Most of us have to read a thing before we know what it's like.'

But Mr Canyot could not be stopped. The consciousness that he was making a fool of himself drove him on.

'Experiments! You talk of experiments. What we want nowadays is *knowledge* and serious hard work.

'It's just the same with everything. I have no doubt Mr Storm is a Sinn Feiner and a pro-Bolshevik, and believes in Egypt for the Egyptians and India for the Indians. Some people are interested in nothing else but experiments; and they'll go on experimenting till everything bursts up. I tell you, what we want in these times is carefully tested first-hand knowledge – not pretty theories; and hard steady work, not ramping around being "original"!'

Nelly's social anxiety to keep the peace was rapidly breaking down now under an extreme schoolgirl longing to burst into an uncontrollable fit of giggling.

The forced smile assumed by Richard and his weary air of abysmal superiority struck her fancy as quite as comic as the excited rudeness of Canyot. She thought within herself, *these poor dears! – how they do go on!* And it suddenly struck her how complicated life is made for women by the mania men have for asserting their intellectual prejudices and losing all interest in the actual details before them. She herself was the 'actual detail' before them now, and here they were, glutting their respective mental vanities on what she knew was a perfectly irrelevant discussion, betraying that as a matter of fact they were really more *interested* in one another's pompous 'attitudes' than in any possible opinion she might profess.

She had once seen, in Arundel Park, two homed stags fighting over a deer. Those animals also seemed to forget the cause of their conflict in the sheer joy of battle.

It certainly did make things more difficult when the very persons who hated one another because one liked them both displayed so much more anxiety as to just how they impressed each other than how they impressed oneself.

That part of the business they both seemed to take for granted!

She found herself wishing that there was a third man in this tea party.

'Surely you will not deny,' she heard Richard saying when her wandering attention returned, 'that the least new ripple of a new point of view, of a new impression of things, of a new tone or rhythm in our reaction to things, has a profound psychological interest, even if, from the highest standard, it remains tentative and formless?'

'I do, I do deny it,' cried the young painter, striking the honey-pot a severe blow with the end of his knife. 'These "new ripples", as you call them, are not the real forward movement of the great tradition. *That*, when it appears, dominates us all, conservatives and modernists alike, by its universal human power. In my art you have a Cézanne or a Renoir. In yours you have a William Blake or a Paul Verlaine. You will notice that Cézanne and Renoir carry on the tradition of the subtlest of the great masters, just as the lyrics of Blake and Verlaine remind you of Shakespeare's—'

Richard's voice violently interrupted him. 'No! No! No! you traditionists are always so unfair to us. You treat us just as the Church treats its visionaries. Blake isn't in the least like Shake-speare, nor is Verlaine in the least like Villon, as you were probably going to remark. And how are you to know, may I ask, when to look for the *new* Renoirs and Verlaines if you take no interest in the experiments of the new people?'

Richard positively scowled at Nelly at that point because he caught her looking with interest at a dog fight in the street. Robert Canyot struck the honey-pot a terrific blow.

'Experiments,' he cried, 'are not achievements! When your new people work hard enough, and study the great men deeply enough, and stop putting down every confounded thing that comes into their heads, they'll force me to respect them. They'll be artists then.

Meanwhile they're just amateur triflers, like the people who fuss over them!'

Richard's face grew dark and his fingers clenched. Was this young puppy actually daring to tell him that his monographs upon René Ghil, Gustave Kahn, Jules Laforgue, Grégoire Le Roy, and so forth, were wasted labour, unworthy of a first-class intellect?

'I suppose you'd class Rémy de Gourmont among your experimenters,' he snarled sarcastically, making a naïvely unconscious movement with his hand, as if to retain the attention of Miss Moreton who had risen from her seat to watch the dogs being separated. But his antagonist was too wary to be caught. 'I know nothing of the person you speak of. No doubt from your tone I ought to, and perhaps I ought. If I ought, some day no doubt I shall; for in the end one always does come across the real achievements.'

'Perhaps that's what these "fussy amateurs" you scoff at are *for*,' flung back the older man; 'in order that these deserving ones shall not have to wait till they're dead for the honour of being appreciated by Mr Robert Canyot!'

At this point – was it with the intention of letting her new friend have the last word? – Nelly Moreton resolutely broke in. 'Sorry to change the conversation,' she said, 'but if we're to get back in time for supper we must really make a start.'

Less shamefaced than they deserved, and avoiding one another's eyes so obviously that the girl couldn't help comparing them to the two dogs who were now being dragged away by their respective masters, the men rose to their feet, and Canyot went to the little desk to pay for their meal.

They moved off together back again up the street which was now golden and mellow with the slanting sunshine.

Richard felt tempted, when the artist had secured his belongings at the close-gate, to suggest that he should accompany them some portion of their way, for the fact of his having, as he felt, put the young man into his place gave him a feeling of magnanimity.

But Nelly Moreton bade him goodbye at that point in so very definite a manner that his project was nipped in the bud. Canyot, pleased at the thought of having his friend to himself for that pleasant walk through the buttercups, shook hands with him graciously, almost apologetically. And Richard himself turned away not unpleased, since her final word to him was emphatic. 'You must come over and see my father.'

It was not till much later in the day, when recalling every incident of that afternoon, that he remembered a sharp piercing look that Canyot had turned upon him and Nelly at one moment during their conversation. *That fellow can't be easily fooled,* he thought.

Chapter 3

It was always a luxurious and pleasant moment for Nelly, when after a knock as gentle as her round knuckles could administer, the all-competent Grace brought her hot water and tea. It was delicious to lie with closed eyes, still half-wrapped in the filmy cloud of sleep, while the sweet airs floated in through the open windows, mingled with the crooning of the dove and the reedy call of the blackbird.

Generally she let Grace put down the tray and the bright-polished can, and carry off her outdoor shoes, without movement or sign. But on the morning after her day in Selshurst she sat up in bed with wide-open eyes.

'I likes to see 'ee with all that pretty hair, Miss Nelly. Mercy,'tis a shame a lovely young lady like you should have to fasten 'un up. None do know, 'cept those as sees 'ee like this and They Above, how winsome a body 'ee be grown into.'

Nelly pushed back her hair with both hands. 'Where's my ribbon?' she said. Grace stooped, picked it up from the floor, lifted the hair carefully from the slender neck and tied it back, giving it a final caress with her great hand as if it belonged to a favourite doll.

'How's Mr Moreton this morning, Grace?'

The maid's countenance became grave. 'He 'ave worked in's study since afore I was up, Miss, I do fear it; working and thinking, thinking and muttering to 'isself. Not that it's my place to sy anything, Miss Nelly; but us remembers what us *do* remember, and how 'twas like this afore 'ee wrote that letter to them great ones wot worrited 'ee so dreadful. I didn't mean like to trouble 'ee with what 'ee do know as well as I, Miss. But I 'eard the Master with my own ears telling Mr Lintot only yesterday that there 'baint no God in Heaven. 'Twas terrible to listen to 'un, strike me blind, if it weren't; for 'a did carry on so about one thing and another that Mr Lintot he up and said he couldn't listen to any more on't. 'Tweren't right nor natural that he should listen to such things, spoke by one of Master's holy profession. There, Miss Nelly, 'ee mustn't take on. What must be must be; what's writ to come'll surely come; and them as calls down Tuesday's rain on Monday's roses will never see the gates of Jerusalem.'

Saying this with a consolatory leer, as if it were a piece of the most cynical worldly wisdom, Grace picked up her mistress's shoes, still all covered with gold-dust from the walk through the butter-cups, and left the room.

Nelly jumped hastily out of bed and pulled the curtains across the open windows. She bathed and dressed rapidly today, cutting short the long leisurely peeps she was accustomed to take in inter-vals of her dressing at the familiar face of the distant Downs.

The little house they lived in had quite recently been 'done over', and as the girl ran down and entered the breakfast room she felt proud of the effect of the labour she and Grace had bestowed upon it. Everything looked so peculiarly cheerful with fresh-painted wood and whitewashed walls and clean chintz covers and curtains.

She had got rid of a drawing room altogether and she and her father had their meals in a lightly furnished south-aspected room which she used during the rest of the day as her own resort.

But the nicest room in the house was her father's study, a large airy place with a low ceiling and french windows opening on the garden.

Here her father kept his natural history collections – cabinets of birds' eggs and bureau drawers full of butterflies and moths – and here he read an endless sequence of scientific volumes.

The Vicar of Littlegate was a lean Don Quixote-looking old man with a long narrow face and melancholy blue eyes. He was very tall and his knotted fingers, as he stooped over his food, touching, the bread as if it were a botanical specimen laid out to be examined, hung from his thin arms like the fantastic hands of a withered ash tree.

On this particular morning Mr Moreton seemed to have no appetite for anything but bread, which he ate in large mouthfuls, washing it down with enormous cups of sugarless, milkless tea. He kept rising from his chair when his daughter needed anything from the sideboard, and was always putting things on her plate and encouraging her to eat, with little friendly exclamations as if she were some pet animal rather than the mistress of the house.

'Some more furniture came yesterday for that little place of Canyot's,' he remarked with a glance at the window. 'He ought to be able to move in in a day or two. It'll be nice for him after the farm. I hope Betsy-Anne's Rose will look after him all right. She'll be able to be there most of the days. She's a funny rough girl; but a good girl I daresay. She comes to the Sacrament.' And he sighed heavily.

'Yes, it'll certainly be much nicer for Robert up there than down at the farm,' responded Nelly, looking anxiously at the old man's troubled face.

'It's what he's been aiming at ever since you and he were engaged,' continued Mr Moreton. 'He's good to me, is Rob Canyot. He understands my difficulty. He agrees with me that I can't go on as I'm going on now. It was because he saw how I love this place for the sake of the plants and the birds and the insects that he first thought of taking it, I believe. It was a good kind thought of his, my dear, and I hope you'll make a good wife to him.'

Nelly's delicate transparent cheeks lost every drop of colour. 'But, dear Father, you don't mean to say that Robert wants us to be married quite soon? I thought – oh, I thought – that it wasn't to be for several years! I didn't dream that he intended *me* to live in Hill Cottage.'

The old man fidgeted a little and looked uneasy. 'Well, I ought to tell you, perhaps,' he said, 'that I did discuss things with Rob Canyot quite openly the other night. I told him frankly that if I resigned my living I should be totally without an income. He agreed with me that at my age and with my book on Sussex flora unfinished it would be wrong for me to try my hand at any other work. And so – to cut it short – he was very kind and said that of course I could live with you at the cottage. He said that his pictures had begun to sell well and that in addition to what he made that way he had a generous allowance from his mother. In fact he told me not to worry about the matter any further, but to consider it settled. He put it in such a way as to make me feel quite happy about living with you – as if my being with him, you know, and our conversations about science and the local flora and the insects and everything, were a real help to him in his work.'

As Nelly looked at her father uttering these words, the old man's fanatical head, with the furrowed forehead and the noticeable wart on the high-bridged nose, took to itself the appearance of some ancient remorseless idol upon whose mechanical decision, entirely divorced from all reason and pity, her whole future depended. Her delicately moulded white face stiffened into a rigid mask of nervous tension and little twitching wrinkles appeared between her eyebrows.

The low-voiced crooning of the doves, in the sycamore outside, teased her as something ill-timed, and the flowers on the table, picked by herself the day before, assumed the curious look which flowers have when they attend on some mortal disaster.

The more she contemplated the fatal cul-de-sac, into which an evil focusing of apparently malleable circumstances had pushed her, the more devastating the prospect looked.

The trap she had so innocently, step by step, walked into, narrowed upon her at that moment with what seemed like iron bands. She felt almost afraid of making the least movement of resistance lest the thing's remorseless teeth should close with a snap. And yet, resist she must! A way of escape in some direction there *must* be. Life couldn't intend to crush her with a stone before she had even begun to live.

'I suppose, Father,' she began, in a voice that sounded like someone else's voice, some voice of a harassed young woman in some unreal story. 'I suppose there's no chance of the bishop being willing to let you keep your work, in spite of your change of views?'

The old man looked fiercely at her. 'Haven't I told you, child? It's not our bishop. It's the authority in London. But it's not really that either. It's my own conscience and self-respect. How can I go on reading the services here when I have ceased to believe a word of it? My plain duty, as an honest man, is to resign.'

The corners of Nelly's mouth drooped piteously. Tears came into her eyes. She bit her lip. 'I don't believe it would have happened – any of it – if mother had lived.'

'Your mother would have completely understood me,' said the old man severely. 'She always did understand me. However, if you're determined to make it harder for me—'

With a brave effort she swallowed her tears and spoke more calmly. 'But, Father dear, I *know* you still believe in Christ. You couldn't *not* believe in Him and consecrate the Sacrament every morning as you do. It is only some theological difficulty you have, quite separate from what is really important. You know what the bishop said when you went to see him.'

The old man rose to his feet before her, a quavering tower of inarticulate passion. His long fingers twisted and trembled as they hung by his side. His hands jerked at the end of his long thin arms. The fleshy portion of his face seemed to draw itself tightly in, over the bony substructure, and his eyes glared as if from a cavernous pit.

'How *dare* you quote that man to me! Didn't I tell you? He treated me like a silly woman with some ridiculous mania that meant nothing. He wouldn't even *hear* what I had to say. He just talked and talked, pretty conventional nothings, and then took me into his garden and showed me his sweet-peas! And I had come to let him know, as my spiritual superior, the deepest thoughts of my soul. His sweet-peas! His episcopal sweet-peas!' and the old man sank down again into his chair, exhausted with his outburst. His face quickly changed from that queer drawn look and assumed his normal expression but Nelly noted a weary world-tired droop about him that startled her. Yes, it was clear that something must be done. His mind was troubled to its very foundations.

She moved over to his side. 'Dearest Father!' she said gently – 'I think I do understand you.' She bent down and kissed his high grizzled forehead, upon which the hair grew rough and stubbly, as one sees it in portraits of the philosopher Schopenhauer.

But after that, she left the sitting room and went out hatless into the garden, and beyond the garden into a cornfield behind the churchyard, where the early rye was already up to her waist. She walked slowly along a little path with the green rye on both sides of her, the ground at her feet tangled with red pimpernel and rose-coloured fumitory and tiny wild pansies. But she had no heart just then for these things. The very song of the skylark above her seemed to harden itself into a cruel screen of mockery, separating her from the heavens and the healing of their remote peace.

Never had her mind been so shaken from its normal quietness. She had known vaguely that her feeling for Canyot was not what she expected from 'being in love'. But like so many others before her, she had, in her ignorance of what that real feeling meant, taken the romance and the passionate idealism of her own heart and woven them around her respect, her admiration, her girlish hero-worship.

And now this sudden coming of Richard on the scene, this mysterious poet from Paris, had revealed to her the limits, the bare, hard, clear limits, of what she felt for her betrothed. It was not that she dared yet to give any name to the obscure attraction she was aware of towards the older man. It was only that his appearance upon the stage at all altered her perspective and revealed the outlines of the trap she had innocently walked into.

And the teeth of the trap, the iron clutch against which she had not yet the courage to press her weight, lest she could not move it, was this new development with regard to her father. Here was indeed a trick, a cunning device, a malevolent ambush of fate, such as she had never expected life was capable of!

It was quite clear that they couldn't be left adrift, without a roof and without a penny. Her father was of course far too old to do anything for himself, except this business with plants and insects which after all was only an old man's hobby. She supposed that in these days of women's freedom she could find something for herself. But she had no experience. She had not even done any serious 'war work'. And how could she support both herself and her father?

They had no relations to whom she could appeal, her father's eccentricity and pride having completely estranged his own connections, whereas her aunts, her dead mother's sisters, were far too poor themselves to be of any help.

Weary and sick in soul the girl turned back to the house to assist Grace in her various household tasks. One tiny faint stream of sweetness, like the up-flow of an inland spring underneath a weight of brackish water, filtered through to her troubled brain through all the bitterness. This exciting newcomer into the circle of her life, this Parisian descendant of old Dr Storm, did undoubtedly seem to want her sympathy.

She knew well enough, by an instinct as direct and sure as that by which the birds build their nests, that the man had grievous need of such as she was, and she knew by the same instinct how angrily he was reacting against his need of her.

Those cynical conclusions of dispassionate scrutiny he called his 'demons' were not by any means so hidden from her as the good man dreamed in his vain masculine aloofness that they were.

Indeed, what really attracted her to him was not the power in him but the weakness in him; or to put it quite precisely the peculiar mingling of power and weakness which made up that troubled essence he named his soul.

That was where the difference lay between him and Robert. Robert was always something to lean upon, something to look up to, something to rely upon and be sure of. But Robert never made any attempt to drag her into the circle of his deepest thoughts. He treated her tenderly but he never confided in her. To him she was a child to be protected.

This man from Paris, for all his heavier weight of years and certainly in spite of himself and to his evident annoyance, could not, it seemed, do anything else than *lay bare his deepest soul before her* – and in doing this he could not prevent himself, in spite of his immense vanity, from appealing to her maternal instinct. Her betrothed was always the strong elder brother, though his years were so near her own; whereas this man, twice her own age, began to look like that grown-up child which, once in every woman's life, becomes her most fatal attraction when, among all the other appeals, he at last takes to himself a palpable embodiment.

Nelly saw nothing more of her father till half the morning was over, and nothing of Robert Canyot. This hardly surprised her, as they had had a serious misunderstanding – if it *was* a misunderstanding – on their way home the night before; and she guessed he had gone off, to punish her, upon some long solitary excursion.

This is what he invariably did when anything clouded their intercourse; and his returns from these excursions had hitherto been marked by their happiest *rapprochements*.

It was in a strangely mingled mood that Nelly busied herself with her various domestic labours that morning. The sense of being most evilly hemmed in remained with her – a feeling as if she were an unsheared sheep pushed from behind down a narrow lane of hurdles towards the fatal jump into the sheep wash – but with it all there moved within her a new delicious thrill, vague and indistinct as the scent of an unknown flower, causing her every now and then to stop in the midst of her work and stand dreaming, seeing nothing, hearing nothing, oblivious to Grace's chatter. Grace came from the West Country and was more voluble and less civilized than the local Sussex maidens. But on this particular occasion she found her young mistress singularly *distraite*. When the morning was well advanced she left the servant to prepare their mid-day meal and went out into the garden. In an old straw hat and a still older apron she set herself to weed one of the flower borders, the one which adjoined the churchyard wall.

The wall was not a low one, but by clambering up on a little ledge created by the collapse of some ancient cement she was just able to peep over it. She found it difficult to prevent herself from repeating this manoeuvre more than once. And every time she did it she had a vague hope that she might catch sight of Richard Storm standing by his grandfather's headstone.

It was somewhere about her seventh peep – she would always henceforth associate that visionary figure with the pungent smell of ivy and its queer bitterness against her mouth – that she became aware, as she rested her chin against the tiny succulent wall plants that grew in the loose mould and moss, that her father had appeared on the scene and was doing something to her mother's grave.

Cecily Moreton had not had a particularly happy life. She had been too hard-worked. But neither had she been unhappy. And Nelly had a clear recollection of a gentle soft-eyed creature bending over her pillow. She associated her mother with the Evening Hymn of Bishop Kern, the courtier-saint of King Charles the Second, and also (such is memory!) with one rare moment of passion in which the lady had flung the big hand-bell, which stood on the hall table, full against the door through which her husband had just passed! The dent in the door, though painted over, still remained. The hand that had thrown it was less distinguishable.

What was her father doing to the grave? He seemed to be prodding at it with a trowel or spud.

She ran round to the gate and hurried anxiously to the old man's side. What he was doing was inoffensive and natural enough. He was planting a somewhat rare wild orchid, of the kind known as 'maculata', in the grass by the side of the monument. He was indeed 'botanizing' on his wife's grave; but with no intent except to do her honour.

He patted the earth down with the trowel and pressed it still more firmly round the drooping plant with his aged knuckles. He rose when his daughter approached, holding the trowel in his hand.

'Come,' he said, 'let's show them that I'm a believer in Christ, whatever I may think about that *Eidolon Vulgaris* they call God.'

He took her by the hand and led her into the church. She noticed that the other hand, the one which held the trowel, was shaking from old age.

It was not the first time he had insisted on celebrating the Anglican Mass at the noon hour.

He retired into the vestry to robe while the girl sat, sad and thoughtful, in the pew she had known since childhood. She almost expected to see him come out with the trowel still tightly clutched in his fingers; but he was quite quiet and self-possessed when he did emerge, carrying with him the sacred elements. He went through the service in English till he came to the words of consecration. These, as he always did in his solitary celebrations, he pronounced in the traditional Latin.

Nothing could surpass in reverence the passionate faith with which he then knelt down before the substance which he believed he had been permitted to transform into the actual flesh of his Redeemer.

Nelly, with her head buried in her hands, sobbed quietly and softly. Her tears were an immense relief to her. Even as she wept she felt a strange thrill of happiness rise up from some unfathomable depth. She was too feminine to fret very much with regard to the unconventionally of the thing. The rite was a mystery to her, not a doctrine; and no irregularity in its administration could lessen its power over her senses and her soul.

She rose from her knees and left the church before the service was over. She knew her father preferred her to come and go as she had a mind. In these matters he had always been singularly indulgent. She thought as she went out how curious it was that the unruly working of the human heart, its deep dark erratic plunges into the unknown, its incurable and obstinate fantasy, could be quelled and soothed as though by some simplicity of natural healing, in the presence of this ritual.

But an idea had come to her as she had knelt there, an idea that she could not help regarding as something put into her mind by what Grace always described as They Above. She would take the opportunity of Canyot's absence to walk over to West Horthing.

She ran into the house full of recovered courage and energy, changed her dress, put on her best hat, and made haste to prepare lunch.

During the meal her father was very silent, evidently brooding upon something. He had recovered his appetite however and looked more resolute and obstinate than unhappy. Nelly could not help thinking how strange it was that such a passionate act of faith in the very secret of love itself, as that service of the Mass amounted to, should leave a person just as little able to enter into the feelings of another person as before!

The old man seemed conscious of no kind of inconsistency, of no sort of betrayal of his high office. Fierce fanatical pride made him prepared to go through anything and remain as he chose to remain.

She looked shrewdly at his face across the table; and she knew that even if she said to him, 'I don't want to marry Robert,' it would not alter his purpose one jot. And yet he had only just changed a morsel of bread into the very body of the Lord! Men are queer creatures!

When the meal was over – he had taken not the least notice of her dress and hat – the old man retired to sleep for a while upon the horse-hair sofa in his own study. Nelly had never presumed to improve upon that sofa. It was all she ever dared to do, just to dust his books and shelves and cabinets.

He stretched himself out at full length, a queer and disconcerting figure of inflexible assurance, his feet, with their great square-toed boots, protruding from beneath an old shawl of his wife's. In repose his face assumed the expression of a very old peasant, worn out with labouring in the fields.

Nelly took a quick glance at him through the french window as she passed down the garden. Poor old man! If only he could analyse her heart as scrupulously as he analysed his Sussex flora!

Quietly and resolutely she opened the garden gate and set out towards the Downs. West Horthing was a village poised high above the great seigniorial park, at the point where the more luxuriant foliage of the lower slopes merges into the sheep-browsed turf of the bare upper Downs.

In less than an hour after leaving her home Nelly found herself seated at the familiar dark-oak tea table, in the dainty drawing room of her friend Mrs Shotover. The old lady was alone and in just the humour to give her whole attention to the troubles of her youthful protégée.

In earlier days, before her engagement to Robert, she had been accustomed to confide all her girlish whims, caprices, hopes and ambitions to the sympathetic ears of the mistress of Furze Lodge. But during the last six months, since she had definitely accepted Mr Canyot, her visits had become fewer and fewer. For Mrs Shotover had from the very first strongly disapproved of the engagement. Nelly had tried to dispel her prejudice. Twice or even three times she had brought Mr Canyot to see her. But it was no use. The painter had refused to be what Nelly called his 'real nice self. He had shown himself taciturn and reserved, brusque and awkward. He had refused to respond to Mrs Shotover's friendly little jests. He had even on one occasion been positively rude. And the old lady's initial prejudice against him, a thing based upon nothing more tangible than that he wasn't Altogether the gentleman', had grown into something uncommonly like hostility. The issue of it had been that Nelly had gradually dropped the habit of confiding in her old friend.

But on this occasion, long before she had satisfied her hunger on the tea-cakes and raspberry jam which Mrs Shotover produced for her especial benefit, she had poured into her ears all her troubles.

She had even, after a momentary hesitation which made the old woman want to hug her to her heart, told her the whole story of her meeting with Richard Storm.

'Number two eh?' laughed the ancient creature. 'Oh, that's nothing. Don't you worry about that, sweetheart. Why, at your age, my dear, it was number five with me. You were too quick to proclaim things. That was all. No harm done. In my time we weren't allowed to make fools of ourselves till Papa and Mamma had studied half the genealogies of the county. You young people are so hasty. On today, off tomorrow – bit like Henry the Eighth, wasn't it? You all want to have religious services performed over your least flirtations. It's the influence of that domestic immoralist Robert Browning. Never marry a man called Robert, my dear. All Roberts are descended from Robert the Devil.'

Nelly interrupted her with a laughing sigh.

'Poor old Robert!' she murmured. 'He'll be really hurt, I'm afraid.' The accumulated stirrings of revolt that betrayed her into this very definite bulletin of the state of her heart frightened her as she uttered it. She had really begun to put her weight, then, against the teeth of the trap? And it seemed as if they yielded a little. Or was it just a passing response to the perilous irresponsibility of her hostess?

'Don't you worry yourself ill over any Robert. They're none of them worth it. Nor any Richard either, for the matter of that! But you may bring number two to see me if you like. I've read something of his in the *Mercure de France*. It pleased me; if I'm not confusing him with that clever Belgian – you know who I mean?'

Nelly hadn't the least idea who she meant, but she begged earnestly to be allowed to see the article in question.

'Not I!' laughed the old woman mischievously. 'I'm not going to corrupt your mind. Does your Richard write in his native tongue as well?'

'Oh yes! He wrote that Life of – of – who was it now?' And Nelly felt a vivid pang of humiliation because at that moment, when she especially wanted to do so, she could *not* recall the Life of Someone, to which reference had been made during their silly quarrel in the tea shop. 'It was those two dogs,' she muttered, blushing.

The old woman looked at her whimsically. 'Dogs?' she cried, getting up from the table. 'You don't mean to say that number two writes Lives of Dogs? Well, that *is* interesting.' She stooped, as they both moved towards the sofa, and addressed a great complacent tabby-cat that lay curled up in the corner of it.

'Do you hear that, Tabbyskins? He writes Lives of Dogs. Perhaps if you're very nice to him and don't show your claws, but only purr, when he strokes your fur the wrong way, he will write your life – the Life of Mrs Tabbyskins Shotover, the great Sussex Thinker. You'll like to have your life written by a real poet, wouldn't you my treasure? Well, my dear– 'and turning to her young guest she pulled her affectionately down by her side and patted her on the knee'–now tell me a little more about this Mr Storm of yours. He's a gentleman, I suppose?'

Nelly smiled. "Yes, I should certainly say he is that,' she answered. 'When you don't notice that they're *not*, they generally *are*, aren't they, Granny?'

In earlier days Mrs Shotover had encouraged her to use this endearment; and it was a sign of reconciliation that she used it now.

'His grandfather was a D.D. and is buried in our churchyard,' the girl added with solemnity.

Mrs Shotover smiled. 'My dear!' she cried, 'I hope you don't think that D.D. is a mark of gentility. They used to make 'em D.D.s when they dedicated their sermons to Queen Anne. Parson Adams was a D.D. and they used to give him his meals in kitchens and places. What was your beau's grandfather's name?'

'Storm,' murmured Nelly, frowning a little. Then her face brightened. 'But it says on the tombstone that Susanna was the daughter of John Molyneux Talbot.'

Mrs Shotover chuckled. 'You've certainly got hostages for his good behaviour in your churchyard! Susanna's a good name. Though if I remember right, one of them found it difficult once to keep herself *to* herself! But Susanna Talbot is a good sound name for anybody's grandmamma. Well, my sweet child, you must bring your Stormy Petrel over here for me to scrutinize. I'll ferret him out, depend on it! I'll show him up if he's a blackguardly villain. I'll storm his defences. What did he do in the war? Did he fight? Was he in the Legion? Of course he's in love with you, my dear! Who wouldn't be? But we must be careful. We must take our time. Who knows? He may have the most obstinate little *ménage* hidden away somewhere! We mustn't have our sweet Nell made unhappy. We must go very slow. Very slow and very carefully.' And the old lady proceeded to put her caution into practice by kissing her companion as mischievously and slyly as if it were the girl's wedding morning.

Nelly replied as freely as she could to all her friend's questions. One thing, however, instinct told her to keep unrevealed; and that was the fact of Mr Richard Storm being so much older than herself.

Let her, she thought, *find* that *out after she sees how nice and young and unspoilt he is in his mind!*

It was a little later in the afternoon, while they were looking at Mrs Shotover's fine roses, that Nelly ventured upon the topic of the writer's desire to secure some quiet lodging in that neighbourhood so as to work undisturbed at some new enterprise.

The old lady laughed uproariously. 'My dear girl you *have* indeed got on! Lodgings in the neighbourhood? What next? Why in my time they used to be satisfied if they came down from town for very short weekends. You're surely not such a dear stupid as to think he'd land himself out here for the summer if there wasn't someone he was after. Of course it *may* not be you. He may have an *inamorata* in Selshurst – though that's not likely. Much more possible he's got some little French friend down at Fogmore. But don't you fool your innocent little heart into believing that bosh about his having to write some great work. They all have to write great works when they want to enjoy themselves!'

Nelly made no reply for some minutes to this tirade. Then, with her hand on the stem of a great cluster of red roses into which she was prepared to plunge her face if what she said became too embarrassing, she uttered a faint protest.

'But Granny, I can't quite understand you. You don't mean that if a man were really immoral, and really had – people – like you speak of – dependent upon him – whether in Fogmore or anywhere else – that it would be right for him to marry?'

The old lady promptly defeated the girl's intention of burying her face in the rosebush after this outbreak, by pulling her back into the path. 'Little goose!' she cried with severe emphasis. 'Get this into your pretty head. There are no such things as moral men in these days – except such dear stick-in-the-muds as neither you nor I could stand for a fortnight! Well! perhaps that's going a little far, considering that my dear old George was faithful to me for forty years. But you would probably have been bored with George. What you girls have to do is to draw the line between honest naughtiness and sheer ill-bred blackguardism. If you're looking for a Sir Galahad, my dear baby, you'd better give up the thought of marrying anybody. What you have to do is to choose some well-bred gentleman who knows the world and make him fall in love with you.

He'll deal with his past life for himself. That'll be *his* affair – *your* affair will be to keep him interested and to bear him children. Men with any sensitiveness are faithful to their children, even if they're not faithful to their wives. The sooner you get over this Sir Galahad business the sooner you'll be a sensible little girl.

'It's a choice between boredom, my sweet, and uncertainty. If the fellow's a gentleman and not a fool, you'll never have anything worse than uncertainty. And the woman who can't live with uncertainty had better go into a nunnery or die an old maid. The wives who go about looking, as they say, "unhappy" are either selfish creatures who're as bad as the men they condemn, in their fussiness over their, precious little selves, or they are unlucky innocents who've never had any Granny to tell them what this world is like. Don't look so wild and scared, child. Things aren't as bad as all that. If your Stormy Petrel has had his little pleasures, as no doubt he has, it's quite likely that he'll make a most quiet companion. The worst ones often do. For my part I'd sooner see you married to a man of the world – that's to say if he were a gentleman – than to some hot-headed boy who'd clear off bag and baggage directly he got tired of you and found some other scatter-brain.'

It was at this point that Nelly was encouraged to reveal what she had hitherto held back. 'He *is* a lot older than me, Granny. His hair is just a little tiny bit grey, at the sides!'

The old woman patted her on the back and chuckled mischievously. 'It'll soon be grey at the top as well,' she threw out, 'if you're as naïve with him as you've been sometimes with me.'

She escorted her visitor as far as the end of the drive, between the old beeches.

'Old Nancy there,' she said, pointing to a little cottage that stood just at the corner where the drive left the road, 'takes lodgers sometimes. But no hurry, my dear, no hurry. Bring him up to see me as soon as you like. And don't let your thoughts run too quickly ahead!' This final word seemed to her advisable, considering the radiant expression that came into Nelly's face when she mentioned the possibility of Nancy's cottage.

'Oh youth! youth!' sighed the old lady as she returned alone to her house, 'but I always knew she was never properly in love with that ruffian Canyot. I wonder if number two does care at all? Oh youth! Oh youth!'

Chapter 4

At the very moment when, in the house of his enemy, his betrothed was drinking tea, the 'ruffian Canyot', as that same enemy had styled him, was seated with his sketchbook on the bank of an old moat-like pond only five or six miles away.

This pond fronted a ruined priory now converted into a farmhouse and was a place of rare imaginative possibilities.

By his side stood a child of about eleven, ugly and untidy, but with large intelligent eyes, eyes that surveyed the young man's face with intent concentrated sympathy.

'We're friends, eh?' said Robert Canyot.

The little girl nodded furiously and frowned a little.

'And you can't tease me and order me about, as most friends do, because you can't speak, eh, Sally-Maria?' Once more the child nodded.

'Because, you know, I found out last night that a grown-up person who I thought loved me best of all didn't really and truly love me; not in her deep-down heart; not as you will love, I hope, someone some day, Sally-Maria.'

The child made a quick sudden movement with her hands as if in protest. Then she stooped down and kissed his sleeve. Canyot patted her gently on the head. 'Yes, when they're grown up they're not faithful and true like you kiddy. Better let them go. Don't you think so, Sally-Maria? No use trying to hold them when they want to go.' He continued for a while sketching in silence, the child watching every movement of his pencil in fascinated absorption. 'How many times have I been here, Sally-Maria?'

The little girl smiled at him at last and held up four fingers. 'As many as that? You've watched with me four times – four long afternoons; and you're not tired of me yet!. You can't be a real girl, Sally-Maria. You must be a bird or a cat or a squirrel. Perhaps you're a goblin. But you can't be a girl. If you were I should be looking about for you everywhere today. I should be saying to myself, "Where's Sally-Maria gone?" And you'd be off with some nice new friend! And then if you did come back, just out of pity, you'd look at me sideways, wondering to yourself how you ever *could* have cared for such a stupid fellow. Wouldn't you, Sally-Maria?'

The dumb child shook her head violently at this and even made a strange inarticulate sound with her mouth – a sound that resembled the whistling rattle of a missel thrush.

'I tell you what I must do. I must come up here tomorrow if it's a fine day, and bring my painting things and try and paint all this. I've sketched it often enough so I ought to make a good thing out of it, don't you think so, little water rat? Ah! that's what you are, a faithful little water rat.' The scene before him was certainly one of remarkable, if somewhat melancholy, significance. Dark laurel bushes were reflected in sombre greenish-black water, and a group of scotch-firs, looking strange and exotic in that Sussex landscape, stood out against the mossy buttressed wall of the farm building. Where the buildings ended there arose another wall, composed not of masonry but of clipped ilex, solid and impenetrable, a living fortress of perennial darkness, at this time of the year lightened just a little by the sprouting of new evergreen leaves.

Between both these walls, the animate one and the inanimate one, and the edge of the pond, there grew in rank profusion a mass of succulent *umbelliferae*, their transparent stalks and greenish-white flowers looking as if they were plants of darkness and moonlight enduring for a while the unnatural rays of the sun, while they waited for the diurnal return of their native obscurity.

'That's what you are, a faithful little water rat!' repeated the painter, looking jeeringly into the great eyes of the ugly dumb child. 'And what's more, I'm afraid you won't have a very happy life unless you learn to betray and change and flatter and tell huge howling lies.'

The child made ghastly movements with its throat and palate and emitted a sound like the noise made by the corn-crake.

'What's that, Sally-Maria; what's that you're saying? You don't *want* to live a happy life unless you can be faithful and keep promises and not deceive? Go and eat hemlock roots then, little water rat, like the great Socrates, and leave this world of human beings to lie and lie and lie and be pretty and happy! Socrates wasn't a beauty, Sally-Maria. He was very very ugly. He was the ugliest person ever born. But he couldn't bear to deceive people. He spoke right out what he thought. Perhaps that's why they turned him into an owl. You hear owls at night, don't you Sally-Maria? Do you remember when we saw that great white one over there? I told you what it was then; I told you not to be afraid. Whenever you hear that old fellow now, when you lie in bed, you must say to yourself: *he's a kind one, he's an honest one, he never eats little faithful water rats. He just hoots and hoots and hoots because human beings are so false!'*

Two men came round the hedge corner at that moment and stopped by their side. 'You'm talking to our little Sal, mister, I see, same's usual,' said one of them, the simple-headed foreman of the place. 'Yes, sure enough. I most always sees 'un talkin' wi' the maidy when 'ee comes hereabouts,' remarked the other, a frail wraith of a man but heavily bearded, as though a human beard should grow upon a ghost-face and be more palpable and real than the countenance to which it belonged.

'Making a picture there I see, mister?' continued the foreman – 'I'd had the old place cleaned a bit for 'ee and polished up like if I'd a' known you was goin' to do it. 'Tis a queer old place like to live in, day in, day out. But, lord alive, we've got to live as well as we may somewheres, so's to die comfortable and as late as us may. That's what I sez to Passon Moreton, I sez.'

'Ho! Ho! Ho!' laughed the wraith-like carter, while his goat-beard wagged and shook. 'That's what a' sez – nothing short o' that. A terrible old hole, a' sez, and his Reverence had to take it from 'un.'

'Live as well, day in, day out, as the belly allows for, in these up-down times, so's to die as late as the Lord be willing,' repeated the foreman, planting his feet wide apart and leering at the universe through little screwed-up eyes. Once more the carter's frail form shook with merriment, at this daring piece of wit. That's just what 'ee sez and Passon Moreton 'eed a got to take it from 'un, 'ee 'ad, meek as a lamb.'

The young artist made as though he would resume his work, but the two men seemed disinclined for some reason to leave his side, Behind his back, as he sat hunched up upon a fallen log, they were now making mute signs to each other, while the little dumb girl stared in amazement at them.

'Tell 'im plain out,' whispered the bearded shadow to the burly confounder of parsons, 'it mayn't be as us thinks it is, anyway knowing is knowing and the written word's the written word.'

The burly man fumbled in his pocket and produced a dirty scrap of newspaper.

The preoccupied painter, glancing up at the child in front of him, caught such a look of alarm upon her face that he turned his head sharply. 'Anything the matter?' he inquired.

The foreman walked slowly round and stood in front of him, while the carter, shuffling uneasily after his superior, peered round at the hedge, the bushes, the pond and the hemlocks, as if expecting a sudden onrush of interested spectators hurrying to witness this dramatic occurrence.

'Us seed 'ee from the yard, us did, mister,' murmured the second man, giving his stammering companion a little dig in the side, 'an us thought the sooner we'd 'a told 'ee what 'twas 'as been and got itself brought to light in them newspapers, the sooner 'ee'd be acquainted with the injured party, like.'

"Tweren't I and'twern't Charley as read about this terrible thing,' murmured the lusty foreman in a tone of profound apology, evidently fearing, as some ancient slave of the house of Oedipus might once have feared, lest the bearer of evil news should himself meet with disaster.

'No! 'tweren't Mr Priddle and 'tweren't I what discovered that your mother had been runned over by a railway train. 'Twas old Miss Stone what lives over the hill 'as told us.'

Robert Canyot leapt to his feet and snatched the bit of paper out of the man's hand. It was a brief statement that a lady who gave a London address had been knocked down by a shunted track at Selshurst Station and had been carried to the hospital. Her name was given as Mrs Canyot of Maida Vale. A horrible cold shiver ran down the spine of the young man and for a moment he felt dizzy. His poor sweet darling mother! She must have wanted to pay him a surprise visit. But why? It was hardly credible that she should do such a thing at her age and with her methodical habits. It couldn't be true! He looked at the notice again, holding it with a hand that trembled. Maida Vale? There could hardly be another Mrs Canyot who lived in that district. It *must* be his mother. And yet – to come like that – without telling him. It was utterly and entirely unlike her. He stood gazing helplessly at the paper in his hand calculating remote chances.

Robert Canyot was an only son. His father had been a wine

merchant, a man of the same type as John Ruskin's father, combining shrewdness, puritanism, and a certain queer turn or twist for what he regarded as 'art'.

The little lady of Maida Vale had done all she could to give her boy everything in this mad world that youth could desire. She had let him run wild. She had sent him to school and removed him from school; sent him to Oxford and removed him from Oxford. Finally she had made over to him half of her income and let him follow the delight of his eyes and the fancies of his heart unrestrained by any responsibility. The result was that the sharp contrast, between his mother's unbounded infatuation and the rough shocks of the world that cared nothing what became of him, made out of quite sound material a sort of cynical misanthropic queer one.

It was not however a very cynical Robert who gazed now, agitated and startled, into the narrow eyes of Silas Priddle and the great watery eyes of Charley Budge.

'Hoping there's no offence, mister, in us having taken the liberty of showing 'ee that there bit 'o news. It *may* be as it's your poor dear Mother what's runned into a railway train, and it may be as 'tisn't. If 'tis, 'tis God's will. If 'tisn't I reckons 'tis somebody else's mother; but seeing how it's upset 'ee like I be afeerd it is as 'tis there writ' down.'

Saying these words the foreman of Toat Farm planted his feet firmly in the long grass, screwed up his eyes, scratched his head, and whistled a few notes of the particular call with which he was accustomed to summon his wife's ducks at the hour of sunset.

'Charley,' he remarked after a long pause, during which the young man read and re-read the bit of newspaper, 'us must be getting on with the beasts, us must.'

'Aye, aye, Mr Priddle,' agreed the other. 'Beasts must be served funeral days same as wedding days, as old Farmer Patchem used to tell us every time 'is missus 'ad a still-born. "Life is as 'tis, Charley," 'ee used to say, "and them as takes it quiet'll last longest and their children's children'll call 'em blessed."'

Having uttered these words of wisdom the two sages moved away. 'The poor lad be dazed-like,' said the foreman. 'Did 'ee mark, Charley, how 'ee squinnied with the eyes o'n, when 'ee got tellin of funerals? A reckon 'ee might o' bashed it out, 'ee did, too point, Charley, than 'ee was. Sort o' bashed it out, 'ee did, too plumb and positive. Maybe the old woman isn't broken up complete. Some of them elderly females is wonderful hard to kill; same as cats I reckon.'

Well! no use standing here, thought Canyot. *I must off to Setshurst. If it is the poor darling, I shall stay the night there. It may be nothing more than a nervous shock, after all. These papers exaggerate so. And it may not be her at all. But if it isn't, it's certainly an odd coincidence.*

He felt a small hand softly and timidly pulling at the sleeve that hung empty. Robert had lost his arm in Flanders and possessed two medals for courage in the field. He looked down and patted the child's head, ashamed of having forgotten her. The little dumb girl was making pitiful sounds with her poor mouth.

'Poor little water rat!' he murmured. 'Poor little Sally-Maria! This is a bad day for us, isn't it? But never mind! Say your prayers for your friend's Mummy. Let's hope that when we meet again all will be well.'

The child put her arms around him holding his sleeve tightly and hiding her face.

'There – there – my little one,' he said, extricating himself from her clinging arms. 'Don't worry any more about it. Run home to Auntie and be a good little kind faithful water rat. We'll see each other again. Goodbye and God bless you!' And he broke from her and started off at a run in the direction of Littlegate. *I'll just tell them where I'm going,* he said to himself, *so if I'm away for the night they won't be scared.* Even to his own heart he used the pronoun 'they', but his thoughts circled round Nelly and the sad walk he had had with her the night before. *I've go to face it,* he said to himself as he followed the pack-horse track along the lower slopes of the Downs. *If she has never really cared for me as she thought she did, I suppose I can't blame her. But if she's simply fickle, and just flattered by that cunning old Frenchy's blarney – well then, to the devil with her! She's no better than a flirtatious little cat!*

The path Canyot followed through the late afternoon sunshine lay through the open country. Its height above the valley gave him a clear view of many outstretched white roads and lanes. As he approached the widespread park-like slopes that rose up from West

Horthing to the crest of the hills he obtained an unimpeded survey over the whole winding length of the narrow chalk track which led from Furze Lodge to Littlegate.

'Hullo!' he cried suddenly and came to a dead stop, breathing hard. 'I seem to know *that* figure! Am I going dotty with all this fuss, or is it really her? It's certainly a girl. How absurd I am! It's probably Betsy-Anne's Rose taking the washing home for her mother. No! It *can't* be Rose. That girl's walking just the way *she* walks.' He ran at top speed for almost five hundred yards. Then he stopped again. 'She's picking flowers,' he cried. 'It's Nelly! and he set off at a tremendous pace across the remaining piece of parkland. Through the patches of newly budded bracken-fern he sped furiously, tripping and stumbling over the rabbit holes and taking the smaller juniper bushes in a series of flying leaps. 'How mad I am!' he said to himself at last, when bursting through a thicket of hazel bushes and skirting a huge clump of gorse that barred his way, he scrambled down a bank into the white sheep-track he had seen from above. 'How mad I am!' *She's probably made up her mind to give me the chuck. She's as likely as not dead nuts on that 'free verse' fellow. Curse his blood, coming here and turning her head! And yet here I am running after her as if she were as fond of me as ever! Running after her to tell her all about mother, as if she would post off to Selshurst with me! I wonder if she will be a little bit shocked and sorry. Maybe she will. Maybe a real shock, and having to sympathize a bit, will do her good.* And the young man suppressed one of those funny inhuman impious thoughts that come to the best of us at certain junctures and crises.

He had as a matter of fact no difficulty at all in overtaking the girl. She was so preoccupied with all the queer opinions recentlyflung at her head that she walked along in a careless absorbed manner, stopping mechanically to pick a wild-flower here and there but twisting her thoughts and her anxieties round every new plant she added to her nosegay. She was resting on a sloping bank, yellow with bird's foot trefoil and cistus when he finally approached her. He lessened his pace so as to recover his breath, and she waved at him the little stick she carried, which he had himself cut from the hedge some months before.

'I knew it was you,' he began when he came up to her. 'I saw you from above West Horthing. I knew you by your walk.' He wavered and hesitated in front of her for a flickering moment. Then he stooped down and took her gently by the wrist.

'Take care!' she said, smiling, as with her free hand she laid down her nosegay; but she allowed herself to be pulled up on to her feet and to be pressed close to him in the old fierce way, at which she used to laugh so gaily, calling it 'the one-armed bear's hug'.

He kissed her cool soft cheeks and her gentle unresisting mouth. He kissed her closed eyelids.

'That'll do, Robert!' she cried at last, making a struggle to release herself.

He gave a sigh and let her go. He had not failed to notice that with the least little movement of her head, in spite of her passivity, she had, before he released her, moved her lips away from his. And even while she had yielded her face to him she had not once kissed him in return.

'Oh Nelly!' he cried. 'My little Nelly! You do care for me just a tiny bit? You haven't got quite tired of me?'

They sat down together on the bank and she let him keep tight hold of her hand. Her forehead was puckered into a miserable helpless frown and her eyes, dry and clear and sad, gazed far away from him over the receding Downs.

'You do love me still, Nelly darling?' he kept repeating in a dull useless chant, as one might go on reading from a book to a hearer who listened no longer. 'You do love me a little bit still, sweetheart?'

She felt absolutely unable to say a word to him. It was one of those moments when women are driven back to grope after some language that is older than the language of words; older, deeper, sadder, gentler; to call upon it, and peradventure not to find it.

'If only you love me, still,' he went on, 'I don't care what you do. We needn't be married, Nelly– not for years and years. We needn't be engaged any more. You can go quite free of me; absolutely free. If only I can feel that it isn't your love that has changed I can bear anything!'

Her lips moved. She drew her head away. She picked up the flowers from the grass and began mechanically sorting them in her lap.

Then, stricken by a sharp pang of remorse, he leapt to his feet.

'Nelly,' he said, taking the piece of newspaper from his pocket and throwing it on to her knees, 'read that!'

She frowned for a moment as she smoothed out the printed scrap. Then, when she had read it, she too jumped up, staring at him with wide horrified eyes.

'Goodbye old girl,' he said, forcing himself to smile, 'it's a bit frightening though, isn't it? I'm off to Selshurst anyway. Of course it may be nothing at all. I mean it may be someone else's mother. But I'm off anyway. Goodbye dear. If it isn't mother I'll let you know tonight, if I'm not back too late. If it is, of course I shall stay with her. Somehow the more I think of it the less I *can* believe it's really her. There might easily be, you know, some other people of our name in Maida Vale. You see it only says Maida Vale; and mother's address is seven Cannerby Place.'

'But Robert, but Robert—' the girl gasped. 'This is dreadful for you. Poor dear, poor dear!' And this time she did herself kiss him tenderly, though only on the cheek.

He tore himself away from her, and started off, without another word, running at full pace. When he was about a hundred yards away, he stopped and threw his sketchbook into the hedge, making a signal to her to pick it up for him. She waved her bunch of flowers; and then with a quick irrepressible movement she kissed her hand.

He soon was concealed by a great thicket of furze bushes and she got no further sight of him. But as he ran, he could not help wondering to himself whether, if it *were* his mother and if she *were* really hurt, this sudden disaster to one person he loved wouldn't turn again towards him, with a deeper understanding, the wavering heart of the other person he loved. Thus did the movements of those little silvery fish of impious thought that rise from the purest soul shock the mind of this youth with their queer leapings.

His anxiety, his suspension of mind, his growing fear, stretching forward towards the prostrate form of the woman in the hospital, blent as he ran with the image of the young girl standing in the path kissing her hand and waving her bunch of flowers.

And what of Nelly's own feelings? The very bitterness of the cruel comedy of things was in her heart. Why *had* she, oh! why *had* she, let him kiss her like that, in the old manner, with the old freedom? And why must she needs have given way to an impulse like that and have waved him so natural, so spontaneous, so loving a farewell? He would naturally think, how could he help thinking – poor dear! – that all her vague flutterings to escape during their walk of misunderstanding amounted to nothing at all, were a mere feminine mood, a mere girlish caprice.

Why couldn't she have drawn back honestly from him, and emphatically and plainly made it clear to him that the whole thing had been a mistake, *her* mistake, her unpardonable, inconsiderate, blind mistake?

But the poor boy, harassed and terrified over this accident, how could she do anything else but pity him and be sympathetic? But she could have been sympathetic, without – without kissing her hand to him! But she *wanted* to kiss her hand to him. She wanted, at that moment – he looked so wretched, poor darling! – to give him a very nice kiss. Was she a bad girl? Was she an unnatural horrid creature, able to love two men at the same time?

Nelly pondered long and deeply as she walked slowly home. So many contrary emotions had seized her and shaken her during the last twenty-four hours that her young brain was in a whirl. This unexpected hesitation in herself, in her own heart, in the very depths of her soul, was a quite new element in the situation. What had happened? Had she got out of her trap, broken its iron teeth, tossed it away from her, only to find herself regretting her freedom? The more she tried to analyse her feelings the more puzzled she became. She had never suspected that any appeal from Robert could move and stir her as she had been stirred. She had imagined him getting angry, calling her evil names, abusing her, and going off in a rage. She had called up all her pride, in advance, to meet the onslaught of his pride.

But it had not been like that at all. He had shown no pride, no anger. He had only shown a pitiful gentleness, a puzzled unhappiness. And it was nice, it *was* soothing and sweet, to be hugged so tight by him and to feel his poor dear unlost arm so strong and firm about her.

What an ironic thing it would be, she thought, if the pity she felt for him as soon as she had made up her mind to jilt him brought her at last, for the first time, really to love him!

She *did* love him, in a way. She knew that well enough. But it wasn't the 'in-love' way. It was different perhaps from his being a brother – but not *very* different. Was it, after all, a horrid and unnatural thing to love a young man one wasn't 'in love' with? Ought one to have *hated* being touched by him, being hugged and kissed by him? She certainly hadn't hated it. She had liked it. But that was only as long as she could stop it just when she liked! But when you were married to a person you couldn't stop these things just when you liked. Therefore it was not right to marry someone you only loved, but weren't in love with – because of not being able to arrange these things! Nelly reached home thoroughly confused, a little ashamed of herself, and very remorseful because she had talked so freely to Mrs Shotover. That had certainly been a mistake! If, as the old adage says, 'it is better to be off with the old love before you are on with the new' it is certainly a very unsafe thing to talk about 'the new one' before you have made up your own mind! She wished most heartily that she had waited a little before going to West Horthing. As a matter of honest fact, if Nelly's guardian angel could have been induced to reveal to us what the girl hid scrupulously even from her own heart, it would have been shown that the cynical assumptions poured into her ears by Mrs Shotover had in an imperceptible manner dropped a tiny drop of poison into her vague delicious dreamings about Richard Storm. She seemed to know where she was so well with Robert, and to know so little where she was with the more shadowy figure of the visitor from Paris!

Chapter 5

An aeroplane traveller armed with a good telescope would have been able to observe from his airy watchtower during the mid-afternoon hours of that eventful day three separate groups of human beings linked together by thoughtwaves but completely ignorant of each other's movements. He would have seen Nelly among the roses of her friend's garden. He would have seen Canyot talking to the farm men by the edge of Toat Great Pond. And finally he would have seen, seated in absorbed conversation under the churchyard wall, the Reverend John Mbreton and Mr Richard Storm.

His telescope would have revealed these various persons and he would have regarded them with the Olympian indifference of the high careless gods of the Epicurean hierarchy.

What he would not have seen – unless he had been a god himself – were those quivering invisible magnetic waves, which it is difficult not to believe must pass backwards and forwards, fast as thought itself, between persons who are linked together by some impending dramatic crisis.

Storm had arrived at Littlegate not long after Nelly's departure for West Horthing and he had boldly presented himself at the vicarage door. Grace, issuing forth, in her young mistress's absence, on an emotional errand of her own, had been reluctantly compelled to turn back into the house and convey the visitor into her master's study. This she hurriedly did with no anterior warning, flinging open the door and announcing in stentorian tones, 'Mr Worm to see you, sir!'

Richard, hearing the door closed with a bang behind him and becoming immediately conscious of a vague zoological garden odour caused by the innumerable stuffed birds and beasts with which the room was crowded, felt for the moment as if he had been pushed into the den of some sort of formidable animal. His consciousness of something odd about it all and a little disturbing was not diminished when he remarked the grizzled scalp of the old man and his wrinkled forehead emerging from beyond the edge of a littered table very much as some horrific 'manifestation' might materialize at a successful seance.

John Moreton did not get up from his knees to greet his visitor. He just blinked at him and frowned, placing one large hand, like a great paw, upon an open sheet of botanical specimens and the other upon a bottle of glue as if he were apprehensive lest the intruder should pounce upon them and clear them away or carry them off.

He looked so exactly like a medieval miser caught in the act of counting his treasure that Richard was tempted to open the conversation by assuring his host that he was not a thief.

Instead of doing this, however, a happy instinct led him to remove from his buttonhole and display to the old man a little flower, quite unknown to him, which he had picked by the edge of a muddy ditch.

This well-omened plant turned out to be a stray specimen of water avens which the old man assured him must have been carried there, in its embryonic state, by some migratory bird out of a neighbouring county.

To investigate the water avens the Reverend Moreton did get up from behind the table and was induced to give a certain portion of the attention demanded by the flower to the guest who held it in his hand.

To retain his hold upon the naturalist's attention, thus with difficulty won, Richard hurriedly began putting questions to him, more imaginative than scientific, about the various stuffed birds hanging on the wall. He began, as a matter of fact, to display a genuine curiosity about some of the less usual among these, and in admiring their beauty made a few allusions to such of their kind as he had seen, or fancied he had seen, in his travels through France.

One naturalistic topic led to another, and it was not long before Storm was examining, this time with actual enthusiasm, the vicar's fine collection of British birds' eggs. It was delightful to ransack the recesses of childish memories in regard to these beautiful little microcosms of the mysterious maternal forces. He suppressed a mischievous desire to ask the old fanatic some wild Sir Thomas Browne question as to the mother of Apollo or the offspring of the phoenix, and he reverently held up to the light, one by one, the strangely scrawled eggs of buntings, the beautiful blue eggs of redstarts, the olive-green eggs of nightingales and that incredibly small rondure, like an ivory-coloured pellet, out of which, if science had not interfered, should have emerged a tiny golden-crested wren!

He made himself so agreeable to the old man by his sincere delight in the beauty of these things, and his modest relish for the pedantic pleasure of 'calling them all by name', that John Moreton did what he very rarely did for any human being – his own daughter not excepted – and invited him to come out into the churchyard that he might show him an inviolate specimen of the nest of a meadow pipit.

Having enjoyed the spectacle of the snug security of the wise pipit's retreat – for the old collector had his full compliment of this species – Richard found no difficulty in cajoling the vicar to sit down with him for a while under the high sunny wall and engage in philosophical conversation.

The writer was indeed quite captivated by the old gentleman's originality and scientific passion. It puzzled him a good deal that his young friend had not told him more about her father, had not made clear to him what a remarkable and unusual man he was. *I bet*, he thought to himself, *that ass of a Canyot has no idea what a treasure this old fellow is! I hope my little girl is kind to him. If she isn't I shall give her a very serious scolding. Scolding? I shall whistle her down the wind, for an undiscerning little impious baggage!*

From general philosophic topics of a semi-scientific character, in handling which Richard found Mr Moreton to be quite as imaginative and daring in his speculations as the boldest modern thinker, they passed by insensible degrees to the great 'sphinx problem' of the unknown reality lying behind it all.

'It would interest me to hear,' Storm at length ventured to say, 'how a man of science like yourself reconciles your priestly functions with what we've been talking about. I've known several scientific priests in France and they do it by keeping the two realms rigidly and inflexibly apart. But I never quite feel as if that were a satisfactory solution. Both views of life are so entirely natural and human; and both, it seems to me, spring from the same fundamental passion in the human soul – the passion to grasp life in its inmost secret.'

The old man looked at him from under his shaggy eyebrows with a look of slow interrogative caution; the caution of an old peasant who hesitates to reveal some piece of instructive local knowledge which to him has a deep inexplicable value.

Richard's direct candid gaze in answer to this peering scrutiny seemed to satisfy the man; for, prodding the ground with his heavy cane, he searched for the exact words in which to sum up his position.

'What I've come to feel,' he said, 'and I speak as an ordinary secular layman in the eyes of the world, for I intend to resign my living (though to myself, as you will doubtless understand, I shall always be a priest), is that there are two entirely separate conceptions – the conception of *God* round which have gathered all the tyrannies, superstitions, persecutions, cruelties, wars, which have wounded the world; and the conception of *Christ* round which has gathered all the pity and sympathy and healing and freedom which has saved the world.

'The conception of Satan has been torn asunder between these two. As Lucifer the Light-Bearer, as the Eternal Rebel, he is an aspect of Christ. As the Infernal Power of malice and opposition to life, he is an aspect of *God*.

'To my mind the world is an arena of perpetual conflict between these two forces, one of which I renounce and defy; the other I worship in the Mass.'

'Pee-wit! pee-wit!' cried the plovers over the old man's head as he concluded this strange statement of heresy; and Richard thought to himself – *On which side would he put the cry of that bird?*

But he answered aloud: 'Your view is not a new one, sir. William Blake seems to have felt something of what you say – and there are modern French poets, too, who have—'

The old man waved his hand in the air with a proud gesture. 'What I've told you, young man, I've learnt from beetles and mosses, from shrikes and redshanks, from newts and slow-worms. It is not a poetical fancy with me. It is my discovery. It is what I've been thinking out for myself, for sixty-odd years. And what I've got to do now is what all discoverers have to do, *I've got to pay the price!*'

'Pee-wit! pee-wit!' cried the agitated plovers, wheeling in circles round the field behind them.

'It seeems to me,' remarked Richard after a moment's hesitation; for his habitual desire to propitiate rather than to contradict made opposition difficult to him – 'it seems to me that you have avoided the chief problem. Surely the human instinct which has in all ages groped after something it calls God is really seeking a re-conciliation between your two forces? Surely, sir, you will admit, constituted as we are, we cannot escape from the notion of some fundamental unity in things? And isn't it a desperate pathetic desire in us that this unity should be essentially good rather than evil, that has led to the theological conception of a Father of the Universe?'

The old man started up to his feet with an angry leap. 'The-ological!' he cried beating the top of the mossy wall with his fists. 'That's just what it is – theological!'

'It might just as well,' muttered Richard, losing his propitiatory manner, for something bitter and personal in the old man's tone irritated and incensed him, 'be called human. For not to *want* the universe to be good at bottom is surely an inhuman feeling.'

'Pee-wit! pee-wit!' cried the plovers in the field behind them.

To their intelligence, the appearance of the old naturalist's grizzled pate, across the familiar saxifrages and pennyworts and kiss-me-quicklys of that old wall, must have been very menacing.

'You will hardly deny, sir,' went on Richard, though a secret monitor in his heart kept whispering to him *You're a fool to annoy him; you're a fool to argue with him,* 'that our Lord himself believed in what we usually mean when we use the expression God?'

The Reverend John Moreton stared down at his visitor with a look of infinite contempt.

'The Christ *I* celebrate in the sacrament,' he said, 'has nothing to do with ignorant repetitions of badly reported misunderstandings. The few great authentic logia which I adhere to make no mention of the *Eidolon Vulgaris* of which you speak!'

Richard had really lost his temper now. 'You are a very good example, sir,' he flung out, 'of what happens when a Church separates itself from the traditions of Christendom!'

'It is reason, it is science, it is common sense!' roared the old man. 'It is a confounded exhibition of obstinate private judgement!' shouted the writer back to him.

'Pee-wit! pee-wit!' cried the birds behind the wall.

At that moment a faded specimen of the butterfly called a painted lady fluttered rapidly across the graves.

Richard's outburst had left him with a sense of shamefaced remorse. He certainly had behaved like an arrant fool in contradicting the old gentleman.

He moved forward towards the dilapidated insect that kept wheeling backwards and forwards over the *orchis maculata*, newly planted on Cecily Moreton's mound.

'What's that, sir? What *ever* kind of butterfly is that? I have never seen anything like that before!'

He removed his hat and made as though he would pursue the swift-winged creature.

'A painted lady!' muttered the old man sulkily. But the naturalist's vanity was stronger in him than the theologian's rancour.

'You've never seen one? You young men are very unobservant! Painted ladies are well known in France.' 'Not *that* kind, sir, surely?' cried the cunning biographer of the poet of the *demi-monde*. Ours in France are lighter on the wing'; and he pursued the faded wanton with more discretion than success.

The old man was completely won over by this boyish display. He stumbled after his antagonist and laid his hand on his arm. 'Let it go!' he said chuckling grimly.'She's one too many for you. Many a time have I hunted them for miles over the Downs. In some seasons they're very rare. They're interesting little things! Very prettily marked when you get a good specimen.

'The North American kind is just a little different. Come in, my boy, come in, and I'll show you how they differ. It must be a case of adaptation. Their woods are thicker, they say – more undergrowth.' And the two men returned towards the house in perfect unanimity. The painted lady had found the secret.

'Yes,' said John Moreton as they sat down together after an exhaustive investigation of marble whites, chalk-hill blues, purple emperors, clouded yellows, green hair-streaks, red admirals; 'Yes, I shall resign my living. But thanks to the young man to whom my daughter is engaged – I have a daughter, sir; she's away somewhere – I don't know where'; and he waved his hand vaguely – 'it will not be necessary for me to leave this village. My daughter and this young man – he's considerate to me; he knows the value of my work – have taken a cottage nearby, north of where we are now, and they propose that I shall live with them. It's a good plan. The young man will have the advantage of my scientific knowledge. He's a painter. And I shall . . . I shall be indebted to him for my humble wants.'

Richard Storm was reduced to a depressed silence by his host's words. He stared out of the french window at the lawn and the trees. He felt miserably tired, all the spirit gone from him and a vague ennui turning everything to emptiness. Of course that was it! He might have known it. He *had* known it. Of course she was engaged to this aggressive youth; and of course her marriage was necessary to her father's happiness!

The point was: did she, in spite of appearances, love the fellow? If so – and it seemed likely enough – there was nothing for him to do but clear off elsewhere. The idea of settling down to write poetry in the neighbourhood of this happy domestic arrangement didn't appeal to him. His attraction to Nelly had gone a little too far for that Confound it all! What a thing life was. The day before yesterday – even yesterday – he had felt that his great new idea, that high mystical doctrine which had gathered in his mind, was the one important thing in existence. Nelly's white fragile face and fair silken hair were only traceries upon the tapestry, no more really essential to him than were the green hieroglyphs at the back of the hair-streak's wings.

But since he had last seen her, at the lodge gate of the close, 'the perfume and suppliance' of her personality had been growing steadily upon him, gathering importance, insinuating themselves into his deeper consciousness.

A horrid thought, black for him as the sooty wings of the rooks he now saw crossing the skyline, flapped down into his mind, trying to find lodgement; the thought, namely, that it might be the fair thing, the honest thing, the kind thing, just to clear off and leave the field quite free for Canyot 'to bustle in'. *Are there any men, he* asked himself, *really so noble and unselfish that when they see that their presence has caused trouble to any human circle, and is likely to cause more, they just move off, say goodbye, clear out?* Yes! he supposed there were such people. He sighed heavily. And how often do such heroic renunciations only cause greater unhappiness in the end? What a world!

His meditations were interrupted by the old naturalist's giving vent to a tremendous snore, loud as the snort of a slumbrous buffalo.

Exhausted with his ardent cicerone work among the dead forms of those filmy winged people of the air, the vicar had fallen asleep.

A desperate desire for tea awoke in the heart of Richard Storm. It occurred to him very strongly that a considerable portion of his present depression arose from the absence of this beverage. He looked at his watch. It was a quarter past five. Tea I must and will have, 'he said firmly to himself,' but heaven knows how I'm going to get it! I can't quite shake the old fellow by the shoulder and bawl in his ears, "Get me some tea!" and I know by instinct there isn't a female in the house.' He stared at the sleeper. The great Schopenhauer-like head looked very noble in its weary passivity.

No! No, he thought, *I can't disturb an old man's dreams to*

satisfy my incorrigible tea-lust. I'll try the farm. If they can put up
with Canyot, they can put up with me. I'll try anyhow.

With these intentions he went very softly to the door, opened it,
let himself out, passed through the hallway on tiptoe, and emerged
into the garden.

Storm strode quickly across the intervening village green and
knocked at the door of the farm. It was a tumbledown, ramshackle
old place, with pigs and fowls and ducks and geese wandering
about, where beds of trim flowers might well have been.

But Mrs Winsome, the farmer's wife, although the grimmest of
women, seemed quite pleased to welcome him.

'Tea? Certainly, sir! Friend of Mr Canyot's? There's been a telegram for him since early this morning. The boy brought it from
Selshurst. Please to come in and excuse everything! Please to sit
down. Kettle's on the boil. Won't keep you long.'

The hard-featured woman did not keep him long. Indeed, before
five minutes had elapsed from his entering her parlour, he was
seated before a charming tea tray pouring out for himself cup after
cup of the divine nectar.

After the first three cups and the first three pieces of home-made
bread and butter, Mr Richard Storm regarded the universe in quite
a different manner. He no longer felt the least inclination to be
unselfish and leave the field to his rival. He felt inspirited and adventurous, ready to deal with many Mr Canyots. He felt that if he
could see Nelly Moreton once more, have her to himself for one
long afternoon in these enchanting lanes and fields, he would be
able to snatch her out of all her past.

As for the 'what next?' which naturally must follow this soul
snatching, he did not at that hour, so irresponsible were the
pleasant fumes of Mrs Winsome's tea, give a thought to the matter.

It was so lovely just to feel oneself growing young again, to feel
all those vague sweet delicious tremors one feared were quite irre-
coverable, once more thrilling one's nerves, that any cold-blooded
virtuous interrogations as to 'what would come of it all' seemed
most singularly irrelevant.

He found himself, in place of any serious thought, just building
up fantastic childish castles in the air. Why shouldn't he, just as well
as this sulky young painter, take a house in this charming spot,

80

marry Nell out of hand, and support the old man for his remaining days?

Having liberally compensated the grim lady of Wind Shuttle Farm for her excellent entertainment and watched her shaking the table-cloth to the ducks and the geese and the chickens, Richard, after a hurried glance towards church and vicarage, started to make his way back to Selshurst.

'Never rush things!' he said to himself. 'Women don't like to be greeted by their male friends when they come back tired to their domestic hearths. They prefer the position of defence, of being prepared on their own ground. Above all never take women by surprise – except when a traitor within the gates beckons to you over the wall!'

Fortifying himself with these maxims, for Richard was a veritable Rochefoucauld, as far as theory was concerned, he swung along the road to the old city in high and boyish spirits.

He was about two miles from Selshurst when he heard behind the sound of one running.

At first he thought it might be a runaway horse or cow, but before the runner came in sight he recognized the steps of a man and of a man in athletic condition.

Funny! he thought to himself. *It can't be the old gentleman? Who can it be?*

His suspense was not very pleasantly ended by the appearance of Robert Canyot.

The young painter pulled up breathless, and saluted him with a couple of gasped-out words of greeting.

'Going to Selshurst?' he panted, wiping his forehead. 'That's where I'm going.'

'So I see,' said Richard drily, 'and going at a good pace.'

'To the hospital,' added the runner.

Storm clutched his arm. 'Nothing wrong at Littlegate, I hope?'

'Nothing that I know of. It's my mother – an accident – at least I'm afraid so. Shall know soon.'

Somehow it gave Richard a most curious feeling to think of this troublesome youth possessed of a mother – and a mother who'd had an accident.

From being an irritating automaton to be kicked out of the way, he suddenly became a human person with a skin that could be pricked, with flesh that could bleed.

'Oh I am so very sorry!' he murmured sympathetically. 'I hope it's nothing serious – but of course, as you say, you don't know. Have you only just heard by wire or something?'

'Walk a little faster, do you mind?' was the youth's response.

Richard quickened his pace. 'I can run with you for a bit if you like,' he said.

'No! No! Get my breath. Can't go it like that all the way. Make no difference.'

'Does your mother live in this neighbourhood?' inquired the older man as they strode along side by side.

'Here?' Oh no! London. Maida Vale. That's what the paper said. That's what's made me afraid it is her.'

And the youth explained briefly to his companion by what chance he had learned of the accident.

Richard insisted upon falling into a dog-trot with him; and thus they soon arrived at the outskirts of the town. 'May I come with you to the hospital?' he asked panting, when they had secured directions as to its whereabouts. 'I don't want to be a nuisance or to intrude – but I might be of service – one never can tell.'

Canyot expressed himself as grateful for the offer; and a little later they mounted side by side the steps of the quiet, unprofessional-looking building where Selshurst tended its sick.

A short hurried interview at the office in the hallway satisfied the young man that it really was his mother who had met with the injury.

'I'll wait for you here,' said Richard, noticing with sympathetic alarm that the boy's face had grown suddenly white when he had finished his interview and obtained permission to see the patient.

Canyot nodded to him in a dazed sort of way, and accompanied by a stolid attendant disappeared in the lift.

The writer sank down on a bench in the lobby and fell into nervous and troubled thought.

From the interior of the newly painted lift, as it carried the youth out of his sight, had been wafted that well-known smell of ether, reminding him painfully of old wartime tragedies.

The coming and going of uniformed nurses, scared white-faced visitors, silent impassive officials, deepened his sense of depression and gloom.

All his recent irresponsibility left him, like something shallow and out of place, and the time-old weight of humanity's bitter lot upon earth laid its burden upon him.

He realized then clearly enough where it was that he had failed hitherto in his attempts after a more enduring poetic method. He had contented himself with isolated 'occasional' poems; forgetting that it is only in a certain accumulated weight of human vision, carried steadily on in a premeditated direction, that any value beyond mere nuances of technique is attained.

And as he sat waiting, full of genuine anxiety as to what the young man might be finding up there in some bare cabin of that great ship of human wreckage, it came vividly upon him that he could never fight quite freely, quite unscrupulously for his own hand and his own pleasure, in a world where all men are bitten by the same adder's tooth.

He made no vow, he registered no purpose, but he made a note of the fact that in a place like this those were lucky, both among such as suffered and such as served, who had hands tolerably clean of their fellows' blood; blood that needed no outward sign of its shedding!

He kept his eye on that fatal lift as it went up and down, the very look of its white paint suggestive of the smell of disaster; and his heart beat a little each time it discharged any person not in hospital dress.

He could not help being thankful that he himself had neither parent nor child – those all too fragile links in the great chain of the world's suffering!

At last the figure Storm looked for did actually appear.

He knew at once from the way the boy approached him that his mother was dead. Two great strands of his tow-coloured hair hung limp over his forehead. His cheeks were tear-stained. His mouth twitched.

He sat down on the bench by Richard's side without a word and stared straight in front of him, his solitary hand resting upon his knee.

Richard in the helplessness of an outsider touched this great fist and closed his fingers over it.

'I am sorry,' he said. 'I'm afraid things are bad.'

'She's gone,' the boy muttered without moving a muscle.

'Did she know you?' asked Richard.

The young man choked and bit his lip to keep down his sobs. With a fierce effort, shaking his heavy head like a bewildered animal, he turned and looked at the writer, great globular tears running down his cheeks and falling upon the collar of his coat.

Yes! she knew me. They say it was a miracle. She *wouldn't* let herself go till I'd come to her. She came down to bring me something; she thought it was fame for me at last; an exhibition in New York – a silly invitation. It was just like her to want to bring it to me herself. But what's the damned thing to me now?'

He made an effort to smile and the contortion of his queer corrugated countenance was piteous. 'Oh mother!' he cried stretching his one arm straight out in front of him with the fingers clenched. Then he pulled himself gallantly together and looked quietly and directly into his companion's face. 'You must excuse me,' he said. She was awfully fond of me. She had no one else.'

A hospital nurse with a kind nun-like face approached them. 'We're ready for you,' she said with a sort of wan smile that seemed to Richard as if it were the final indictment of a grief-exhausted planet, addressed to the Unknown.

The youth moved away with her and then suddenly turned and came back.

'Thank you very much,' he said, holding out his hand.

Chapter 6

The sudden catastrophe that had overtaken Mr Canyot produced many drastic effects upon the lives of those whom destiny had entangled with his life.

Soon after his departure to London to superintend his mother's funeral and to settle his business matters and the disposal of the poor lady's small possessions, Richard received a surprising letter from him, addressed to the Crown Inn.

'Dear Mr Storm,' the letter ran. 'It may seem to you a laughable thing that I should write like this, but I want you to feel quite free as far as I am concerned. You well know what I mean by free. I've written to Miss Moreton, sending back certain little things she'd given me, and have asked her to do the same. It is not your fault that you've come between us. It has just happened so. I am writing to you like this because Miss Moreton seems for some reason reluctant to return me what I asked for and I attribute her reluctance to pity. She *pities* me. This I cannot endure. I will not be the person to take advantage of a great loss to soften a girl's heart where it really belongs to someone else. I shall come down and say goodbye before I start for America; by which time she will have to choose definitely between us. But I did not wish, especially after your kindness to me at the hospital to leave you with the feeling that you also, out of pity, must leave things as they were. I don't want pity from anybody. I don't want to bind anybody. I've lived till now for my work; and I can continue to do so. If however, by any chance in which I *cannot* believe, you are trifling with Nelly, you may count on it you will have me to deal with. She has no mother and you have seen what her father is like. But I won't have our engagement kept on out of pity. I won't have it! Yours, with gratitude for your kindness, Robert Canyot.'

There was a postscript appended to this letter which read as follows:

'You'd better use my rooms at Mrs Winsome's. I've paid in advance up to August. Board included.'

This singular epistle, and especially the postscript to it, gave Richard Storm an extremely uncomfortable day. He had well understood Nelly's shyness about going up to Mrs Canyot's funeral and was not surprised when in the end she had not gone. But since that decision of hers he had made few efforts to see her, and moreover when they *had* met, both of them had been so nervous and ill at ease that it had been impossible to talk with any kind of intimacy.

Richard took Canyot's letter with him into the cathedral close and pondered long and wretchedly over it.

The situation was certainly an awkward one. What an extraordinary letter! No – he wasn't conscious of 'trifling' with Nelly Moreton. What the devil *was* this 'trifling'? But on the other hand he certainly did not feel committed, or as if he were involved with her in any irrevocable way. What a blundering, clumsy, roughshod fellow this Robert was! He felt a very decided anger against him. It was so childish – so ridiculous. Was the boy entirely ignorant of the ways of the world? Or was he, Richard, out of touch with the habits and manners of the middle classes in England?

He fumbled in his memory among his early impressions and ran over hurriedly the English novels he had read since. Did they do this kind of thing in this provincial island? Or had the war produced a new England with queer new customs? The boy wrote to him as if he were his superior officer warning him not to seduce some maiden of a conquered country! It seemed an incredible letter from one artist to another artist, from one nomadic Bohemian to another nomadic Bohemian.

Wasn't one free to strike up a casual friendship with a charming girl without bringing down upon one the wrath of a furious fiancé?

Return her little gifts to her? Confound the fellow! If he were as touchy and jealous as all that, the child was indeed well rid of him.

But had they quarrelled? That was the point he wanted enlightenment upon. And if they had, had they quarrelled about *him*? But if they *had* quarrelled, because the girl had talked to him and seemed to like him, how did he know that she wished to have her engagement broken off on such ridiculous grounds?

She might be thoroughly in love with Canyot still and just hurt in her pride by his hot-headed silly violence. She might even be putting it all down to his upset nerves, to his grief for his mother. It looked as if she cared for him still – her reluctance to send back his ring. But it might also be a very natural refusal to be jostled and hurried and bullied at a moment's notice.

Choose definitely between us! the fellow said. Never had such rough, boorish, crude, impolite usage been applied to a young woman! They would be lucky if she didn't whistle them both down the wind!

The whole thing was particularly annoying. Little had he expected that before he had been in England a fortnight he would receive a threatening letter handing over into his keeping an unprotected female!

This letter of Canyot's putting the matter so bluntly and grossly broke up like a bombshell the delicate sentimental dreamings he had begun to weave around the girl. It drove him to drastic issues and decisions; and he wasn't at all ready for drastic issues and decisions. Nor was Miss Moreton ready for such things; he felt sure of that. The more he thought of it all the more angry he became with Canyot. Hot-headed conceited young prig! Because he had lost his mother did he think he could dictate their behaviour to half the world? It was extraordinarily annoying. It put both himself and Miss Moreton into such an absurd position. It made the girl look ridiculous and it made himself seem an ill-bred lunatic who had paid court to another man's sweetheart before he had been two hours in her company.

For, after all, what had Canyot to go upon? Nothing at all. Absolutely nothing. He had not been alone with Nelly for a minute except those hours in the canon's garden and the cathedral – except their encounter in the little church.

Was England so queer a place that one couldn't talk to a girl for three-quarters of an hour without having her flung at one's head?

She must have had an awful quarrel with the boy; there could be no mistake about that! But surely, surely, she couldn't have told Canyot that she had ceased to care for him and had begun to care for *him* – a man she'd only just seen for the second time! It was unthinkable that she should have forgotten all modesty and decency to an extent as fantastic as that. The whole thing was Canyot's damned hot-headed blundering jealousy. If he'd been a Frenchman he would no doubt have challenged him to a duel. The stupid ass! And then this postscript about the room at the farm . . . It was all so extremely laughable that it was difficult to take it seriously. That girl, who was a thoroughly sensible girl, showed clearly enough that she didn't take it seriously by refusing to send him back his gifts.

She must be furiously angry with him though, if he had written to her in the style he had used to him!

Thus, with the surface of his mind, as if before a jury of people of the world, did Richard pour righteous oil upon his embarrassment.

In that deeper, subtler portion of his being, the part of him that did not condescend to use reason or logic, he was less sure, far less sure, of his position. Down in *those* depths, without any words, some honest cynical demon told him that Canyot was fatally near the truth. Of course there *had* been, directly he and Nelly met, and every second they were together, a thrilling vivid undercurrent of sympathy, of understanding. Canyot would have been a very insensitive lover if he hadn't sensed that. He would have been a fool if he hadn't seen it. No doubt he saw things in her expressions, in her tones, in her gestures, that made him know, with the breath of fate itself, that his hour was ended.

No doubt he had challenged her – and, poor innocent inexperienced thing as she was, she had not been able convincingly to meet his challenge. Without meaning to do so, teased and persecuted in his bullying, she had betrayed herself to him. This subtler voice, among Richard's interior demons, was supported in its conclusions by his vanity.

It was as agreeable as it was touching: to think of a sweet young creature like this being driven into a corner till she admitted being more than a little interested in Mr Richard Storm!

Finally, as he rose from his seat under the lime trees, crushing Canyot's letter into his pocket the better, more normal Richard in him decided that the young man had recognized more quickly than either Nelly or himself which way the wind was blowing, and apart from the least admission on her side and simply from devotion to her interests, had brought matters to a head in this erratic manner.

All that day and a good deal of the next was spent by Richard in meditating what he should do in this curious imbroglio. The end of it was that he decided to do nothing at all, except to leave Nelly Moreton alone for a while.

To leave the neighbourhood was out of the question. It would be like running away *for the second time*.

He replied in a friendly but quite non-committal manner to Canyot's letter and said he would be very glad to see something more of him before he sailed for America. He avoided any mention of Miss Moreton's name. His policy of remaining in retreat for the present and leaving the girl alone was made easier for him by a certain rush of energy in the sphere of his writing.

He wrote steadily for several long uninterrupted mornings and afternoons making a conscious effort to keep the image of Nelly, as well as that *other* image, far back in the recesses of his consciousness.

What, he thought fantastically to himself on one of these calm days, do these insidious phantoms of people, that for the time being we don't want to think about, these bodiless haunters of our suppressed world, do with one another in that queer twilight? Do they gibber and squeak at one another – these Elises and Nellys – or are they, like the Queen of Carthage in the Elysian fields, silent and disdainful?

He found, as he wrote, that it was possible to reduce all these human entanglements to a vague far-off world that hardly infringed upon the world he visioned in his present humour. *This* world, of his mystical consciousness, was a world in which the immediate pain of things and the immediate thrill of things were both held back to a certain distance. It was a world in which *his* immediate pain and *his* immediate pleasure were taken up and absorbed in the great stream of all the pleasures and pains of the human race.

What he sought to give an enduring expression to, as he took his available words and squeezed out their subtler meanings and tried to make his thought clothe itself, rhythm within rhythm, with these delicate essences, was the large flowing tide of human experience as it gathered in great reiterated waves, under the old pressure of the old dilemmas, and rolled forward and drew back along the sea banks of necessity.

What he groped after was an entrance into some larger consciousness, not remote from this earthly world, but carrying forward, generation after generation, the faint surmises, the dim guesses, the broken half-glimpses, of men and women and, with all these gathered up within it, itself growing more and more responsive to deeper vibrations from the Unknown, more and more aware of itself as the true Son of Man, as the true logos, into whose being had been poured all the thwarted and baffled aspirations of all souls.

It was not that he wished to find some mere mystical sensation, inchoate and indistinct, and try to express the feeling of just that, in lulled and monotonous rhythms. It was that he wished to take the many poignant 'little things', bitter and sweet, tragic and grotesque, common and fantastic, such as the earth affords us all in our confused wayfaring, and to associate these, as each generation is aware of them before it passes away, as he himself was aware of them in his own hour, with some dimly conceived immortal consciousness that gave them all an enduring value and dropped none of them by the way.

It was, so to speak, some tentative, hesitant, as yet only half-conscious soul of the earth, to which he sought to feel his way, a kind of half-human, half-elemental logos, nearer the Goat-foot Pass than any vague dream of the old Gnostics, and yet with a music in its being, beyond the breath of any reed of the marshes.

It was comparatively easy to let the faint magic of his view of things ebb and flow before his mental vision in these long golden mornings in Selshurst, where the very streets were full of the fragrances of the fields. It was a very different matter when he came to attempt the task of putting all this into poetic form. How, in that little bedroom of his, opening on the light breaths of rosemary and balsam and newly budding lavender, where every now and then came lively voices from the back parlour, he wrestled with the obstinate mystery of words!

Why not put these thoughts of his into the simpler cadences of prose? Because there are certain things that refuse to be expressed in prose, that demand the austerer rhythms, the more oracular gestures, the more broken, fragmentary, evasive hints, of poetry.

But 'Oh Prince, what labour, oh Prince, what pain!' For the rhythms of poetry, expecially of the *vers libre* he was working in, are of such a kind that not only the general swing of the verse had to leap forth as the very exhalation of his own especial soul, but each separate line, nay! every word he uses, must fall into its place, not 'by taking thought', but by an indefinable movement of the energy of music in himself. The syllables have to form an essence compounded of strange subtleties; and as for the thoughts, they must be bitter and sweet, full of the mysterious saps and juices of the blood of life, cool-breathing, redolent of undying mornings and evenings, sprinkled with eternal dews.

Day followed day without any interruption to these mental and psychic labours. 'I have not run away a second time,' he kept saying to himself; but that was the very thing, as he well knew in his secret heart, that he *had* done! To fall suddenly after those vibrant and thrilling first meetings with her, into dead silence, was nothing less than to abscond, to quit the field, to bolt.

He did not attempt to bring into honest daylight the queer

shadowy motives that tumbled over one another, like shifty hump-backed weasels in a rabbit hole, down there in the darkness of his hidden mind. But somehow by not actually clearing off, by not leaving Selshurst altogether, he satisfied the scruples of one part of his nature, while by offering the girl nothing but this profound silence he made a definite break with what had begun to occur between them, and in a queer sort of indirect way hit back at the meddling Canyot.

It was all the more easy to hide himself like this just because that 'threatening letter', as he called it, of the impulsive painter had quite definitely broken up the special kind of sentimental attraction he had begun to feel for the young girl. In those first days he never thought of her without thinking of buttercups, and celandines; but now whenever he thought of her he thought of that 'choosing definitely between us'; until the fair face of the maiden floated, in his mind, above a horrid iron prong, that jerked and prodded him into that lamentable arena of duty where decisions are made!

One morning, however, after more than a week of this recluse existence, his whole line of action was scattered to the winds by a letter from the girl herself.

'Dear Mr Storm,' the letter said, in a firm clear round rather childish hand. 'When are you coming to see us again? – or have you left Selshurst? If you have gone away I hope they won't forward this because it's only a dull invitation which it will be a bore to receive in Paris or wherever you may be. It's to ask you to come over to tea tomorrow, to meet my friend Mrs Shotover. Please try and come if you can, as my father took a great fancy to you; which is rare with him as you can guess. But of course if you *have* left it's no use. In that case may I say I'm sorry we didn't say goodbye?' And the letter ended with an evident hesitation between 'Sincerely' and 'Very sincerely', avoided by a manufactured blot and a hurried 'And with best wishes for the success of your work – from Nelly Moreton.'

It is extraordinary what power a direct personal appeal has, to break up a whole fabric of moral speculation! The look of the letter, the way she had worded it, that blot at the last with the unconventional ending – all these things thrilled Richard as if they had been the very touch of her hand. 'Ha! Ha! My good friend,' one of his slyest demons whispered to him, 'so, after all, the real reason for this retreat of yours was pure jealousy! You thought she did still care for Canyot!'

Tea tomorrow? That means today – this very afternoon. And Richard rushed out of the Crown Inn passage, into the street, sans hat and stick, and made his way to the leafy cathedral close, walking upon air.

He left an admirable lunch, that noon, very imperfectly dispatched, and found himself chatting to barmaids, gardeners, ostlers, boot boys, even to that old insinuating toper, half-beggar, half local-celebrity, who went by the name of Young Bill, with the most eager interest. –

'I may as well start early,' he said to himself. 'It's so horrid to meet people when one's hot and rushed.'

He started indeed so extremely early that it was hardly half past two when he arrived within a couple of miles of the place. *I can't appear yet for hours!* he thought, and tried to settle himself down in a pleasant corner of a field, taking out of his pocket a little volume of *Songs of Innocence and Experience*. He got as far as the title on the cover, which struck his fancy as being singularly appropriate; but the words inside the book might have been written in Chinese, for all they conveyed to his mind.

'Confound this waiting!' he said to himself. 'It makes a person nervous. Maybe I'd better take a bit of a detour.' This diplomatic move had the effect of so entangling him between hedges and ditches, and hayfields where he knew he mustn't tread down the grass, that it was quite four o'clock before he made his appearance, decidedly hot and very muddy, at the door of Littlegate Vicarage.

Mrs Shotover had arrived, and with John Moreton and Nelly was standing on the lawn outside the vicar's study.

Richard's joining them was the signal for Grace to bring out tea, preparations for which had already been made under the shelter of a wide-spreading sycamore.

Nelly had blushed scarlet on first seeing him and had been so nervous that in introducing him to Mrs Shotover, she said the one thing which she had made up her mind she must on no account say, the one thing that it would be 'perfectly awful' to say. 'Mrs Shotover,' she said, 'has been teasing me about you. She calls you my Stormy Petrel.'

As soon as she had uttered the words she could have bitten off her tongue. *Some devil must have said that through my mouth!* she thought.

A voice within the man she addressed did certainly not fail to point out that the jest was an ill-timed if not an ill-bred one; and that it was not pleasant to be the subject of 'teasing' between ladies. But this was only one voice among many that were uttering fantastic and carping comments in Richard's brain; and the real Richard was very little affected by them. Indeed the girl looked at him so shyly and so wistfully after this blunder, that she could have said something far worse than that and he would have forgiven her.

'I found a knapweed out this morning,' remarked the vicar, after the first settling in seats and pouring out of tea had subsided. 'I've never found one so early before; not in thirty years. It's a remarkable season.'

'Father always finds the first flower,' said Nelly quickly. 'He seems to know by instinct where to go for them. It's quite queer sometimes. You'd think that no sooner were a new flower out, than it made a special signal to Father, over miles and miles, to come and see it.'

'Mr Storm must come and see my garden,' threw in the lady from West Horthing, 'and I've got a few things in my house that no doubt would interest him still more.'

'What things do you mean?' asked Nelly with genuine curiosity. But her friend shook her head at her. 'It's Mr Storm I'm going to show them to, not you, dear. When *you* come to see me it's all gossip and scandal, isn't it? We've no time for serious things. Do you think it's really true, Mr Storm, that women are fonder of gossip than men?'

It was the old naturalist who unexpectedly replied to her.

'Women, Betty, gossip out of pure malice; in order to satisfy their spitefulness and spleen. Men gossip out of a philosophical interest in human nature.'

'I would put it rather differently.' said Storm. 'Men gossip about their enemies – women about their friends. Women think themselves privileged to abuse their friends.'

'Mr Storm! That isn't true,' broke in Nelly. 'Don't interrupt him, dear,' said the old lady. 'He was going to say something else. I saw it coming.'

What do you think yourself?'inquired Storm, looking straight into her satiric screwed-up eyes.

'I think we all gossip as fast as we can find subjects for it. Women's subjects are more limited than men's; so they're bound to make more of them.'

'Tell me this then—' began Richard.

'Oh no catechisms, I implore!' cried Mrs Shotover. 'That's where you literary people are so unkind.'

'I hope you don't mean *so boring*,' said Richard.

'No, please, Granny dear; let Mr Storm finish his question. I'm sure it was thrilling. Ask me instead of her, won't you?' And Nelly smiled at him with a tender quiet little smile that seemed to say, 'I love your catechisms!'

'It probably wasn't a proper question to put to you,' chuckled Mrs Shotover. 'Well, go ahead, young man, and be as unkind to the old lady as you like.'

'I only meant – but there! we've driven your father away I'm afraid—' and he stopped abruptly, as the vicar, nodding benevolently at them all, got up and shuffled across the lawn.

'Oh no! Father never stays after he's had his tea,' cried Nelly. 'Now Mr Storm, *do* finish your sentence!'

'I only meant,' Richard went on, cursing himself for having launched into the topic at all, 'that it's queer how women scold so bitterly and vindictively people that they're really all the time actually in love with.'

Mrs Shotover put back her head, dropped her lorgnette, and dropped into a cackling high-pitched laugh. Then she leered at Richard with her head on one side like some wicked very old fowl. 'Do they do that? My goodness! You notice, Nelly, what experiences Mr Storm has had.'

Richard glared at her angrily. 'I'm afraid it wasn't an original remark of mine,' he retorted. 'It's that old well-known poem of Catullus I was thinking of. I hardly liked to bore you with it in Latin.'

'In Latin!' Mrs Shotover clapped her hands. 'Oh Nelly, do put down that cake. You know you don't want it. And listen to Mr Storm quoting Latin.'

But Nelly's face was very serious. It would never do for Mrs Shotover and Richard to quarrel at this juncture.'You two dear nice people!' she cried, rising to her feet in order to deal more adequately with the situation. 'How you do fight over these absurd problems! As Mr Storm says, I don't think we need much experience to know what people are like when they love and hate at the same time! But I don't think it's only women who torment the people they care for. I'm sure men do it. I don't know whether you'd count Father as an example? But he certainly does it. Well? Shall we go round the garden?'

As they moved away Nelly thought to herself – *The poor absurd darling! how sweet he looked when he got angry because she laughed. And how solemnly he began that old tiresome business about loving and scolding.*

What pompous vain conceited things the nicest of men are! But oh I'm so glad to see him again – and there's the same feeling between us – just the same – he feels it and I feel it. How wonderful it is!

And Richard thought in his heart – *That vulgar impertinent old woman! Trying to make me look a fool before Nelly! But the sweet thing came to my rescue instead. Bless her heart! She may be innocent, but she's got more intellect, any day, than that old harridan with false teeth and a grin like a hyena! Bless her heart! I was a silly ass to keep away all this time. What days I've wasted!*

And as he followed the old and the young woman round that pleasant little garden he smiled to himself to notice how naïvely and simply he had thought of those even days of work at the main purpose of his life as 'wasted' – because he had hidden himself away from a girl of twenty-two.

Chapter 7

Richard did not succeed in securing any private word with Nelly before he felt it incumbent upon him to say goodbye. The 'laughing hyena', as he named Mrs Shotover to himself, grinned her obstinate determination to 'stick him out' and be left alone with her young friend. He was only thankful she had a coachman and dog-cart; so that there was no question of his having to walk back with her to West Horthing. He cordially detested her; and made up his mind to attack Nelly on the subject, and express his wonder as to what she could see in such a spiteful and silly old creature!

That's the worst of England, he thought. It's such a confounded individualistic country, that a horrible old woman like that as long as she has money and 'knows the neighbourhood' can go on indefinitely making herself a general nuisance. In America, he supposed, she would have been put into her place and forced to mend her manners. Well! Well! After all, perhaps, there was something to be said for a system that encouraged everybody to grow into a 'Character', either a charming one or the reverse! It was better perhaps to have 'laughing hyenas' than monotonous herds of sheep!

The next day was a day of pouring rain and Richard made no attempt to do more than visit the cathedral. He took the opportunity of carrying his notebooks there and reading to himself what he had written. On the whole he was not displeased with the result of his week's work. He had composed about two hundred lines of this uneven dithyrambic 'litany of the earth-soul', its slow growing into consciousness, its use of the sentiency of all living things, its vague 'dreaming on things to come'.

He became conscious how deeply he had abandoned himself to these English fields and lanes and hedges, to these mossy walls and historic buildings, to these old quiet immemorial traditions.

His return to his native land had stirred a thousand atavistic feelings in him, tastes and prejudices, devotions and queer old attachments.

The lines he had written were full of the sounds and scents of the English country, and the more conscious, more human element in them was religious in the calm reserved English way and was rootedly, but not feverishly, pagan. Dithyrambic in its broken ebb and flow the poem might be; but the music of it was rich and slow and a little heavy – not by any means a song of air and flame! The thing might not be passionate and exciting; but the bleating of flocks was in it, and the sweet breath of cattle, and the patient labours of simple people under the sun and the rain, and the faint sad strange murmurs, like the winds at night, over summer grass, of the dead generations that found their survival in those who came after them.

He returned to his inn late that night, having wandered far through the fields as the evening cleared, along the old canal bank, towards the sea. It had come upon him, as he walked there, especially in passing a particular group of poplar trees, pale and soaked with rain, shivering in the night wind like something human against the orange-coloured skyline, that he had known all this before. Yes, long before, under some other name perhaps, in the unending sequence of the great wayfaring, he must have stood, just as he was standing then, watching those trees whispering to each other with sad tender voices!

And that night he pulled his chair close to the open window and sat for a long while looking out into the silent wet garden, where the darkness itself seemed to exhale an old forgotten fragrance, carrying the mind back to dumb deep-buried memories.

It was one of those hours when a man feels the presence of all the days he has lived through, gathered up and folded together like the crowding of soft innumerable wings; an hour when what is to come hangs palpably imminent, like a vast pregnant shadow, before him, beckoning to those sheltering wings that they should let him go, let him move forward to his fate.

Winnowed and purged by his days with the secrets of words, their mysterious alliances and treacheries, his soul seemed, as he sat at that window, reluctant to break the spell, hovering consciously between a past that was over, its wounds healed, and a future on whose threshold he wavered and hesitated, full of unknown things – beautiful, terrible, pitiful!

He left the window at last with a sense as though he had made, for good or for evil, some great decision; as though at some dark crossroads he had chosen his way, and now could never, through all that should subsequently happen, retrace his footsteps.

Never had Richard sunk into so deep a chasm of dreamless unconsciousness as he slid away into, almost as soon as his head touched the pillow. He awoke the next morning with a feeling as though he had slept not for seven hours, but for seven centuries; he wondered vaguely if he would ever sleep quite in that way again. Was it the very sleep of the 'earth-soul' he had been writing about into which, like a child entering the spaciousness of a mother's dreams, he had been allowed to pass?

He had the queerest feeling as he washed and dressed as though it were necessary to move very quickly, very stealthily and solemnly, about the room. Was some shadowy dead self, some phantom corpse of everything he had been before, actually lying on the bed he had quitted?

He ran downstairs anyway with a distinct feeling of relief from psychic tension and oppressipn. And on the table in the breakfast room, lying on his plate, he found a letter from Nelly. He opened and read it standing by the window, while Trixie Flap, the Crown housemaid, watched him shrewdly, her hand on the mahogany sideboard.

The letter was brief enough.

'Dear Mr Storm, Please come over and see me. *At once*, if you don't mind? It's impossible to tell you more in a letter. I must talk to somebody. I am very worried, so please come as soon as you get this. In the morning if possible. I'll look out for you. I am sorry to trouble you.'

And the letter was hurriedly signed, 'Nelly'.

Richard looked at his watch and then at the self-conscious back of Trixie Flap who was now fidgeting with something on the sideboard.

'Let's have some tea at once, Trixie, please,' he said, seating himself at the table and beginning to cut the loaf. 'Never mind about the porridge. I'm in a hurry. I've got to go somewhere.'

When he next looked at his watch it was after ten and he was already halfway to Littlegate. He could not have given any lucid account of what trees or beasts or rustics he had passed on his way. He might have passed much more remarkable things than early flowering knapweed and they would have been unnoticed. That phrase *I'll look out for you* with its pathetic confidence in his friendship had stuck a dart into his heart whose sweet rankling made him oblivious of all outward objects.

He came upon her quite suddenly, leaning against a gate, staring with woebegone eyes in front of her, without hat or gloves. She turned when she heard his step and leaped forward to meet him, her cheeks burning.

She gave him her hand. She made a little hesitating movement as if she would have given him both her hands. Instead of that she gave him the loveliest smile that Richard had ever seen on a human countenance. 'Thank God you've come!' she said with a sigh of content.

They instinctively moved to the gate which Richard rapidly opened, untwisting its rustic defences with a trembling hand.

'Let's get off the road,' he said. 'Then we can talk better.'

They risked the wrath of the farmer and crossed the field to the shelter of a large ash tree which grew in the hedge bank. At the foot of this tree they were isolated from the whole world.

It was a hot, still, thundery day, the sun having a semitropical feeling in it owing to the rain that had fallen.

'I'm afraid the grass is damp,' said Richard. 'With that thin dress . . . ' He looked at her tenderly. 'Oh, I know!' he cried impulsively, and taking off his coat he spread it upon the ground.

The girl looked grave. 'After getting warm walking . . . ' she murmured, 'I don't *think* you ought to—'

'But just feel how hot the sun is – burning hot!' And he made her sit down by his side; even going so far as to give her a little friendly pull closer to him when she seemed shy of taking more than the minutest share of the tweed jacket spread out beneath them.

Nelly sat with her legs stretched straight out in front of her, Richard with his knees under his chin; and when he told her that it was like sitting together on a magic carpet that only needed one talismanic word to transport them both to some Happy Valley out of reach of all annoyance, she nodded in contented agreement.

The hot thundery heavy sunshine fell upon them like an actual stream of attenuated gold, as though the very father of gods and men were blessing them with full hands.

'Well – now we are alone and safe,' said Richard, hugging his knees with his clenched fingers and letting his eyes rest on the childish indoor shoes she was wearing, strapped with a thin leather strap above the instep, 'let's hear the worst. Out with it Miss Nelly! I can tell you in advance, by a sort of presentiment, that I shall be able to find a solution. Out with it Miss Nelly!'

'You may drop the Miss – if you like,' said the girl in a low voice, plucking a long feathery grass blade and pulling it to pieces on her lap.

'Well, out with it, Nelly!' he repeated.

She drew in her breath as if for a great burst of volubility; and then suddenly, instead of telling him anything, she broke into a flood of tears. Richard longed to take that fair forehead with its pearl-white transparent skin, its delicate blue veins, its exquisite arched eyebrows, and those wet cheeks hidden in her hands, and comfort them with caresses; but it seemed somehow as if it would be stealing an unfair advantage of her just then. So he just laid one of his hands lightly on her shoulder. 'Come, come, little one,' he said. 'I'm certain we can settle all these things if you only tell me.'

She made a gallant effort and stopped crying, turning to him a look of almost frightened apology. 'Don't be angry with me,' she murmured. 'I really don't often give way like this. I think it must be the thunder in the air. It's so hot and close isn't it?'

Richard hurriedly assented. 'Oh awfully close! But do try and tell me now. I'm sure I'm the right person to be told.'

'It's about Father,' she said quietly. 'He's written several times to London lately and he's written to Selshurst. And now it's all decided. They've accepted his resignation. Someone's coming from Selshurst to take the service. And there's to be a new vicar. He's not to be allowed to officiate in the church again. In fact it's more like being turned out than resigning. There'll only be one more quarter's salary coming in; and that's the end. After that we've got nothing! And we've not saved a penny. God knows what we shall do. What hastened all so and brought things to a head was some parishioner from over the hill complaining to the bishop – no Little-, gate person would have done it. I believe it was the foreman at Toat Farm. He's a silly officious old fool. He's always been a trouble. He must have told them about Father's leaving out prayers and things. Whenever it says *God* in the service he changes it to *Christ*. It's very, very cruel – happening like this. But I suppose it was bound to come sooner or later. I suppose it *would* sound odd if a stranger heard him. He didn't always change it to *Christ*. Sometimes he changed it to *Lord* but he always changed it – except when he was thinking of his butterflies or something, and then he forgot and said it like anybody else. I suppose it couldn't go on like that, could it? Though the people here didn't seem to notice any difference.'

She stopped breathlessly and looked at her companion with appealing eyes.

Richard felt compelled to confess to her that it did seem a little

Strange for a priest to expurgate the syllable *God* out of the Christian worship. He admitted that he did not very clearly see how it could 'go on' quite like that.

'But cannot your Father make any special use of his scientific knowledge? He seemed to me a man of unusual mental power. Couldn't he get a biological position in some college?'

Nelly frowned just a tiny bit at this, and thought in her heart, *How curiously stupid the nicest of men are! Any woman who'd seen Father would know at once that he was quite hopeless in things like that. I suppose the truth is all men are a little hopeless themselves. How any of them do any practical work I can't think!*

And she sighed and smiled, and then frowned again.

'No. I suppose that's out of the question,' said Richard and stared helplessly at the little crossed ankles lying in the grass beside him, over which the ash leaves above their heads threw a tracery of delicate shadows.

Sitting there in his shirtsleeves he felt as though he were prepared to undertake any quixotic labour on behalf of this young girl. But what form could it take?

'I think perhaps I ought to tell you something else,' said Nelly gravely. 'Perhaps you've guessed I'm engaged to be married to Mr Canyot?'

'Yes,' said Richard with a beating heart.

She was evidently making a tremendous effort to be entirely frank with him and he felt a wave of vibrant pity for her in her manifest embarrassment.

'Mr Canyot's been so different since he lost his mother. He misunderstands things. I mean he confuses things. But it's all too much my own fault!' She pulled up a large handful of sun-warmed grass and threaded it around her fingers.

Richard could not help noticing that she still wore the ring which he had from the first day assumed to be her engagement ring.

'I ought to tell you that we had a bad quarrel that day when we walked back together from Selshurst.'

Now we come to it! thought Richard.

'And the quarrel,' she went on, 'if you want to know, was absurdly enough about *you!*'

'About me?' cried Richard, putting a good deal more astonishment into his tone than he actually felt. What he really felt was something much more like the edge and fringe of extreme fool-ishness; for he began to fear that he had exaggerated altogether the link between her and himself.

She is treating me as her father confessor, he thought. *She is talking to me about her love affair.* And a very cynical and rather bitter emotion passed through him.

'Yes, it was about you, about *us*,' the girl went on. It was a faint comfort to him to remark that she did blush – she blushed so quickly; it was the misfortune of her transparent complexion – at the word 'us'.

'He was troubled in his mind because I liked you, because we liked each other. He said I looked at you and talked to you differently from the way I did with him. Well! you *are* different, a lot different, from Robert, aren't you?'

Richard dryly admitted that he did differ from Mr Robert Canyot.

'We quarrelled over that all the way home. He was rude to me. He was really angry. And I'm afraid I got angry too and said things that hurt him.'

'Things that hurt him,' repeated Richard, helping her out.

'I said I had a right to choose my own friends. I said . . . more than I ought to have said!' And she gave Richard that same inde-scribably lovely smile that he had received from her three times before.

I wonder if she looks at Canyot like that? he thought. *If she doesn't, I'm blessed if he is her choice! At any rate as long as she gives me that look I know we've got something very deep between us.*

'I said,' she went on, looking down now at the grass-blades twisted round her fingers and smiling to herself a quaint elfish enig-matic smile that seemed to separate her in some queer way from all possible lovers and turn her into a mocking sexless thing of childish unapproachableness.

'I said I *did* like you very much indeed; and that, if he wasn't careful, I should fall in love with you, and fall out of love with him – I said *that*, on purpose, to annoy him. I wanted to annoy him as much as I possibly could.'

'I see,' said Richard. 'You said *that* to hurt your lover as much as ever you could, to punish him for being, as you say, so absurdly jealous.'

Again there flickered over her downcast face that peculiarly detached, mischievous and elfish ripple of merriment.

'And what did he do?' inquired Richard, feeling like a man who squeezes a nettle tighter and tighter in the hope that the smart would diminish if he only squeezed hard enough. 'What did he do when you said *that* to him?'

She laughed aloud then, a ringing peal of reed-throated laughter like a blackbird in the rain. 'You won't be too horrified if I tell you?' she asked.

He promised hurriedly to receive, any account of this incident with complete equanimity.

'He shook me!' she cried with another ripple of reed-like merriment. 'Shook me ever so hard. Till I rattled like a pea pod.'

There was really nothing for Richard to say or to do in response to this – unless he were prepared to shake her himself.

A little unkindly – but he surely had some excuse – he brought her back to the point from which she had commenced this narration. 'You say his mother's death has not improved things between you?'

She did become grave at this; very grave and quiet. 'Poor Robert!' she sighed. 'Yes, it upset him completely. He made it difficult for me to go to the funeral. And he has been writing me such strange letters since.'

Her face assumed an unhappy and puzzled expression. 'You don't suppose,' she said, turning to Richard with that peculiarly wistful look that had disarmed him at the beginning, 'that the death of a person's mother can really unsettle a person's mind?'

'I hope not, I'm sure, Nelly,' was all he found himself able to say to this. Then the temptation arose violently in him to tell her about the letter he had himself received from Canyot. He fought this down with resolute energy. *No! it would be a caddish thing to do – I must play fair in this business.*

He recompensed himself for this piece of virtue by a very mischievous move.

'Do tell me,' he said, 'while we're talking so frankly together, what you told Mrs Shotover about me. I'm sure you must have given her your most real impression. There was no reason for pretending things to "annoy" *her*.'

If he had wanted to cause his companion agitation and discomfort he certainly succeeded. Nelly pulled up her knees beneath her frock, gave a little twist away from him, dug one of her hands into the ground to support herself, and jumped up on her feet.

'I don't think you ought to have asked me that,' she said, frowning down upon him like an accusing angel.

Richard jumped up too, and picked up his coat.

'I don't see why not,' he retorted. 'You admitted she'd been teasing you about me. People don't tease people about things like that out of a blue sky. Besides, you said she called me funny nicknames, making puns on my name.'

There were burning spots of colour in Nelly's cheeks by this time; but they were roses of anger much more than roses of shame.

'I don't think you ought to have said that to me. I don't think you treated Mrs Shotover at all nicely. She's an old lady. She's nearly seventy. And you spoke quite crossly to her in that silly argument. It isn't that I minded your having different opinions – but you needn't have been rude.'

'I thought it was your friend who was rude,' retorted Richard.

By this time they had, as if by mutual consent, left the friendly shelter of the ash tree, and were retracing their steps towards the lane.

'I don't know why it is,' observed Nelly, addressing her remark to the air and the grass and the hot thundery sunshine which beat down on them with a benignant indifference to their dissension, 'but men seem so tiresomely serious and pedantic in their arguments sometimes. I think it's absurd to quote Latin at a tea party.'

To cover her retreat from his ill-timed reference to her friend – oh! how she wished she had never said a word to Mrs Shotover about him! – Nelly had certainly succeeded in reducing their happiness to a low ebb.

He trailed along at her side so sulkily and morosely now that she was tempted to give him yet another stab.

'It was silly of her, of course, but one couldn't expect her to like you after your being so brusque to her. But she *did* go a little far. She said you had a *clerical* way of talking – that you reminded her of a certain archdeacon she knows.'

Richard burst out at this. 'She reminded *me,*' he cried, 'of a certain animal I know! I think she's a most unpleasant old person. I can't understand your making a friend of her.'

The girl turned clear round. 'I choose my friends as I choose,' she cried, her grey eyes turning quite dark with anger; 'but I see I must ask leave in future from Mr Storm!' They had reached the gate by this time and Richard without a word moved forward to open it for her. He closed it again meticulously behind them.

'Well?' he said, looking straight into her eyes. 'I suppose I'd better say goodbye now.'

She gave a little gasp and moved back a step. For an infinitesimal moment of time they looked darkly and strangely at one another, as if measuring swords. But the man had already played the winning card, the old eternal masculine trump card in these contentions.

She thought to herself, puzzled, startled, bewildered, frightened, *He* cannot *surely mean that? He cannot mean just to go away, without a word?*

'Goodbye—' she whispered in a low voice scarcely moving her lips, and stepped back yet further. Then, still facing him, she leaned against the gate, stretching out her arms behind her so that they rested on the top bar. Her wide-open eyes, darkly blue now in her alarm, fixed themselves upon him out of an immobile white face.

'Goodbye,' she repeated. And the whispered syllables went floating away over the leafy hedges and the tall waving grasses.

The situation had reversed itself, like the sudden turning of an hour-glass.

She had had complete advantage over him in her unscrupulous power of wounding. He regained the ascendency in his equally un-scrupulous power of just leaving her alone.

Neither of them at that moment had the mind to analyse these things. Their whole consciousness was absorbed in their indig-nation against each other. His emotion was complicated by the great woolly flock of interior vanities and self-respects which he had to protect from outrage. Her emotion, far deeper than his, had nothing to complicate it.

The situation hung suspended in this way for a perceptible moment. Then the masculine diplomatist in Richard, with its heavily acquired sense of order and decency and its hatred of shocks and scenes, led him to take the line that really was the meanest and most cowardly he could take.

Had he accepted her little tragically whispered 'goodbye' and gone straight back to Selshurst, he would have struck that white face a remorseless blow; but the account between them would have been balanced up, and the look in her eyes which would have gone with him would have given him no peace.

Instead of that, he proceeded to override her with a forgiveness that was no forgiveness; to secure himself against remorse and yet to keep his grudge intact and the hurt to his vanity unhealed.

He moved up to her side. 'Come, Nelly, we two are just making fools of ourselves quarrelling like this. Are you going to ask me to lunch? I want to meet your father again so very much. It would never do to come as far as this and go back without seeing him. I didn't see half his collections, you know – only the butterflies.'

She had to submit to this. There was no other way. And thus led, as it were, captive, harnessed helplessly to that elaborate social propriety which women are supposed to be responsible for, but which in reality is man's protection from the passionate sub-civilized woman-soul, she meekly walked by his side, passive, quiet, subdued, unhappy, along the road by which she had come that morning hoping for unspeakable comfort.

'I ought to tell you,' she said as they went along, 'what Mr Canyot has proposed for us; because Father is sure to talk about it and you'd wonder I'd said nothing. So you must let me bore you with just one or two more family details.'

'Don't be sarcastic, Nelly,' he said gently. 'How can I give you advice if I don't know the situation? And you *did* ask me to help, you know!'

She flashed at him one quick look of bitter mockery; and then went on in quiet unemotional tones.

'Robert suggested – he and Father talked about it without my knowledge – that when we were married, which he wanted to happen very soon, we should live in Hill Cottage – that's a place you haven't seen yet to the north of the village – and my father live there with us. Robert had nearly finished furnishing it when . . . when you came. It's a pretty little house. It would really suit us very well as far as I'm concerned and Father would be happy there.'

She stopped speaking and they walked on for a second or two in silence. 'Please go on,' said Richard. 'Please tell me everything. You don't know what a magician I can be sometimes! Let me know every aspect of your difficulties.'

'And then you came,' the girl burst out; 'and then his mother was killed. And now his poor head seems to have got the wildest notions into it. I can't understand his letters!'

'He told me at the hospital,' threw in Richard, keeping that 'threatening letter' from approaching the tip of his tongue only by a resolute effort, 'that it was about an exhibition in America that his mother came to see him. Has anything more come of that?'

Nelly looked round sharply. 'I didn't know you knew that,' she said. 'Well, I expect, as you say, if you're to give me advice you must know everything. Yes. He talks now of going to America quite soon; in two or three weeks in fact. But what's going to happen to Father while we're gone, heaven knows!'

'Then he wants to marry you at once and carry you over with him?' Richard threw back at her, in a hard, firm, unemotional voice.

Nelly saw that she had been pushed into a corner. She had been tempted, she hardly knew why, to fling at him that assured 'while we're gone'. It was a sort of raft of refuge for her at the moment, that significant 'we', but she had no sooner uttered it than she felt as ashamed as if she had been caught in a palpable falsehood.

She wasn't in any sense conscious of playing off one man against another. Whichever way she looked she saw perils and disasters. But it was intolerable to have to admit to Richard that Canyot had sent her a practical ultimatum, telling her she must choose between them and announcing that he would 'come down soon to hear her decision'.

It was being left stranded like that, thrown out of her home without a moment's notice, with her father on her hands, that created this misery, these wavering equivocations.

She, like Canyot himself, had no wish to be taken by anybody 'out of pity'. Her painter, she knew, needed her, wanted her, loved her single-heartedly, loved her passionately – his wild jealousy proved *that* – and as long as she leant upon *him* her pride was quite unhurt. But the idea of having to confess to Richard the drastic nature of those letters she had been receiving, with their refrain of 'choose' – 'choose' – 'choose', was altogether unbearable. No girl could say to a man, 'I *must* have one of you – now, which is it to be?'

The whole thing seemed to be a welter of bitterness and misery. And it had been so beautiful, so thrilling, that first encounter with Richard! This miserable problem of money, of necessity, of her father, put her into a completely false position. It spoilt all her happiness with Richard. It made her irritable; it made her say things to hurt him; it made her *hate* him.

She felt convinced that he didn't believe that all was as well in her relations with Canyot as she had tried to make out. She had practically lied about it. Canyot had never suggested taking her to America. And she divined that Richard suspected her of lying. But what could she do? She *had*, at all costs, to protect both Richard and herself from the humiliation of her being driven into his arms by Robert and her father!

Life was certainly much more cruel to women than she had had any idea of before these last months. And it had been so lovely, so indescribably lovely, that first delicious vague consciousness that there was 'something' between herself and Richard different from anything else in the world!

And now this wretched money business, and the question of her father, had come in to spoil it all! And of course, poor darling Robert. But curiously enough it wasn't, just now, her anxiety over any broken heart of Robert that filled her with gloom. She had a queer instinctive feeling that she could always 'deal with' Robert, whether she married him or not; 'deal with' him and quiet him and satisfy him and make him happy or at least content. It was as though she felt that merely for her to be alive on the earth at all was in a sense enough for Robert!

The case of Richard was completely different.

And what, when it came to that, had she appealed to Richard for in her desperation? He had come to her and they had quarrelled. He was so tiresomely touchy and vain. And was that to be the end?

What was it, when she had written that letter, that she had had in her mind? He was by her side now and she must protect him from herself, from pity for herself, by making it seem that all was well between her and the painter. Why must she do this? Because she was a woman; and women were not allowed to say straight out, from a clear unclouded sky, 'I, Nelly Moreton, love you, Richard Storm.'

Instead of this they had to protect these impulsive susceptible creatures from their own emotions, from *their* emotions too! *Why* had they to do this? Why was the whole weight and burden of everything put upon them? Because they were women; and life had been arranged in that manner, by God, by nature, and by men!

'Well,' she said to her companion as they observed the figure of her father crossing the garden to meet them, 'you must give me your magician's advice very quickly; because I know Father intends to walk back with you to Selshurst after lunch. He has to make his final settlement today with the people there.'

She turned to him as she spoke and he noticed that though she lifted her eyebrows with a touch of quizzical humour her underlip was trembling.

'The magician's advice to the enchanted princess,' said he, 'had to be given in parables: *It's better to get drenched by the rain than to shelter where the lightning is attracted. But it's best of all to wait under the nearest hedge till the rain is over.*'

Her response to this was that same puzzled, bewildered, appealing look that had followed him in his first departure from her after she had watched him light the candles in Littlegate church and they had waited behind the bolted door.

Chapter 8

The look with which Nelly had received his evasive parable haunted Richard all the next day and the day after.

He set himself to examine his own feelings and to try, if he could, to sound hers.

He was unable to write a line; and was thankful enough when his correspondence arrived from Paris and gave him something definite to do apart from poetry.

He had learnt from what John Moreton said, as they walked to the town together, that in no less than a month's time they would have to move from the vicarage, so that the place might be made ready for his successor.

It was a wretched situation and the one thing that would have made his own way clearer, if not quite clear, a definite knowledge that Nelly really cared for him and did *not* care for Canyot, remained as obscure as ever.

He saw shrewdly enough the diabolical trap in which the girl was caught, with nothing except immediate marriage as an escape from a struggle for bare life with a helpless parent on her hands. He saw too that whoever *did* step in and rescue her, whether it were Canyot or himself, there would stiil be the difficulty of her pride and that horrid suspicion – *was it out of pity?*

On the third day after his walk with the old man, Richard set out, in the morning, to see Nelly again. He was in a bitter, miserable frame of mind; for a letter had reached him from Paris with that signature he knew so fatally well and he had broken his resolution by reading it. He had meant to destroy it, but he had read it, and it punished him cruelly now with its sweet passionate clinging sentences, soft and electric, like the fingers that had penned it.

This letter and the vibrations it had stirred, coming on the top of his trouble about Nelly, wrecked completely his peace of mind.

He tore the great dancer's characteristic syllables into tiny bits and flung them from him into the hedge as he went along.

The contradictory emotions that swayed him – Nelly's white face and great childish eyes and those monumental heathen gestures of the body born to kindle undying desire – broke up his whole inner integrity.

In vain he sought to associate first one and then the other with his new mystical faith.

'I am nothing in myself,' he said to his heart, seeking to quiet its angry agitation. 'I am merely one momentary pulse of consciousness of the great earth-life that struggles to purge itself, to free itself, to enrich itself with a thousand new subtleties, to pass into the *something* else for which there is no name but the name of God.

'This perilous woman and this rare child are mere incidents in the love life of a wretched chance-driven wanderer. I take one. I

110

take the other. I leave them both. It matters nothing in the final issue. All that matters is that this personal life of mine should lose itself in the larger life that flows down the generations; that I should *become* that life and let it become me. And then that I should express its beauty, its tragic wonderful cool-breathing eternal beauty, in such words as I can hammer out!'

He said these things to himself as he strode the now well-known lane. But these things brought him no peace. That white face with the troubled eyes remained more important to him than any earth-soul. And those noble limbs moving in incomparable rhythms against the black curtains of the Théâtre des Arts refused to be reduced to the temporary and the irrelevant.

They pressed upon him, that girl's face and that woman's form. They demanded that his philosophy should include them, account for them, reconcile them. Ah! it could never *reconcile* them. That was, he thought with a bitter smile, precisely where philosophy broke down.

He half expected, as lovers do, that he would meet the girl where he had met her before; but he arrived at the vicarage without having caught a glimpse of her.

He found the door of the house open and he could see the buxom Grace at the further end of the kitchen garden pulling up lettuces.

He knocked. There was no answer. He knocked again. Still there was no answer. He wondered if he should shout to Grace and command her to announce his presence. He looked at his watch. It was a quarter to twelve.

'They must both be out,' he said to himself. Then it occurred to him to look into the church, where he had first seen her.

Yes! There she was; kneeling in the very spot where he had sat when he had lighted those candles to the memory of Benjamin and Susanna.

The old atheist priest – if so reverent a worshipper of Christ could be called an atheist – was celebrating what was certainly an unorthodox and probably an illegal Mass. *Maybe for the last time too!* thought Richard, as he slipped quietly into the building and knelt down at the girl's side. She had lifted her head at the sound of his footsteps and as he took his place and she moved further into the pew to make room for him she gave him a smile so radiant, so full of spontaneous happiness, that it redeemed in one moment all the past days. It was certainly from a sincere and contrite heart that he muttered his 'mea culpa, mea maxima culpa' during that ancient rite, the one flawless work of art, whatever else it might be, of the passionate mutterings of the old man – and Richard noticed how often his heretical old lips blundered inevitably into the great word he loathed – it seemed to both of them that in a sense beyond anything they had ever felt they were lifted above the troubles of brain and flesh and nerves. 'Lifted into what?' the man asked himself, as they remained on their knees, with the passion of the thing upon them, as the unfrocked priest carried away the vessels he had used. 'Not into any mere soul of the earth! Into something that belonged to the whole stellar system. Yes! and beyond that! Into something that belonged to the life which was behind and within life, from whose unknown heart the souls of men and gods and planets and stars drew the rhythm that sustained the universe.'

By a mutual impulse they moved out together without waiting for the old man. Nelly showed him her mother's grave, upon which the *orchis maculata* now put forth tiny red buds. '*Cecily*', murmured Richard, 'what a delicious old-fashioned name! It seems to smell of herbaceous borders and box hedges!'

'It's my name!' cried Nelly, laughing. 'Eleanor Cecily Moreton,' she repeated solemnly.

'I should like to have known your mother,' he said earnestly.

'You'd have liked her much better than me,' she responded. 'She would have never said horrid things to you.'

They moved on to the grave of Benjamin and Susanna. It gave them both a peculiar satisfaction to feel how they were linked by this churchyard.

'Why didn't they call you Talbot?' she asked.

'They must have known what a rebel I was going to be. It wouldn't do for a friend of revolutionaries to be called Talbot.'

'Are you a revolutionary?' she inquired. 'You seem to me most awfully conservative – much more conservative than I am.'

'I don't know what I am,' said Richard. 'I met a man in Paris who'd have made a Red of me if I'd seen much more of him. I'm afraid I'm too easily influenced.'

'I like people who can be influenced,' she said gravely. 'Father certainly can't and I don't think Robert can – except by me!'

This last phrase was thrown in after a pause and was accompanied by that mischievous elfish smile which had puzzled Richard before.

Leaving the grave of Dr Storm they moved together towards the house, Nelly silent and preoccupied, pondering something.

Suddenly she turned to him with shining eyes. 'Do you know what I'm going to do with you?' she cried. 'I'm going to take you for a picnic! I often do that with my best friends – with Mrs Shotover for example–' and she shot a whimsical glance at Richard which was received, this time, very amiably. 'Grace will look after Father. He hates picnics. Besides, he'll want his rest after lunch. And we'll go off and have all the afternoon to ourselves till tea time! Shall we do that? Would you like to? Unless you'd prefer to look at the painted ladies again!'

Richard's contentment at this proposal was so evident that it did not need his feeble joke, 'I prefer them unpainted!' to show her what he was feeling.

Gay and radiant, with a happiness in their hearts only permitted once or twice in a lifetime to the sons and daughters of men, they went together into the kitchen and assisted Grace, who leered at them both like the sly Shakespearean wench she was and even winked at her young mistress, in preparing sandwiches and cake and bread and butter and jam.

Hearing their voices and laughter the old naturalist came in too after a while. Richard was surprised at the friendly humorous chuckles he bestowed on the expedition and at the alacrity with which he added to their basket of provisions, a flask of wine from his study cupboard.

'A shame to leave any of this for the good man who comes after me!' he said, with chuckling unction and maliciously twinkling eyes. 'It's what I use in *my* Mass; and if you young people drink it up, there won't be any left for the *Eidolon Vulgaris!*'

He escorted thme to the gate and wished them good luck with such mellow and ironic benevolence that Richard could not help thinking of the dignified *bonhomie* of the Rabelaisian Grangousier.

Nelly did not hesitate for a moment as to the direction they should take. She led him along a little secluded path bordered by blossoming elders which emerged after a mile or two of circuitous ascent upon a high ridge of arable upland, covered at the season by a waving sea of green rye and barley.

She led him across these cornfields, walking with swinging youthful steps in front of him along the narrow chalk path; every now and then stopping and turning round to point out to him how red-bright the fumitory was and to indicate to him some little plant associated with her earlier memories.

When they reached the further brink of this ridge, where the ryefield ended in a thickset hedge and the path in a three-barred well-worn stile, Richard cried aloud with delight at the beauty of the valley that lay stretched before them. It was enclosed on the further end by a wood of oaks and hazel; and the edges of it, sloping down by soft degrees to a grassy level floor, were covered with thyme and cistus, milkwort and trefoil.

'Don't you like it?' cried the girl in a voice of such thrilling happiness that it made even the turtle dove's crooning seem less golden in contentment. 'I call it the Happy Valley. I never come here unless I'm in my best mood of all.' And she added after a pause, 'I haven't been here for two years!'

Richard helped her over the stile and they lifted the basket across. 'How heavy it is!' she said with a quick frown of solicitude. 'I oughtn't to have let you carry it all that way. How thoughtless I am! I quite forgot the old thing. Here, let's hide it under the hedge. We don't want it yet do we? We can come back for it when I've shown you the Happy Valley.'

Richard was certainly relieved to get rid of the weight when it actually was out of his hands, but he had not been conscious of it as a burden. He felt that day as if all the baskets in the world might be piled on his back and he would be oblivious to it.

They ran down the thyme-scented slope hand in hand, and when they reached level ground he pressed her fingers so tightly in his own before releasing them that poor Canyot's engagement ring hurt her severely.

It may have been the sharpness of the ring bringing melancholy thoughts, or it may have been the shy happiness of a heart too full for expression, but she walked very silently by his side through the rest of the Happy Valley. It was Richard, not she, who exclaimed with astonished delight at the huge masses of budding honeysuckle that overspread the bushes above them. It was Richard, not she, who pointed to the sprays of wild roses, the first he had seen that year.

When they reached the end of the valley, where the path they were following entered the wood, they stopped by mutual consent and leaned over the old weather-worn gate covered with a minute grey lichen and looked into the cool leafy shadows.

'Why don't you take off your hat?' he said suddenly, in a voice that to himself sounded strange and forced. 'Like you did in the Selshurst garden,' he added in a louder tone, making an effort, so it seemed to himself, to conceal the wild beating of his heart.

As he spoke he flung down his own hat and stick on to the bracken fronds beside them.

Her breath came unevenly, in funny little gasps. She put her hands feebly up to her head and pulled out the hat pins one by one; and then holding the hat on the top of the gate stuck the pins she had removed into it, one by one again, her fingers visibly trembling. High up in a beech tree above them a little invisible warbler kept uttering its own name in a monotonous chant, as if drunk with the sunshine and the pride of its well-hidden nest. 'Chiff-chaff! Chiff-chaff! chiff-chaff!' that invisible owner of those leafy solitudes kept repeating.

Richard took her hat and laid it gently down, balancing it carefully upon a last year's plant of hart's tongue fern, still glossy and unfaded.

As he did so one of those weakly fluttering pale-coloured moths, which frequent shadowy places and move so helplessly when they're disturbed, flew against his face.

When he turned to her again he noticed that her eyes were so large and bright that it was as if a disembodied spirit was gazing into his very soul. The slight movement he instinctively had made towards her was stopped suddenly by that look and he clutched the top of the gate and drew a deep breath.

Then it was that the brightness in her eyes softened, melted, grew infinitely passive and tender, and by an impulse that seemed to come from some power outside themselves they threw their arms around each other and clung together, their lips joined and their hearts beating as if they were two hearts in one body.

'Chiff-chaff! chiff-chaff! chiff-chaff!' repeated the little invisible lord of the sanctuary they had invaded, giving to their encounter the winged blessing of the very Eros of the woods.

Very gently the girl released herself and a sigh of happiness that seemed beyond even the happiness of that place of enchantment rose from her lips and floated away among the leaves.

Then she nestled against him, her head bent so low that he could not see her face.

For a long space they stood thus silently together, he leaning against the gate and she leaning against him. Then with his hands on each side of her fair head he lightly lifted up her face as if it had been a delicate white flower and holding it away from him kissed her with a long silent kiss that seemed to throw so strange a trance upon them both that even after he had released her and she leaned, with her head on her hands, against that confederate gate-bar, and he rested motionless beside her, his arms about her body, they seemed like people drugged, spellbound, magnetized, 'entoiled in woofèd fantasies'.

'Chiff-chaff! chiff-chaff! chiff-chaff!' repeated the relentless warbler; and neither of the two to the end of their lives forgot that particular sound. It blended with the faint, relaxed, indescribably sweet languor that took possession of the maiden, and it blended with the infinitely tender if less deep emotion that filled the heart of the man.

At length she moved aside from his caresses and put up her hands against him as he tried to kiss her again.

'Give me my hat, dearest one,' she said. 'We must be good now. We've so much to think of. I feel as if I ought to think of everybody now, for the rest of my life. I've been so happy with you, my dear!' She surprised him by suddenly lifting up one of his hands and pressing it against her lips. The gesture touched him more than anything she had ever done. A great wave of tenderness rose up in him, so that at that moment he would have willingly marched straight to death for her sake.

But as she dropped his hand her old mocking-elf's smile flickered over her white face. 'Poor old Robert,' she murmured. 'Look! I've still got on his ring.'

She held up her fingers so that he might see his rival's gift. It was a simple enough matter – a little turquoise set in pearls; but Richard regarded it with gloom. It brought back to him with a rush of painful thoughts all the troublesome circumstances that hemmed them round.

'Are you going on wearing it now?' he asked as she put on her hat and they turned away together leaving the little chiff-chaff in possession of his leafy paradise.

'I'm not going to take it off *today*' she answered. 'It's unlucky to take off one ring till you've got another!' And she laughed a naughty child's laugh at his discomforted face.

Her response irritated him. It seemed the sort of thing that a well-bred girl oughtn't to say. It was a silly servant-girl remark, he thought, and he teased himself in sulky silence over it till they were halfway back through the Happy Valley. It somehow made him think of Mrs Shotover. Had that confounded old woman really corrupted the girl? Had she put coarse, common, cynical notions into her head?

Observing the effect of her words, Nelly gave way to an irresistible temptation and did what she could to make it worse. 'How do I know,' she said, with a mocking little laugh, 'that you won't feel quite differently tomorrow? I'd better not throw Robert away *too* quickly.'

If she had intended to wound him she certainly succeeded. His swarthy face darkened and he raised one of his brown thin hands to his mouth, an instinctive habit of his when seriously annoyed. If the gesture was caused by a desire to hide a certain ugly, cruel, revengeful curve of his lips, it hid nothing at all from her; and she went still further . . .

'Robert has faith in me,' she said, 'whatever I do and whatever I say, too. Oh you don't know what things I've said to him! And he's taken them all like the dear lamb he is. Poor old Rob! I've been a bad girl to him I'm afraid.'

'What a wonderful mass of honeysuckle!' Richard cried in a sort of desperation, anxious to do anything to put an end to this miserable estrangement. 'I'm going to get you some.' And he proceeded to clamber up the bank and make his way into the middle of the brushwood. He derived a savage pleasure from the nettle stings and thorn pricks through which he struggled. He felt as though in forcing his way through these obstacles towards the resplendent fragrant clusters above him he were fighting back to those delicious moments of love which her teasing had spoilt.

But how *could* she drag in that business of 'dear old Robert' and his turquoise ring? A 'lamb' did she call him? A confounded old tiger! But how *could* she, after kissing him like that and being kissed, drag things down to banality and commonness and silly servant-girl superstitions? Or was she, after all, quite a different person from what he had imagined, from the Nelly he had fancied himself so fond of? Was she, really, playing the two of them off against each other and ready to take which ever seemed the more desirable catch? He was able for the moment – perhaps the thorn pricks and nettle stings helped him – to think of her thus grossly without the Feast shame; and he thought to himself how queer it was that the fact of men and women being thrilled by one another's caresses did not in the least really bring them together. They seemed indeed to pay the penalty for that momentary unity by a more absolute relapse into their separate hostile identities when the rare moment was past.

Then he thought within his heart, *But after all I love her. But this 'love' or whatever it is, seems to have no influence upon our clashes with each other, as fierce separate units of nature, each struggling for its own purposes!* He derived, as men of his type do, a revengeful satisfaction from this sort of pedantic analysis.

That he could analyse the girl thus and detach himself from her so quickly after their first embrace gave him a malicious satisfaction and soothed his vanity like a costly ointment.

On the strength of it he tore and rent at the reluctant tangles of yellow and rose-pink sweetness, pulling down huge trailing sprays of it, heedless of scratches upon face and hands, and gathering it in his arms in massed confusion, all mixed up with bindweed and bryony.

From the grassy level below Nelly watched his movements. 'Bless his heart!' she said to herself. 'I love him! I love him! I love him! This is not a dream. This is really true. I am standing in my Happy Valley watching my man pick me honeysuckle.'

Then she thought, 'I mustn't tease him. I won't tease him. I'll be sweet to him when he comes back. But how *could* he get so angry when he's just found out I love him? When we've just been together like that?

'How peculiar men are! Everything seems on the surface with them – how you behave, how you look, what you say. As if it mattered what you *said*! Don't *they* ever say things by opposites? Don't *they* ever rage and stamp and scratch and bite and tease without it meaning anything at all; anything except – oh! I don't know – a sort of stretching out of one's arms and legs, after sitting in the same position too long? No I suppose they don't. I suppose they *can't* be superficial, however much they try! I suppose their surface is the same as their depth. I suppose they're *all* surface!

'Mrs Richard Storm. It sounds rather nice. I don't think I shall want to keep him in Littlegate. It would be lovely to have a flat in Paris. But Father can't be left. Oh how annoying it is not to be entirely alone in the world! No! Father can't be left. And I must make Robert completely understand that I really shall belong to him much more when I'm married to Richard than I am now. Because he gets on my nerves now with everything unsettled and I can't love him as much as I do really without his wanting to marry me. But when I'm married to Richard he can't want to marry me, so I shall be free to be as lovely to him as ever I like. For I won't stand it if Richard gets jealous. If he has me altogether that must be enough for him. I won't allow him to be jealous! I won't have it.'

When Richard did finally come scrambling down the bank to her side his arms were so full of honeysuckle that he looked like a moving bush.

'Though Birnam Wood be come to Dunsinane!' cried the girl running to meet him, and with feminine mischief kissing his face through the masses of honeysuckle before he could catch hold of her. 'Well done! How perfectly beautiful! How sweet they are – intoxicating.' She pressed a spray to her face and inhaled the heavy fragrance. 'Oh Richard how happy I am! What a day this is. Oh! my dear, my dear—'

Her words died away, as dropping the great scented bundle at their feet, he clasped her slim form tightly to him and kissed her on the mouth, cheeks, eyelids and chin. Then, while he held her close with one arm round her body, he passed his free hand caressingly over her forehead.

'You do really love me, sweetheart?' he said, searching half-angrily, half-tenderly, for that absolute conviction of certitude in those soft feminine eyes for which the whole human race since the beginning has sought in vain.

She answered with so passionate and clinging a kiss that it was difficult to retain the questioning mood, and with the masses of golden-pink sweetness, like an offering to them from her own special gods of her Happy Valley, held in both their arms, they moved slowly back to where they had left their basket.

Their meal was unspoilt by any further difference. Bareheaded they sat opposite each other on a bank of thyme and milkwort; the now un-analytical Richard insisting on twisting a spray of his treasure trove round her head, and round her neck too, while in eager solemnity she untied the provisions.

They ate hungrily and happily, enjoying themselves without thought of past and future, dividing lettuce sandwiches and jam sandwiches between them with the laughing greed of lovers who can afford to play with the lower appetites, as children play with toys.

Having drunk to the very dregs the liberal bottle of milk supplied by Grace they discovered at the bottom of the basket, lying by the side of the vicar's flask of port wine, nothing less than Nelly's silver christening mug.

'Let's christen our meeting with this!' cried the girl; and jumping to their feet they filled the little cup to the brim.

The sun shining upon the red wine made it glow like the blood of a god; and when they had both drunk of it and kissed each other 'with purple-stained mouth', they poured out what was left as a heathen libation to the powers – whatever they might have been – who had brought about their encounter.

In queer unlovely places, many months after this, in sordid streets, in depressing offices, on crowded pavements, Richard Storm had many occasions to remember that moment of his life, when wreathed with honeysuckle, round head and neck and waist, this girl, the very incarnation of youthful passion, poured out the wine cup upon the earth.

Chapter 9

Robert Canyot showed himself more of a man over the affair of Nelly's marriage than anyone who had known him would have expected. He put off for several weeks his voyage to America so that he might himself give the bride away.

Mrs Shotover denounced the whole business and refused to be present at the wedding. She was positively rude to Nelly on the subject; accusing her, in very pointed language, language more suitable to the age of Fielding than of Hardy, of having made up her mind to keep both the men. There was certainly this much justification for the old lady's wrath, that Nelly refused to give up her former fiancé's ring – the turquoise with little pearls – and wore no other except the thin golden one that proclaimed her a wedded wife.

The old woman only got one chance of giving vent completely to her feelings and that was not to Nelly but to her husband.

If she was 'eighteenth-century' in her explicitness to the bride, she was positively 'Elizabethan' in her outpouring to the bridegroom. Richard however was far too content with his lot at that moment to do more than lead the woman on and tease her with an exaggerated serenity.

He was as a matter of fact perfectly serene. It suited him in every respect, this devoted and very practical waiting upon her of his bride's former betrothed. It was precisely one of those situations that Richard's peculiar nature was eminently adapted to sustain with aplomb and indulgence. He felt thoroughly sorry for his defeated rival and it eased his conscience in the only way his conscience *could*-be really eased by giving him every facility to make the best of the rind, so to speak, while he enjoyed the fruit.

A man is never displeased to see his mistress adored by another when he feels she is entirely his own; and there was not the remotest shadow of doubt that Nelly was his, just then, from the top of her head to the sole of her foot. The sweetness of her complete abandonment to him during those first days was indeed the most thrilling and delicious experience he had known in his whole life – so wonderful and flawless that he felt it would be an ingratitude to the gods not to dispense in his turn as much happiness as he could.

Canyot's shadow on their pleasure would have been much worse than his real presence, for the painter seemed to have the power of reducing the pain of his loss to a minimum as long as he was not driven away and forgotten.

The truth was that neither Richard nor Nelly had the least idea of what was going on in the young man's mind. He showed no outward sign of bitterness or moroseness or jealousy.

He was gentler in the expression of his opinions, quicker-witted it almost seemed in his response to their high spirits; and there was not the least tendency on his part to take advantage of the serene indulgence with which Richard tolerated and indeed encouraged his friendship with the bride.

They were married in Littlegate church by the old naturalist, and the service that united them was the last he was permitted, as priest of the church, officially to perform.

They went down to Fogmore for seven days' honeymoon, during which time the devoted Canyot helped Grace and the old man to settle into Hill Cottage.

On their return from Fogmore the painter informed them that he had decided to put off his voyage to a yet further date, giving as a plausible enough reason that he would be too late now for the Philadelphia exhibition of his work, and that the New York one was not to occur till five or six weeks later.

Instead of leaving them therefore to enjoy their *vita nuova* in complete isolation the extraordinary young man proceeded quite calmly to settle down again at Wind Shuttle Farm.

This unexpected move of his was not entirely agreeable to Richard but it would have been much more disagreeable to him to have seen the least cloud on his young wife's face; and she, it appeared, was entirely pleased with the arrangement.

He could not altogether find the clue to her attitude to her old lover, but he contented himself with putting it down to Nelly's maternal instinct and her girlish desire to soften as far as was possible the boy's feeling of loss in Mrs Canyot's death.

'She wants to "mother" him,' he said to himself. He derived a certain self-flattering moral unction from the thought that he was being singularly and unconventionally magnanimous to them both.

Thus did those golden June weeks pass by, in almost perfect

felicity, for Richard; in whatever mysterious happiness a young girl derives from the satisfaction of her heart's passion, for Nelly; and in fierce persistent wrestling with new problems of his art, for the recluse at Wind Shuttle Farm.

The only cloud upon the horizon, if it could be called a cloud, was the estrangement between Mrs Richard Storm of Hill Cottage and Mrs George Shotover of Furze Lodge. But this cloud had already broken in two rain-storms of strange language from the latter lady; there now seemed no reason to doubt that among the scanty parishioners of the newly appointed vicar of Littlegate none was more clearly marked out for an unruffled life than the daughter of John Moreton.

It was only the scurrying white-tailed rabbits and the great black-winged rooks haunting the long summer twilights between Furze Cover and Horthing Down who could have predicted any sort of evil omen upon the wind; and these could only have done it had they possessed enough superstitious intelligence to give credence to the angry mutterings of a lonely old woman, deprived by nature's tricks of the one thing she loved.

The weather continued to bestow upon the newly married couple, as the season drew on towards the longest day, its most wonderful largess of ample sunshine and cool-breathing balmy air. A few heavy showers in those moonless nights kept the light chalk soil from becoming over-dry.

In the lower pastures the lush grasses were already laid level with the ground; and the murmur of the mowing machine, like a great invisible bumble bee laden with summer spoils, made a constant background to the crooning of the doves in the massive-foliaged trees.

On the uplands the green rye was already up to the height of Nelly's waist as she went afield to gather the first red poppies, while the green barley was up to her knees and the wheat well above her ankles.

The blackbird's reedy cry was heard seldom now; its place in the feathered orchestra of the lanes and fields was taken by the thicker-throated 'muggy' and the hot sun-burnt ecstasies of finches and buntings.

There was a perceptible change in the mood of Robert Canyot as the time drew near for his departure to America.

He saw less of Nelly and hardly anything of Richard.

He went out, morning after morning, for the whole day taking his lunch with him and not returning till late in the evening.

It was always to Toat Farm that he went, for he kept his precious easel-picture, now near completion, of that sluggish pond and those sombre ancient walls in the cottage of Sally-Maria's aunt. He had become a close friend of this woman, a person almost as silent as her dumb niece; and Charley Budge and Mr Priddle had grown so accustomed to his presence that they gave him their most familiar nods and 'how-be-gettin'-on-then' as if he were an established institution like old Miss Stone or the grocer's cart from Selshurst. When it was a Sunday that he was there, there used sometimes to be quite a group of farm hands round his picture, Charley having brought Tom Rattle and Jimmy Roebuck to see 'how 'twaren't like a common school-marm job – more like what 'un sees in shop windies and them show places'.

And on these occasions the men in their tightly fitting, uncomfortable cloth suits, with a flower stuck in both buttonhole and cap, would poke at the picture tentatively with their sticks as though it had been Farmer Patchem's dangerous sow.

Canyot had put the very 'body and pressure' of his soul into this picture and the rustic wonder it excited gave him more pleasure than any virtuoso's praise. He held, like Molière, that the first test of good art was that it should arrest the attention of the simplest. He had concentrated all his powers upon the reflection in the water of that rank herbage and those mossy walls, indicating as well as he could the shadowed presence there of a spirit of the spot, carrying the mind down a long dim vista of obscure memories, gathering itself, out of the colours and shapes of the moment, into a kind of eternal vision – a platonic archetype, that was more than a crumbling wall and a bank of hemlocks.

It was on Canyot's last Sunday in England that he presented himself soon after breakfast at Hill Cottage and bluntly asked Nelly to accompany him that day to his favourite haunt. He wanted to put the very final touches to his picture and he wanted also, so he told her, to make her acquainted with Sally-Maria, so that he should feel that the child was not left quite friendless at his departure.

His abrupt request fell like a sharply flung pebble into the smooth waters of the little *ménage*.

Richard had been enlarging upon the fact that they had not yet revisited their Happy Valley and he had secured a promise from Nelly that they should walk over there that afternoon.

He looked at her therefore very emphatically, when in their small garden, among the phloxes and sweet-williams, Canyot sprung his intrusive request. Nelly looked silently and nervously from one to another. Her mind recalled Mrs Shotover's upbraidings. Was she really, as the old woman had said, behaving as no decent girl ought to behave in 'hanging on to two men'?

'I'm afraid I can't, Robert,' she said; 'you see we've arranged to go out this afternoon and take our tea out so as to give Grace a free day. I shouldn't like to disappoint Grace, you see. And if we left Richard alone she'd never let him get tea for himself. She looks after him better than I do. No, Robert, I'm afraid it's impossible.' The little invention about Grace and her 'day out' had brought the colour to her cheeks; and the young painter did not hesitate to fix his eyes sternly and passionately upon her.

She looked tantalizingly soft and sweet, hovering there in her embarrassed hesitation.

She looked the very incarnation of English girlhood, some idyllic blending of earthiness and innocence such as might well make a jilted lover 'grow pale and spectre-thin' with unsatisfied longing. Canyot was neither thin nor pale at that moment, however. His muscular form was very erect and straight. His tanned, corrugated face scowling gloomily at her showed no inclination to be the only sufferer that day. His empty sleeve too had its own voice in the matter. He was one of those who had left 'something' behind in France; as he stood before her, subjecting her to the concentrated reproach of his gaze, there was that about him that made it very difficult for Nelly to hold to her decision. She felt a sudden immense pity for him and her heart nearly yielded. The freemasonry of youth was between them, adding a curious poignancy to her maternal instinct, and the very tenderness and softness of her mood just then, though due to her abandonment to Richard, made it all the more difficult for her to be hard and austere in dealing with her former lover.

'My wife will be delighted to see your picture some other day, before you leave us,' remarked Richard, conscious for the first time since his marriage that he and Nelly were at cross-purposes.

Nelly had looked up with a quick flush when he began to speak but her eyes dropped and she bent down over the flowers when she realized the import of his words. Why couldn't he have been generous just then? She would have rewarded him for it. She would have loved him with an added love. Why couldn't men understand these things? Why must they always be so legal and exacting, when what was wanted was the impulse of self-effacement?

She kept her head bent down for a perceptible moment of embarrassing suspense, inhaling the heavy scent of the phloxes until it became a thing that was no longer a perfume at all, but a thought – a wild reckless thought in her brain.

The beauty of the yellow day-lilies against the curves of her bending figure made Canyot sigh bitterly and worked like a sort of angry fever in his blood.

'Well,' he said, almost roughly, 'I've got to go back anyway to Wind Shuttle to get my things. I've got to pass by here again. It's on my way. So if you change your mind look out for me. Do you understand? I'll be back in half an hour but I won't worry you if you don't want to come. I've only a week more, you know. Then I shan't trouble you any more.'

He took no notice at all of Richard's movement to open the gate for him but strode surlily off down the slope of the hill.

At that moment the little gate swung open again and the ex-priest entered.

'What's that, Father?' cried the girl, noticing a letter in the old man's hand.

'It's for your husband, my sweet,' remarked the naturalist. 'I met the boy bringing it up. It came by some extra post. It's a foreign one.'

Nelly snatched the letter from him. 'Oh! it's from Paris. I do love the French stamps. They're so much more exciting than ours. Here you are!' She handed it over to her husband who, seeing the hand it was written by, placed it unopened in his pocket.

Nelly put on her spoilt-child air at once, the air so natural to youthful twenty-two married to middle-aged forty-five.

'Don't hide it away!' she cried. 'Nelly wants to see it. Nelly likes foreign letters!'

Richard turned just a little bit pale. This was a most unlucky trick of the imps of chance! 'It really wouldn't interest you, sweetheart,' he said; 'it's not an exciting letter. A friend of mine – not anything thrilling.'

The old man who had been watching this scene, with a shrewd interest unusual in him, now broke in. He laid his hand on his son-in-law's arm – 'Show it to her, boy; show it to her,' he said. 'Never keep letters away from them. They don't like it. It's a bad beginning.' And he sighed heavily, thinking of one of his own early quarrels with his dead Cecily.

Richard turned paler still. He found himself stammering some quite fantastic irrelevance, about its being a literary secret.

Nelly made a quick movement and snatched the letter from his pocket. 'You make me curious,' she said. 'I must have just a tiny little peep.' And she made as though she were about to open it.

When he recalled later every little detail of that scene it seemed to him as if a terrible eternity elapsed between that movement of hers and what he did next. During that eternity of seconds he seemed conscious of jet-black icebergs crashing together in a darkened sea.

Then, in a desperate inspiration, he acted.

He snatched the letter from her and tore it, unopened as it was, into four thick pieces. 'There!' he said in a husky voice. 'Come here, Nell!'

She glanced at her father and raised her eyebrows a little.

The old man made a gesture as much as to say, 'Go in with him, my dear, but it's a bad job!' And then she followed him into the house. 'Here, Nell!' he called and she followed him into the kitchen.

He lifted the round iron cover of the kitchen grate, with the implement appointed for that purpose, and thrust the four torn pieces into the fire. Then he replaced the iron lid.

Grace was quick to notice by both their faces that something was amiss. 'Lord, Miss Nelly!' she cried. 'What be up to then? Burnin' weddin' scrips and holy promises? Lord! Mr Richard, sir – look to her now! Goodness save us! what fine cantraps and unlawful doin's is this? Miss Nelly darlin', now don't 'ee be takin' on like that! Don't 'ee, dearie!'

And she put her stalwart arms round her mistress who had suddenly turned a deadly white and was supporting herself against the table.

Grace almost lifted her on to a chair. 'Don't stand starin' like as you a' seed the Devil, Mr Richard. Get the dear darlin' a drop o' water!'

He put a glass hurriedly under the tap, obeying the wench 'meek as any dazed sheep' as Grace commented afterwards. 'Gi'e it to I!' she cried. 'Bless the man! it's the hot water tap 'ee's a-turnin'. Here, gi'e it to I!'

But Nelly waved away the glass. 'I'm all right now,' she said, 'thanks all the same Gracie dear!'

And certainly her colour began coming rapidly back.

Richard stood anxiously and wretchedly before her, twisting his fingers backwards and forwards and slowly nodding his head, as was his habit when utterly nonplussed.

She raised her eyes to his face and smiled a bitter, cruel little smile. It gratified and pleased her to see him look so entirely foolish.

Then she sprang to her feet. 'All right now Gracie!' she said. 'It was the heat, I suppose.'

'Hope 'tweren't no wills nor testaments nor birth certifications you've a-throwed away like that and burned to cinders? I keeps this 'ere stove as hot as Pharaoh's Furnace, I do, else the darned thing don't cook nothin'; but I ain't a-heatin' kitchen fires for to burn weddin' dockiments and citations!'

'That's all right, Gracie. It was nothing. It was just a letter from a friend. It was nothing important.'

'Well, it be ashes now, sure enough, whatever it were!' Grace returned to her cooking with a philosophical wink.

The husband and wife went back to the front of the cottage. They found the old man anxiously awaiting them in the porch.

'Nothing serious I hope,' said he. He looked at Richard gravely. 'Never keep letters from them. And never explain anything to them. Obey your own conscience. Go your own way. And if they want you to change your mind, just you hold your tongue and go on as you are. They'll come round all right, sooner or later. But never argue with 'em. Do what you have to do; never hide your letters, and never argue!'

'There's a lot in what you say, sir,' said Richard very solemnly, propitiating the old man.

When the ex-priest had returned to his own room, the husband and wife moved by common consent into the garden. They both seemed conscious of a craving for air and sun. But the magnetism of their quarrel held them together and drew them towards each other.

'So you still keep up with at least one of them?' said Nelly, bending down, precisely as she had done half an hour ago, to smell the phloxes.

'Yes, I keep up with one of them,' answered Richard. 'If to "keep up with" means to burn letters unopened.'

She lifted up her head at that, and her eyes flashed from her flushed face like two steel-blue blades. 'Don't lie, Richard! It's not worth it. You know you've never burnt *one* of that woman's letters before! And you wouldn't have burnt that one, if you hadn't been scared of my reading it. It's no use lying. We may just as well face it. If you *must* keep these things going on, you must, I suppose. If you're made like that, well! you are. But it's rather a shock to me, my dear – just at first – you know.'

Richard had never felt so miserable, so uncomfortable, or so much of a complete fool as he did at that moment.

He did not know whether to be angry or relieved when the figure of Canyot, carrying a basket, appeared outside the gate.

Nelly gave him one quick glance – and then she waved to him and shouted: 'Wait, Robert! Please wait! I'm coming with you.'

He waited just where he was without making a sign. He began picking the long grasses out of the hedge and sucking the sweetness from their stalks. He whistled as he did this and flicked away the flies from his forehead. He took no more notice of Richard than if the man had been one of the posts of the gate.

'We've thought better of it, you see,' said the writer, after a moment's pause in which he gathered all his wits together to carry the thing through somehow.

Oh how he hated these tense undignified scenes! *In France*, he thought, misquoting Laurence Sterne with a miserable inward laugh, *they do these things better*.

'I'm sailing on Saturday,' was the only response he got from Canyot, who now began nibbling the little sticky leaves of a briar rose.

Richard turned and went into the house. He knocked at the door of the room he shared with Nelly.

'I'm just coming,' the girl called out. 'May I come in?' Richard pleaded, turning the handle of the door. The door was locked from the inside – for the first time!

He walked back into the garden feeling thoroughly miserable. He had hoped for one swift all-obliterating all-forgiving embrace. She had deliberately forestalled this intention. She intended to go off for the whole day with Canyot, leaving the rift between them raw and unhealed.

There was his rival, stolid and impassive, an ugly one-armed sentinel at the gate of their lost paradise. He had the end of a dockleaf in his mouth now. Would he eat up the whole hedge?

Nelly came flying past him with tripping steps. She pretended that the haste of that moment was extreme so as to avoid having to give him a farewell kiss.

She was out of the gate before he could open it for her, and instead of pausing then she ran past the young painter and up the hill-path crying as she ran, 'Come on, Robert, we shall never get there if you're so slow. Come on! I'll race you to the top!'

Canyot picked up the picnic basket provided for him by Mrs Winsome and strode after her. About ten yards away he stopped and looked back, waving his stick at Richard. 'Sailing on Saturday!' he shouted and turned again to pursue the girl whose light mauve dress was still visible from the garden moving rapidly among the elder bushes and furze.

Richard waited till they were out of sight and then went straight into the kitchen. 'Grace!' he shouted, but Grace was in the rooms above and did not hear him. *I can't stand a lunch alone with the old man*, he thought and began mechanically putting together some bread and cheese. This he crammed into his pocket along with some small cakes. 'Grace!' he shouted again. This time she heard him and came running down, her heavy West Country tread shaking the whole cottage. 'You must look after Mr Moreton, today, Grace,' he said, in the most offhand, easy manner he could assume. 'We shall all be out.'

'Nothing wrong, Mr Richard, I hope, begging your pardon? Nothing to do with burnin' any certifications or such like? 'Tis a queer world and summat of the likes of they things do bring terrible trouble on folks' heads. I knew'd 'ee and Miss Nelly had had a bit of a ruption. And what's more I could have told 'ee 'twere comin', this very mornin', if 'ee'd a listened to I. 'Twas that girl hedge pig the Master brought in the house. I never did hold wi 'bringin' the like of them stinking pricklies into Christian families. I knew'd it 'ud mean trouble soon as I set eyes on 'un. Master ain't as careful as 'a should be over these 'ere pick-ups. 'A kind o' forgets that 'tis you and Miss Nelly's kiss-luck time, when men and maidies be growin' into married folk like, and lovin' natural and unthinkin' by night and by day. 'A shouldn't a' done it. 'Twere a temptin' them as is Above. A girt lousy prickleback, with a snout like Satan and little squimsy eyes. Do 'ee tell 'un of it, Mr Richard, do 'ee tell 'un of it. I can't abide them stinkin' things. Sparrerhawks and flitter-mice be all very well. They be honest fellow creatures, they be; but them hedge pigs, 'tisn't behavin' right to the Dear Lord to go meddlin' wi' the likes o' they!'

'I'll do what I can, Grace,' said Richard when the woman stopped for breath. 'But you know what Mr Moreton is. Well! you'll be able to see for yourself that he only collects lucky things today. I may be back by tea time and I may not. Goodbye, Grace.'

'Don't 'ee go bein' sour and angered agin' our young leddy,' whispered Grace. 'Don't 'ee get argufying with 'un. The way to manage us womenfolk is to be one thing or 'tother. Kiss us soft and sweet or let's have it hard so us knows what's what. None of this burnin' o' dockiments and bidin' the time. Out w'it, straight and forrard; that's what I do say to my Jim.'

'You say very well, Grace,' responded the writer. 'I'm sure I hope you'll always be with us to keep us in the right path.'

'And don't 'ee let Miss Nelly go gadding off with young Mr Robert. There ain't no maid nor wife in God's kingdom what's perfect sure of 'erself when't do come to them carryin's on. We be all meanin' for the best; but girls be girls and young fellers be young fellers and 'tis hard to be stiff as a poker on haymaking days.'

Richard looked gravely into the young woman's face as if he were on the point of asking her what she really thought about his wife's attitude to Canyot. But he turned away with a smile. 'Well! Grace,' he said, 'you and I must make her so happy here, that she won't be in need of any friends but us. Goodbye Grace!' And he left the house and began walking gloomily and thoughtfully in the direction of the Happy Valley.

*

Old Mr Moreton was not altogether pleased when he found he was destined to spend a lonely Sunday. On weekdays he never expected much society. It seemed quite natural that they should all be occupied with their own affairs. But on Sundays it was rather different, because he felt a vague tradition in the air against going on just the same with his scientific work; and it was pleasant, as a change from that, to see something more of those he lived with.

He ate the admirable meal prepared by Grace in rather melancholy silence which was not made any more cheerful by the servant's comments on the events of the morning.

'It ain't nice of Miss Nelly and Master Richard to leave 'ee lonesome and solemn-like of a fine Zunday. It don't seem kind o' natural; and I be lorn to see 'ee so. I just out and told 'un straight how it do seem to I. There'll be sad goin's on, present, I sez to 'un, when the Missus and that young man get too fond like. Kiss and be friends, I sez to 'un, and don't fall into the sin o' pride.'

'Your mistress is in a difficult position, Grace,' said the old man; 'and I'd rather you didn't talk about it. Mr Canyot has always been very considerate and civil. It's a difficult position for her. But the young man is going away in a few days so we shall be quieter then. We shall go on quietly and as usual then. But Mr Canyot is always very civil to me—' John Moreton sighed heavily – 'very civil and considerate.'

When the meal was over and he was thinking of returning for his usual rest, Grace, who came to take away what was left of the gooseberry tart for her own consumption, surprised him by saying, 'Why don't 'ee go and see Mrs Shotover, over to Furze Lodge, sir? She be an old friend of your'n I reckon and a good friend o' Miss Nelly's. Maybe she'd be able to hearten' 'ee up a bit, in a manner of speaking.'

The old man raised his head and stared at the maid. 'Eh? what's that, Gracie? Go to see *her* again?' He blinked with his deep-set grey eyes and knitted his shaggy eyebrows. 'But she and Nelly have been quarrelling since she was last here. But after all, *that* doesn't matter; that's nothing to do with *me*! I go quietly on my own way whatever fuss the womenfolk make, don't I, Grace? Well perhaps I *will* walk up in Furze Lodge direction when I've rested a bit. I do feel as if I needed a little change today. One can't work seven days a week.'

Well pleased with the result of her audacity the Dorsetshire maiden retired to the kitchen.

''Twill do the Master a gallon o' good,' she said to herself. 'What with one thing and another the poor old gentleman do look mighty doddery. 'Twill hearten 'im up like, to pass the time o' day with that old rappity-tappity.'

The afternoon of that June day proved hotter than Mr Moreton had anticipated. The old man found the way long and exhausting. It was most of it uphill and bare of trees; the scorching sun struck fiercely upon his lean black-coated figure.

He stopped frequently to rest and sat down at last in the middle of a cornfield, overtaken by a fit of dizziness.

As he sat there, seeing the green world of innumerable waving stalks about him, the world as it must always appear at that season to field mice, partridges, hares and rabbits, the old naturalist felt a profound melancholy enter his heart like some jagged piece of iron.

He knew nature too well to be able for long intervals to enjoy her external charm in the epicurean manner familiar to his son-in-law. As he hugged his dusty-trousered knees and blinked out of his deep-set eyes at those myriad green stalks, there came into his nostrils the smell of death. By shifting a little upon his haunches he was able to detect the cause of this smell; and what he saw did not diminish the prod of that iron in his soul.

Near him lay on its side the dead body of a small rabbit gazing horribly and vacantly into the burning sky out of a great eye socket which was nothing but a dried-up hole of rusty blood. The old man knew at once that he was looking at one of the normal atrocities of creative nature, a rabbit killed by a weasel.

He got up laboriously to his feet and tottered on, the beautiful sun-bathed world about him darkened for him and poisoned as if by a universal smell of murder. As he struggled forward in the fiery heat, the soles of his boots as hot as the cracked chalk earth beneath them, it presented itself once more to his mind that the only religious symbol in the world capable of covering and including the pain of this cruel chaos was the symbol of the Mass, where the wounded flesh and the spilt blood of the God-Man becomes an eternal protest, for those who enter into it, against all this blind suffering.

At the gate of his old friend's drive he was compelled to sit down once again to rest himself and he sat down on one side of the drive, resting his back against a sycamore tree. Here in his exhaustion he dozed off into an old man's heavy sleep. He was aroused by a high-pitched feminine voice and he saw himself confronted by Mrs Shotover. The lady was bare-headed and carried her favourite tabby-cat in her arms. She was taking the air after her early tea. She scolded Mr Moreton for attempting that walk in the heat. She scolded him with the familiarity of an old friend and with the burnt-up malice of an old 'flame'.

'So you've come at last,' she said in a gentler voice when, having got him safely into her drawing room, she made fresh tea for him which he drank with avidity. 'I thought you and I would never see each other again.'

He smiled feebly at her, his old half-ironical half-benevolent smile; but he was too tired to reply.

'It isn't quite like old days is it, John Moreton?' she said. He nodded, smiling still, and then shook his head and sighed.

'When you and I worried the life out of my George and your Cecily – dear innocents that they were!'

He refused her offer of anything to eat with a wave of his hand. 'You're the same as ever, Betty,' he said.

He looked so bedraggled and helpless, lying against her cushions, so caught by the red-tongued hounds of the years, that she stepped up to his side and kissed him on the forehead. 'Poor old John!' she murmured, running her jewelled fingers through his stubbly grey hair.

He grew a trifle more rested as time went on; and the obscure shadows across his face receded before the ancient cajolery of her voice.

'What a world it is, Betty!' he sighed at last. 'What a world! You know I've come to a stage in my life when, except for hearing Nell laugh and seeing her look happy, I don't care much what happens. My work interests me still, in a way, Betty, in a way. But not as it used to. If it wasn't for the church and the Mass I couldn't go on, Betty. I should just give up.'

'But they don't let you do *that* any more, you poor old heathen, do they?' asked Mrs George Shotover.

He gave her out of his cavernous eyes a most whimsical look.

'Someone must remember the rabbits killed by weasels and the sheep slaughtered by man and the trees killed by ivy and the mice killed by owls and the flies in spiders' webs. Someone must remember these things, little Betty!'

'And the butterflies caught by John Moreton!' she laughed mischievously at him.

'And the butterflies, too,' he said. 'But they would have died anyway,' he added. 'And my killing-bottles only send them to sleep, you know. I wish you'd put *me* into a killing-bottle, Betty!'

'But surely they don't let you say Mass any more, you dear old lunatic? I can't imagine the Reverend Sugary Salt, as I call him, allowing such a thing!'

The late Vicar of Littlegate regarded his hostess with a glance full of suppressed and chuckling amusement. 'Have you never heard of a Midnight Mass?' he said.

The old lady's face grew very grave. '*That's* what you've been up to, John Moreton, is it? Well! You just listen to me. That sort of thing's got to stop. Do you hear? Got to stop and stop at once!'

She paused and looked at him very anxiously, with tears in her eyes. 'So it's pranks of that sort has brought you downhill so fast, is it?'

She got up out of her chair and stood in front of him, scowling at him with knitted brow and quivering lips.

'John Moreton! John Moreton!' she cried, waving her forefinger at him. 'I'm afraid you're no better than a muddle-headed old fool!'

But he smiled at her so reassuringly and made his next remark in so quiet and normal a manner that she relaxed her tense expression and resumed her seat.

'Dear old Betty!' he said. 'It's not such a very nice world, after all, that old people like you and me should want to live on indefinitely. Why don't you smoke your cigarettes, Betty, as you used to? You haven't reformed, I hope?'

Comforted by his tone she did light a cigarette then.

'John Moreton,' she said after a pause, sending a puff of smoke through her daintily curved nostrils, 'do you believe in a life after death?'

Her ancient admirer looked at her rather wistfully.

'As keen on life as ever, Betty, I see! Oh, my dear, I don't know!

And to tell you the honest truth I don't greatly care. The whole thing is such a bitter sorry business that we should all be well enough out of it, to my thinking. But there *may* be another life. Oh yes! certainly there may be. I think Christ is alive. If I didn't think *that*, I should go crazy.'

They chatted on, after that, on less serious topics; till at last Mrs Shotover spoke what was rankling in her mind. 'I shall never forgive Nelly,' she said. 'I shall never forgive her. To turn on an old friend for the sake of a man! And what did I say to her? Nothing but the plain truth; that she's turning your house into I don't know what, with her husband and her lover!'

The old naturalist rose slowly to his feet. 'I must be walking home now, Betty; and you *mustn't* talk like that.' He staggered a little as he spoke and leant against the table.

'Of course I shall have Thomas drive you back,' said the lady. But you may take this from me, John Moreton: it's your fault; it's your going and getting yourself turned out of your living that has brought your girl down to this miserable mess-up. You may say what you please but the truth is you have driven that girl into all this. Canyot is a ruffian and this other fellow is a sly, sneaking, self-satisfied, conceited prig. And here the silly girl is, married to one of them, and hanging on to the other! You've brought about a pretty kettle of fish, John Moreton, by your pranks and your manias!'

The old man wilted under her storm of words like an ancient hollyhock bowed down by a cruel wind. He made a feeble movement with his hands and sank back upon the sofa.

'Ring for your Thomas, Betty dear,' he gasped. 'That walk's been too much for me. I am no doubt very much to blame – very much to blame. But we must forget and forgive, Betty; forget and forgive.'

Chapter 10

Nelly was glad that it was Canyot's way to make her walk fast by his side. She was glad that it was his way to be silent when he was strongly moved. The effort of keeping pace with him soothed her; and his silence made it possible for her to collect her thoughts and arrive at some sort of understanding with herself.

It had been the most unpleasant shock she had ever known, this business of the letter. It was not only a blow to her love, to her pride, to her happiness. It was a blow to something deeper than these; to that innate respect for life as a thing of quite definite aesthetic values, which made up the very illusion of her soul.

Except for the young man by her side now, she had never known anything of love or lovemaking; and though Mrs Shotover had riddled her with cynical advice she had not really been roused from her illusion by the old lady's words.

She kept going over in her mind every incident of the scene. *It must be some woman that he cares a good deal for*, she thought, *otherwise he would have shown me the letter and just laughed at its sentiment. It must have been one particular letter in a long correspondence; or his surprise at seeing an unexpected hand would not have disarmed him. He must have known that it would reveal to me the whole story. He must have been thoroughly terrified of my seeing it.*

'Not quite so fast!' she was compelled to cry out to her companion when, having reached the smooth turf of the crest of the hill, Canyot quickened his pace still more.

He turned round and looked at her.

They were alone in the midst of a wide treeless expanse, an expanse unbroken by any other human being, unbroken by bush or shrub or animal. Above their heads the larks sang; large cool shadows, one after another, floated over them, thrown by slow-travelling clouds, and from the little patches of thyme at their feet arose that peculiar faint sun-burnt pungency which more than anything else seems to be the attribute of the Downs.

The immense undulating upland, along the crest of which they were now moving, was like some huge wave of the sea struck into immobility. This great green wave held up their two figures, isolating them completely from the rest of the world; carrying them through infinite blue ether on the planetary motion of the round earth.

He stopped at her words and looked at her. Her cheeks were flushed and she was drawing her breath in little gasps.

'Let's sit down here,' he said.

They sat down side by side, the smell of the thyme becoming vividly distinct and little groups of blue butterflies chasing one another backwards and forwards across their feet. Her hands lay on her lap and Canyot possessed himself of one of them, holding it grimly, tightly, passionately.

She could hardly release it without an exertion of moral force for which at that moment, as she panted for breath, she lacked the energy.

She had not realized· how easy it would be for Canyot to repossess himself of such a privilege. She had not realized how the mere physical habit of lovemaking may outlast the emotional importance of it.

He on his part took what was a mixture of pique with Richard, physical exhaustion, the revival of old habitual gestures, and real· affection for himself, for something much deeper in her. He had grasped her fingers so fiercely, just because he had not supposed for a moment that she would let him retain them. She did let him retain them; and his passion gathered intensity.

'I hate human beings,' she said after a few minutes' silence. And in her heart, she thought, *What does it matter if I do let Robert hold my hand? Richard has got some woman in Paris who writes to him letters that I'm not allowed to see. He is evidently entangled still with her or* he would have told me the whole story. *And it doesn't seem fair that I should keep Robert at a distance when he goes on with his Paris entanglements.*

'I hate all human beings,' she repeated, 'because they always spoil everything. I do it myself, I know. I spoil things for myself.'

Canyot gazed in a kind of sombre ecstasy at her downcast profile.

'You've spoilt everything for me, Nelly,' he said; 'but I don't hate you for it. I like things to be spoilt! There's something in me that is glad when things are spoilt. I'm glad you're married. I'm glad I've got to leave you in six days. I'm glad you are tormenting me at this moment with your speeches and your ways.'

His tone was too familiar to her, and the peculiar mood he was in too reminiscent of former times, for Nelly to be shocked or startled.

She gave him a little flickering smile. 'Dear old Rob!' she said.

He lifted her hand to his lips but did not release it.

'I don't know whether you can possibly understand me,' he continued. 'You probably can't. But the fact is I've come to the conclusion that if you can't be glad of everything that happens to you, of everything that happens in your life, you'd better kill yourself at once. It's one or the other, Nell.'

'It's certainly one or the other with you, Robert,' she answered; 'but you needn't hurt my hand, whichever way it is.'

He did not release her fingers even then; he went on in the same strain.

'You can't get back from me, you know, any of the things that have happened between us. Every kiss you've ever given me still remains mine and no one else's.'

'I see you put my kisses with all the other horrid things you're glad to have happened to you,' remarked the girl, in a voice full of a teasing affectionate mockery; 'but to keep true to your present theory, what you ought to remember best are the times when I've been most bad to you.'

'You've never been bad to me,' he said. 'You couldn't be. You can hurt me and hurt me and hurt me. You can marry a hundred Richards. I shall only like you the better. And it'll be part of what I have to put into my paint box.'

'Oh there's a ladybird!' cried Nelly suddenly. 'Do look!' She took advantage of his disarmed attention to release her hand.

'What do you mean by your *paint box*?' she inquired when the ladybird had flown away.

'I mean,' said Robert, making a futile effort to regain her lost fingers, 'that my painting draws its life from every single thing which destiny takes away from me.'

The girl looked at him in whimsical gravity. 'Then if you had *had* me,' she said, 'I shouldn't be in your paint box any more?'

'The *Nelly* part of you wouldn't,' he answered solemnly, 'but your soul would – because I should never have got hold of that!'

'But the *Nelly* part of me *is* my soul,' she protested; 'that's what I am really and truly.'

He looked at her grimly and sardonically.

'No! No! my dear,' he said. '*This* is Nelly,' and he touched her shoulder. 'And *this* is Nelly,' and he touched her knee. 'But the thing in you which says "I am I" isn't Nelly at all. It isn't even a girl. It isn't even a human being.'

She smiled somewhat uneasily. 'What is it then?' she asked. 'I don't at all like the idea of being something that isn't myself.'

'It *is* yourself. It's the self that nobody in the world can ever take away or invade or imprison, as they can *this* Nelly,' and he gave her propped-up knees a vicious little shake. 'But it's something that *I* could never, never get hold of, even if I had you absolutely for my own.'

She looked frowningly at the hot grey-green turf at her feet where a heavily winged brown butterfly was fluttering aimlessly.

'What *is* it you really care for in me?' she suddenly inquired.

The thoughts that had led her to this were queerly complicated. That discovery that Richard corresponded with some Paris woman and received letters which he dreaded to show to her had stained with a sort of muddy tincture the whole outlook of her mind. It not only spoilt Richard for her. It spoilt herself for herself. It muddied up, as it were, the whole business of love between human beings. It made her doubt her own integrity, her own charm. If she didn't satisfy Richard, if her love couldn't work the miracle of making them really *one* – mustn't that be because there was something wanting in herself? She felt a horrible suspicion of her own nature. She realized for the first time how cruelly alone everyone is in the world; how one doesn't evoke love simply by being what one is without any effort.

It was at that point in her train of thought that she said, 'What is it in me?'

Her question completely broke down Canyot's self-control. He jumped up from the ground. He took her by the wrist and swung her up upon her feet. He threw his arm round her and embraced her passionately; kissing her so brusquely, that he kissed the tip of her nose, and her open mouth and her lace collar, in one rapid series of indiscriminate hugs.

When he let her go he was pale and trembling and hardly dared to look into her eyes. But the effect of his violence upon Nelly was not to make her in the least angry with him. She saw his remorse. She bent forward and gave him a quick affectionate little kiss upon his cheek. Then she smiled sadly and tenderly. 'You'll only make yourself unhappy by *that*, Robert dear, and it doesn't do any good. I do love you; but I could never like your doing that. So what's the use?'

He stood staring at her, like an animal that has been punished for some unknown fault. The colour, coming slowly back into his face, covered it with funny red blotches.

'I'm a fool,' he muttered, 'a damned fool! Let's go on now.' And they resumed their rapid stride, side by side.

They reached Toat Farm without any further personal conversation. The weight of the basket of provisions he carried wearied him and reduced his speed; so that when they arrived at the place the girl was quite cool and collected and able to be nice to Sally-Maria and Sally-Maria's aunt.

They ate their lunch in the woman's cottage and she made them tea. The dumb child seemed hostile to Nelly, for she refused to accept a morsel of food while they remained there and a queer inarticulate anger against them both was obviously smouldering in her sullen eyes. 'She is jealous, poor little thing!' whispered Nelly as they went out, and the whole complicated misery of human emotions swept over her in one drowning wave. Was there no such thing in the world as disinterested love?

But Canyot's picture impressed her much more than she had anticipated. The artist had managed to communicate to those shadows in the water a strange passionate beauty full of wistful hints and intimations; the wind that stirred the rank-growing melancholy hemlocks seemed, as the girl gazed at them, to be the very wind of fate itself carrying the burden of old sorrows, of old baffled longings, out of some deep unknown into some still obscurer future.

She understood, as she looked, fascinated and silent, at what he had done, something of what he really did mean by his queer phrase about the 'paint box'.

It was not till quite late in the afternoon that they prepared to leave Toat Farm. At the last minute Robert discovered to his dismay that Sally-Maria was missing. Her aunt called loudly for her and they all searched for her in the places where the child generally was accustomed to play. But in the end they had to leave without saying goodbye to her.

If her aunt's final conjecture was correct, she had run off; as she usually did when she was unhappy, to the cottage over the hill where lived Old Miss Stone'. With this explanation Robert had to be contented.

The incident of Sally-Maria's disappearance threw a gloom over them both as they walked back slowly across the Downs; and nothing that Nelly could find to say to her companion seemed able to lift it.

She herself was occupied with the very difficult question as to how the broken and ruffled stream of her love for her husband could be restored to its former level course.

She surprised herself by the bitterness she felt about it, by the anger she felt towards him.

Her present desire, which she herself did not dare to bring into the light of complete consciousness, was to excite his jealousy to the breaking point.

She wished to make him suffer exactly the same pain that she herself was suffering. She wished to have him not only begging for her forgiveness, but in a blind helpless manner – the clearness of all human issues tarnished and stained – *doubtful as to her love.*

Meanwhile as she walked by Canyot's side there slowly settled down upon her the consciousness that things could never be quite the same. If she had actually caught him in the act of making love to this Paris woman, she could hardly have felt more deceived, more betrayed, more disillusioned. And yet in one part of her brain she had known that it was almost certain that he had entanglements. Woman-like, she had suppressed that knowledge, thought it down, thought it away, thought it into faint unreality.

Everything about her present feeling towards Richard puzzled and bewildered her. She was surprised at herself for not being more hurt than she was. She recalled how as a young girl she had often imagined herself in just this very position – the position of a betrayed wife – and how she had always, in imagination, felt a kind of passionate passivity in suffering, a sweet tenacious clinging devotion to the erring one that nothing could shake. In place of this she found herself sickened with the whole business of life, dulled and stupefied, as if with a species of nausea. What especially surprised her was that the strong, clean, pure flow of her own love for her husband seemed to have received some disastrous alloy, some influx of poisonous bitterness.

Was she, after all, she asked herself, something different from the devoted, passionate, tenacious Nelly, in whom she had believed?

Was she, as Mrs Shotover had so bluntly told her, no better than an intriguing flirt whose infatuation for a man turned to gall and wormwood at the first catastrophe?

Or had Richard, by his miserable business, really poisoned with a fatal poison the well-spring of her love?

It is strange, she thought, these terrible little accidents of betrayal – what they can destroy! Like some evil acid thrown upon sensitive flesh, they seem able to bite to the very bone! Nelly sighed, as she walked, from a heart most 'sorely charged'. It seemed so ridiculously small, the whole matter of this clandestine correspondence, of this burnt letter, revealing a sequence – so she told herself – of letters that had not been burnt! A ridiculously small matter! and yet it seemed to have given to the very essence of her being a strange organic shock.

She felt as if since he had thrown the thing into the fire two or three long bitter years had passed over her head instead of a few hours.

When they reached the top of the hill above Hill Cottage they were surprised to see a small motorcar standing by the gate.

'Who's that?' said Canyot brusquely. 'If it's a visitor I shall clear off. In fact,' he added, 'I think I shall be off anyway. I don't feel in a mood for meeting people.'

He gave her his hand and looked into her eyes, hoping for some final glance of tenderness; but her gaze was fixed upon the unusual object at the gate. 'Goodnight, Robert,' she repeated, almost mechanically, as with a wave of his hand he strode away.

She was met at the door by her husband. Directly she saw him she knew that something was wrong. 'Is it Father?' she asked. Richard nodded without speaking and stood aside for her to go in.

Her father's bedroom was upon the ground floor. Its door stood wide open.

Directly the girl stepped across the threshold she knew that the old naturalist was dying. By his side stood the doctor, a quiet self-contained young man with an expressionless face; at the foot of the bed sobbed Grace, her big tears streaming down her rosy cheeks and falling upon her apron.

'What is it?' whispered Nelly to the doctor. 'Is it his heart?'

It was Richard who answered her question. He stepped up close to her side and put his arm round her waist. 'It was a sun stroke it seems,' he said. 'He was brought back from West Horthing in Mrs Shotover's carriage. He must have become unconscious on the way. Grace was alone. Mrs Shotover's man carried him in and then went for the doctor. I have been several times to the top of the hill to look out for you. I found him like this when I came in and he has not changed since.'

The old man was lying on his back with his eyes closed. His breath was loud and unnatural, resembling the sound of water in an iron pipe. His mouth was wide open and every now and then a convulsive spasm crossed his face.

Nelly went up to him and bent down above him – 'Father!' she whispered. And then in a louder tone, a tone full of a sudden desperate fear, 'Father!'

Her voice seemed to reach the dying man's ears; for he made a little feeble movement with his hands.

The young doctor drew a step back.

'Can't anything be done to make that breathing easier?' whispered Richard with something like a tone of reproach. 'It must hurt him to breathe like that.'

Suddenly John Moreton opened his eyes and gazed at his daughter. The girl fell upon her knees and kissed his hand as it stirred faintly on the counterpane. Wildly and strangely the old man looked at her. His breathing grew shriller, harsher, huskier. It became the most dominant thing in the room. It became a living separate entity, a palpable horror that pressed with a ghastly weight upon them all; that tyrannized over them all. It was as if, in that repulsive sound, Death itself – the old eternal antagonist – was mocking them, was menacing them with an unintelligible threat.

Nelly spread out her arms over the bed and hid her face. It was not easy for her to look into those bewildered wild eyes with their inexplicable appeal. An unnatural longing suddenly seized Richard that he might rush from the room and escape, escape into the largeness of the evening, from this pitiful struggle. He felt as if every breath the dying man drew rent and tore at his own throat. He felt stifled; as if it were he himself that were wrestling there with an invisible enemy.

The impassive young doctor contemplated the scene with serene detachment. He had seen hundreds of deaths in France and this particular death had less effect upon his emotional capacity than the shooting of an aged dog.

Nelly's head, buried in the white counterpane, was full of a turmoil of remorse. Why hadn't she been a better, a kinder, a more considerate girl? Her sobs shook the bed and mingled with the horrible rattling in the old man's throat.

Suddenly John Moreton jerked up his head from the pillow and held it erect. The young doctor was reminded of a similar movement in the neck of a frightened tortoise.

Inside the old man's mind, at that moment everything was absolutely clear. In a flash he saw the whole scene. He saw the impassive doctor. He saw the weeping servant. He saw his daughter lift her tear-stained face from the bed and gaze at him with desperate love. He caught in Richard's eye a look of fidgety irritation, a look that said 'let's get this melancholy business over and go for a walk on the Downs'.

And in a flash he knew that this was his last moment of what is called *life*. He gathered up in a bundle all his inveterate thoughts – the *Eidolon Vulgaris* popped up on its pedestal before him as he had grown accustomed to envisage it. It nodded at him amiably from the top of his bookcase like a leering Punchinello. He did not think of it as the great illusion of humanity. He saw it as a whimsical but not unfriendly goblin whose feelings he had hurt by his contempt. He felt inclined to bid it goodbye and to apologize to it.

Yes, his brain was clearer than it had ever been in his life. The only thing that puzzled him was that the human arms of that crucifix which hovered just above poor Gracie's head were not fastened to anything but were waving in the air like the wings of a butterfly. What butterfly was it? That was the one thing that troubled him. He would like to know that, before darkness covered his eyes. He felt extremely happy, happier than he ever remembered feeling. Was that because Cecily and Betty were making it up? He knew they were making it up, though he could not see them. Those butterfly wings were doing it. They were hidden under the shelter of those wings; and as the wings waved they were growing smaller and smaller and smaller.

Everything was growing smaller now, smaller and further away. And yet they were not leaving him. They were leaving themselves. He himself was getting further away – a stupid old man breathing like a cracked steam engine. He was *there*, and they were *there*, far off, far away – four unhappy people bending over a grotesque old entomologist stretched out on a bed. Why couldn't he communicate to them what a delicious thing it was to be fanned by butterfly wings?

Never had his brain been more clear. But it was annoying that he couldn't remember the name of that butterfly! And it was annoying that he couldn't remember what his opinions were about the immortality of the soul. He ought to be thinking about that now; not enjoying this unphilosophical happiness!

He was just on the point of dying. That was certain. This happiness was nothing less than death. What a curious discovery! And he was quite unable to explain this to any of these dear agitated young people. This was the queerest experience he had ever had in his life; it was teasing not to be able to speak.

The immortality of the soul? What was his view upon that problem? He hadn't the least idea. He had no idea of anything except of floating in a lovely blue space – a blue space that grew darker and darker. Then he recalled one single word out of a great many. It was the word *annihilation*.

That was the secret then; John Moreton was being annihilated. He wished this being annihilated would never stop. It was the happiest sensation he had ever known. He loved everyone; only he couldn't speak to tell them so. Annihilation had something to do with love, then? It must have. And it was beautiful beyond expression. But what was the connection between annihilation and the immortality of the soul? He wished he could remember what the immortality of the soul meant. It was a musical sentence. It must have meant something once to him when his brain was clouded. But his brain was clear now and it meant nothing at all!

How heavy his eyelids were growing; and how nice it was to love everyone, every single person – even foreman Pringle! Yes, his eyelids were very heavy. It would be still nicer when this blue space in which he floated got quite dark! He was going to sleep now; going to sleep upon velvet-black butterfly wings.

Someone was weeping. It wasn't Cecily or Betty or Nelly. Who was it? It was the darkness of space. No! it was his mother.

At that moment he uttered a strange croaking cry like the cry of a bullfrog in a swamp. It seemed to himself that he shouted 'Mother!' in an ecstasy of indescribable peace; but to the four figures watching his death it sounded as if he had uttered the meaningless syllables 'Blub-blub'. His head sank back on the pillow after that; the young doctor in a quiet discreet voice informed them that he was dead.

Chapter 11

The day following the old naturalist's death was a day of supreme discomfort for Richard. His feelings were those of natural sympathy with Nelly; on his own account he felt a certain sense of loss and bewilderment. The little cottage seemed to have changed its character. The old man lying upstairs dominated every corner of it with his silent presence; and it was difficult to understand exactly how Nelly was reacting to that wordless motionless appeal.

She went about her domestic duties as usual. She comforted poor Grace and kept her from any further outburst of grief. But what, all the while, was going on in her own mind it was impossible for Richard to guess.

Canyot came round in the morning after breakfast, and Nelly took him up at once to the dead man's room. A little later, when they were all three loitering miserably and awkwardly together in the little garden, ostensibly engaged in picking flowers to make 'that room' as cheerful as it could be made, they were disagreeably startled by the appearance outside the gate of Mrs Shotover's dog-cart.

Richard went to help her down.

'I know all about it,' she said. 'I telephoned to the doctor last night. Thomas told me he had fetched him. How do you do, Mr Canyot— 'this was in recognition of the young man's opening the gate for her.' And my dear, dear child!' She embraced Nelly with tender effusiveness. 'And there is Grace! Take these things, Grace, will you? It's eau-de-cologne, my dear, and some of my best roses. I thought he would be glad to think I'd remembered to bring them. And now you'll take me upstairs at once won't you? Well, Mr Storm, I'm afraid all this is very sad and disturbing to you. It must be terribly upsetting to you writers, when something really human breaks in on your inventions. Dear, dear child!' She still continued to retain tight hold of Nelly's hand while she addressed her words to the two men. 'And you, Mr Canyot, you've had your own loss of course; and no doubt you know how to comfort our little Nell. It is very nice that she has both of you to fall back upon. It would have been doubly sad if she'd had nobody but an old friend like me . . .

'Yes, Grace. In water, Grace. It would be a pity for them to wither while we can fancy he enjoys them. Ah my dear, my dear' – this was addressed to Nelly again – 'we old people must seem very tiresome sometimes to you young ones. But when it's all over I dare-say you miss us. Yes; at once if you please. Yes; do take me up at once.'

Preceded by Grace and escorted by Nelly, Mrs Shotover walked solemnly up the little creaking stairs. What did actually go on under that high forehead and behind that elegantly poised head no human being will ever know. She shed no tear at the sight of her old friend. Very gracefully, and like a great actress in a play, she stooped, and kissed him; once on the forehead, and then with a quick bird-like movement, a sort of fleeting afterthought, on the bloodless lips.

Nelly thought she detected a furtive glance into the mirror as they went out together after placing the roses on the table; but her rush of cynical thoughts was dissipated in a wave of sympathetic feeling when she noticed that the hand which rested on her arm as she helped the old lady downstairs shook like a leaf in the wind.

'Very beautiful and very peaceful,' she said, addressing the two men when she came out into the garden; for the one thing that Nelly wanted to avoid at that moment was to be left alone with her.

'And now you two must come back to lunch with me,' she said. 'I'm sure Grace will be glad to have you off her hands. She doesn't look as if she was fit to do a thing more. I daresay Mr Canyot will be available if he's wanted. Oh yes you *must* both of you come. It would be quite the dear man's wish, I'm certain of that. You must let me take you all in hand. He would wish it. You see I *did* understand him. Mr Canyot is just the right person to take care of dear faithful Grace. Aren't you, Mr Canyot? An artist like you is always so nice to simple natures. Have you thought of taking a death mask? No, I suppose not. Oh, there's just one more thing – if you don't mind, Nelly dear. No! No! I'll be down in a minute. Just one little thing. You must humour an old woman, my pet. One minute!' And with more alacrity than she had yet displayed Mrs Shotover went up for the second time to the room above.

What passed on this occasion between those ancient friends only the invisible watchers of life and death will ever know. When she came down again the old lady was a little quieter.

While she was away, Richard had whispered to Nelly – 'Do you really wish to go with her?' Nelly had nodded. 'And you'd like me to come too?' Nelly had nodded again. 'I don't want to be alone with her today; and we can't hurt her feelings. She was Father's friend.'

So Nelly climbed up by Mrs Shotover's side in the front of the dog-cart; and Richard held on at the back in company with Thomas.

Never had the author of *The Life of Verlaine* had so uncomfortable a drive.

He felt as though Mrs Shotover had ears in the back of her head and heard every word he said to Thomas; Thomas, in any case, was the most taciturn of feudal servants and had already acquired a prejudice against him as a foreigner and not quite the right sort of gentleman.

The lunch passed easily enough; for after the stress they had been through, and the long jolting drive over the Downs, they were both hungry. The uncomfortable time for Richard came afterwards, when they lingered over the coffee in Mrs Shotover's drawing room.

Nelly clung resolutely and tenaciously to her husband. She seemed to have made a vow not to be separated from him for a moment; their hostess, whether she liked it or not, had no alternative but to submit.

So Richard became aware of the enormous importance, in events of this kind, of the right fabrics to be selected for a young woman's mourning.

Of course you'll leave it all to me, 'said Mrs Shotover.' I'll drive you in to Selshurst tomorrow and have you fitted. They keep the medium sizes practically made up, you know. And you're a good medium, my dear. Just a few touches here and there, and that sweet little Mrs Fortescue will fit you to a nicety! I'd have had her over here this afternoon, if we'd only known in time. You needn't look so pompous and reproachful, Mr Storm. Need he, Nelly? Your dear father never minded my little jokes.

'Ah you modern men, you modern men! You're always grave when you ought to laugh; and you chuckle like wicked ogres when you ought to be grave.

'The question of Nelly's looking nice at her father's funeral, when quite a lot of the neighbourhood may be there, is not a thing to laugh at. No gentleman ever laughs at a woman for her seriousness about dress. That kind of humour is just pure vulgarity and shows simple ignorance of life. It's like the bucolic laughter of stupid rustics when they see well-dressed people coming out of church.'

'I haven't been in an English drawing room for quite ten years,' remarked Richard, in an effort to change the conversation.

'So I imagined!' was on the tip of Mrs Shotover's tongue; but she substituted for it, 'Dear me! How glad you must be to be civilized again!'

'I don't like drawing rooms,' said Nelly. 'I've never had one. I think men's rooms are much nicer.'

'That's what all the young people say now,' cried the old lady. 'You'll turn England into a dreadful place soon, where there's no more society and no more good manners and no more good conversation. You should have seen the tea parties we used to have at Fixden Manor in my young days. *There* was a drawing room for you! And the men were witty too. I can remember old Lord Trace-bridge, how he used to flirt with my aunt, Lady Gower. That room had no less than seven mirrors. One of them got cracked one day; and the Bishop of Sodor and Man said to Grandmamma – but that's too naughty a story to repeat before Mr Storm! I'll tell it you tomorrow, Nelly, when we're driving to Selshurst'

Richard looked round Mrs Shotover's drawing room with an eye of unmingled contempt. There was not one single book to be seen in any direction except a great morocco-covered edition of the poems of Lord Byron, lying on its side on a tortoiseshell slab, and a tiny volume of151 *Dodd's Beauties of Shakespeare*, used as a letter-weight on the lady's rosewood writing table.

To make up for the lack of books there were endless vases of flowers of every conceivable size and colour; there were plants in Japanese pots and plants in Chinese pots and plants upon little stands of old English pottery.

On the mantelpiece and on every available space in the room were an incredible assortment of objects that could hardly be called *objets d'art*.

The most harmless of this gallery of knickknacks were portraits of elegant human beings, nearly all of them in full dress, varying from the dark ancient daguerreotypes in silhouette down to the latest modern photographs of young soldiers and young society belles.

'I see you're looking at my things,' said the owner of this pretty collection. 'The work of a lifetime, young man! The work of a lifetime! My French novels I keep upstairs. But we won't talk of *them* now! All the same I wish you'd make Mr Storm write something really amusing, Nelly. Something witty, for one to read at night when one goes to bed. I read a lot in bed. It's the only place where I get a moment's time.'

'Oh, here's a picture of your father when he was a young man. You've seen it before? Yes? It's rather nice I think, don't you?'

She replaced the object carefully in its former position and sighed deeply, looking at herself as she did so in one of her innumerable mirrors.

'Poor dear John! He never minded my bad little ways. I've told him before now the most terrible stories. You've heard him laugh, haven't you, love, when we've been together in his study? Well! he's past laughing now, poor darling. Why don't *you* ever laugh, Mr Storm? For I can see you never do, does he Nelly? He "grimly smiles", as the novels say, and that's all. I must confess I like a man who can laugh. You modern writers take life so horribly seriously. One would think you were always in pain. Are you in pain when you "smile grimly" like that, Mr Storm? I hope Nelly looks after your stomach. I always used to advise her father to take castor oil, didn't I Nelly? It was quite a joke between us. And other things too. Heigh ho! And the dear, dear man is lying there all alone. Well! I see you're anxious to be off and I won't keep you. But what is *your* opinion of these modern authors, Mr Storm, and their spiritualistic nonsense? I say that when we are dead we're in good society. In these days you have to die to be in good society. Oh my sweet little Nell, how I am rattling on! Well! you must excuse me. I am an old woman and hardly see anybody nowadays.'

'It was very kind of you to bring us over,' said Nelly, rising, 'but really you mustn't trouble about tomorrow. I've got several black dresses.'

'Nonsense, child, nonsense. You talk in the way your mother used to. Black dresses indeed! I hope, Mr Storm, you won't let her get silly and dowdy now she's married. But I'm sure you won't. I expect you'll be getting her all sorts of things from Paris. That's what she married you for, you know, not to hear sermons about art! And do let me hear you laugh sometimes. I suspect serious faces. I always have. I advise Nelly to watch you very carefully when you're silent like that and looking out of the windows and into the bushes. You may try to make her believe you're composing lives of the poets or something; but I know better! You bad sly man! You're probably thinking of some naughty little girl in Paris! There! Don't look so sad, Nelly. It does him good to be teased a bit. These modern clever men have no sense of humour. Well! goodbye my dear one. You *will* walk back, eh? I could easily get Thomas to drive you. Oh dear, dear! What a thing life is. Well! be a brave girl. That's what'll really please your father. I'm sure the dear man is safe in heaven by now. If he's *not* there, the Lord may send Betty Shotover to the other place!

'You *will* walk, then? Well, goodbye, and God bless you! I'll be over tomorrow early.'

They shook hands with her at the door; and Richard threw up his arms and beat at the laurels with his stick as soon as they were out of her sight.

'What an awful woman! What a perfectly horrible old woman!' Then, as if to relieve his feelings, he proceeded to make a goblin-like grimace in the direction of Mrs Shotover's drawing room,

'Don't, Richard,' said Nelly. 'You hurt my feelings; and it isn't pretty of you. I don't think it's ever nice to despise people quite like that, when you've been enjoying their hospitality. Besides she was a friend of Father's.'

'Damn her hospitality!' cried Storm, letting loose the stored-up venom of his outraged vanity. 'She only asked me there to annoy me. She might just as well have had you by yourself. She has always hated me from the first time we met. Her Fixden Manor! Her aunt, Lady Gower! What a disgusting old snob. I expect she saw I saw through her from the very start. That's why she loathes me. We know how to put people like that into their places in France.'

'Perhaps she sees through *you*, Richard!'

'What do you mean?'

'I only mean that when it comes to *seeing through* people, we're all at bottom much of a muchness.'

'Don't for God's sake, Nelly, use those awful expressions. I know they're supposed to be arch and debonair and genteel in England; but I detest them. We're not living in Wonderland or Looking-Glass-land.'

'I wish we were!' cried Nelly looking at him with a little surprised tilt of her eyebrows. She was still in the dark as to what had really ruffled him; for it was inconceivable that a person of his intelligence could take poor dear Aunt Bet quite as seriously as that!

Had she possessed a little more insight into her husband's character, she would have known that he was engaged in a secret and not very human struggle to exploit in the interests of his own scheme of life every one of the events which were now occurring, centred round that old dead man lying at rest. And into this vision of things, where the old man's death and Nelly's own grief fitted so beautifully, Mrs Shotover and her drawing room came as a bombshell of irrelevance.

He wanted to act the part of a wise and tender philosopher to his young wife just then. He wanted her to give him an opportunity to comfort her, to explain to her his views upon death, to soothe her mind by large and noble sentiments. He wanted her to remember to her dying day how beautifully he had said just the right thing with regard to her father, how tactfully, how spiritually, he had entered into her feelings!

And here she was, actually amused and diverted by the silly chatter of this old featherbrain, and even by her ridiculous rudeness to himself!

It was not a very cheerful walk that they had together, that afternoon, back to where the dead man awaited them.

The tension between them was relieved for Nelly – while it was increased for Richard – by their overtaking a young visitor who was on her way to leave her card at their place. This was an acquaintance of Nelly's for whom, though he had only seen her twice, Richard had acquired almost as strong a dislike as he had towards Aunt Bet.

Their meeting in just that way seemed to Richard extraordinarily awkward and unfortunate. One surely, in reserved and discreet England, managed to avoid acquaintances and condolences when one's father was still unburied?

What would the caller do now, since she *had* met them? Would she hand her card to her friend with a polite curtsey, and say, 'I'm sorry your father's dead,' as one might say, 'I'm sorry your potatoes are blighted'?

These little niceties of social intercourse always filled Richard with chilly embarrassment. His own feelings were so seldom simple or direct that it was a matter of terrible self-consciousness to him how he should behave where the conventions did not act as direct signposts.

As it happened on this occasion, whether conventionally or not, Olive Shelter walked with them as far as their gate and simply said goodbye. As far as Richard could make out, she didn't so much as refer to the dead man. Their conversation as they crossed the cornfields was lively and interesting. Nelly was evidently challenging the girl about some male cousin of hers in whom gossip reported she was interested.

'There's absolutely nothing in it, my dear,' Richard heard the girl saying, 'and you know that there isn't. How often must I tell you before you believe me that I've never been interested in anyone in my life? When my uncle dies I'm going to take a poultry farm and earn my own living. Perhaps when people see me in gaiters and knickers they'll let me alone.'

'But, Olive!' cried Nelly, 'lots of us wear things like that just to attract men!' 'They won't be attracted to what *I* shall wear,' said Olive smiling. 'I'm perfectly sick of this stupid idea that we've all got to have love affairs or husbands. I don't see things that way at all.'

'You're not going into a convent are you, Miss Shelter?' Richard threw in without taking very much heed to what he said. The girl's clear-cut sharp-featured brusqueness had little appeal for him.

'A convent? Oh dear, no!' she replied, giving Richard a quick satiric glance which seemed to say 'as usual!' 'That's just what everybody thinks,' she went on. 'It seems incredible to people nowadays that a girl should prefer to be unmarried just as a man prefers to be a bachelor. Whenever I talk of my poultry farm, everyone always smiles and sniggers – as much as to say "she'll be married in a week and then you'll see!" And if they don't do that, they look at each other and become grave and sympathetic, as much as to say "she must have been badly jilted, poor little thing!"'

Richard became faintly interested at this point. 'But you don't mean to say, Miss Shelter, that you really intend to live alone all your life?'

'Certainly I do!' she laughed back at him. 'Though I *might* of course take a partner, if I could find some girl of my own sort.'

'Ah! a girl, a platonic friendship,' laughed Richard super-ciliously. 'Not a bit of it!' replied Olive, giving him a quick, almost angry look and flushing a little. 'A business partnership between good comrades,' she threw out with a toss of her head.

Richard became puzzled and silent. It seemed incredible to his mind that there should be any alternative between a passionate devotion to religion and a passionate devotion to some shape of flesh and blood. To rule out the attraction between human bodies and souls and not to substitute for it some exclusive passion of religious faith seemed to him weird and strange.

He looked at Olive with an unexpected interest. She was certainly a new type to him of what England could produce. Was it really possible, he wondered, for life to go on being thrilling and exciting, without the stimulus of either religion or sex?

Olive was by no means a bad looking girl. Her features were a little hard; but her complexion was soft and childlike. Richard was quite glad to take her hand when they said goodbye. It was a cool and a firm hand, the hand of a woman who, like Natalia in *Wilhelm Meister*, loved 'never or always'!

Chapter 12

John Moreton was buried on the following Wednesday by the side of his wife Cecilia.

Mrs Shotover came to the funeral; she thoroughly scared the new vicar, patronized Richard before the whole neighbourhood and offended Nelly very seriously by being rude to Robert.

The news which Canyot received that week about his exhibitions made it possible for him once more to postpone his journey; for it appeared there was to be a second New York show of his things which promised to be of far greater importance than anything that had been done hitherto; there was no need for him to cross the water until July.

He stayed on therefore at the farm, painting as he had never painted before, painting at a furious speed and with a gathered weight of feeling and intensity.

He wanted if possible to have at least half a dozen more pictures to carry over with him and he dreaded to lose the peculiar value of the kind of power which was now coming to him, snatched out of the electric air of his relations with Nelly.

He felt obscurely that all was not perfectly right between the husband and wife; he felt that Nelly needed him and in some mysterious way clung to him at this juncture, almost as if he had understood what she felt about her father better than Richard did.

Richard himself was making at that time a concentrated effort to recover the interrupted sequence of his own work. He found this surprisingly difficult. The roots of the thing were there, firmly planted in his new feeling; but the temptation to enjoy that lovely countryside, to fall into a sort of vague half-sensual dreaming over the sounds and scents of those unequalled fields, was still fatally strong.

The sweetness of Nelly's initial surrender to him still remained, an intoxicating drug among these other enchantments, and his pleasure in her grew more and more material, more and more a thing of the thrilled and exacting senses, less and less of an emotional or spiritual passion.

Nelly was occupied in arranging the natural history treasures in her father's study; she went about this work with a greater weight of gloom upon her mind than she had ever known. She had not separated herself from her husband; nor had she referred again to the matter of the letter; but even while she submitted to his caresses, even while she passionately responded to his caresses, there was a weary disillusionment in her heart. She tried to forget this, just as she had tried to forget her father's loss, by abandoning herself almost fiercely to her love; but the whole thing was different. Her very love seemed to herself much more a thing of the senses than it was before; a thing from which some peculiarly subtle essence had been withdrawn. She knew only too well what she was trying to do. She was trying to forget her father and she was trying to forget the old 'dead' Richard, by plunging recklessly into the mere material thrill of the chemical attraction that existed between them.

She was playing the courtezan, so to speak, in the temple of her pure love, so as to drown, if she could, that bitter underlying consciousness that something was wrong between them.

It was very painful to her to think of her father at all, so guilty did she feel towards him. The actual pain of missing the old man was made so much worse by the miserable feeling that in a hundred ways recently she had neglected him for her own pleasure. And the only distraction that seemed able to make her forget this remorse was the distraction of Richard's caresses.

The unfortunate thing was that in proportion as Richard made more sophisticated love to her and she responded to his lovemaking, Richard himself in his own brain and nerves began to lose something of the original delicacy of his attitude towards her. The more feverishly she tried to forget her troubles in his arms the less rare and exquisite did the link between them tend to become. This tarnishing and blunting process was not, of course, a thing of a few days, but it began to have its effect upon Richard's character. This effect showed itself in two ways.

His wife became more of an obsession to him in a physical sense and very much less of an inspiration to him in a spiritual sense.

The situation was a singularly cruel one; for had the girl loved him less, had there been less magnetic attraction between them, the charm of her personality, apart from flesh and blood, would have grown more powerfully upon him. Nelly's physical beauty was indeed Nelly's own rival in this matter, and a rival who was absorbing and devouring the very thing in the man she loved that had originally drawn her towards him.

What was happening to Richard was indeed the very thing he had fled from Elise Angel to avoid. He had fled from it because he knew how dangerous to his peculiar temperament this sort of erotic obsession was – how it sapped the very life blood of his soul. He had married Nelly for a conscious and also an unconscious reason. Consciously he had wanted her as a living symbol of what he was aiming at in his work. Unconsciously he had been attracted to her with precisely the same sort of purely sensual attraction as he had felt towards Elise Angel. He had not known that at first. But now he did know it and it had a fatal effect upon the freedom of his brain. The sweetness of his English wife and the sweetness of the English scenery became between them a dangerous euthanasia, a drug-induced trance, the death of his better self.

And the thing did not stop even there. For the very lowering of the moral atmosphere of his life produced by his uxoriousness led to a subtle undermining of his resistance to the image of the dancer. The more absorbing did his present voluptuousness become, the less .did he expel from his imagination the attraction of the other woman. Both he and Nelly were deliberately seeking to drug their differences by exploiting their attraction to one another.

That this kind of abandonment must eventually lead to satiety and reaction they did not seem to realize. That it was destroying the more exquisite moments of their life they did vaguely feel; but they felt it without understanding what they felt. And by slow degrees there entered into the fabric of their love some black threads of abominable hostility which came very near to hate. They loved and hated because they loved without restraint. They put poison into their love, because they separated love from life.

Had not Richard been twice as old as Nelly this ruining of the delicacy of their relations might never have occurred. What he was really guilty of was the exploitation of her emotions by his sophisticated senses. He was 'seducing', so to speak, his own lawful wife and turning her into a more delicate reproduction of his Old irresponsible amours. The worst of it was that while these former excesses had in no way interfered with his old work, his *new*, more spiritualized purpose was most seriously imperilled by what was occurring now.

The engaging, ingratiating charm of that insidious Sussex land-scape lent itself with fatal ease to the process of spiritual deterioration. He bathed himself in the beauty of those rolling hills and those rich pastures. He drank in, through every pore of his skin, that magical air, those blue skies, those soft languorous mists, those warm, fragrant rains. And the girl he loved became for him the material medium through which he worshipped all this, through which he lost himself in all this. In loving Nelly he was loving the trees, the hedges, the lanes, the meadows, and the thyme-scented grass. In embracing Nelly he was embracing the very body of the sweet earth which, just then, was so luxuriously responsive.

It is true that there came to him certain moments when he was seized by a vague uneasiness. These moments were generally connected with Canyot; for, sure as he was of his wife's material fidelity, he was by no means so sure now of her mental interest, of her spiritual *rapport*. She seemed to escape him, even while he held her, and that obscure disillusionment at the bottom of her eyes fell away sometimes into a region of thoughts and feelings to which he had no entrance, the clue of it quite lacking and all its ways dark.

Physically she was his without reserve; mentally she had slipped aside into a land of her own; it was at the moments when he suspected that this land of her soul's escape from him was not barred to his rival, that he was seized with a vague uneasiness and discomfort.

One morning, early in July, Richard intercepted the postman in the outskirts of the village and received from him another letter from Elise Angel.

The fact that he had every intention of reading every word of this communication, and that he put it away in his pocket with a thrill of furtive delight, was an evidence of how far he had drifted from his original purpose, of how he had changed in these brief two months.

He actually took it with him, without any feeling of shame, to the secluded shelter of the overarching hazels of the lane that led to Nelly's Happy Valley.

Here, sitting under the hedge, he read it with absorbed unre-strained fascination.

It was a characteristic scrawl, written in the dancer's bold imperious hand; its passionate words, conveying like a far-flung torch a trail of fire into his languid senses, thrilled him with forbidden longings.

She told him that she had accepted an engagement at a New York theatre that would begin sometime in October.

'I shall be there till Christmas,' she wrote, 'couldn't you possibly come over?'

He tore this letter into the tiniest fragments and poked it with his stick under the dead leaves, into the soft mould.

As he did so there came over him a sense of shame at this concealment, at the furtive cowardice of this action.

'It's *their* fault,' he said to himself, apostrophizing women in general. 'If they weren't so damned jealous, if things were really free – as they will be, perhaps, in two hundred years! – there would be no need for these tricks.'

Then it occurred to him to wonder what he would feel if he caught his wife in the act of kissing Rob Canyot. 'Hang it all!' he muttered in the retired honesty of this sudden soliloquy with his soul; 'I'm cursed if I should like *that* very much! I don't think *that* would be very nice!'

Then he turned his attention to Elise and tried to conjure up a situation in which he surprised *her* in some amorous colloquy with another person. 'The devil!' he confessed to himself. 'I shouldn't like *that* very much either!'

What did he want then? The answer was certainly naïve in its veracity. He wanted to move agreeably and openly, as if it were quite the accustomed thing, between Nelly his wife and Elise his friend! That, and nothing less than that, was precisely what he wanted. Was he no better, then, than an oriental Turk? No! he was no Turk; he was a civilized heathen. He wanted them both; but certainly not together in one house! *There*, at any rate, he had advanced in refinement upon the devotees of Allah.

But how would he like it if both Nelly and Elise moved 'agreeably and openly' between himself and two other men?

'The devil!' he muttered. 'I couldn't put up with that! I should run away from that.' 'But,' whispered his cynical demon, 'suppose *that* were the recognized custom in your two-hundred-years-hence community?'

I should find someone who really satisfied me, he thought, *and persuade her to break this confounded custom. She and I would be the only faithful ones.* This new line of thought led him to the conclusion that what he really wanted was not Nelly in England and Elise in America, but some wonderful 'Elise-Nelly' with whom he would be completely contented on both sides.

Having reached this conclusion he promptly rejected it with disgust. Such a double-natured female would be an odious monstrosity, like a peewit with the hooked beak of a sparrowhawk!

Then where *was* he, after his rambling meditation? Precisely where the bulk of humanity was, after its experiments of four thousand years!

It seemed, that particular July day, as though the hot sun on the ripening corn and the blazing red poppies had roused a feverish ferment in more than one human cranium. For no sooner had Richard reached the churchyard, where Canyot armed with a billhook was cutting the grass under the wall, while Nelly, perched on the top of the wall, with bare head and swinging legs, was watching him mischievously, than he became aware that their conversation was tense and startling.

At his approach Canyot rose to a perpendicular position, billhook in hand, and surveyed him frowningly and intensely. Nelly fixed upon him a glance of the most mocking and mysterious elfishness.

'You've just arrived at the right moment,' she remarked. 'Robert has been proposing to me that we all go off to America together!'

'Why to America?' said Richard lightly, leaning back against the wall by her side and giving her skirt a little discreet pull so that it should conceal her ankles.

'She understands my work,' threw out the young man. 'I want to work over there . . . new impressions – new world – sky-scrapers.'

'But perhaps *I* don't want sky-scrapers,' said Richard with a smile. 'Perhaps I prefer Sussex.'

'Go ahead Robert!' cried Nelly mockingly. 'Explain yourself. I told you how absurd you were.'

'It's like this, Storm,' went on the tow-headed youth, screwing up his eyes and prodding the wall with the tip of his billhook. 'It's like this, Storm—'

'Well, my friend, what is it like?' inquired Richard blandly, laying his hand familiarly on his wife's knee. 'Do you intend to carry us both off with you, or are you thinking of kidnapping Nelly?'

'She understands my work, Storm. She knows nothing of painting, of course—'

'Thank you, Rob dear!' cried Nelly from her perch on the wall, giving him a kick with her foot. 'You can leave out the "of course".'

'But she understands what I am aiming at. She helps me. You can't work without one person who knows what you want to do.'

'I don't know in the least what he's talking about,' cried Nelly. 'And please don't think I put all this into his head.'

'Of course he knows you didn't!' protested the painter. 'He knows only too well you didn't!' he added with a profound sigh.

'Well then,' began Richard, feeling extremely well pleased with this queer turn of fate but prepared to get the full credit for magnanimity, 'it appears that you want to drag me to America with you as a sort of necessary item, troublesome but inevitable, in the train of my wife?'

'Don't try and be sarcastic like that,' interrupted Nelly. 'It annoys me and it goes completely over Rob's head.'

Richard at this removed his hand from her knee. Her words irritated him more than, at that moment, he could have guessed was possible. In his heart he roundly accused her of ill-breeding and he revenged himself on her by reverting with a sweep of his imagination to the large heroic gestures of Elise Angel.

It was one of Richard's weaknesses to dislike beyond everything else the flick or sting or smart of a well-placed rebuke; especially if administered by a woman he cared for. His temperament had a certain equine sensitiveness to the lash of the human tongue. He himself was singularly slow of wit in these verbal encounters. Externally he kept his temper, to avoid looking a fool; internally he revenged himself out of all proportion to the affront. And he never really forgave.

'It's like this, Storm,' repeated the young painter, dropping his billhook and coming nearer to the man he addressed. 'If you and your wife don't come with me on this American trip my work will stop dead. I shan't do another stroke of the brush. I can't work without her. I can't deal with my thoughts without her. I can't cope with existence without her. I can't endure it without her.'

His words came out pellmell, one on the top of another. He seemed all in a moment to lose control of himself. His clenched hand quivered at his side. His voice became shrill and harsh. His lips trembled. 'I can't endure it without her,' he repeated. 'I know you don't understand my work, but you said it was good. You know it is good. You know I shall go very far with it. If you take her away from me now it'll be the end. It'll finish me. I can't stand it. I shall chuck the whole thing and just go off.'

'But Robert dear—' began Nelly.

He raised his hand. 'I know all that,' he said. 'I used not to mind not seeing her; but she's too much for me. I can't bear it any more. I *must* see her. I *must* have her within reach, where I can get to her. I thought I could sail without a word. I can't. I can't go away. If she doesn't go with me, if you two don't go with me, I am done in. I'd better give up at once. Without seeing her I can't do my work; and without my work what's life or anything in it to me? I hate it all! So you see you *must* come with me, Storm.'

It gave Nelly a strange and curious feeling to hear herself spoken of as if she were not present. A chilly sense of ghostliness fell upon her and she looked at Canyot's agitated features with a queer mixture of compassion and remoteness.

'If you two don't come with me,' the young man continued, 'it'll just finish me off. I thought I could bear not having her – I gave her up.' He still kept talking of Nelly in the third person. 'I didn't know myself. I was proud of letting her go. But I can't do it. I've found that out. I can't do it. So you *must* come. I only want to be somewhere near her – on the same side of the sea. But I can't do without her. Life is short. Everything else is unimportant. I only want just to see her – I – I love her too much! It's like that, Storm. I love her too much!'

'Well?' murmured Nelly looking at Richard with inscrutable eyes. 'Well?'

Richard was simply and directly touched. Canyot's feeling was so genuine and so deep that it swept him off his feet. It was one of those moments when he showed the best that was in him. He was awed and he was impressed; a real impulse of generosity stirred within him. He would have made the same response had there been no Elise Angel in the world. At that moment, oddly enough, he actually wished that Elise Angel was *not* in America; so that his response could be disinterested. The power of that passion passing like a tornado across the artist's twisted and corrugated countenance shamed him, disarmed him, liberated him from himself.

'Well?' repeated Nelly.

Richard bowed over the girl's hands as they lay in her lap and taking one of them into his own kissed it with a grandiose gesture.

Then he turned from her to Canyot and laid his hand on his shoulder.

'Of course I'll bring her. Of course we'll come, Robert,' he said. 'I've always thought I ought not to settle down without seeing America, and Nelly's never been out of England. Of course we'll come. I like Nelly to be of use to a real artist.'

Canyot's expression when he heard this was one of such rapturous relief that Richard had a reciprocal thrill of emotion.

The young painter blurted out some inarticulate words of gratitude and then without a glance at either of them strode off over the graves, his heavy shoulders shaken with childish crying.

'That was nice of you, Richard,' the girl whispered. 'At least I *think* it was nice of you. But I never quite know. You are not an easy person to understand, my husband!'

'It *was* a little bit nice of me, sweetheart,' he responded. 'But I quite sympathize with your difficulty in understanding me. I'm damned if I understand myself.'

'*I* wouldn't have let another woman come with us,' Nelly continued, 'certainly not that woman who wrote that letter!'

This was indeed a sharp thrust. Richard's mind visualized that little hole under the leaves into which he had prodded Elise's last communication. In one brief moment he was hurled down from the heights of magnanimity.

'I don't know that I would have agreed,' he said, 'if he hadn't been what he is. But he's a real artist and one must do what one can when it's a question of that. You really do seem to have been an inspiration to him. Yes; his work *is* good. Canyot's a genius in his way; with his mother dead, one couldn't very well do anything else.'

'Well! It's nice of you. It *is* nice of you! I only hope I shan't be seasick. But it'll be fun anyhow. I shall enjoy it. Come, dear! Aren't you going to lift me off this old wall?'

He took the opportunity of kissing her before he set her on her feet again. They were still sufficiently in love for these snatched embraces in unpromising spots and queer moments to be very pleasant to both of them.

Hand in hand they drifted to where the old naturalist lay; as if anxious to receive his benediction upon their erratic impulse.

That afternoon Richard deliberately slipped off after tea so as to leave his wife a free field to discuss the details of their departure with the young man. She had told him she had to go down to the farm to get some eggs from Mrs Winsome and he took it for granted that the painter would be expecting her there. A faint glow of self-righteous magnanimity still hung about him and his knowledge of the dancer's being in America still remained a vague exultation far away in the back of his mind.

He thought to himself, as he followed his favouriievhazel path, that these difficult relations between men and women were really growing a little more adjustable nowadays. The war had left its impress, he thought. Old rigid conventions were breaking down. Human beings were learning to be more generous to one another, less tenacious of their legal rights, more flexible, more reasonable.

He was inclined to attribute the thrill of new happiness which he felt, as he swung along the lane under that leafy roof, to the spirit of his own generosity to Canyot. Something of it was perhaps due to that. But if he had analysed his feelings down to the bottom he would have found that it was not at all disagreeable to him to have Canyot there, somewhere about, so that when he was in a mood for solitude he could hand over Nelly to him and go his own way. He liked to go off for long walks alone. He was still obsessed with Nelly as a lover; but he was not perfectly satisfied with her as a companion. There *were* moments, especially after he had made love to her a great deal, when he was decidedly bored with her society. The companion he really loved best was, after all, none other than Richard himself. Richard alone with Richard was what really gave him the deepest satisfaction.

He branched off after a while down a lane to his left, which led ultimately by shadowy byways to a small country town to the west of Selshurst. He had never been precisely this road before and the absence of any old landmarks made the path full of fresh and new impressions. The fact, too, that he was destined to leave England so soon again gave an added attraction to every little omen of the way. The jerk to his mind of this impending adventure shook him out of the half-sensual half-mystic lassitude into which he had insensibly fallen and he found himself thinking and feeling with more clear-cut subtlety.

He paused at the entrance to a long avenue of ash trees that led away across a marsh into the very land of the sunset.

What was it in a road of that kind, bordered by those twisted weather-beaten trees, that caught his mind up and carried it so far?

There came over him, just then, a feeling that he had only known once or twice in his life before; a feeling far too evasive to be put into intelligible words.

It was as if the obscure emotions of many lonely travellers upon many lonely roads, the fragments and morsels of their intercourse with the low–bowed branches and the gleaming pools, with this particular patch of moss and that particular bed of reeds, had mingled strangely together and had waited for him, had been waiting for him, precisely at the turn of the road, so that he should respond to them and give them a sign of recognition.

It was as if they became for him, at that hour, a solitary signal, a beckoning intimation, something that emerged out of long lonely expectant nights, nights full of soft-falling rain and rustling wind and the sound of shaken leaves.

It was a feeling that was only possible in a very old country, a country where generations of men and women, one after another, had mixed their human sorrows with the wistful loneliness of marsh and mere, of moorland and wayside. It was a feeling that could not have endured for a moment either in the uproar of a city or in the inhuman desolation of jungle or desert or mountain. It was the evocation of a strange marginal purlieu, lying midway between the loneliness of solitary human beings and the loneliness of inanimate things, things that had been witness, in their long centuries, of the passing of many such wayfarers and had become the accomplices of many vaguely floating thoughts.

Richard turned back at that point – he was already some three miles from home – but the glimpse he had been permitted that day into the very secret of his native soil went with him as he retraced his steps.

He felt humbled and saddened. He realized that he had in these days of lovemaking lost some clue, some contact with the unknown, that it must to one of his motives to rediscover.

That half-sensual half-mystical communication with nature, such as he had blended with his love for Nelly, had not been subtle enough. Certain more delicate voices had grown inaudible, had passed over his head, had been drowned in the grosser monotony of his material sensations.

Towards Nelly herself, how dull, how insensitive he had been! Towards her and towards poor Canyot too!

It was likely enough, he thought, only too likely, that there were aspects of Canyot's work deeper, more clearly emphasized, nearer the great withheld secret of things, than anything he had himself ever written. And how little he *had* written, of any kind, during these recent months! He had betrayed his better self; and in doing so he had betrayed Nelly also.

He had not retraced his steps very far when he observed a dog-cart driving rapidly towards him, with a couple of dogs running beside it.

It pulled up with a jerk when it reached him and he perceived that the driver was none other than Mrs Shotover.

'How do you do, Mr Storm,' said the lady. 'It's a pity we're going in opposite directions. I'd have offered you a lift. I'm going to Fern-ham Beeches to fetch a bitch pup I've just bought – such a little darling. Well! how's Nelly and everything else at the cottage?'

Richard put his hand on the side of the cart. Her horse chafed and stamped and fretted; and the two dogs barked at his legs. The wheels of her smart little vehicle smelt of new paint. Mrs Shotover was dressed in a tightly fitting tweed suit and her grey hair was well tucked in under a cloth hat. She looked the typical Englishwoman, out for a race meeting or an agricultural show or, as was actually the case, to visit her dog fancier.

With her champing and stamping horse, her barking dogs, and the taciturn Thomas sitting on the back seat, she broke in upon the writer's thoughts like an image of the 'verdict of society.'

'Oh, Nelly's very well,' he said. 'I have been for a long walk. I often go for long walks.'

'Too long,' Mrs Shotover hazarded. 'It's a mistake! Married men ought never to go for long walks. They ought to take their young wives out – to see people and all that kind of thing.'

'To buy terrier pups, eh?' said Richard.

'To buy the good opinion of people that count,' rapped out the lady. 'Oh no, my dear Mr Storm, you really must be seen a little more, you and your charming Nelly. There's that adorable Lady Wincroft; why, she's asked me over and over again why Nelly hasn't returned her call. Of course I say it's her father, and so forth – but her father, poor dear, is out of it now.'

'I don't see why I should break my usual habits, Mrs Shotover. I married Nelly Moreton, not the society of West Sussex.'

'That won't do! That won't do!' cried the lady, and she sat so bolt upright in her seat and looked so fierce that Richard began to feel as if he had encountered the chariot of the sternest of the Eumenides.

'You're a great deal older than she is,' was her next remark; Richard could not help wondering what comments upon all this the coachman's imperturbable profile concealed from the world.

Then his mood suddenly changed. A mischievous spirit of schoolboy levity took possession of him. *Confound the woman!* he thought. *What right has she to talk to me like this?* And in order to see what she would do, and out of pure maliciousness, he burst out with what was in his mind.

'You'll be pleased, then, I expect,' he said, 'when I tell you that I've decided to travel with Nelly for a bit.'

Mrs Shotover did indeed look startled. 'Oh excellent! very excellent!' she cried. On the Continent, I suppose? To Paris first, no doubt, and then to Switzerland? I am delighted you can afford to give my dear child this happiness!'

'I think of taking Nelly to America,' he said, with a malicious emphasis. 'Robert Canyot has some exhibitions to look after over there; and he has persuaded us to go with him.'

Mrs Shotover did indeed show 'the mettle of her pastures' at that moment. She became extremely quiet, and flicked a horse-fly from the flank of her impatient steed.

'Ah!' she muttered, drawing in her breath with a little hissing sound. 'Ah really!'

'Yes; we think of going quite soon. Nelly will be sorry to leave Hill Cottage of course. But we may be able to let it for a few months. We are both so interested in Mr Canyot's success.'

In her heart Mrs Shotover thought bitterly – *Who is the one to be exploited in this abominable affair? What a couple of ill-bred cads these fellows are! Poor, poor, poor Nelly!* But aloud she only said, 'How nice it is for the dear child to have *two* men of genius to support her! I expect you and Mr Canyot will both find America very much to your taste. I *hope* Nelly will. It's rather a terrible place isn't it? But no doubt there are *some* nice people there. You won't get anything to drink, of course, but I suppose none of you will mind that. What's their word for those horrid mixtures they all swallow? Soft drinks! Well, I hope you'll enjoy the soft drinks, Mr Storm. But don't kill my dear child between you. Give her my love, please! Goodbye.' And she flicked her horse viciously and was off at a gallop, almost throwing Mr Thomas into Richard's arms.

She had successfully destroyed the filmy threads of his meditation. 'It is to escape from women like that,' he said to himself, 'that people emigrate. Oh England, England, you certainly allow many troublesome persons many strange privileges!'

Chapter 13

The newly broadened Varick Street, now a continuation of Seventh Avenue, is one of the most characteristic thoroughfares in New York. It is characteristic of that city by reason of a queer blending of the dilapidated 'old' with the harshly and rawly 'new'. The old is indeed rapidly disappearing, but it lingers on in a diffusion of chaotic litter; bits of ancient Dutch houses, roofs and sheds, old wooden walls, little ramshackle staircases, fragments of antiquated sidewalks and old tobacconist and barber shops, clinging pathetically enough to the great new erections, just as the small narrow streets in that vicinity seem themselves to cling with a tenacious persistence to the huge new thoroughfare that cuts its proud straight path through the middle of them.

It was at the corner of Charlton Street and Varick Street that Richard and Nelly at last installed themselves.

They had a bedroom, a sitting room, a bathroom and a kitchen, on the second floor of a small house that must have been at least a hundred years old.

The place was already furnished; and they possessed themselves of it on the understanding that they could leave it when they pleased.

Robert Canyot had taken a studio on a year's lease in another part of the city; in a street adjoining Central Park, of whose trees he could catch a distant view as he worked.

Nelly had found the heat of New York with its accompanying humidity rather exhausting when she first arrived, but the amusement and interest of housekeeping under these new conditions prevented her from losing her good spirits.

Her first view of the great group of colossal buildings gathered round the Woolworth Tower, as they entered the harbour more than a month ago, had been forever associated in her mind with the discovery that she was to be a mother.

She could see that same Woolworth Tower as soon as she left her little apartment and turned into Varick Street; for Varick Street led straight into the city district and lost itself among those iron and marble monsters.

It always struck her when each day she saw the huge erection as she went on her housekeeping errands that the thing resembled some gigantic temple, built to some new god of this new world, a god who demanded the service of innumerable men and women but whose own especial angels and chosen ministers were things of iron and stone and steam and electricity.

It a little terrified her sometimes to think that she was destined to stay in New York until her child was born; but they had let Hill Cottage before they left England; Grace had married her young man; it would have meant an uncomfortable hunt for a new abode if she insisted on returning. She had no desire that her child be born in America, but she dreaded, in her nervous state of health, the effort of the voyage.

There were other more subtle reasons to account for her acquiescence when Richard proposed to take this apartment. She associated Hill Cottage with that fatal letter from Paris and it pleased her to think that New York was further away from Paris than was that little garden where she had inhaled, together with the scent of white phloxes, her first taste of the cruelty of sex jealousy.

And she had a longing, too, that she might put off her return to her father's grave till she had received – as she believed she would receive in time – some sort of absolution for what she regarded as her sin in neglecting him when she first married.

If I'd married Robert, she thought, it would have been to give Father a home. I did give him a home with Richard; but it wasn't the same. It was for my own pleasure, and I hardly saw anything of him during those weeks.

In the subtle workings of her brain she had come to associate her Littlegate haunts with a certain complicated sadness – the sadness of her first taste of the bitterness of life and the sadness of her father's wasted powers.

The upbraiding shadow of Mrs Shotover also menaced her from those Sussex fields. *I suppose I ought not to have let her go, she thought. I suppose I was cruel. But she was impossible. She was mad.*

In spite of her nervous condition and in spite of certain moods of timid apprehension as to all that was before her, Nelly was really extremely happy during those hot airless days. She suffered physically from the heat; but her husband had never been mentally so close to her; their mutual interest in their new surroundings seeming to have brought them together on a deeper plane.

She was very happy too in her frequent visits to Canyot's up-town studio; and the conversation about life and art which she had with the young painter, seated by his side in some gallery of the Metropolitan Museum or on a bench in the Central Park, lifted her out of herself into regions which she had never supposed she would be able to enter.

She admitted Canyot into the secret of her condition with a sure feminine instinct as to the effect the news would have upon him. And in this she was completely justified. The final loss of her, in a physical sense, thus emphasized by her prospect of motherhood, seemed to act as a sedative to the young man's passion, seemed to purge it of all possessive jealousy.

Canyot himself was steadily advancing in power and originality. He was surprised by the recognition his work received. Not only did he experience no difficulty in selling his pictures, but he found himself accepted as a desirable personage by the whole aesthetic fraternity of that enterprising cosmopolitan city. He turned out to be the only artist in New York whose methods of work were untouched by modern French fashions; this very fact appealed to the American craving for novelty; it was just the moment when a reaction was impending against the more extreme European schools.

It was not the prospect of Nelly's giving him a child that brought Richard nearer to her, it was the effect upon him of America. Like some great wedge of iron this tremendous new world, bored its way through the thick sensuousness of his nature and laid his deeper instincts bare. It was a process of spiritual surgery, painful but liberating. There were no lovely fields or leafy lanes here in Manhattan; as he trod its hot pavements and passed down its echoing canyons of iron and stone he was compelled to fall back upon his own soul for vision and illumination. Nelly's ways and Nelly's feelings and Nelly's little enjoyments became a sort of oasis to him in a stern stark wilderness where he wandered alone, stripped and defenceless.

Things were thus arranging themselves for all these three persons when an event occurred which changed everything.

Richard received word from Paris to the effect that his publisher there had gone bankrupt, leaving him without hope of any further income until arrangements could be made with some other house.

It became necessary that he should at once find work; for he had already spent what he had saved.

While he was looking for work he was compelled to borrow a couple of hundred dollars from Canyot. This loan was the beginning of evil, for by making him his rival's financial debtor it introduced a new element into their relations full of dangerous possibilities. Insensibly he began to hate the successful painter as he had never hated him before. He threw out malicious and carping observations when Nelly went to see him. He got into the habit of grudging her her uptown visits. He vented his feeling of humiliation by all manner of sarcasms upon 'successful people who cater to the American taste'.

The money that had passed into his hands became a slow poison, ruining the new understanding between himself and his wife. He brooded gloomily and morosely upon his situation as he went about looking for a job. He felt himself to be a failure. He was tempted to borrow more money and clear off to Paris; but he did not dare to suggest so drastic a move.

The late summer was a bad time in which to look for work. The pitiless sunshine made those vain interviews with journalistic underlings in stuffy offices peculiarly depressing.

Week after week passed; in spite of rigid economy the two hundred dollars ebbed away, and still Richard had found no job. Canyot kept pressing him to accept another loan. Once, to his unspeakable chagrin, he found that Nelly *had* accepted a cheque for fifty dollars from her friend. This incident led to the first quarrel between them that had occurred since they landed. The fierce manner in which the girl, when teased by his reproaches, cried out, 'My child shall not be starved while Robert has a penny to give him!' pierced the skin of his deepest pride. To revenge himself on her he deliberately reduced his own diet to an absurd minimum, refusing meat and milk and eggs and living almost entirely upon bread and tea. The result of this was that he began to suffer from acute dyspepsia which was aggravated by his miserable and hopeless hunt for work.

He found that he had overrated his reputation as a writer. In America he was practically unknown; the French estimation of his critical power amounted to almost nothing with the New York publishers and newspapers.

His great poetic purpose upon the substance of which, both in manner and in matter, that first month in America had produced a profound change, pruning it of accessories and giving it a sterner, more drastic tone, was now completely laid aside. He began to curse the day he had ever entered upon this too ambitious undertaking. He began to regret the light facility and the easily won local fame of his pre-war achievements. He felt himself a charlatan and a fraud; was almost tempted to destroy every word he had written under the stress of his new spiritual purpose. He felt as though he had completely deceived himself as to its quality.

At last he did succeed in finding something. It was not much of an opening, considering his former Paris reputation and his recent poetic schemes; but it was something – a ledge to cling to, a shelf of rock to hold by, in this tidal wave of adversity.

It was in the middle of September when he found it; an engagement with a newly organized magazine called *The Mitre* for which he had to furnish weekly articles upon the more definitely Catholic writers and poets of Europe. His salary amounted to forty

dollars a week; but with the rent they had to pay for their apartment, this meant a very rigid economy. It meant, as a matter of fact,
that he continued to underfeed himself so as to give his wife as little
excuse as possible to accept any further help from the painter.

He went each day to the office and did his work there – though he
might have worked at home – partly because he found it increas-
ingly difficult to concentrate his thoughts in their small apartment,
and partly to avoid the irritation of being harassed by his wife on
account of his fantastic experiments in diet.

The result of this was that Nelly, being lonely and restless at
home, resorted more and more to Canyot's studio. By gradual
degrees the custom arose that she should prepare for the young
man and for herself a substantial lunch in his 'kitchenette' while
he worked at his pictures.

These picnic lunches in the painter's apartments were some of
the happiest hours Nelly knew in those days and she solaced her
conscience for accepting them by posing for him in various drap-
eries during the afternoon.

Her evening meals with Richard grew more and more gloomy;
for though she forced him to share certain little dishes which she
took a pride in making, he never would really eat enough; and his
persistency in this aggravating mania became a constant cause of
friction between them, which was not lessened by his knowledge
that in spite of such economy she still continued to accept Canyot's
help.

Things went on in this unsatisfactory manner till the end of September, the girl drifting further and further away from him and
concentrating all the attention that was not bestowed on Canyot
upon the care and protection of the new life that was germinating
within her.

It was a curious thing that this same new life, which had not
drawn Richard as strongly towards her as it should have done, did
not draw her either towards him.

It almost seemed, as time went on, as though it estranged her
from him. It certainly absorbed her to such a degree that she could
not make the effort to overcome his nervous irritability or to put an
end to this ruining of his digestion by ill-chosen food.

She was touched and grateful to him for the way he stinted himself in his favourite luxury of cigarettes and she was distressed and

worried to see him grow constantly thinner and older-looking. She seemed to live in these days in a self-concentrated dream, so that it was only the outside of her mind, as it were, that stirred at all. The more passionate elements in her were all taken up and exhausted in the slow process of maternity.

She could not have described to anyone what she felt in her inmost heart all this while. What was happening to her mentally was happening in some deep subconscious region out of reach altogether of any intelligible analysis. To her conscious self her attitude to Richard remained unchanged; and she was only dreamily and faintly aware that she regarded his coming and going with an abstracted eye, taking his presence for granted, like a background that varied slightly in colour but was always *there*.

It seemed as though the tenacious unscrupulous egoism of that new life was asserting its blind formidable unconscious will, careless as to whom it sacrificed, careless as to the spiritual havoc it caused, careless as to the human agencies to which it owed its being; asserting its will, as it rose out of the unfathomable reservoirs and groped forward towards the light, asserting its will, as it drew its nourishment from the body that protected it, isolating that body and treating the consciousness that animated that body as of no account at all save as it answered to its physical needs.

And Richard, while day after day he set off, with growing disinclination, to the office in East Twenty-seventh Street and settled down to his task of selecting, from piled-up Catholic books and brochures, the few things that interested him, felt as though his personal self were of no more weight than a floating straw borne on the tide of great irrepressible forces.

This feeling was precisely the one most naturally engendered in New York, where the crowds of men and women scourged by economic necessity seemed to dehumanize themselves and become just one more mechanically moving element, paralleled to the iron and steel and stone and marble, to the steam and electricity, whose forces, brutal and insistent, pounded upon it, hammered upon it, resisted it or drove it relentlessly forward.

Richard was puzzled in the profoundest depths of his nature by Nelly's attitude towards him. He expected her to be nervous and capricious. He expected her to cling to him, to depend upon him, to share every subtlety of her emotions with him. This strange

shrinking away from him into herself, into that dim obscure unfathomable workshop of organic creation where her soul now
brooded in its solitude, startled and bewildered him.

He wondered how she behaved with Canyot and whether *he*
suffered from the same mysterious aloofness.

And Nelly's remoteness from him, her escape from him, was
only one more additional element among the blind tremendous
forces which seemed invading the last recess of his mind; and then
passing on their way, indifferently.

Much of Richard's depression arose from sheer physical weakness, from his saving money by cutting down on meat and milk and
eggs; but a good deal of it was due to a horrible doubt that began to
invade his mind – a doubt as to whether he had not made the one
irretrievable mistake of his life in marrying Nelly at all.

With the toning down of the more physical elements of their
attraction to one another, the accompanying difficulties of the present situation seemed to fill the whole field. Richard became
vaguely aware for the first time in his life of a serious deficiency in
himself. He fought against this recognition and threw it aside but it
kept returning; what it amounted to was that a certain human
warmth, a certain tender fidelity, apart from either spiritual or
physical excitement, was lamentably lacking in him. His great
poetic purpose had been so thwarted and baffled that he found it
difficult any more to take refuge in it; but he had to face the fact
that all that was best in him was roused and stirred by that kind of
thing alone. Apart from that kind of thing, he felt himself to be
something hopelessly ignoble, untrustworthy, irresponsible, below
the emotional level of ordinary humanity.

He did not attempt to conceal from himself that this ill-balanced
economy of his was not really undertaken for his wife's sake. For
her sake – if *that* was what he was about – he ought obviously to
take every care of his health. The real motive that prompted him
was a kind of voluptuous self-cruelty, mingled with an angry hatred
of her dependence upon Canyot.

When he was quite alone, seated in the overhead railway or
struggling with the crowd on Sixth Avenue, all sorts of inhuman
egotistic feelings came upon him. Where had his intelligence been,
that he had let himself be led into this trap? He had not the least
desire that Nelly should have a child, He wanted *Nelly*, not Nelly's

children. If he could not write wonderful new poetry, poetry that would be read hundreds of years hence – why, then, his old Paris life brought him quite enough fame and pleasure to satisfy any man! And what had he got now? Nelly's body was dominated by Nelly's child; Nelly's mind was dominated by Canyot. He had nothing for himself but odious duties and harassing responsibilities. He supposed that most men were thrilled with joy when the woman they loved had a child by them. Well! He was not thrilled. The idea of having the responsibility of a child gave him not the remotest pleasure. He wanted his name to be perpetuated not by children but by poetry. Children were nature's will and pleasure. Poetry was the attempt of the spirit of mankind to rise above nature and extricate itself.

Richard had just begun to make a few acquaintances among the literary and theatrical circles when this blow fell. But he let them go now; and they were not sufficiently interested in him to take any trouble in seeking him out. His wife was meeting Canyot's friends but that did not mean that Richard met them.

As long as he did his work in the office he felt that he had fulfilled every duty that was demanded of him.

Each day he seemed to care less what happened; the promise for the future which his wife was bearing within her seemed to coincide in its growth with the steady loosening of his own hold upon all that he valued in existence.

There were no fields or lanes in Manhattan where he could recover his spirit by drawing upon the deep earth forces. All about him were iron girders and iron cog wheels and iron spikes. All about him were the iron foreheads of such as partook of the nature of the machinery whose slaves they were. And the iron that entered his soul found no force that could resist it; for all the days of his life he had been an epicurean: when the hour called for stoicism he could only answer with a dogged despair.

Chapter 14

One day, about the middle of October, Richard left the office between half-past one and two o'clock to get some lunch. He had been trying to extract the elusive quintessence from some especially recondite Catholic poet in order to make a popular article out of what was the last refinement of subtle and sceptical credulity.

He felt sick of his work, weary of himself, and beaten down by the noises of the street. Between the elaborate sophistications of this Parisian trifler with the faith and the raw harsh brutal aggression of the vortex of ferocious energies that swirled around him there seemed no refuge for his spirit, nothing that was calm and cool and simple and largely noble.

He made his way slowly up Sixth Avenue, searching for some little refreshment room or café where he could eat and read in quiet. He passed many of these places with a shudder. They were crowded and unappealing. The people inside them seemed as though they were eating for a wager, watched by the whole world through plate-glass windows.

He felt hunted by iron dogs whose jaws were worked by machinery and whose mouths breathed forth a savour of 'poisonous brass and metal sick'.

He crossed street after street, threading his way through the automobiles and the great motor-lorries, jostled and hustled by the crowd. He held grimly to Sixth Avenue, knowing that there alone, in this quarter of the city, could he find any sort of inexpensive retreat. Above him rattled with clanging roar the trains of the elevated railway, supported on a huge iron framework, the very shadows of which, as they broke the burning sunshine, seemed to exude a smell of heated metal. The paraded objects in the store windows leered aggressively and jeeringly at him through their plate glass. Every material fabric in the world, except such as suggested quietness and peace, seemed to flap and nod and make mouths at him. Every man he passed seemed to flaunt an insolent cigar, held tightly between compressed lips, and every woman seemed to jibe mockingly at his decrepitude from under her smart hat.

Suddenly, when he began to feel actually faint and dizzy and was on the point of entering a glaring cavern of marble tables, he caught a glimpse of the front of a theatre down one of the streets on his right hand. It was some distance away but certain well-known words emblazoned on a huge placard made the blood rush to his head.

ELISE ANGEL, proclaimed this placard to the tide of traffic, ELISE ANGEL IN HER FAMOUS ATTIC DANCE.

All his dizziness disappeared in a moment and the iron wedge that had worked itself into his brain during these miserable weeks seemed pulled out by invisible hands and flung under the wheels of the crowded street.

He rushed to the theatre entrance, paid for a ticket in the second row and was led to his place by a damsel in apron and cap, whom he smiled at with a smile of a drunken man entering paradise.

The house was not particularly full that afternoon and it was not long before the performance began.

It was a vaudeville entertainment and the great dancer's 'turn' was the last on the list. It was indeed nearly an hour and a half before she made her appearance, the longest hour and a half, but in one sense the very happiest, that Richard Storm had ever known. He saw and heard all that preceded her entrance as if he was in a trance.

At last she appeared, with the familiar background of plain black curtains; and out of infinite depths of obscure suffering his spirit rose up, healed and refreshed, to greet her.

She danced to some great classical rhapsody, tragic, passionate, world-destroying, world-creating; and the harmonies of the dead musician lived a life greater, more formidable, more liberating, than humanity could have dared to dream they contained. Her arms, her limbs were bare; her nobly modelled breasts, under some light fabric, outlined themselves as the breasts of some Phidian divinity.

Once more, as if all between this moment and when he had last seen her were a dark and troubled dream, she lifted for him the veil of Isis. In the power of her austere and olympian art, all the superficial impressions that had dominated him through that long summer dissolved like a cloud of vapour.

This was what he had been aiming at in his own blundering way;

this was what he was born to understand! The softness of ancient lawns under immemorial trees, the passion of great winds in lonely places, the washing of sea tides under melancholy harbour walls, the retreats of beaten armies, the uprising of the multitudinous oppressed, the thunder of the wings of destroying angels, the 'still small voice' of the creative spirit brooding upon the foundations of new worlds – all these things rose up upon him as he watched her, all these things were in the gestures of her outspread arms, in the leap and the fall and the monumental balance of her divine white limbs.

Her physical beauty was the mere mask of the terrible power within her. Her spirit seemed to tear and rend at her beauty and mould it with a recreating fire into a sorrow, into a pity, into a passion, that flew quivering and exultant over all the years of man's tragic wayfaring.

But her dancing was not the wild lyrical outburst of an emotion that spurned restraint. Beneath every movement, every gesture, binding the whole thing together and realizing the cry of the beginning in the finality of the silence of the close, there was the stern intellectual purpose of a mind that was consciously, deliberately, building a bridge from infinite to infinite, from mystery to mystery.

The scattered audience that watched her was largely composed of poor people, many of them unknown unrecognized artists of both sexes, mingled with a sprinkling of wealthy virtuosos, mostly young men and women.

It was to youth – that was plain enough – to the youth of these after-war days, that she came with this great new art, an art that changed former values, an art that created the taste that was destined to understand it.

And how, for one man at least who watched, white-cheeked and still as a statue in his place, the important things became the unimportant and the things that had been half forgotten became everything that mattered!

All the complicated weight of sensual sensations, of refined *sensuous* sensations even, which had hitherto meant so much, seemed to be torn away from him. New York had loosened them from his heart already – those insidious pleasures! New York had cut at them and prodded them, had hammered them and crushed them, with its iron engines and the howling arena of its energies.

But New York had left his soul naked, helpless, flayed and bleeding.

With these divine gestures that seemed to arise out of some tremendous unseen victory over all that was in the path of the spirit, Elise Angel clothed that wounded soul of his with the garments of new flesh and blood.

She had never danced quite like this in the days when he had known her in Paris. He felt she must have endured strange tribulations while he was taking his pleasure in green pastures and beside still waters. And this new phase of her unconquerable art was the result of what she had gone through!

When it was over and the curtain fell, Richard felt like a man to whom has been manifested at last the hidden god of a lifetime of hopeless prayers.

He rose to his feet when they began applauding her and stared at her without a movement. In his eyes were tears, but they did not fall. On his lips was a cry 'Elise! Elise!' but he did not utter it. He only stood motionless and white as a ghost, staring at her, his whole soul one inarticulate ecstasy of gratitude. He knew, all of a sudden, that she had seen him; for the frank infantile smile of delight at the shouts that rose from every part of the house changed in the flicker of a moment to a quick agitated look of troubled concern. She must have found him sorely changed! She made an imperceptible movement towards him and gave him a direct sign of recognition. He smiled faintly in answer to this and moved at once from his place towards the theatre door.

Out in the street his dizziness came upon him again; so that it was all he could do to stagger up the little dark passage that led to the stage entrance. Here he sank down upon a flight of wooden steps and closed his eyes. He only prayed that he might not lose consciousness before she came out.

She came at last, hurriedly, anxiously and unattended.

'Richard, Richard!' she cried, bending over him.

He struggled to his feet and she gave him both her hands. 'What's happened, my dear? You are old, you are ill, you are horribly changed! What have they done to you? Didn't you get my letters?'

He could only smile at her with perfect happiness and contentment. Then he staggered and sank down again on the wooden steps.

'*Mon Dieu!* You *are* ill,' she cried. 'Oh I must get you away from here. I must get you to my rooms. Stay where you are. Don't try to move. I'll be back in a moment. Ah! there's Tommy!'

A tall thin man in fashionable attire approached them from the street. 'Tommy dear,' she began at once in a pleading, cajoling voice, full of a vibrant plaintiveness. 'This is the great critic Richard Storm, the friend of Richepin and Barrès. Have you got your car there? I must beg you to help me get him into it. He's going to dine with me. The theatre was too much for him.'

The gentleman addressed as Tommy obeyed her with courtly alacrity.

Between them they supported Richard to the street and got him into the automobile. Then 'Tommy', after giving his chauffeur the dancer's address, bowed to Elise and bade her goodbye. 'I shall be here tonight,' he said. 'You can tell me then how your friend is.' With a farewell wave of his hand the man was gone and Richard was alone with Elise.

She made Tommy's servant help her to get him up the single flight of stairs that led to her luxurious apartments.

Once safely ensconced here and laid out upon the cushions of her divan she hurriedly brought him a glass of cognac.

When he had drunk this she told him to rest for a bit; leaving the door between the two rooms ajar she retired into her bedroom and changed her dress for a long loosely fitting tea-gown.

Appearing again in this more intimate array, and with purple-coloured oriental slippers on her feet, she called softly into the lighted corridor. To the elderly duenna who obeyed her call she gave some quickly whispered order; the woman presently returned with a heavy silver tray upon which were a pile of sandwiches and a bottle of champagne.

Having filled their glasses, this invaluable attendant, mute and competent, observing everything as though she observed nothing, went out as silently as she had entered; Elise, seated on the divan by Richard's side, made him eat and drink.

It was not long before the wine brought back the colour to his cheeks and loosened his tongue. He made a feeble effort to rise.

'It's you who ought to be resting now,' he said, 'after what you've done; not a great hulking fraud like me!'

She forced him back upon the cushions and kissed him tenderly on the forehead.

Then she refilled her own glass with champagne and rallied him because his was still only half-empty.

'You never could drink as I do, *mon vieux*,' she murmured. 'Come then. Let's smoke for a bit!' And she lit a cigarette and gave one to him.

'Well! speak to me, old friend; tell me what they've been doing to you? I can see you're in the hands of some female person! Only a woman could reduce a man to the state you're in. Getting grey and withered, upon my life! Come on, *coeur de mon coeur*, and let's hear the whole miserable story! But do please tell me, first of all, why you ran away from me like that? That wasn't very nice of you, was it? Why did you do it, Richard? No! you shan't get out of it by kissing my hand. Why did you do it, Richard?'

She spoke with a caressing infantile *naïveté*, which many another had found irresistible, and she sidled up to him on the couch, letting her fingers stray through his hair and across his thin cheeks. The softness and warmth of her flexible form enveloped him like a hovering cloud that follows every contour and every rigid outline of the hillside against which it nestles.

'Why did you do it, Richard?' she repeated, putting all the plaintiveness of a child's appeal to be loved into the intonation of her voice. 'Why did you do it?'

There seemed to be no answer to this except the one inevitable answer to all such questions and he let his hand slide round her waist and drew her closely against him.

Vaguely in his half-conscious mind – such is the eternal hypocrisy of the male conscience when confronted with the unscrupulousness of women – he justified himself for this yielding by putting all the burden of it upon her. He let her lips be the first to seek his lips, and the fact that it *did* happen in that way seemed, to his half-extinguished loyalty, justification enough. The only alternative would have been that he should have struggled up to his feet and shaken off, with a brusque unthinkable violence, her warm arms and caressing fingers.

Having been so long without food it was no wonder that the wine she had given him disarmed his scruples quite as much as her insidious beauty. It threw him back upon a sort of delicious helplessness and weakness out of which he clung to her blindly, while her love lifted him up, like something strong and immortal into a paradise of peace, pressing against its breast something hurt, wounded, frail and pitifully human.

It was indeed with a certain innocence of real tenderness that they clung together then; and with their kisses was mingled for both of them a kind of infinite relief, as if they had been for aeons of time torn apart and separated, and as if some living portion of their being had gone through the world suppressed, dumb, fettered, stifled, until that liberating hour.

It seemed as if only a few minutes had passed, so rapt and absorbed had they been, when Elise leapt up to her feet and announced that it was time for her to dress.

She called to Thérèse and scolded her for not having brought in dinner; and she insisted, when the servant did bring it, that Richard should begin his meal while she changed her clothes.

While he ate she kept running in, in her dressing gown and with loosened hair, to make sure he was doing justice to Thérèse's cooking. She snatched her own meal by hurried mouthfuls in this way; Richard never forgot the mingling of childish excitement and royal graciousness with which she filled his plate and his glass and bent over him with fleeting kisses as she did so, her bronze-coloured hair hanging in heavy braids upon her white shoulders.

They had just time for a last cigarette together before she had to leave. Richard, laughing at her protests about being too heavy, drew her down upon his knees and teased her about the shameless way she had reddened her lips. 'It's your fault,' she whispered. 'You've kissed away every bit of natural colour out of me!'

She would not let him enter the theatre again that night, but before they parted at the stage door she made him promise to come to tea on the following day.

'It doesn't matter how early or how late you come,' she assured him. 'There's no performance tomorrow and I'll keep myself free for you from four o'clock on. So don't get worried. Come just as soon as you can get away.'

It was not till he found himself in the Seventh Avenue subway that Richard remembered that he had been expected home at half-past six.

It occurred to him then, as he sat staring at advertisements of soap and toothpaste, cold-cream and hair-wash, that Nelly was to have made some especial vegetarian dish in his honour, the recipe for which she had obtained from one of her uptown friends.

He got out at Sheridan Square and walked down Varick Street.

Far off, in front of him, he could see the colossal bulk of the Woolworth Building, in and out of the very body of which the huge procession of wagons, drays and motor-lorries, which poured up and down from north to south, seemed to be moving. Normally this stream of rattling trucks and wagons, driven by reckless brawny youth, some of them still clothed in heterogeneous patches of khaki, was a cause of nervous misery to him.

He gazed in astonishment at the unmoved equanimity with which the tiny school children, going to the high school in Hudson Square, crossed that roaring street. American children, he thought, must be born with some self-protective membrane, impervious, like the shell of the oyster, to all rending shocks of noise!

But today he seemed to possess within himself a resistant power more effective than any oyster shell, inasmuch as it was able to carry, so to speak, the war into the enemy's camp and find grist for its mill in the most rending and tearing sights and sounds.

As he swung down Varick Street brandishing his stick – a stick bought under the shadow of Selshurst Cathedral – he actually exulted in all the sights around him. He exulted in the rawness of the iron frameworks, in the great torn-out gaps, like bleeding flesh, that were being laid bare in the sides of the old Dutch houses, in the subterranean thunder and the whirling puffs of air and dust that came up through the subway's gratings. He exulted in the huge grotesqueness of the gigantic advertisements, in the yells of the truck drivers, in the flapping clothes lines, in the piled-up garbage, in the hideous tenements and vociferous children. He suddenly became aware that in all this chaotic litter and in all this reckless, gay, aggressive crowd, there was an immense outpouring of youth-ful energy, an unconquerable vitality, a ferocious joyousness and daring.

The individual separate person, with his ways and his caprices, was certainly hammered and battered here into a horrible uni-formity. But the stream of humanity, considered in its ensemble, had a tornado-like force and swing and amplitude. If the exquisite was pounded out of existence, the fidgety, the affected, the meticulous, the conceited, was certainly allowed no mercy.

He stumbled along the rough uneven sidewalk and finally threaded his way through a long line of arrested vehicles to the corner of Charlton Street.

He opened the door with his latch key and ran upstairs.

He found Nelly extended on the sofa white as a sheet and with her eyes tight shut.

He rushed to her side and falling on his knees took her hand and called her by name.

She opened her eyes and looked at him with a bitter smile. She snatched her hand away and drew back from his touch.

He was so relieved to find that her immobility was a deliberate and not an unconscious thing that he got up from his knees and began talking loudly and freely, walking up and down the room.

'I was very lucky tonight,' he said, using the crude diplomacy of his earlier days and trying to undermine her suspicions by a mask of nonchalant candour. 'I met an actress I know and got treated to a wonderful dinner; champagne and all that sort of thing. Upon my soul I believe it made me a bit tipsy. I'm not used to this wining and dining.'

Nelly's face had changed from its ghastly pallor to an unnatural flush. She moved her head and made a little gesture with her hands that might have meant anything or nothing.

'But I thought,' went on Richard, still walking up and down the room as if to gather confidence by the sound of his own footsteps, 'that in our present state of finances it would be absurd to leave a good dinner unenjoyed.'

'You left *my* dinner unenjoyed,' murmured his wife. 'I had it ready for you by half-past six: I waited and waited for you. And then, when I did eat, I was faint and sick. I waited so long. I got nervous and scared. I was afraid something had happened. Kiss me Richard please, and don't tell me any more.'

He stopped by her side and bent over her and kissed her tenderly. The particular scent used by Elise Angel still hung about his clothes and she drew away from him with a quick start.

'You've been making love to someone!' she cried. 'Oh Richard, how could you do it?'

That refrain 'how could you do it?' – hadn't he heard it, just an hour or so ago, on the lips of the other?

'My actress reeked with every kind of scent,' protested Richard. 'They all do, you know. Why, you yourself were buying something of the sort the other day. I expect we shall have you using rouge soon!'

His air of bullying levity did not conceal from Nelly the fact that something quite serious had occurred to him. He was a different person from the Richard who had left her that morning.

'You've been making love to someone,' she repeated. 'But it doesn't matter. I'm too tired to talk about it now. So don't tell me any more. I think I shall go to bed if you don't mind. It upset me a bit waiting so long. It isn't nice to have to wait so long.'

She raised herself up with a weary effort as she spoke. 'No, no, my dear,' she repeated, 'you can't fool me like that. You've been making love to someone while I was waiting and waiting for you. You had quite forgotten my existence.'

'I don't see,' said Richard, beginning to assume an irritated and scolding tone, 'why I shouldn't have my friends just as you have yours. How do I know what people you see up there in Canyot's studio? I don't ask you inquisitorial questions when you come back to me.'

'You have no need,' she answered with a sad little smile, sitting on the edge of the sofa and propping her chin upon the palms of her hands. 'But it's no matter. I don't care what you do. I don't want you to tell me anything. All *that* came to an end long ago when I found you were writing to someone. I ought to have known something of this kind would happen. I suppose I couldn't expect anything else. I *did* think, though, just a little, that since I am as I am you wouldn't have done anything like this – yet.'

He was just about to pour forth a torrent of false asseverations when there came a ring at the street door. 'What's that?' he whispered looking at her in a frightened nervous way. He vaguely expected some drastic agitating message from Elise Angel.

She got up quickly and walked with steady steps to the mirror. 'Open the door, Richard, will you please, and bring him in.'

'Who is he? Is it Canyot?'

She smiled at him out of the mirror, as she arranged her hair –

her old mocking elf-smile. 'Bring him up and you'll see, my dear. No – it's not Robert.'

Greatly puzzled but at the same time a little relieved Richard ran down and opened the door. He came up escorting a tall slender girl, quite unknown to him, who was at once greeted by Nelly as 'Catharine dear'. 'Where is Ivan then?' she asked. 'I thought it was *his* ring.' Catharine Gordon looked round the room with an expression of amused suspicion. 'You're not hiding him up somewhere are you?' she said. 'This is Mr Storm, I suppose?' And she gave Richard a firm boyish grip and fixed on him a pair of laughing grey eyes.

'Oh, I suppose Ivan's gone off somewhere else,' she said; and without further invitation proceeded to take off her hat and fling herself down in the only available armchair. She seemed to exercise a kind of fascination upon Nelly, who promptly seated herself on the arm of her chair and began toying with her silver bracelets, the weight and number of which gave to her long brown wrists an almost oriental appearance.

'What will you do if you don't see him tonight?' inquired Nelly.

'What shall I do?' repeated Catharine Gordon. 'What would *you* advise me to do?' And she turned round suddenly upon Richard whom Nelly had just now a tendency to treat as if he were thin air, rather than a tired, excited, agitated, uneasy man of forty-five.

Richard who was standing at the window drew near to her and surveyed her curiously. She had the longest legs of any girl he had ever seen and she stretched them out now in front of her as if they had been the legs of some young athlete.

'You must tell me more details,' he said, indicating by the way he looked at her and by the interest in his voice that she had made an impression upon him.

'Don't tell him anything,' threw in Nelly. 'Why should you? It'll do him good to get a little bewilderment. Just go on talking to me.'

'But I should like to tell him,' said Catharine, crossing one leg over the other and clasping her long brown fingers behind her head. 'I should like to hear what he'd say.'

Nelly at this got up from the arm of the chair. 'Oh well,' she said, 'if you're going to start confessing your sins to Richard I'd better make the coffee.' She retreated into their little kitchen.

Catharine did not seem the least perturbed by this outburst. On the contrary, she turned to Richard with quite an intimate gesture.

'Come and sit down,' she said; 'there's plenty of room for two thin people like us.' Then she added in a low quick whisper, 'You must be very kind to Nelly these days; the poor darling looks worried.'

Richard had a taste that evening of what real Bohemian life in New York is like, and it amused him that it should have come to him through Nelly. *If these are the sort of people she meets in Canyot's studio*, he thought, *I certainly needn't agitate myself about Elise.*

'. . . And so I said I'd be down here tonight and he said he'd look in too, though he had to be some place else for dinner; the French Pastry Shop I think it was, or the Five Steps Up, and I knew he *might* change his mind if Lucretia dragged him round to her rooms, but the chances are she'd hardly dare to do that, as it would be breaking up the party and leaving Tassie Edstein, and even Lucretia would scarcely go *quite* so far, so I fancy he'll turn up all right; it's absurd if he doesn't, because he knows he'll have to make it up sooner or later and the sooner he does it the less I'll punish him; have you a cigarette? Oh, imported English ones! That's lovely.'

Richard's mental confusion was not greatly cleared up by this breathless discourse. A certain Lucretia was evidently no prude and a certain Tassie was evidently a maiden who couldn't be left unprotected in the streets of New York.

He hazarded a leading question to this long-legged damsel whose athletic person was giving him at that moment what children call pins and needles, as she leaned against him as if he were a convenient piece of furniture, completely devoid of normal sensibility.

'Who is this you are speaking of, this man you are expecting here?'

'Who is it?' She jumped up from his side and ran, or rather bounded, into the kitchen. 'You've never told him about Ivan!' she cried indignantly. 'Here have I been chattering on for the last half hour and I find he doesn't know who Ivan is! Do you and he go round with different crowds?'

Nelly's answer was interrupted by such a burst of laughter that Richard could not catch its purport. The two women then launched into a whispered colloquy punctuated by little smothered shrieks of amusement.

What children they are, he thought, stretching himself out in his big chair and lighting another cigarette. *If it were Canyot and I making that coffee, we should be either propitiating one another's vanity with the most pompous earnestness, or we should be quarrelling like the devil!*

They came back into the room at last, with the coffee not quite spoilt by so elaborate a preparation. At that very moment the doorbell rang again. Richard ran down to open it, full of curiosity to see this much talked-of Ivan. As he descended the stairs he could not help thinking with what completely different an eye he regarded everything in the world, now that he had seen Elise.

He opened the door to the stranger; who walked in with hardly a gesture of thanks. When the door was shut he turned upon Richard and showed himself under the electric light of the little hallway to be a man of about thirty with a pointed black beard and a head of small stiff black curls. His eyes were at once dreamy and alert; dreamy on the surface of them and profoundly alive beneath the surface. 'Is she up there?' he inquired.

Richard lifted his eyebrows. The man's manner irritated him. 'Is it our place you're looking for? Please come up, will you? We're on the next floor' – and he proceeded to lead the way.

Halfway up the stairs the man caught Richard by the arm. 'Is she angry with me?' he whispered. 'Has she told you about me?'

The long rambling discourse he had just submitted to, squeezed so very close to the young person in question, rose confusedly in his memory.

'I really don't know,' he answered drily. 'But please come in. I'm sure my wife will be delighted to see you.'

They entered together and Nelly greeted the newcomer enthusiastically. He was introduced to Richard as Ivan Karmakoff. Catharine, who had once more taken possession of the armchair, extended to him a long languid brown arm without making any attempt to rise.

They all sat down and began drinking coffee.

Catharine concentrated herself upon Richard, and in order to face him more directly she swung her legs over the arm of the chair, displaying a greater length of openwork silk stocking than he had ever associated in his life before with any respectable conversation.

'You've seen Fancy Goring in *The Way of all Souls*, I suppose?'

she asked. 'She's a good actress, but her personality is terrible. Oh, and have you seen Keenie Trench? She does that innocent-little-girl business adorably – a regular young Greuze, don't you think so? But what you *must* see, if you haven't yet, is Jack Candid in *The Blue Mirror*. He's a bit wobbly in the serious parts but he does that harlequin stunt to absolute perfection. What a pity Charlie Guelph didn't do the set for that thing! Don't you think so? He's the only one of that Broadway bunch who's got any gumption. It was real creative stuff that he did for Ralph's *Banbury Cross* – those conventional trees, you remember? and that market place? They say he's never got another job since his affair with Lena Hastings. Kind of pulled him to pieces, so they say at Aunt Flouncy's. Disintegrated him. Broke his spirit. Lena's mad about Jack Candid now, who'll hardly speak to her. Serve her right, I say. But she's very unhappy. Jack Candid's the last person a girl ought to get involved with. I like him myself. We have splendid times together. But he knows he can't be at all personal with me. And so he treats me quite decently. She's a little fool I think. And I'd tell her so, for a cent! Oh, and have you seen Elise Angel yet?'

This unexpected question coming bolt out, at the end of a rigmarole that Richard had quite lost the thread of, made him give a palpable start.

Like one greater than himself and on a very different occasion, he lied bluntly and deeply.

'Elise Angel? No I've never seen her work. What is she? an imitator of Clarice Darling?'

Catharine Gordon clasped the arm of the chair and bounded to her feet. She forgot all about her difficulty with Ivan and turned to him with something like a shriek of excitement.

'He's never seen Elise Angel! Is it possible? He says he's never heard of her!'

There was a general movement of aesthetic consternation. Richard felt that he had damned himself for ever with the initiated of Manhattan.

Even Nelly attacked him – 'But surely, Richard, surely—'

'Why,' cried Catharine. 'Nelly told me you'd spent years in Paris. It's only Paris that really understands Elise. She gets outrageously wretched houses over here. She hates this place and I don't blame her. But her time will come. They'll be sorry for it. Why, my good man, she's the greatest artist in the world. She and the Duse. Tell him about her, Ivan. It's incredible he shouldn't know!'

'I can only tell him,' said Ivan, speaking very slowly and deliberately, 'that her genius has revolutionized the whole modern theatre. Her influence is behind everything – not only dancing, but everything. The Russian Ballet of course – they've admitted *that* themselves. And everything that's been done since! It's her ideas, they say, that started Charlie Guelph with his best sets.'

Richard began to curse himself for his treachery to his goddess. Never had his diplomacy blundered so abominably. He felt instinctively that Nelly was watching him very closely in his discomfiture. He felt that his power of self-control was on the point of abandoning him. He felt that just because it was all so impossible he might at any moment blurt out the truth.

In desperation he got up from his seat. 'Well, some of you people must take me to see her,' he muttered. 'Yes, I think I *do* remember hearing of her in Paris. But this office work today has put everything charming out of my head. And I had too good a dinner tonight – that's another thing – a dinner uptown, you know? I scared Nelly when I came in. I really wasn't quite myself. They gave me champagne.'

'Who's *they*?' cried Catharine Gordon, flinging out her long arms and seizing Richard by the shoulders. 'Shall I make him confess, Nelly?'

Richard looked helplessly at the arms that held him. They were bare except for the loose short sleeves of the smock she was wearing, and their skin looked brown and soft above the elbows like the skin of a young gipsy.

He threw them off almost roughly. 'I think I must go out for a bit of air,' he said. 'I seem to have been indoors all day. You people will look after Nelly till I come back, won't you?'

Ivan Karmakoff walked to the side of the room where he had left his hat. 'I think I'll come with you, if you don't mind,' he said.

'That's lovely!' cried Catharine putting her arm round Nelly's waist. 'Then I shall have this sweet thing to myself. But don't forget, Ivan, that you've got to take me home. Be sure you bring him back, Mr Storm. Don't let him run off.'

The men went down the stairs together and out of the house. 'Do you mind if we go to the river?' asked Karmakoff.

Richard assented passively; crossing Varick Street and Hudson Street they made their way to the waterside.

There was a heavy wooden jetty, used for transferring garbage from the rubbish carts to the barges, that stretched out into the river just at the point where they struck the wharf.

Karmakoff led Richard out along the edge of this, in placid disregard of the evil odours that emerged from the cavernous recesses.

When they reached the end they sat down on some wooden crates and contemplated the lights of the river and the lights of Jersey City on its opposite bank.

At their feet the tide was rolling in from the Atlantic, dark and swift and stormy; an evil-looking volume of formidable water, out of whose blackness arose gurglings and whisperings, capricious splashings and strange indrawn sucking gasps, like the swallowings of an indescribable monster.

Karmakoff lit a pipe, and Richard got a truer glimpse into the secret of his personality, here by the water's edge, than he had obtained in his wife's apartment.

A lamp suspended from the mast of a small coal steamer adjoining the jetty where they sat threw a flickering light upon them both. Ivan's black beard, sulkily sensual lips, and heavily lidded beautiful eyes fixed themselves upon Richard's mind as objects with which he was destined, whether he liked it or not, to become more closely acquainted.

Karmakoff began talking quietly and bitterly about America. He described its ways, its weaknesses, its inmost pathology, like a surgeon dissecting a corpse.

As Richard listened to him he began to wonder what his relations could possibly be with that brown-armed Indian-looking girl who called herself Catharine. Was all that fuss, as to what temper she was in and so forth a mere social *convenance*, proper to that particular circle, but meaning nothing at all to the man's real identity?

The fellow attracted him and repelled him simultaneously. He deliberately lit a cigarette for no other reason than that, by the light of the match, he might get a clearer glimpse of those extraordinarily beautiful eyes.

There was something a little equivocal and menacing about the kind of sensuality betrayed in the man's mouth. But his eyes were, without any doubt, the most beautiful eyes that Richard had ever seen in the head of any human being, whether man or woman. They actually seemed to be a woman's eyes, as he looked at them under that steamer lamp. Had not the black beard on his chin decided the matter Richard could have sworn that he was a girl in disguise. Even as it was, he caught himself hazarding a fantastic speculation as to whether it was possible that the beard was a false one and that he was on the track of a wild romance. But no! Ivan's voice was not a woman's voice. It was deep and low and purring. It was a seductive voice but the voice of an eminently masculine mind. It had a caress in it but it also held out danger signals. It was curious to Richard how he felt about this man. It was as if he had seen him before. But he certainly had never seen him before. What *was* the attraction he exercised? By degrees it occurred to him that the explanation was that Karmakoff was his direct psychological antipodes – his fatal opposite – with vices, virtues, nobilities, ignobilities, made up of some chemical compound that was the extreme antithesis of all that he was himself.

Karmakoff soon drifted into political and economic problems; and Richard, before he quite realized what was occurring, found himself listening to a most subtle and convincing argument in support of the dictatorship of the proletariat.

As the writer listened to one clear-cut argument after another, lucidly and modestly suggested, hinted at, made way for, rather than flung dogmatically down, he became conscious that he himself had hitherto barely touched the fringe of these drastic issues.

Karmakoff's purring, caressing voice, between long puffs at his pipe, the stem of which acted as a sort of pointer to his argument, flowed rhythmically on, above the flow of the dark water at their feet.

There was certainly nothing personal in his argument. It was almost inhuman in its impersonality. It might have been addressed by an inhabitant of Mars to an inhabitant of Uranus; for all the appeal it made to ordinary human prejudices. It seemed to use all human passions, all human pieties, as if they were pawns upon a gigantic chessboard.

Richard, whose Parisian experiences of the revolutionary spirit were of a very different nature, was astonished at the absence of personal animosity in what the man advanced. He effaced his own tastes. He effaced the tastes, passions, prejudices, hostilities, of the proletariat he represented.

Everything was reduced to a logical inevitable sequence of cause and effect, which could neither be hastened nor retarded, but which in its own predestined hour, to the discomfiture of some, to the relief of others, would reveal a new order of society.

Richard felt, as he listened to him, as though he were present at some demonic unclothing of the hidden skeleton of the universe – a skeleton of cubes and circles and angles and squares, of inflexible geometric determination!

The steady flow of the tide beneath them, with its gurgling and sucking noises, seemed to gather the man's reasoning into its own flood and become a living portion of the fatality he represented.

Storm could detect no flaw in Karmakoff's logic, wherein all that was personal and arbitrary seemed slowly to be obliterated, as if under the power of a remorseless engine. Nature was reduced to a chemistry. Human nature became mathematical necessity. A sublime but cheerless order, irresistible and undeviating, swallowed up in its predetermined march everything that was the accomplice of chance, the evocation of free will.

Deep within his own heart, Richard hid away from the beautiful eyes of this terrible logician, the secret exultation of his own free will, wrought upon by Elise's great dance. *Art*, he thought to himself, is anyway safe from this man's logic. There, at least, will always be a refuge for the free creative spirit that lies behind all this cause and effect. The image of Elise, dancing her dance of the Eternal Vision, became at that moment his only counterpoise to what the Russian was saying. He hid this image away deep in his heart, very much as some crusader in medieval times might have hidden away his piece of the True Cross from the eyes of some conquering Saracen.

In his imagination he seemed to see this great city of marble and iron as some huge Colosseum, in the arena of which the art of Elise wrestled with the science of Karmakoff.

He felt vaguely and obscurely that the mind which could bring these two tremendous forces into some vital relation with one another would be the mind that would dominate the world.

Karmakoff meanwhile was comparing the huge cosmopolitanism of New York harbour with what he had seen at Southampton.

'Could anything be more English?' he said. 'You sail straight in between parks and fields and country villages, and are landed right at the bottom of a quiet provincial street, where nurserymaids and butchers' boys congregate to watch your exit! You English are a queer race. You seem to have acquired your precious empire without leaving your sheepfolds and rose gardens. You seem to have marched from Cairo to Baghdad in your sleep, without so much as having a single theory that'll hold water, except with regard to the breeding of terrier dogs. Come now, Mr Storm, I've been talking all this evening to you and you've hardly spoken a word. What is *your* theory of the economic problem?'

'I'm afraid I haven't gone into the matter,' replied Richard, rising from his seat. 'My economics are terribly personal.'

Karmakoff laughed softly. 'How English! Everything you do and think and feel is personal. Do you know, my good friend, you English are so individualistic that I wonder sometimes that any of you manage to get born at all!'

'Isn't *that* rather a personal matter?' murmured Richard.

Karmakoff positively stared at him. 'Personal?' he said. 'You don't mean to say you still think – wait a little. Wait a little. You evidently have never been in love.'

'What are you talking about?' asked Richard, almost petulantly.

The man laughed aloud. 'I'm talking about the utter *impersonality* of the most devastating force in the universe! I should like you to overhear Catharine Gordon when she's got her knife into me. Don't you know what it is to worship the flesh of a girl and to hate her for it? Do you know nothing of *that* malice? But I beg your pardon. You're an Englishman. The great forces of the world are your child's toys. Well! It must have something in it, your little method. Everything must be genteel and well-behaved and respectable and personal. But good Lord!'

Chapter 15

About a week after Richard's reversion to his old love, Nelly according to her custom was preparing lunch for herself and Canyot in his studio in Seventy-fifth Street.

His model, a handsome girl from Siena, beautiful as that purest Italian race is beautiful, with a certain glowing and yet chaste voluptuousness, was resting from an exhausting pose, and eating cream chocolates.

The two were conversing together without embarrassment, though the richly coloured garment that half-swathed her was more in harmony with a picture by Veronese than with a New York apartment.

Nelly, through the open door leading into the little passage containing the kitchenette, joined amicably, when she could, in their conversation.

'Amelia swears she's never had a lover and never means to,' remarked the young painter, raising his voice a little. 'Did you hear that, Nelly?'

'She's a sensible girl, then,' came the, answer from the passage.

'You see? The lady agrees with me!' cried the model, selecting another chocolate with exquisite care. 'It's all nonsense this, about love being so important. I do my work. I help artists. I put myself into pictures. I *make* pictures. And then I go home and look after the little mother. I cook us a good dinner – a very good dinner. I smoke cigarettes. The little mother smokes cigarettes. We go to the theatre together. We go to hear the singers. And then we go home and sleep till morning and – that's all!'

'But haven't you ever fallen in love, Amelia, dear?' inquired Canyot, putting a dab of crimson lake upon his canvas and retreating a little to observe its effect.

'Why should I fall in love? I know what men are. I know what women are. Chocolates are much better. And when the great Caruso sings – *basta!* I don't want to think of such things. I go to Mass too, and I love Our Lady. Our Lady didn't need to have a lover. Her Son was enough for her; and the little mother's enough for me.'

'But Amelia darling, don't you find it rather difficult to be so good? I should have thought with your profession—'

'That's just where you're wrong, Mr Canyot. You're a good man. *You* don't have any lover or any woman about, except Madam, and anyone can see how good she is! And I can tell you that lots of the people I work for are like that. Artists are good men. They love their work. And I'm part of their work.'

'But haven't you ever, not *ever*, seen anyone you'd like to marry?'

'Don't tease her so, Robert,' came the voice from the passage.

'It's all right, lady,' cried the girl from Siena; and then, in a lower voice: 'If there ever was *anyone*, it was that Russian gentleman who talked to me about the strike in Milano in this very room. Now don't you go and tell him what I've been telling you, Mr Canyot! Of course I'd never really have him, because of mother. Mother doesn't like Russians. But I think he was beautiful – as beautiful as St Anthony.'

'Well run away and dress now, Amelia; I shan't want you any more this afternoon.'

When the girl reappeared in her street costume she still looked adorably handsome; but no one would have guessed how flawlessly classical her limbs were.

Nelly begged her to stay and share their meal; but she flatly refused to do this. 'I always go to Castignac's to get my dinner. They cook me little yellow omelettes, full of red jam. I love Madame. She has a great heart. I am her protector.'

When Amelia had gone, Canyot said to Nelly, 'I wonder what it is about that fellow Ivan that attracts women so? You're a woman, Nelly, you ought to know what it is.'

'You'll have an opportunity of watching his effect upon me very soon,' Nelly replied, as she carried in her dishes and arranged them on the table. 'He's going to come round at two o'clock; so we'd better hurry up and get our meal over.'

'What's he coming here for? I can't stand the fellow. He must know I detest him.'

'Oh my dear,' cried Nelly, regarding him with an affectionate smile across the plate she held in her hand, 'no one minds the way *you* detest them! Of course he's coming because Catharine is coming.'

'I don't like Catharine,' remarked Canyot pulling a chair up to the table and making his guest sit down while he went to fetch the knives and forks.

'Why don't you like her?' asked Nelly giving a sigh of weariness.

'I don't like her because she pulls you about so and makes such a fuss over you. I don't like her arms or her legs.'

'Poor old Cathy! She can't help *that*, you know. I like both of them. I think she has a very interesting figure.'

'I don't like the way she treats that fellow Ivan,' Canyot went on, eating his food in great hungry mouthfuls but keeping a still hungrier look, full of infinite tenderness, fixed on his friend's face. 'Why doesn't she take him altogether or let him go altogether? I can't stand all this messing about and playing around.'

'It *is* a bit hectic, her life, I admit,' said Nelly. 'But I'm not at all sure Ivan loves her.'

'Loves her? He's mad about her. He follows her everywhere with those confounded woman's eyes of his.'

'He may be mad about her. But that's not the same thing as loving her. Do you know, Robert dear, I think that there are very few men who really love their woman – love her for herself, I mean, and not for the sensations they get out of her.'

Canyot glanced meaningly at the grey eyes that met his own across the table.

Impulsively Nelly stretched out her hand and, seeking his, gave it a tight squeeze.

'I'm not thinking of you, Robert,' she said. 'You're one in a thousand. I'm thinking of all the rest.'

Canyot frowned savagely as was his wont when his love for her troubled him.

'Men and women want different things of each other,' he muttered, 'and always will.'

'But would we want different things – if things had been different with us?'

As soon as she had uttered the words she would have given anything to recall them, for she saw the pain upon his face.

'Oh yes, I suppose so!' he replied wearily. And then after a little pause: 'I could never have satisfied you, Nelly – my darling!'

She thought in her heart, *How can I tell him that I love him with everything that is best in me? How can I tell him that I love him* because he is strong and good; and that I love my poor Richard because he is weak, and anything but good?

And she also thought in her heart, *Am I different from other women and much less moral? Am I doing something callous and selfish in sitting here eating Robert's food while I am still Richard's wife?* And then, sweeping aside both Richard and Robert, there rose up within her that fierce blind instinct to protect the unborn at any cost; to take from one, to take from another, to exploit them all – if only this flesh of her flesh, this bone of her bone, might live and grow in peace! And she thought to herself, *How little, really, is anything in the world important except the creation of life!* This idea had come to her several times during these last weeks as she listened to Canyot's conservatism and Karmakoff's radicalism. 'These men understand nothing!' she had heard her heart whisper. 'All their theories are superficial! All their words leave the truth untouched!'

'It is destiny, Robert dear,' she said at last. 'I certainly little thought in those old days that we should be sitting together like this this autumn united by your faithfulness, separated by my . . . nature!'

They finished their lunch in silence after this; then he made her lie down on his studio couch, while he washed up the things.

At two o'clock punctually Karmakoff turned up. He was excited beyond his usual wont. There had been a police raid upon some peculiarly inoffensive Russian utopians, and one Herculean Irish official had used his baton savagely. 'The absurdity of the whole thing is,' he said, 'that these people were not political revolutionaries at all. They were a sect of mystical Tolstoyans – quiet nervous saintly men, like medieval hermits – the sort of people that in any other community would be protected by the populace, as innocents sacred to God.'

'What annoys me,' remarked Canyot in his most surly manner, 'is the way all you fellows appeal to what you call *bourgeois justice* and *bourgeois morality* as long as you are persecuted. And then, directly it's your turn to be the upper dog, to the devil with such scruples! It's then a case of *saving the revolution* at the cost of any bloodshed. If you are allowed by the moral law to save your revolution by breaking heads, why isn't the capitalist allowed to save his system by breaking heads? With both of you it becomes a sheer matter of who can use the greatest force. I never can see what right either of you have to appeal to these moral principles, principles that are just simply human, and quite outside your class struggles.'

'Nothing,' replied Karmakoff, smiling patiently, recovering his normal poise; 'nothing is outside the class struggle. The class struggle is the very thing that has given birth to all these abstract human principles you're referring to. The principle of the sacredness of property, for instance, is simply the enforced will of the people who have possessed themselves of property. And all these doctrines of justice and order and legality and so forth are really nothing at all but just the will and pleasure of those in possession of power.'

'Order is the one essential thing!' cried Canyot. 'How can anyone work or think without order? What becomes of art without order?'

Karmakoff bowed his head politely. 'I entirely agree with you,' he said. 'It's you who're the anarchist, not I. Certainly we must have order. The question is who are to enforce this order – a privileged few or the whole community?'

'The whole community can enforce nothing,' cried Canyot controlling his anger with difficulty, his face growing flushed and wrinkled. 'The whole community is a set of silly sheep!'

'Precisely,' replied the other in his most purring voice. 'And the whole question resolves itself, then, into what set of people are to give this desirable order to these silly sheep. Are they to be people with sheep's blood in their veins – old horned rams for instance, like myself? Or are they to be wolves in sheep's clothing? I believe it will be found in the long run that the silly sheep prefer the former!'

'I wish,' broke in Nelly, 'that the day would hurry up and come, when the sheep stop being silly and throw you both overboard!'

Karmakoff laughed heartily at this. 'The woman speaks!' he said. 'But seriously, you know, Mrs Storm, you and I are in much closer agreement than you and Mr Canyot. I am perfectly ready to admit that the dictatorship of certain representatives of the proletariat is only a temporary and transitional thing – an interregnum of horned rams, shall we call it? – until the sheep grow accustomed to power. Mr Canyot would have the poor wretches left for ever at the mercy of the wolves.'

At this point there was a rapid tap at the door and without waiting for a reply Catharine Gordon swung into the room. She had just bought herself a new smock of the very latest futurist design, and though it was so early in the afternoon, she wore a black silk skirt.

'Ha! you're here first, then!' she threw out at Karmakoff while she gravely shook hands with Canyot, who at once, turned away and busied himself with his palette of colours.

Then she rushed across to Nelly who still reclined on the couch. 'I've got a job! I've got a job! I've got a job!' she shouted, throwing herself down on the floor by the end of the couch and possessing herself of Nelly's hand. 'It's what I've always wanted. The very nicest thing in the world. Try and guess what it is, Ivan!'

'Not anything on the stage?' Karmakoff inquired.

'Oh dear no! I'm sick of that. I'm not vulgar enough for Broadway; and I know too much about the theatre for the art people.'

'Is it dancing, my dear?' asked Nelly. "I've always thought if you only got a chance—'

'No! it's not dancing. That may come later, of course, and probably will; but it's not dancing yet. Shall I tell you what it is – oh, and I've got something else by the way to tell *you*, Nelly, in private, presently, something very comical, something about your husband – well, I'll tell you. It's that I'm to be secretary to Elise Angel!'

There was a general exclamation of surprise. Even Canyot turned round from his work. 'I didn't know you could typewrite,' he said.

'I can't! That's just the fun of it. But Elise said it didn't matter a bit. She liked her letters written in ordinary script. She made me show her my hand and liked it awfully!'

'Do you mean that she liked your hand or your handwriting?' inquired Canyot.

'Both! She made me write on a piece of paper. And when I had written my name, she took my hand in hers and played with my fingers, and said she liked their longness. And – just think – when I said goodbye she kissed me. Yes! kissed me. Oh, isn't it lovely? I've been kissed by Elise Angel! And I'm to go to her this very night to begin!'

'Surely she doesn't Write her letters by night?' growled Canyot.

'Are you going to live with her?' inquired Karmakoff gravely.

'Oh no. I'm not going to live with her. She doesn't want me to do that. I'm going in the daytime, in the morning, in the evening – any old time; just as she wants me, you know.'

As the girl spoke she fixed her eyes steadily upon Karmakoff. The Russian walked up and down the room, frowning, his hands behind his back. Presently he stopped in front of her. 'You'll have to introduce me to Elise,' he said. There is a chance they might invite her to Moscow to take charge of the whole art movement there.'

'What?' cried Canyot in a loud voice. 'It's impossible! She wouldn't contemplate such a thing.'

It's hard to predict what a person like Elise will do, 'said Ivan quietly.' But you may be quite right. It would be a sacrifice in some ways.'

Catharine, who had fallen into a sort of meditative trance with her chin propped upon her knees, now struggled to her feet. She bent down and taking Nelly by the wrists tried to pull her up from the couch. 'I've got something very amusing to tell you my dear and I'm sure you wouldn't want me to say it out before these two.'

Nelly, rather reluctantly, submitted to her violence and allowed herself to be led into the passage. 'Don't let Ivan run away,' shouted Catharine to the painter before she closed the door.

'I always say,' remarked Karmakoff, sinking down on the couch vacated by Nelly and lighting a cigarette, 'that it's you *honest* conservatives who do more to retard the progress of the world than any other people.'

'I don't believe in the progress of the world,' replied Canyot drily. 'Life swings backwards and forwards. Everything has a beginning and an end. It's all the same old mad game.'

'Then why,' murmured the Russian, puffing out a cloud of smoke and arranging himself on the couch with a certain feline grace, 'why do we fuss ourselves about anything?'

'I *don't* fuss, myself,' growled the painter stepping back to regard his canvas, upon which was emerging a revel of satyrs and nymphs; 'it's just a matter of taste. My taste objects to cruelty and disorder and lechery. I am old-fashioned, that is all. It doesn't really matter. But I'm not comfortable when I've behaved like a cad.'

Karmakoff smiled pleasantly. 'I suppose you're thinking at this moment that I've behaved like a cad to Catharine?'

Canyot moved up to his canvas and gave it a resolute splash with his brush. His gesture was so drastic that it looked as if he would have greatly enjoyed dabbing that brush across Ivan's smiling countenance.

'Heaven forbid,' he said, 'that I should interfere between you two. I expect you are perfectly agreed as to what the limits of life are.'

'What do you mean by the *limits of life*?'

'Oh, I don't know,' murmured the painter indifferently, 'something about life extending a little further than the five senses, I suppose. You mustn't press me. I'm at work.'

At that moment the passage door opened with a violent outward fling and Catharine burst in upon them. 'She's upset. I've upset her dreadfully. It wasn't my fault. I didn't know she cared.'

Canyot dropped his brush upon the floor and came forward, his face convulsed with anger. He flung Catharine aside as if she were some intrusive stranger, and rushed to the back of the passage where there was a small box-room filled with spoiled canvases. Here he found Nelly seated in a dark corner shaken with smothered sobs.

'Darling! my darling!' he whispered, kneeling beside her and putting his arm around her. 'Tell me what's the matter. No! no! never mind! I don't want to hear anything. Nelly, my darling – I can't bear to see you like this.'

The girl gently but obstinately pushed him away. 'Leave me alone, please, Robert,' she gasped. 'I'll be better soon. I'm silly to make such a fuss. It's nothing really. Please go back to them, Robert, if you don't mind? I'll be all right in a minute.'

He obeyed her so far as to move to the further end of the passage. But he would not open the studio door. She made a desperate effort to control herself and rising to her feet passed her hands over her hair and pressed her knuckles into her eyes and against her cheeks.

'Robert,' she murmured in a whisper. He came quickly up to her side. 'Get my things for me, please, my dear, will you? I don't want to see them like this. I'll go straight home I think. And don't let Catharine talk to Karmakoff about me. But she's sure to do it. She's sure to do it!' And her sobs began to break out afresh. Canyot ached to press her to his heart and soothe her tears with kisses from his very soul, but he kept a rigid hold over himself.

'She shan't say a word, my dearest one – not a word. But won't you let me take you home, Nelly? I'll just say you're unwell and we'll go straight off.'

She looked at him quickly, a rapid tender look, full of affectionate gratitude. 'No – no, Robert, I don't wish that. It's sweet of you, old friend, but I don't wish it. Get my things, please, dear. I shall be quite all right.'

He saw that her mind was made up and he went straight into the studio and possessed himself of her hat and cloak. Catharine was huddled on the couch, clinging like a great frightened child to Karmakoff. 'How is she?' she whispered. 'I'm so sorry I told her! I'd no idea she'd take it like that.'

'She is going home alone,' said Canyot, turning away with her things on his arm. 'We must let her do exactly what she wishes. I'll come back when I've seen her into the subway.'

'She knows how to change at Grand Central?' asked Karmakoff quietly.

'The shuttle to Times Square, you mean?' said Canyot. 'Yes, I'll tell her. If by any chance I *don't* come back you'll make yourselves comfortable here won't you? You know where my tea is Catharine?' And once more the door was shut between the studio and the passage.

Nelly did not let Canyot go a step further with her than the entrance to the Lexington Avenue subway. She made him leave her at the top of the steps.

'Sorry for having made such an idiot of myself, Robert,' she said as she gave him her hand. 'I knew Richard was having an affair with someone. It was only a shock to me to hear Catharine talk about him – you know? – in the way she does. I'll be all right now, my dear. Goodbye – God bless you, Robert.'

He turned sadly up the street, and feeling himself singularly disinclined to go back to his studio he made his way into the park and walked blindly, engrossed in miserable thoughts, across its least frequented spaces.

Nelly got out at the Grand Central and made her way through the conflicting streams of people to the little shuttle train for Times Square. She had to stand, during this short journey, clinging to a leather strap, and the mass of indifferent humanity that were jammed against her weighed down her spirit with an infinite discouragement.

It was even worse when she emerged at Times Square. *Well*, she thought, *has this place been named!* In those underground corridors extending indefinitely in every direction, with their little green and black arrows pointing backwards and forwards, and their confluent streams of people, it certainly did seem as though she had arrived at the spot in the universe where time and motion became identical.

As she struggled against the crowd, she experienced the queer feeling that her real conscious mind was somewhere out of all this, and that the Nelly thus pushed and jostled was a mere helpless automaton among other automatons. A horrible feeling of mechanical indifference seized her. Her real mind seemed to have escaped out of her flesh, leaving nothing but a mass of quivering exposed nerves that could suffer passively without end but could take no initiative. She found herself thinking with relief of the quietness of her father's body lying in Littlegate churchyard, 'free among the dead'.

Confused by the bewildering corridors and stairways she got finally swept by the crowd into an uptown train on the Seventh Avenue subway instead of a downtown one.

Her first intimation of this mistake came to her when the train was just leaving the next station marked Fiftieth Street. She got up from her seat and looked around her in dismay. Her eyes had such panic in them that one man whispered to another; a little old coloured woman who had been sitting next her hazarded the remark, 'Wrong station, honey?'

Other, less sympathetic observations reached her, such as, 'She's up against it!' 'Some girl, too!' with various humorous asides which were quite unintelligible to Nelly's English ears.

She got out hurriedly at the next stop which proved to be Columbus Circle – another symbolic name! Here a hopeless weariness descended upon her and when she had climbed the steps and emerged into the great open space near the entrance to the park she leaned against the edge of a newspaper stand and began to cry without caring who noticed it.

A man who was buying the *New Republic* raised his hat. His head was large and powerfully moulded, his figure of corresponding weight and dignity. 'Can I do anything for you, lady?' he said kindly. Nelly pulled herself together with a gallant effort and dried her eyes. 'I'm so ashamed of myself,' she murmured. 'I'm not often like this. I'm not feeling very well.'

'Won't you let me get you a taxi?' said the tall man whose face seemed vaguely familiar to Nelly, though where she had seen him, or anyone like him, she could not remember. While addressing her he continued to hold his hat, which was a soft broad-brimmed felt one, in his right hand, while with his left he stroked her jacket reassuringly with the *New Republic*.

A sort of blackness began now to descend on the girl's eyes, blackness crossed by little vibrations of white light. She nodded eagerly however and the tall man stopped a passing taxi and assisted her into it. He handed the driver a couple of dollar bills; only after he had done that did he put his head into the window and ask her for an address.

By that time the blackness was very dense around Nelly Moreton's brain and without realizing what she said she uttered the words 'Elise Angel'.

The man's friendly physiognomy became illuminated with a new interest. 'Ah! you're one of *her* girls are you? *That's* where you belong, is it? Well! tell her that Pat Ryan says she must give you some of his especial cognac.' And he shouted an address in clear terms to the driver who started his car without further question.

Nelly sank back on the cushioned seat, too faint to realize in the least what was happening and too dizzy to breathe another word.

The air beating on her face through the open window saved her from becoming actually unconscious, but she felt too wretched to think anything or even to feel anything. A blank numbness, inert and obscure, took possession of her and sealed up her mind and senses.

They stopped in front of the well-appointed apartment house where Elise Angel had her rooms.

The driver got down from his seat and approached the door of the taxi. He mechanically held the door open, gazing down the street and meditating upon matters in no way connected with cabs or houses or fares.

While he stood thus, waiting in professional indifference for her to emerge, the door of the house opened and Elise and Richard came down the steps.

Richard looked straight into the taxi window. He was laughing at some remark Elise had just made and his eyes were bright, his cheeks flushed. Elise, sweeping majestically down the steps just behind him, laid her hand at that moment upon his arm. She bent towards him as she did so and whispered something which made him laugh yet louder. Then he turned his head and they both moved down the street.

Richard, had he been challenged, could not have told what vehicle it was that was waiting there. His heart was full of excitement and happiness. He was in a trance of obvious delight.

But he had smiled straight into Nelly's wide-open bewildered eyes; and when the other whispered to him and putting her hand on his arm led him away, an ice-cold stab of an emotion the girl had never known before pierced her heart.

The sight of Richard had brought her consciousness back; but it was only brought back to be startled into sharp incredible pain at what she saw. To her bewildered mind it seemed as if her husband had recognized her, had laughed in her face, and in callous disregard of her distress had gone off, jesting about her with his new love.

But her brain was working only too normally now and her fit of faintness was gone.

'Number sixty-six! Where I was told to go to, Marm,' repeated the driver. To the end of her days Nelly would associate that particular number with the stark desolation of that moment.

'I've changed my mind,' she said quietly. 'Will you please go to number one Charlton Street.'

The man looked slightly surprised at this order, but closed the door again and mounted his seat. He was considerate in his demands upon her purse, however, when they reached her own house, exacting only sixty cents in addition to what Mr Pat Ryan had given him.

Nelly mounted the stairs to her room with chaos in her heart. One wild notion succeeded another in her brain. She would leave Richard, she thought. She would go off somewhere into the country and stay there till her child was born. She would borrow money from Robert, risk the voyage, and go back to Sussex. She would seek refuge with Mrs Shotover who, no doubt for old acquaintance sake, would take her in.

All these ideas surged through her mind as she climbed the stairs. When she reached her own floor she was a little surprised to find the door of her apartment standing ajar. She must have forgotten to close it when she went out that morning.

She pushed it open and entered quickly to discover, to her immense surprise, a completely unknown young man smoking a cigarette in Richard's armchair.

The stranger rose at her entrance and began stammering and apologizing. 'I am Roger Lamb,' he said. 'You don't know me, but I'm a cousin of your friend Olive Shelter. My grandmother was a Shelter and we've kept up the connection. I've never seen Cousin Olive – I've never been to Europe – but she wrote to tell me you were here.'

There was something so grave and quaint about this youth's manner that Nelly felt drawn towards him at once. She begged him to sit down while she took off her things and tidied herself up. Incidentally she slipped into the kitchen and lit the gas under the kettle. 'I *must* have some tea,' she said to herself; then she gazed at her face in the looking glass as she used her brush and comb.

Presently she laid down these objects and began smoothing out the little wrinkles round her mouth and eyes with the tips of her fingers.

She was shocked by the drawn look of her face; as if in these last hours the skin had grown tighter and less soft.

A faint shadow of her old elfish smile flickered back at her from her staring disillusioned eyes.

Then her face hardened into a mask of bitterness and a strange expression of recklessness passed across it. The queer thought came into her head – *Richard's got tired of me. He has this other woman. What does it matter what I do now?* It was with this reckless expression still upon her face that she returned to her guest.

In the first few minutes before she got the kettle to boil and the tea poured out the conversation between herself and her visitor was broken and perfunctory. When they had drunk a few cups, however, they began to grow quite intimate.

Roger Lamb persuaded Nelly to try one of his own cigarettes which were a different sort from those Richard smoked. Settled comfortably in the deep armchair listening to his whimsical talk, the girl felt as if she were recovering from an anaesthetic.

It appeared that her young visitor was a journalist – a dramatic critic – attached to one of the largest of the New York evening papers. He seemed to know all the people Nelly knew and a great many she had only heard of by name, and she was struck by the way he spoke of them, without any of that tang of spiteful disparagement which she had come to associate with artistic people.

Of Catharine Gordon, for instance, he spoke with peculiar respect. 'She has the heart of a child,' he said. 'She would be the happiest thing alive if she were less generous-minded. People take advantage of her.'

'Don't you think she's a little affected?' said Nelly.

'Not a bit of it! She has her own manner; why not? but that's natural to her. It's a cruel thing she should be so involved with Karmakoff.'

'Don't you like him?' said Nelly, a little startled. 'I thought everybody liked Ivan.'

Roger Lamb laughed. 'Of course I like him,' he responded. 'But I can't honestly say I think he's very good for Catharine. She's an elemental; and he's a fire spirit. He withers her up.'

With an irresistible impulse Nelly led the conversation round to the problem by which she herself was confronted. 'It's all so wretchedly mixed up, this business of men and women. Don't you think so? Whether for instance a man who knows a girl is false to him should go on just the same, or should have it out with her and make her confess? Doesn't it seem to you that it's disgusting when a man knows he's being deceived and made a fool of and he just does nothing?'

Roger Lamb became very grave. He got up from where he was sitting and walked about the room. Nelly began to fear that in her indirect hovering round her own situation she had prodded an open wound.

'We're all too touchy,' he burst out at last, 'over this business of deception. Our idea is that when a person we love loves someone else they triumph over us unless they confess everything. But, you know, if they *did* confess everything we should regard them as heartless and callous beasts. We should accuse them of abominable bad manners. It's all frightfully difficult. But I don't believe myself that a woman who deceives a man enjoys doing it or derides or despises the man she deceives. I think if we were a little more generous lots of these people who "deceive" us would come back to us all right. It's often a mere passing attraction. It's *our* bitterness and jealousy that drives them on.'

Nelly made a little grimace at this point. 'But it's so disgusting–the idea of *sharing* a person! I'm sure I should despise anyone who tamely submitted to that sort of thing. I should feel they'd no self-respect.'

Roger Lamb bit his underlip and threw back his head like a restive horse. He had fine eyes and a sensitive mouth but his nose and chin were shapeless and badly moulded.

'Oh, this self-respect!' he burst out. 'It's the cause of half the misery in the world. Have you ever met Pat Ryan, by the way? No relation to the great financier.'

The introduction of this name gave Nelly a bitter stab.

'Yes,' she said quietly. 'He reminds me of someone and I can't think who it is.'

'It's William Jennings Bryan, of course! Everyone notices that. But what I was going to say was this. I know Pat well; and he's got a very difficult wife, and he himself is a very – what shall I say? – amorous kind of person. But they get along quite happily. They go their own way, but always come back; and they've got no children either. I think that Pat and Mary are models of what married people should be – unless they're *naturally* good and faithful.'

Nelly sighed deeply and bitterly. 'Are there any faithful ones in the world? Oh, I think life's a terrible thing. They ought to warn women before they're born what they've got to expect!'

The girl's visitor looked distractedly at the shaded electric light. 'I don't think many of us have got at the secret of life yet,' he remarked. 'The worst of it is we've nothing to go upon and no proof that there's a secret at all. But I think there is; and I think it has nothing to do with self-respect.'

For a moment Nelly was stirred by his words and by his manner into an obscure response. Then she relapsed into her habitual feminine contempt for all these vague generalizations that seem to do little to ease the hurt of the iron teeth of the great trap.

Chapter 16

'Nelly – listen to me,' said Richard, standing behind his wife that night as she was combing out her silky fair hair and tying it together with a black ribbon. 'I swear to you on my dying oath that I didn't see you in that taxi! Whatever wrong I may have done you I *couldn't* do a thing like that.'

Their eyes met in the mirror and he was the first to turn away.

'I believe you,' she said.

'Well, *do* do more than just believe me! Do smile at me and say something like your old self. Don't let's hurt each other any further.'

Nelly did swing round at this. With a flash of clear-eyed indignation and with a tilt to her chair so that she could face him, she flung out her challenge.

'Are you going to give up that woman and never, never, *never* see her again?'

She gave a sharp little tap. to the floor with her slippered foot as she uttered these words. Deep in a somewhat ambiguous portion of her heart she was almost sorry that he had *not* jeered at her in that taxi. That would have been a definite gross brutality and she could have held him in contempt for it. Now, after he had confessed to her about Elise, there was nothing she had against him except the fact that he loved someone else; and Nelly, in spite of her bitterness, recognized that she could not hate him with the intensity he deserved, as long as this was his *only* fault.

Richard certainly was staggered by the violence of her words and the directness of her demand. It did not seem to him that his attitude to her had changed at all because of the appearance of Elise upon the scene. He loved her still. He loved both of them! It was the old recurrent dilemma, into the real psychology of which women seemed debarred from entering. With them the state of being *in love* was a clearly outlined condition with sharply defined edges. One either was in love or one was not; that seemed to be their code; and one couldn't by any possible means be in love with two people at the same time! And yet, he thought, it is unfair; because Nelly herself in a sense loved both himself and Canyot. Why then, couldn't he be allowed to love Nelly and Elise? Because the element of passion entered into it. Yes – he had to confess to himself that there was a difference! He knew perfectly well that Nelly's affection for the young painter was entirely free from the last sensual element. But suppose he had loved Elise in an absolutely platonic manner, would that have reconciled Nelly to their association? It might; but he doubted if it would. She would never believe that it was possible to love a passionate provocative woman, with a body predestined for heathen dalliance, in a manner that was entirely chaste. Yet Richard knew that it only needed that Elise's own wayward heart should be ensnared by someone else for him to have just that pure devotion to her. For even now the deeper portion of what he felt was a thrilled and grateful response to her genius as an artist.

In his own mind he was able to separate into two distinct worlds his emotion towards the dancer. On the one hand she appealed so overwhelmingly – and that was what had made him leave her at the beginning – to his sophisticated senses. On the other hand she inspired in him a pure flame of hero worship, such as any critic might feel for any creative spirit.

The spell she exercised over his senses could hardly be called 'love'. It was the old immemorial heathen craving for the beauty that troubled the blood, that aroused insatiable desire. And though he craved for her in that way, he knew very well that he hated her also in that way. He was not blind to the secret law that makes love and hate so evilly interchangeable when the senses are once enslaved. All these thoughts whirled through his mind as he leant back against the little chest of drawers in their bedroom and looked into Nelly's reproachful eyes.

By throwing out at him that violent ultimatum she had recklessly forced the issue. She had dragged them both to the edge of the precipice. He felt angry with her for it and yet he felt guilty too. Beneath both these emotions was a vivid sense of revolt against the accursed law of things that made such drastic dilemmas possible.

How lovely she looked at this moment with her fair hair bound up so chastely under that black ribbon, and her slight girlish frame, as yet but faintly indicative of the promise within her, so delicately fragile!

The silence between them prolonged itself remorselessly. Her sharp cry, 'Never, *never*, see her again' hovered in the air and became a menacing and disturbing entity. He could hear his own Waterbury watch ticking, ticking, ticking, where he had placed it on the dressing table. Damn the ticking of watches and the issuing of ultimatums by resolute young mouths!

For one moment Richard seemed to catch a glimpse of what women meant by love. For one moment he seemed to see that mysterious bond, the unbroken attachment of a man and woman, like a visible thread of light over a dark gulf. Then his masculine logic broke into this sudden vision; and he reasoned with himself that this fierce claim of hers for absolute loyalty was a wild demand of insane possessiveness that no human soul had a right to make upon another.

Yes – she had dragged them both to the edge of the precipice, to the very brink of the parting of the ways, by this fierce claim upon him.

He could see that thin film of white light, the link that bound them together, quivering and vibrating in the darkness.

Then a sort of crash came somewhere in his brain; and he had a cold terrible sensation of irrevocable choice, the kind of sensation out of which, it may well be, the human race has evoked the idea of perdition.

'You have no right to ask that of me, Nelly,' he said in a low husky voice. 'It's too much. It's more than a man is allowed to promise. A certain freedom of movement *must* be left us. We cannot bind ourselves like that, whatever we've done, whatever we deserve.'

He was conscious that the colour left her cheeks and that the angry light faded from her eyes.

'Ah!' she murmured, drawing in her breath. 'That'll be the last time I shall ask it of you.'

She gave her chair a little jerk with her hands and turned away from him towards the mirror. Mechanically she picked up her hair brush and mechanically raised it to her hair. The gesture struck Richard to the heart as piteously pathetic; for he knew well that she had done all that was required to that silky head.

He made a half-movement towards her and then checked himself. What was the use in insulting the better spirit in both of them by an unworthy lapse into sentiment that anyhow must miss the mark? It would be like trying to make love to the dead.

He went back into the sitting room and changed into his night-things there, as he usually did. He sat for more than half an hour after that, silent and motionless in the armchair, wrapped in his dressing gown, too deep in thought even to smoke a cigarette.

Life seemed flowing past him in great irrevocable waves and he felt as though he were stranded upon a remote shore watching a ship gradually disappearing over the horizon. The ship of Nelly's and Richard's love!

When, after giving a slight knock, he entered their bedroom again and looked hurriedly towards the place where their two beds lay side by side, he saw at once that she had separated these by the introduction between them of a little table containing her favourite books and a photograph of her father, a thing that until that night had always remained on the further side of Nelly's bed.

The electric light was not turned out but the girl lay far round on her side, only the outline of one white cheek and ear visible, for her hair was thrown round the top of her head now, and the bare nape of her neck looked touchingly childish as she hid her face from him in the pillow.

Richard went over to her side and bending down kissed the top of her head. But so softly did he do this, that whether or not she was aware of his doing it he did not know.

Then he went round to his own side of the divided beds and put out the light.

Chapter 17

'You are cold, *mon ami*. What's the matter with you? Are you tired of me already?'

Elise drew herself out of his perfunctory embrace and moved across to one of her deep wicker chairs, leaving him alone on the sofa.

He had thought in his simplicity that he could transform his relations with her at his arbitrary will and pleasure, 'and nothing said'. He was destined to discover his mistake.

'You are the same as you always were, my dear,' she flung at him, settling herself among the cushions with a sort of crouching movement, like a beautiful lithe animal among jungle branches and leaves. 'You were always afraid of committing yourself. And that's what's the matter with you now. You're afraid of love. You hate love. You're scared of losing something of your precious personality. As though one lost one's personality that way!'

'It isn't that at all,' protested Richard feebly. How *could* he tell her about his conversation with Nelly? Elise laughed, a bitter cruel little laugh.

'Oh, of course you'll lie. You always have lied to me. You lied to me when you left me like that in Paris. I know now why you did leave me. For precisely the same reason that you're in your present mood – fear of committing yourself!'

Teased by her words and foolishly anxious to justify himself at any cost, he burst out then with the one thing he had particularly made up his mind not to say.

'It isn't that at all. It's nothing to do with that! It's only that I have sometimes a touch of remorse when I think of my wife.'

Elise laughed more maliciously than ever and her eyes gleamed. 'No not a bit of it! All excuses! That's just what you always do. You use masks and screens and blinds for everything. You are not in the remotest degree concerned about your wife. You're just simply afraid of committing yourself to *me*! You're afraid of love. You have a mean soul, the avaricious ingrowing soul of a peasant – and you're afraid of losing something if you let yourself go. I don't know what you're afraid of losing. Your precious soul perhaps – if you believe in the soul; but I sometimes doubt if you really believe in anything.'

Richard jumped up from the sofa and rushed towards her.

For one flicker of a second she must have thought he was going to strike her; for she put up her hand as if to protect herself. The movement was accompanied by a quick change of colour in her eyes as if they had been the eyes of a wild animal seized with sudden alarm. Perhaps if Richard's purpose had been to reduce her to submission, to softness, to amorous response, it would have been to his advantage to strike her. But he was very far from anything of the kind; all he did was to kneel at her feet and press her hand to his lips. She tore it away in a moment and her eyes flamed at him.

'Never think you can play *that* game with me!' she cried. And the look of dark fury which she gave him made him get up from his knees and walk back to his former place.

'Did you actually suppose,' she said, leaning forward, with her long white hands clutching the arms of her chair, 'that I would let you pick me up and put me down at your pleasure like a paid courtesan? Did you think you could have me when you were annoyed with your wife and wanted to be revenged on her; and then drop me when you made it up again and were good little children? Did you think I'd submit to that kind of thing, Richard Storm?'

'Elise! Elise! *Stop!* How can you say things like that? I can't understand you.' And he stared at her with contracted brows as if she were some kind of extraordinary animal.

'I suppose,' he began, in a meditative voice, 'this weird mood of yours comes from that accursed possessive instinct which all you women have. I suppose you are really just simply jealous of my wife.'

The crouching position she had assumed became still more pronounced. She drew in her hands slowly, along the edge of the chair, and her greenish-hazel eyes, staring at him out of her pale face, seemed to darken almost to blackness.

'How little you know me! How little you know anyone! It's your gross, heavy, blind complacent vanity!'

Richard mechanically drew out of his pocket a packet of cigarettes. Then, seeing what he had done, he deliberately and consciously selected one and lit it.

Do women, he thought, never give the real reason of their sudden angers? Is it an inveterate tendency with them, like a dog who turns round before he lies down, to give their fury some moral basis completely removed from the point at issue?

Why didn't she scold me for my 'gross, blind heavy vanity' yesterday, when we were happy together? I was much vainer and more complacent then – the Lord knows – than I am today!

But how magnificently beautiful Elise looked! He couldn't help admiring her in spite of his sense of injustice. Her hands pressed against the sides of the chair straightened her Attic torso, under its filmy drapery, into lines and curves that were worthy of Praxiteles.

He couldn't resist a faint smile, through his clouds of cigarette smoke, as he looked at her sitting there in her dark smouldering feline sulkiness. *If she was less dangerous and less irrational*, he thought, *she wouldn't be so lovely*.

'Come, my dear, my dear,' he said, 'it's absurd for us to quarrel like this. It's not fair to make me tell you my thoughts and then to pounce on me for them. Of course I'm bound to have moments with you when I feel a little guilty. You know what I'm like. You know my troublesome ridiculous conscience. It's just because I'm so happy with you that I get these moods. I can't help my nature. I was made like that.'

Her eyes darkened yet more and her face paled yet more. Before she could find her voice, her lips quivered, opening and closing like the petals of a sensitive plant. *"Made like that!*' she hissed at last, her beautiful head swaying on her long white neck like the head of some angry Lamia that might at any moment revert to its primitive shape. 'Oh, how English you are, Richard! That's what we other races have to accept is it, and just conform to? *Made like that*. And we have to unmake *ourselves*, and change our very skins, so as to adapt ourselves to this thing that cannot alter!'

'Elise – Elise – you must be mad to talk like that! You know that with us from the very beginning it's been the attraction of opposites. You don't change, you can't change, any more than I. If I weren't so English, as you call it, so heavy and gross and all the rest of it, do you think you'd have ever cared for me? Not a bit of it!'

'Well, I don't care for you now, anyway,' she flung out. 'I hate you!'

There was just a faintly perceptible softening in that 'I hate you!' which was not concealed from Richard. By laying the stress upon the faults of his character and keeping his wife out of it he had evidently succeeded in turning the course of her thoughts. He got up and threw his cigarette into the grate.

Her incredibly sensitive mouth with its twitching lips looked irresistible to him and he suddenly loved her with a fierce deep strange love such as he had not felt for any living person in his life before.

He went straight up to her, seized her by her wrists and pulled her up upon her feet. Then he kissed her as he had never before kissed any woman. He kissed her with an emotion that was neither sensual nor spiritual. It seemed to him as if his soul *required* her soul, and the only way to obtain it was by draining it through those quivering lips.

When at last, after what seemed a blind eternity of feelings beyond any analysis, he let her go, he noticed that her eyes had changed from that dark look. They were strangely beautiful still but it was with a different kind of beauty. As he took her on his knees and caressed her Grecian head, pushing back the heavy bronze-coloured braids from her broad low forehead, it seemed to him that her eyes resembled the leafy shadows of cool rock caves overhung with ferns and moss. He had never realized their depth or what soft greenish lights were hidden in them.

'You know how to treat us!' she said with a low tender laugh that had something in it of the sigh of a wild animal that submits to being petted. 'But I don't love you any better for this.'

'I don't care whether you love me better or not,' he said, 'as long as I've got you still. I should be much more agitated about your moods if I wasn't with you, if it were a case of writing letters to each other.'

She looked at him almost as intensely and questioningly as he had looked at her a little while ago.

'I've been reading those poems of yours,' she said, with just a faint flicker of malice, 'and I cannot say that I think they're worthy of you. They are so overloaded with sensations that one doesn't get any emotion at all from them.'

'I must have a cigarette if I'm to talk about poetry,' said Richard, lifting her off his knee and walking over to the chimneypiece to get a match. 'And you must free yourself from the burden of your critic's weight too, it seems!' she retorted, as she settled herself alone in the wicker chair.

'What do you mean by sensations?' said Richard walking up and down the room with impatient strides. 'The whole purpose of what I've been writing is to get into it the very essence of the English country – and that's a "sensation", isn't it?'

'It may be to an Englishman, my dear,' she replied. 'It isn't to me. All this indiscriminate piling up of flowers and trees and grasses, all this business about lanes and fields, seems to me just heavy and dull. It seems to get into the way of something.'

'That's because you're an American,' he threw at her indignantly. 'Any English person reading what I've written would be reminded of the happiest moments of his life.'

'And what are they, if I may ask?'

Richard looked at her with a scowl. A red flush came into his cheeks. 'It's no use trying to explain to an American things of that kind,' he said. 'The happiest moments of a person's life in England are associated with old country memories, with just those lanes and gardens and fields that you find so dull. If you don't care for things like that, of course my poems are nothing to you!'

'But my dear Richard,' cried Elise, 'surely the whole purpose of art is to make such impressions universal, so that everybody feels them? If you're content to write about ponds and ditches for the benefit of English people – well! you may please yourself of course; but I cannot allow you to call such a thing *art*. It's the merest personal sensation of one individual!'

Richard looked as if it would have given him immense satisfaction to box her ears.

'Isn't art always a personal sensation?' he protested.

'Not a bit of it!' cried the dancer. 'Art's an emotion not a sensation. It's an emotion that expresses the only really impersonal thing in the world.'

'And what may that be?' asked Richard sarcastically.

'Ah! my dear,' murmured the dancer with a sigh, 'if you don't know what that is, if you don't care to know what that is, you'll never be a great poet.'

'Well, at any rate,' said Richard, 'I've only done in my poetry what English poets have always done; that's to say, tried to get the magic of the earth soul into words that are not too vague or mystical.'

'My dear, my dear!' cried the dancer, laughing at him quite frankly now. 'You don't mean to say you think you have rivalled Shelley and Keats in these verses? They are very beautiful and right, those old poets, but you can't do that sort of thing twice. You've got to go further. You've got to start where they left off. You've got to say something new.'

Richard came and stood in front of her, glaring and lowering. She had stirred the very depths of his self-love. She had entered a chamber of his mind deeper than all his indolent acquiescences. She had given him the sensations of someone poking with a hayfork into the most sacred recesses of his soul.

'*New!*' he threw out at her with infinite disgust. 'You're the victim of your confounded country, whatever you like to say!

Everything has to be new, always new! My poetry deals with those elemental feelings that the race has always had. My *earth soul* is not a bit different from Wordsworth's earth soul or Virgil's either, or Plato's for the matter of that!'

She looked at him with a queer deep enigmatical look that puzzled and irritated him.

What was she after? Did she want to rake into his very inmost being? *Had* she raked into it, and found rank weeds where she hoped to find delicate and rare plants?

He felt angry and humiliated. A vague feeling of misgiving mingled with a raging sense of injustice. Was he destined never to love a woman who responded to every movement of his mind? Of course it was her cosmopolitan life, without roots in any soil, that made her so difficult! Naturally she could not understand the subtle and exquisite pleasure that he derived from every stick and stone in England. Where could he get in touch with anything deep if he didn't go back to those old delicious sensations connected with lanes and fields, with gardens and hedges?

He solaced himself hurriedly with these thoughts, but was not reassured. He was bitterly hurt and startled. After all, in her own work she was a great artist. She had done what he certainly had never done: she had put her whole life into her work. Why couldn't he, too, do that? Was she right in her attacks upon his mystical sensationalism? Did that kind of thing really act as a sort of drug, numbing the finer and rarer energies?

Troubled through and through by what she had said, his self-love obscurely conscious of a deep wound, letting in air and light from very alien spaces, he hovered in front of her, with his hands behind his back, like an erring soul before some tutelary spirit.

'It's like this, my dear,' she went on. 'Though I don't want to annoy you. I think you *have* great powers. But I cannot say I think this poetry of yours has done justice to them. I believe you inject into it, as you read it to yourself, a great many vague feelings that are not conveyed to anyone else. Your poetry is a kind of self-indulgence. It is the expression of a good deal in you that is merely personal. It is too self-satisfied, too unruffled. It's as if you had never really wrestled with life!'

He looked so completely miserable under her words that she took him by both his hands and pulled him towards her.

He responded to her caress almost savagely, seeking to recover his ascendency over her and to regain his self-respect in the oldest of primitive ways.

As he made love to her he withdrew his soul from her, letting it escape down some long corridor of reservation. His pride found a way to recover itself in this manner. Without actually formulating the malicious thought, what he felt in his mind was a derisive sense that she did not know at that moment how far his soul was wandering from her.

When the hour arrived for her to return to the theatre she was called for by Pat Ryan in his green Studebaker. They separated therefore at the door, Richard's vanity completely reinstated upon its secret throne. 'She is only a woman,' he said to himself as he walked towards the elevated station. 'Her art is instinctive, not intellectual. She does not understand the quieter, cooler, more magical kinds of poetry. She wants everything to be emotional and dramatic. In some ways Nelly has a truer feeling for beauty than she has. But Nelly's childish impishness spoils her insight. Nelly laughs at her own soul.'

As he ascended the crowded steps to the little platform, Richard felt in better spirits than he had felt for many a long week. It was a relief that Nelly knew of his affair with Elise and apparently had no intention of doing anything about it. It was sad that it made her unhappy. It was sad that she insisted that all lover-like play between them should cease. But she clearly had made up her mind not to sulk; and they had had – even since her discovery of his unfaithfulness – some not uncheerful hours.

There was thus a base unction, a shallow satisfaction, a sleek slurring over of all deeper issues, in Richard's mind as the elevated railway carried him down Sixth Avenue, the car in which he sat moving parallel to the third-storey windows of the larger shops.

It seemed as though the malicious revenge he had taken upon Elise had punished him by removing from his nature, in that hour, all nobler, all subtler feelings.

He had never caught himself in a mood quite so cynical, quite so brutal and crude, as he caught himself in then. It was a mood that seemed to fall into odious reciprocity with the external aspect of the New York thoroughfares at that evening rush hour.

Those pale-jowled rigid-faced men, those handsome self-assertive metallic-voiced women, pushing, jostling, scrambling, hurrying, driven by that elemental necessity of which Karmakoff had discoursed to him, seemed to fall in with this mood of his, to blend with it, to hearten it, to justify it. It was with a kind of prolonged snarl of predatory exultation that he – one of their number, one of the male animals of this wrestling tribe – chuckled to himself as he thought of the desperate struggle of life and how he was playing, in his dunghill isolation, his own little game against all these! Two women were 'interested' in him, two exceptional women, a great artist and a sweet-souled girl. How easily it might have happened, in this evil vortex, that no feminine creature worth a moment's thought might have cared one jot what became of him! But two of the most exquisite *did* care, and in this alone he had surely attained something! One after another the little stations passed, each numbered by the number of a street, crossing Sixth Avenue. When the train stopped at Twenty-third Street two young businessmen got in, in company with an older person, an elderly woman. The three were quarrelling about something, and continued quarrelling as the train moved out. The woman's face was gentle and very sad. The two young men were causing her some peculiar shame by the vulgarity and crudity of their discussion. Richard caught her eye, the eye of a hunted thing, looking desperately out of the train window, and then he caught her reverting her gaze into the interior of the car as though driven back by the menacing heartlessness of those glaring lights, gaudy advertisements and obtrusive store windows.

There swept over him a drowning wave of sudden remorse. Had he, in this eternal division between the sensitive and insensitive, slipped over to the wrong side? Had he ranged himself with the glaring advertisements and brutal sounds, with the lights and the iron and the paint and the roar, against the deeper voices that alone gave life any beauty or meaning?

Was he actually – he, Richard Storm – exulting in his possession of these two women as if he were a gross fool of a numbskull roué, devoid of all finer instincts?

Eighth Street! It was necessary for Richard to get out here, if he wished to walk through Cornelia Street and Le Roy Street to Seventh Avenue.

As he made his way through Greenwich Village with its laxer, easier, more careless atmosphere, he became conscious that there did exist in New York, hidden away among its iron buildings and its chaotic litter, many charming backwaters of friendly humanity.

In this particular quarter were artists of all the nations of the earth, writers, painters, journalists, bric-à-brac dealers, revolutionists, virtuosos, charlatans, dilettantes, actors, bachelor women, women workers, wealthy connoisseurs of the theatre, aesthetic dabblers, art-book dealers, literary recluses, imagist poets, futurist sculptors, popular mystics, cranks, faddists, philosophers, humbugs, devoted humanitarians, art-movement leaders, and many quiet solitary thinkers living between uptown fashion and downtown greed, intersected by wedges of every sort of foreign element. There was certainly a large, free, easygoing casualness in the air that seemed powerful enough to maintain itself unspoiled, in defiance of both economic necessity and social convention.

It was naïve and simple, this *Quartier Latin* of the New Atlantis; it was crude and self-conscious, but something of the great ocean spaces that surrounded it, something of those free winds and that high unclouded sky, had got into its manners and habits and usages. It was certainly primitive and unsophisticated in its ardours and devotions to what it proudly called 'creative work' but its very primitiveness preserved its love of beauty intact and pure, unspoiled by the cynical disillusionment of the traditional Bohemians of the Old World.

Here, if anywhere, wedged in between foreign tenements and big business, breathed the lungs of whatever mental and spiritual freedom that iron Manhattan could offer to her children!

When he reached the Charlton Street apartment he found that Nelly had already got their supper ready. She permitted him to kiss her, only turning her head a little to one side so as to avoid giving him her lips.

How blint and clumsy, how brutally callous and dull he had been, he thought. This avoidance of his lips made him suddenly aware of the infinite subtleties, the world of shy emotional reactions, so deep and so clear-edged, that women associate with this simple symbol. He was made obscurely conscious that he had hurt something in his wife's soul of a different character, of a more sensitive texture, than anything which he possessed in his own.

Does any man, he thought, really understand what this touching of the lips implies in the heart of a woman?

He felt at that moment as though there was a region of delicate, evasive, exquisitely attuned vibrations in Nelly's spirit, of which he might suddenly awake to discover he had lost the clue for ever; to discover that he had lost it, when it was too late to get it back.

As he chattered superficially with her, of this piece of gossip and that piece of scandal, over their meal, there slowly grew upon him the bitter cruel sense that he had, in his clumsy sensuality, thrown away something much more exquisite and precious than any merely physical thrill. After all, he *could* have given himself up to the divine genius of Elise, to her inspiration, her great instinctive art, without dragging her down to the level of an odalisque, a courtesan, an amorous plaything.

There was no reason to suppose that if he had made it clear to Elise that he loved his wife and intended to remain faithful to her she would have rejected his platonic friendship. The passionate paganism of Elise was a thing quite uninvolved with her deeper nature and a few clear indications of loyalty to Nelly would have placed his relations with the dance on a basis much more honourable to both of them.

Every mouthful he took at that meal, as he sat facing the delicate being whose love he had deliberately set himself, so it seemed to him now, to trample on and to kill, tasted of miserable remorse.

Had she sulked, had she thrown out sarcastic speeches, had she been vituperative and vindictive, he could have hardened his heart in his unfaithfulness. But as it was, thinking his self-accusing thoughts beneath their friendly chatter, it seemed to him as though he had dragged down and exploited in sheer stupidity of sensuality both these finer spirits. His remorse about Nelly diffused itself over Elise too, and he felt he had betrayed them both. The great creative spirit of life – the only god he worshipped – had given him Nelly's love and the child *she* carried within her; had also given him the friendship of Elise and the child she carried within her, that incomparable art of hers. And what had he done to both these mirrors of the eternal vision? Tossed them down, flung one against the other, tried to see his own egotistic countenance in each of them, and clouded and blurred them in the effort.

He sought, absurdly enough, on this particular evening, to soothe

the smart of his conscience by an exaggerated consideration. He helped Nelly clear the table, he helped her to wash up; it was only afterwards, when seated near her in their small living room looking out on the quiet houses opposite, that he was made starkly aware how futile such catchpenny offerings were.

He found himself leaning forward and touching her hand as she worked at the piece of sewing spread over her knees. 'Nelly – my dear – my dear, can't you bring yourself to forget and forgive? It's more than I can stand, this way we're living now. It makes me homesick for the old days. It makes me long for Sussex.'

She let his hand stay where it was, but her fingers lay passive and cold within his own.

'What can I do, Richard?' she murmured, looking at him gravely and quietly. 'What can I do that I haven't done? I haven't inter-fered with your pleasure. I haven't made a fuss or tried to leave you. Many women would have . . . well! you know! But when you ask me to be just the same, as if nothing were going on, when you're still seeing that person, I can't understand quite what you mean. Sometimes, my dear,' and she looked at him with a puzzled look that almost flickered into a faint smile, 'sometimes I doubt whether you've ever grown up. You seem to be so blind to certain things; as if you actually *didn't* understand, as if you were not quite an ordi-nary human being; as if you were hurting me without knowing that you were hurting me. You can't expect me to laugh and smile and encourage you to go off to someone else.'

He moved a little nearer to her. 'But you *do* love me still, my darling, my darling?' he whispered.

Her forehead puckered up into a concentrated frown and her lips quivered.

'You don't think *I* like the way we're living?' she broke out. 'But how can I bear it differently? What can I do? When I asked you that first day whether you'd give this person up, you wouldn't answer. And of course I know you haven't given her up. I know you see her every day. I know you came straight from her this very night. And how can I feel as if it were just the same – when it's like that? I can hold myself in, from saying any more. I *must* hold myself in, for our child's sake. But I can't help feeling bitter. You can't expect me to go on just the same. It takes a little time to make a person's heart numb and dead. I don't think you *know* – that's what I keep saying to myself – I don't think you know what a woman feels. I don't think you *can* know. You couldn't have done it, you couldn't have done it, if you did.'

Her voice broke at this point but she controlled herself with a pathetic struggle, and got up from her chair. 'You mustn't expect too much from me, Richard,' she added. 'I'm not made of wood and stone.'

The direct cause of her rising was the sound of the doorbell accompanied by a sound of quite a number of voices in the street.

'Here they are!' she cried, moving to the window and drawing aside the curtain. 'They've come all together. Let them in, will you Richard? You've got cigarettes for them? We'll have the coffee at once. I've got two of those cakes.'

He ran downstairs. A few minutes later the little apartment was full of tobacco smoke and lively conversation.

Roger Lamb sat by Nelly's side on the sofa. Robert Canyot established himself on the windowsill, his long legs dangling awkwardly, and his dusty boots looking large and prominent.

Karmakoff and Catharine shared the armchair; while Richard seated at the table before his coffee cup munched one piece of cake after another, as if by the mere process of devouring this sticky substance he fortified himself against unhappy thoughts.

'It's all very well for you to speak of Russia as if nothing but sweetness and goodness emerged from it,' said Karmakoff suddenly, throwing the remark like a hand grenade straight at the head of Roger Lamb. 'Russia's no better and no worse than the rest of the world. All this sentimentality is as false as all this savage abuse.

'Where we Russians differ from you people is simply that we've no false shame. We express everything – all that there is to be expressed – and a good deal more sometimes!' He laughed a rather bitter laugh.

Nelly made an unconscious little movement of her hand towards the young man as if to protect him from this frontal attack; but Roger Lamb seemed quite unruffled.

'I apologize,' he said. 'I ought not to have dragged Russia into it at all. It was a lapse. It was only that Mrs Storm seemed so awfully pessimistic. I just reminded her of the nicer side of things – of human nature, you know? I was trying to explain my own feeling about it. Russia was a by-issue and a silly one. I apologize to Russia, Ivan.'

'Oh Roger,' cried Catharine Gordon, 'while I think of it Elise wants you to write her up in *The Manhattan*. She's getting sick of the rotten notices they give her.'

The colour rose in Nelly's cheeks at this name. Karmakoff deliberately pinched Catharine in the arm. Richard put an enormous piece of cake into his mouth. Canyot, kicking the wall with his heels, remarked surlily, 'She gets better ones than she deserves as it is. I'd leave her alone, Roger.'

Nelly, who had bent her head over her lap, raised it at this. '*The Manhattan* ought to have something about her,' she said calmly, looking straight at her husband.

Roger Lamb smiled. 'I don't think any of you know much about the difficulties of journalism. I've been trying for three months to get her a satisfactory write-up. The old man won't have it. He says we're too modern as it is.'

Karmakoff, who had been regarding Roger Lamb with a fixed scrutiny for some minutes, moved a little away from his companion in the armchair and, leaning forward, startled them all by suddenly saying – 'Something's wrong with you, Roger. You're not well. What is it?'

Richard rose from his seat at the table. 'Shall I get you a glass of water or anything, Lamb? Ivan's right. You look pale and worried.'

Nelly turned towards the young man at her side with a look full of solicitude. Catharine Gordon leapt to her feet and rushing up to him took his head in both her hands and gazed into his face. 'You're not ill are you? No you can't be ill. I won't have you getting ill!' She slipped down beside him at the very end of the sofa and hugged him with her strong young arms.

The general disturbance produced by all this concern on his behalf did not seem to ruffle Roger Lamb. He drew himself gently out of the young girl's embrace and rising from his place moved over to the chair vacated by Richard. With an amused and friendly smile he rejected the glass of water which this latter offered him. 'You can give me a match if you like,' he said and proceeded to light a cigarette.

Catharine Gordon possessed herself of Nelly's hand. Canyot returned to his place on the windowsill. Richard sat down by his wife's side.

'You haven't answered my question yet,' resumed Karmakoff who had not ceased to regard the journalist with a searching scrutiny.

'Don't tease him, Ivan!' cried Catharine. 'You're looking at him as if you were a magician or one of these horrid psychoanalysts. Don't – don't look at him like that!' And she waved her arm backwards and forwards in the air as if to break the spell.

'He doesn't tease me,' remarked Roger Lamb. 'I love Karmakoff's way of looking at people. And he is quite right too. He's found me out. He's called my bluff, as they say. I hadn't meant to tell any of you anything about it. But it was silly of me to hide it up – a sort of pride I suppose. I don't know! One does these things sometimes. Perhaps it didn't seem so real to me as long as I kept it to myself. But Ivan has found me out with his confounded Slavic intuition; so I'll confess . . .'

There was a perceptible hush in the small apartment as he said these words; his youthful figure, in its trim dark-coloured suit, seemed to isolate itself from the rest. His queer-shaped skull under its closely cropped hair assumed the appearance of an archaic statue as it emerged from the clouds of his cigarette smoke. His grey unhappy eyes looked quizzically round him as he paused in his speech; and his sensuous mouth with its impassioned red lips seemed more than ever as if it had been carved out of his white face by the hands of some insane god, forgetful of all proportion.

'Don't tell us! Don't tell us!' cried Catharine Gordon suddenly, putting her fingers in her ears. 'I hate you for this, Ivan. It's a cruel thing. And you're a devil to do it.'

Karmakoff smiled at her with a smile of infinite indulgence. A strange contest of looks passed between them full of complicated vibrations;

'If it's anything to do with your nerves, Roger,' said Canyot earnestly, 'I'd much rather you didn't tell us—' and he looked anxiously at Nelly.

Roger Lamb interpreted his glance. 'You needn't be afraid, Robert. It's nothing that could scare anyone. It's simple enough. It's only that I am—'

'Don't tell him! Don't tell him!' cried Catharine again, pressing her fingers wildly into her ears.

But the young man proceeded without regarding her. 'It's only that I learnt from the doctor this morning that if I don't have an operation at once I've no chance of living; and that the operation I've got to have is a ticklish matter, a matter of even chances.'

There was a moment of embarrassed silence in the room. Catharine, who seemed to have understood his words, took her hands from her ears and covered her face.

'How long does he give you without the operation?' asked Karmakoff.

'About a week,' replied the other smiling. 'Just about a week.'

'And you've arranged to have it?'

'I go into the hospital tomorrow.'

'Which one?'

'The Postgraduate.'

'I am very glad you told us this,' said Nelly quietly. 'I should have hated not to know.'

'How does this affect your old pessimistic apathy?' inquired Canyot from the windowsill, speaking roughly and almost harshly.

'I shouldn't have thought that he was either pessimistic or apathetic,' protested Richard.

'He isn't! How can you say such things, Robert?' reiterated Nelly.

'Speak up, Roger, and tell them I'm right,' cried Canyot. 'You know you've always said that down at the bottom, except for the theatre, you cared nothing for anything in life; that you'd just as soon be dead as be alive.'

The brusqueness of this question flung so crudely at the young man produced a curious jar and jolt among them all. Nelly looked reproachfully at the painter. Richard scowled and sank into gloomy silence. Karmakoff lay back in his chair and shrugged his shoulders, smiling a little.

'I can't understand what you mean,' remarked Catharine. 'Roger's always so amusing. He's naughty of course and funny; but I can't think how you can call him pessimistic. He always puts me into a lovely mood when I come across him.'

'Thank you, Catharine,' said the journalist, looking affectionately at her.

'You're wrong all the same,' persisted Canyot; 'and Roger knows it, only he won't admit it. You haven't answered my question yet,' he went on, almost brutally, his eyes flashing from beneath their heavy brows.

'Robert dear!' protested Nelly softly.

But the atmosphere of tension in the room after the journalist's revelation seemed to have gone to the painter's head.

'Why don't you answer?' he growled. 'You know perfectly well I'm right.'

Roger Lamb buttoned his jacket with quiet fingers and crossed his legs.

'Are you really going to the hospital tomorrow?' cried Catharine. 'It's dreadful. It's like a dream.'

'Yes, you're quite right, Robert,' replied the condemned young man, frowning a little and opening his eyes very wide with a sort of humorous grimace. 'I *have* never cared very much what happened to me. A sort of inertness – a silly kind of disillusionment about everything – I don't know! but it's always been *here*, somewhere or another, like a marble slab.' He tapped his forehead with his long second finger.

'But, Roger, you have helped me so much at different times,' protested Nelly softly.

'And me too – you poor darling – you've been an angel to me always,' murmured Catharine Gordon.

'But how has this operation news affected your indifference?' Canyot persisted.

'How can you go on teasing him like that?' cried Catharine, stepping up to Canyot's side and seizing his arm with her hands. 'Stop it, I say! Stop it!' And the young girl positively shook the painter in her indignation.

'It has had absolutely no effect at all,' answered Roger Lamb. 'It's all right, Catharine. Robert and I understand each other perfectly.'

'He ought to be beaten!' cried the young girl retreating to Nelly's side and clutching her hand.

'Absolutely no effect,' the journalist repeated, bending down to straighten out one of his purple-coloured socks. 'But I confess I'm a bit scared of that hospital. I always have been terrified of institutions. The most agitating moment of my life was when I first went into camp.'

'But Roger dear,' cried Catharine, 'the army isn't an institution.'

'Is marriage an institution, Catharine?' asked Karmakoff.

'Not for you or me,' the girl replied, giving him a strange quick look.

At that point Roger Lamb arose to his feet. 'Well! I think I'll be making my way home,' he said.

They all made an involuntary movement towards him; and while Richard was searching for his hat and stick they surrounded him awkwardly, in a silence full of unsaid things.

His slim figure and closely cropped skull seemed to grow almost terrifyingly alien from them; seemed to repel them, for all his gentleness, as if with a stern and menacing gesture.

He shook their hands quietly enough when that moment's embarrassed pause was over; the passionate sympathy of the embrace which Catharine Gordon gave him broke the spell of the general discomfort.

'You'll take him home, Richard, won't you?' said Nelly, and added a hurried 'of course he will! No, Roger, he *must* go with you. You *must* let him. He'll see you to bed and then come back to us.'

As Richard walked by the side of the doomed boy, up Varick Street and across Sheridan Square, in front of the Greenwich Village Theater, he became conscious of the extraordinary power of Lamb's self-possession.

This might well be the last time the youth was destined to walk through those well-known haunts, the last time through an inconceivable eternity; and yet he seemed to look round him with his usual whimsical gravity, noting the passers-by and the various familiar scenes without a sign of dramatic self-consciousness.

They went into one of the innumerable Village cafés for a cup of coffee, and Richard was amazed at the urbanity and aplomb with which his companion greeted some casual acquaintances of his, Dulcie Foster and her strange friend Siegfried Stein, the mad musician. When finally, an hour afterwards, he left the room in Waverley Place where he had seen the young man safely to bed, he felt himself impelled to walk round Washington Square in order to collect his thoughts before returning home.

The night was a little damp and chilly, although the day had been hot. The trees in the square had already changed their tints and many of their leaves had fallen. As he strode beside the familiar arch, whose classic facade is so curiously adorned with two statues of the same Father of the Country, and let his eyes wander up the long perspective of Fifth Avenue, he realized how tremendous was the mere weight of sheer material substantiality in this astounding city. The death of a fragile man-of-letters, the death of many men-of-letters, what were they amid the palpable projections of this tremendous scene?

As he moved up close to the masonry of the arch, to shelter himself from the tornado of whirling automobiles that rolled past him, he visualized this harsh raw emphatic city as a sort of deliberately flung-out challenge to the march of the feet of the destinies. It was like a great flaring advertisement sign, this city, hung up here between the deep sky and the deep ocean, with a sort of defiance to all the old submissions and resignations. These immense marble-and-iron structures, blazing with a million lights, seemed to flaunt in the face of the gods a certain bravura of splendid levity.

The Old World with its time-bleached pieties had accepted those gods' austere decisions and had bowed low before them in patient fatalistic ritual. But this reckless New World seemed to claim, in daring impious flippancy, the right to deny the whole traditional order, its solemn sorrows as well as its solemn assuagements, and to fling forth a sort of profane adventurous challenge to the whole system of things.

The death of a man, contemplated in the light of the illuminated perspective of Fifth Avenue, dwindled into a kind of negligible accident. So many men must have died in order that this huge shout of defiance should reach the planetary spaces.

Love and friendship and religion and loyalty, these things were proper subjects for the old forms of art; but here in New York these things seemed to fall into the background and other manifestations of the life force seemed to assume prominence.

In a different mood Richard might have been tempted to condemn these other manifestations, as part of the primordial brutality in things, but in some queer way the influence of Roger Lamb had altered his feeling about them. The journalist had thrown out to him so many capricious fancies as he prepared for his last night in his own bed, that Richard began to wonder whether it was possible that this huge chaotic welter of a world might after all be destined to evoke some completely new attitude to life; some attitude in which camaraderie took the place of love, honesty to one's self the place of loyalty to others, cynical courage replaced submissive piety, as a reckless indifference to death did the old sad resignation.

As he walked slowly back to Charlton Street through the familiar quarter with its voluble crowds and its lighted fruit shops great splashes of crude warm colour against the darkness, there came upon him a dim feeling that there was something here, some mood, some attitude of the spirit, some breaking up of ancient barriers that it would be perhaps unwise wholly to harden one's heart against.

At any rate he was able in that hour, as he had never been able before, to gather up into some sort of perspective his former life in Paris, his marriage to Nelly, and his love affair with the dancer. *I will make this night*, he thought, as he passed the illuminated front of the Greenwich Village Theater, *a new start for my poem. I will get some of that young fellow's fancies into it. And I will tell Elise that she was right and I was wrong.*

Chapter 18

Two days later, after Richard had left for the office, Nelly was called up on the telephone by Catharine Gordon who told her that she and Ivan were at the hospital and that Roger Lamb was dead.

Catharine informed her that Karmakoff was taking her down to Atlantic City to get a breath of sea air, and that she had already spoken to Richard 'over the phone'.

Nelly got a queer startled sensation from Catharine's words which had ended with incoherent emotion. She stood for a few minutes by her kitchen tap, fumbling with the breakfast things and mechanically putting into the water some plates which she had already washed. An infinite sadness invaded her heart. It seemed incredible that this self-possessed boy, who had talked to them so quietly in that very room only forty-eight hours ago, was now as far divided from her as her own father.

The news about Atlantic City was a shock to her too. She wondered if Karmakoff and Catharine had secretly got married. If not – was this naïve passionate creature self-possessed enough to risk the sort of transient affair which such an excursion suggested?

Nelly had come to feel a maternal tenderness for the erratic young girl; and though Ivan was no pleasure hunter, she could hardly imagine him committing himself to any lifelong attachment.

She did not go so far as to accuse Karmakoff of exploiting the girl's emotional agitation over Lamb's death to his own amorous advantage; but she wished Catharine had come straight to her from the hospital instead of going off like this.

But perhaps it was only for the day. There were plenty of late trains back from the famous resort and, after all, it was likely enough, in the easy moral atmosphere in which they lived, that all the harm that could happen had happened already.

She turned with a heart full of vague forebodings to her house-work in the little apartment. She could not quite explain to herself the sort of melancholy which descended upon her. It seemed something more than the boy's death, more than Richard's unfaithfulness, more than Catharine's danger, more than her natural apprehensions about her own future. She reverted to each one of these matters, trying to get at the secret of what she felt, but it escaped her each time. It seemed to be something impersonal, a sort of universal misery in things, a kind of freemasonry of tragedy into which, by the medium of her own distress, she had been formally admitted. Whatever it was, it seemed to grow upon her as the morning went on, gathering in intensity and volume, as if actual vibrations of misery were rolling, wave after wave, over her brain. She had felt something like this once before, during the war; but she had got rid of that by digging frantically in her father's garden. Here, in a New York apartment, there was no garden to dig in. It was about half-past eleven. She was already vaguely beginning to wonder whether she had the spirit to cook herself any lunch when the telephone rang. Lifting the receiver she was surprised to hear her husband's voice.

Richard hated telephoning. This was the first time, as it happened, that these two had ever talked together in this way.

She was still more surprised when she heard him say that he thought of following Ivan and Catharine down to Atlantic City and spending the night there. She was indeed so startled by the tone of his voice, which sounded abrupt and strange out of the receiver, that she could do nothing but say 'yes – yes – yes—' without any comment. He must have been anxious enough to avoid any comment, for he rang off suddenly in the end, having told her that the train he intended to take left at three o'clock.

Nelly sat down on the nearest chair, nonplussed, puzzled, bewildered, indignant. Had the death of Roger Lamb affected Richard as much as Catharine? But why Atlantic City? There were surely other places, country places in New Jersey, he could have rushed off to? Had Lamb's death driven them all crazy? Surely Karmakoff and Catharine didn't want him down there with them? And then, all in a moment, it dawned upon her that he was using the two lovers merely as a clumsy excuse, as an awkward blind, for his own devices. What he was really up to, no doubt, was going down there with Elise Angel! Lamb's death had made him restless and defiant, as it had made these others restless and defiant, and he had resolved to follow their example and take some wilful plunge. It was curious that that boy's death, instead of lifting them all into a calmer, clearer state of mind, seemed to have driven them into fiercer acts of self-assertion than they had ever dared to risk before!

The girl felt almost tempted, as she sat on the high chair by the table resting her chin in her hands, to attribute all these feverish movements to some influence of Roger Lamb emanating from the invisible world.

Was this capricious and chaste spirit trying to communicate to them all some utterly subversive doctrine of human relations, some secret of the abyss that contradicted all the normal traditions? Was the real law of the system of things nothing less simple than that every living person should fight unscrupulously for his own hand?

She rose to her feet and moved to the window. The little street below her was quiet enough; but from the great neighbouring thoroughfare came the roar of the motor-lorries carrying their merchandise from the warehouses and wharfs of the downtown quarter to the uptown department stores.

Along with that harsh persistent rumble, the very beating of the bold heart of the adventurous city, came a sort of challenge to her courage. Dared she too, as these others had done, shake off the fatalism of the Old World and strike resolutely and swiftly for what she wanted?

She turned from the window and looked at the clock on the

mantelpiece. It was only a quarter to twelve. Richard's train did not leave for three hours yet.

She stood in the middle of the room biting her lip and pondering deeply. Then with a sudden start she rushed into her bedroom and began putting on her outdoor shoes and her best hat.

A great and desperate resolution had formed itself in her mind. She would go and see Elise Angel.

The effort with which she prepared for this daring move was the most extreme she had ever made. It was like the effort required by an unarmed hunter who walks straight up to a crouching tiger, seeking to dominate it with his eyes.

She was out of the house by the time the chimes in the Metropolitan Tower sounded twelve o'clock. She took the subway at Houston Street and sat bolt upright in the crowded car, her lips tightly compressed and her heart violently beating. What she felt in her inmost soul was that she was fighting for her unborn child, and this thought gave her a defiant courage.

She got out at Columbus Circle and proceeded to walk resolutely eastwards, skirting the southern edge of Central Park.

She was not oblivious to the aggressive newness of everything round her and the crushing challenge of the huge hotels and the portentous apartment houses.

Through the iron railings she could see great blocks of huge grey stone emerging from the midst of enbrowned grass and melancholy shrubs.

It was as if the skeleton bones of the primitive rock basis of all this grandiose architecture were insisting upon its own share in this orgy of triumphant matter. Nelly felt as though all this iron and marble and stone were consciously piling itself up against her frail human weakness. She touched the park railings with one of her hands and a stain of dusty rust came off upon her glove. Never had she felt so entirely alone in the world. She experienced a sickening sensation of nostalgia, of longing for her Sussex hills. Tears came into her eyes as she thought of her father, unable to help her, however desperately she called for help. The longing for home grew so intense as she moved on, between the rocks of the park and the mountainous buildings that she was conscious of a definite pain in the pit of her stomach, something quite distinct from the sense she had of bearing the burden of her child.

But in spite of her weakness she moved steadily on; and when she came to the great hotels that surrounded the flamboyant gilded statue, the most unsympathetic spot on the face of the globe, she found herself able to cross the pretentious avenue and turn northwards along it without losing her self-control.

Compared with this terrible centre of uptown fashion, how warm and friendly and human and mellow was that unassuming Greenwich Village which she had left!

She had never till this moment realized what the prodding thrust of unmitigated newness, armed with the arrogance of wealth, is able to do to the frail human heart into which it drives its wedge.

She turned eastwards at length, out of the great avenue with its palatial enormities, into a comparatively quiet street that seemed to her to possess something of the massive reticence of London.

It was a quarter to one when Nelly finally arrived at the door of the apartment house where her rival lived.

She was by this time so physically exhausted that a sort of obstinate recklessness took the place of her former agitation.

She rang the bell and asked to see Miss Angel.

'What name?' demanded the braided official.

Nelly had one second of hesitation and then she said quietly, 'Mrs Richard Storm.'

She had a moment of faintness while the man clicked at his telephone board and talked to the apartment overhead; but a few moments' rest on a polished bench and a drastic effort of her will saved her from collapse.

'Miss Angel says will you please go straight up,' announced the man presently. 'Second floor and first door on the left.'

She entered the elevator, worked by a Negro boy, and emerging at the designated level knocked at the dancer's door. She was admitted by Thérèse and ushered straight into the luxurious sitting room with its oriental rugs and settees.

The servant closed the door behind her and she found herself alone with the owner of the apartment.

Elise rose from one of the cushioned lounges and advanced towards her with an air of regal indulgence.

'I'm so glad to make your acquaintance, Mrs Storm,' she murmured, with the sort of inclination of the head that some barbarian queen might have given to a casual prisoner doomed to die. 'Please sit down. No! No! This one's much nicer. There! we'll sit together here. What a child you are; and oh! how pretty you are! I don't wonder Richard's so in love with you.'

She made a half-movement as if she would have touched Nelly's hand, but something in the face that was turned towards her cut her gesture short.

'I came to see you,' Nelly began in a voice that sounded hard and strange, 'because I wanted you to know exactly what you're doing, what you've done.'

'My dear child, I've done nothing. You've come to me on a wild-goose chase. Your husband and I must have been old friends when you were in short frocks. How pretty you must have looked in those days!'

'I came to see you,' Nelly repeated, completely disregarding her words, 'because I wanted you to understand things; and not be able to plead ignorance of the ruin you are causing.'

Elise Angel lifted her eyebrows. 'What a dramatic little person you are! I don't myself see this ruin you talk of. *You* don't look in the least "ruined". And as for Richard – why he, even *you* must admit, looks a great deal better since I first picked him up. It wasn't your fault I daresay. It was simply want of money. But when I think of how wretchedly thin and miserable he was that day, and how happy he looks now, I can't say I feel as if "ruin" were the right word for what I have done.'

A look of such strange intensity flickered over Nelly's face as she opened her lips to reply to this, that the great artist by her side drew in her breath and stared at her in a sort of puzzled wonder. The girl seemed hardly to have heard what the other actually said. It was as if her look answered some unspoken word, some word that passed between them quite independently of any uttered sound. Nelly spoke again:

'You don't really love him. I am glad of that. That clears up a great deal. If you really loved him I should feel differently to you. I don't know whether I should hate you or not, but I should feel differently.'

Elise looked at her with a deeper bewilderment than ever. There was something about Nelly's self-possession that took the situation out of her hands. As long as it had been a matter of dramatic gesture and physical dominance she had held the lead; but the lead was taken away from her now, the girl of twenty-two seeming to represent an older, deeper experience of life.

'So you came to me to find out *that*,' said Elise Angel.

'I came to you so that you should know what you've done to me. You've killed something in me that can never revive. You are a successful woman, Miss Angel; you're what the world calls a genius. But you are a cruel woman and a heartless one. You are just as much a murderess as if you'd killed me. You *have* killed me, in a sense. I don't suppose you care. I know you don't care. But I wanted you to know once and for all how one person feels about you. I feel towards you as I should feel towards any other perfectly heartless criminal, towards any other person who is capable of killing things. You've killed my life, Miss Angel; though no doubt I shall go on *living*. One does, you know.' Nelly's voice had shown no sign of nervous tension as she uttered these words. There were no tears in her eyes. When she had finished she clasped her fingers tightly together and sat very straight, looking in front of her. Her attitude seemed to say, 'I have spoken for my own satisfaction rather than for any desire to make you understand me. And *now* I may just as well sit here and think, as sit anywhere else.'

'I suppose it's never occurred to you,' said Elise Angel, 'that I was a friend of Richard years and years before you came on the scene. One has to judge things by their general effects. And I can't say his life with you seems to have made him so very happy. He left me full of radiant spirits to go to England; and I find him here thin, miserable, half-starved, working in a wretched office! Of course I know he has to support you; but it seems to me when a man gives his name to a woman he deserves at least to be looked after a bit.'

Very slowly Nelly unclasped her tightly locked fingers, and turned her head towards her rival. The thought flashed through her mind, *He has been telling her about Robert*, and for the first time during this interview there was aroused in her a ferment of real vindictiveness. Out of the depths of her being this evil poison rose to the surface, corroding her more honourable indignation and turning it into bitter gall. It rose to the surface from that deep cistern of malice which is one of the unfathomable secrets of mortality.

As usually happens in these cases the cause of this particular anger was a misunderstanding. It was unfair. It was unjust. For Richard had far too much pride to breathe a word to Elise on such a matter as Canyot's relations with his wife – those picnic lunches in the painter's studio were quite unknown to the dancer.

'He lost his money,' said Nelly. 'The Paris people failed him. I've had to go short of things as well as he. But it's no use trying to explain. It doesn't matter. Nothing matters very much now. It's a mere incident to you of course; but incidentally it has destroyed a thing that was really beautiful – quite as beautiful I daresay as your wonderful dancing.'

Elise rose slowly to her feet at this. 'That's the worst of you good domestic women,' she said. 'There's always a point where you begin to scold like fish-wives.' She walked to the mantelpiece and back again, the texture of her gown hanging about her figure in clinging folds, folds that were as statuesque and classical as those that fall about the figures known as the Three Fates among the Elgin Marbles. 'It's all sex,' she went on, standing erect in front of her visitor and looking down upon her. 'Your anger against your husband; your anger against me. You talk of my heartlessness and cruelty. Do you suppose I *asked* your Richard to make love to me? Do you suppose I'd care a jot if he stopped making love to me tomorrow? I don't care a fig about *that*, one way or another. *That* means nothing at all with men. You ought to know it means nothing; and you would know it, only you are blinded by sex. Suppose *I* were married to him and he was playing with *you*, I might be furious; I probably should be, but I shouldn't deceive myself about it. I shouldn't use grand language about it. I should know it was all this wretched sex illusion, his unfaithfulness and my wretchedness about his unfaithfulness – both of them illusion.'

Having uttered this tirade Elise looked at Nelly as if challenging her to respond. Nelly did not even lift her eyes. She seemed to look through the goddess-like figure before her as if it had been a thing of transparent mist.

'You have killed my happiness,' the young girl repeated. 'You have killed it without scruple or thought. You have no human kindness in you. You are thoroughly heartless. You will always be a bad selfish woman, a woman without pity. And sooner or later your dancing will end. You will get stiff and heavy and dull. And then perhaps you will remember the girl whose heart you killed and who came to tell you what you had done!'

She rose from her seat as she spoke and the two women stood looking at each other with that deep look of infinite understanding and infinite contempt which is one of the most characteristic achievements of nature's laws.

Elise, the artist, felt herself in this struggle weaker and less implacable than her more normal rival. And it was her sense of this advantage in the other that made her toss her proud head and burst into a bitter laugh.

'You silly pretty child!' she cried, moving towards the door.

Nelly followed her; but when the door had been opened and she stood on the threshold, the accumulated indignation within her burst forth. 'I'm glad I came to you,' she said bitterly. 'I know you now for the kind of thing you are.'

'What you really came for,' retorted the dancer, 'was to try and persuade me to give Richard up.'

'You can't give him up – because he's never belonged to you. You've never loved him, not one little bit! And *he* – he's only infatuated with you, as he might be with any other woman of your sort. There's no real link between you and there never can be.'

'There's a much closer link between us than *you* can understand. But goodbye – I wish you joy of your preciouls possession.'

The dancer's eyes were blazing with anger now. But Nelly looked straight into her face. 'It may interest you to know that Richard and I are expecting to have a child. I ought not really to have risked the shock of this interview. You can better understand now, perhaps, how impertinent and ill-bred you seem to me in coming between us just now. You talked of illusion. But it seems to me that the illusion is yours and a crude and vulgar one. It is the illusion of thinking that you could do anything worse to me than destroy my happiness. *That* you have done by your interference. But your power for evil stops there.'

Having flung this parting shot the young girl turned her back on her enemy and without waiting for the elevator ran down the two flights of stairs and walked out of the building.

She moved now with a very different step from the one with which she had approached the place. Some curious power of battle seemed to possess her, quite different from anything she had felt before. She emerged into the great gaudy avenue with her nerves strung-up and her heart bitter and hard.

There was a child leaning over the stone fountain in front of the Plaza Hotel whose appearance made her, for a moment, recall what she herself had once been; a flicker of faint amusement crossed her face as she thought of those early days and how far she had travelled since then. Had all this happened in Sussex, she thought, would she have had the courage to fight so fiercely for her own hand as she was prepared to do now? Was she too, like the rest, acquiring a new spirit in this New World?

She paused and looked at the watch on her wrist. It was nearly two o'clock. She remembered that her husband's train left at three. From where did these Atlantic City trains start? The Pennsylvania Station! Yes, that was it. She had seen someone off from that very place only a few weeks ago.

She mounted to the top of one of the green buses, and then left it at Thirty-third Street for a cross-town car.

Walking down the stately arcade of the grandest of all railway stations, she paused at the top of the great flight of granite steps leading into the enormous concourse.

She was impressed, even in the midst of her agitated thoughts, by the superb magnificence of that imperial architecture. The feelings that passed through her must have resembled those of some un-happy Celtic captive, conveyed with her unborn child into the forum of the classical city. In spite of herself she was conscious of a sort of exultation as she looked at these huge columns and em-bossed roof. Something in the tremendousness of that weight of primitive stone, measured and carved in such grand outlines, lifted her above herself and beyond herself. Here at any rate was a beauty and nobility that had something in common with her Sussex Downs.

What amazing cooperation between brain and hand had been needed to produce a thing like this! She found herself thinking suddenly of an argument in support of Karmakoff's theories; an argument based on the difference between this building and the vulgar individualistic palaces on the avenue she had just left!

She lifted her head and tried to read the time by the huge clock which hung above her; but she was too close beneath it for the great hands to be intelligible. She felt as if she had indeed reached some

243

fulcral or pivotal point in space where time issued its mandates but was itself obliterated by some formidable super-time.

She looked at her own watch. It was twenty-five minutes past two. The thought struck her, how living and human a thing a time-piece was, whether large or small, and how terribly like little goblins – so nice or so hateful – these 'ones' and 'twos' and 'threes' and all the rest of them were!

Suddenly she remembered she had had no lunch. After hesitating for a moment between the spacious restaurant on one side and the lunch counter on the other, she hurriedly entered the latter place. Seating herself on one of the revolving stools she ordered a cup of coffee and a roll. She was not sufficiently accustomed to this kind of public feeding to be quite at her ease. The long counters were not crowded; but to her English fancy every eye there was regarding her with a questioning stare, and the Negro who waited upon her embarrassed her by his Southern affability.

She kept her eye on the clock while she ate, anxious to make sure she caught her husband before he went past the barrier to his train; and at twenty minutes to three she paid her bill and ran down the granite steps.

It was only when she reached the iron gates marked ATLANTIC CITY EXPRESS that she realized how vague her notions were as to what she would do when her husband did appear.

She had come here blindly to see him, just as blindly and instinctively as she had gone to see Elise. In neither case had she formulated any project. In both cases a vague fighting spirit had driven her on.

Would Elise be with him when he came to the train? She had not precisely thought of *that*, though she had suspected that they were going down there together. But how could the dancer escape from her engagement at the theatre? *That*, again, was an aspect of the affair that she had not considered.

Without losing sight of the iron barrier, whose gate was already opened now, Nelly ran quickly to a newspaper stand and possessed herself of an *Evening Post*.

Returning to her place of observation she rapidly turned over the pages of this paper until she came to the theatre announcements.

She had no difficulty in finding the theatre notice she wanted and the first thing that met her eyes was the phrase, 'Change of Programme'. The name of Elise Angel was not mentioned at all! Hurriedly she scanned the opera and concert notices. Yes! there it was. Beginning next Saturday at the Morgan Hall,' a series of Classical Dances by the famous Elise Angel from Paris'. So the woman was just now entirely free, and that was the reason why Richard was hurrying down to Atlantic City!

As the full force of this discovery dawned upon her she realized how far she had been from actually grasping the situation in its true meaning. She had, after all, only half believed it. She had, after all, really expected to find her husband *alone* here – and either to persuade him not to go, or to go down with him herself.

It was now suddenly borne in upon her that he was actually coming, with Elise, here to this barrier, to go off together to the great pleasure place.

By one of those sudden telepathic flashes of insight which remain at present inexplicable, but to which women are more subject than men, and women in Nelly's condition most subject of all, she knew in a single moment that her husband and Elise were, at that very second, coming down the arcade.

With an instinct of desperate panic she fled across the aisle of this cathedral of commerce and slipped into the waiting room. Here, pressing her face to the glass, she watched the iron gate she had just quitted, her body cold as ice and her hands trembling.

Yes! There they were. There they came!

She drew back from the window as if she had been shot and, covering her face with her hands, sank into one of the waiting-room seats.

Here she remained absolutely motionless; her body heavy as lead, a curious dull pain in her forehead, and all her pulses numbed.

The last traveller of the three o'clock train hurried through the closing gates. The trainmen on the platform, below the iron stairs, blew their whistles . . . Richard and Elise, seated opposite one another in a Pullman car, sighed a mutual sigh of miserable tension, half-relief and half-remorse; while the great clock above the steps moved forward its hand, oblivious, indifferent, worked by punctual machinery.

Chapter 19

Three days after their departure from the Pennsylvania Station Richard and Elise were walking together on the sands by the edge of the sea. He had sent a telegram to his office begging them to give him a brief holiday and promising to send them all necessary copy by mail. He had written briefly to Nelly – a letter full of half lies in which he announced that he would return with Ivan and Catharine in a few days.

His time with Elise had been a turbulent one, full of violent quarrels and passionate reconciliations. As they drifted together now, side by side along the water's edge, they were engaged in bitter recrimination.

Above them, supported on wooden trestles, stretched the famous board-walk, frequented even then, at the end of the autumn, by a gay and noisy crowd.

On the further side of the board-walk a long line of small wooden shops offered the visitors to that newfangled promenade every sort of fantastic novelty.

Richard and Elise, absorbed in their quarrel, moved along the brink of the ocean until these shops began to thin out and disappear. But even beyond where the shops ended, that immense board-walk continued to extend its length. It was borne in upon Richard's mind that by use of its ironwork and its woodwork the American public loved to separate itself from nature and to dominate nature with a certain brutal contempt.

Not a living soul except themselves was to be seen walking upon the sand or close to the water. Directly the actual bathing season was over, during which, in their super-moral costumes, they had lain about in the hot sunshine, all the visitors to Atlantic City congregated upon those high-erected boardings and peered triumphantly at the elements in the intervals between moving-picture shows and flirtation.

Where Richard and Elise were now walking, the noises of traffic and entertainment had ceased; the high bare boards had a look quite peculiar to themselves and different from any other inanimate objects in the world.

They were curiously melancholy, these projections of woodwork, but not melancholy in the manner in which most new human erections are depressing and sad when contrasted with so old a thing as the sea: they were full of peculiar loneliness and desolation of their own – and one not devoid of an appeal to the imagination – but it was a desolation quite different from that produced by deserts or moors or marshes. It was a negative desolation, wherein the mere absence of humanity in a place obviously built for humanity evoked something peculiarly forlorn.

Still exchanging words of cruel and wounding bitterness, such as only those who are physically attracted without being temperamentally congenial are capable of flinging at one another, the two lovers were soon out of reach of the town altogether; the famous board-walk had dwindled to a narrow plank path.

Here they found themselves in a world of more attractive melancholy. Beyond the sea bank there stretched a vast expanse of reeds and rushes, and by the edge of the sand dunes where they were now wandering grew all manner of glaucous sea growths mingled with wild purple asters.

Every now and then they might have seen a long line of wild geese, travelling at an enormous height in the air, and sending down that peculiar sound, by the creaking of their wings, which can be only expressed by the syllables *hank-hank or honk-honk*.

But they did not look up at the sky at all just then; and the lines of flying wild fowl meant nothing to them; and the vast grey plateau of the ocean meant nothing to them; and the shells upon the white sand meant nothing to them.

They were two human beings, engaged in the immemorial occupation of sticking poisoned arrows into one another's hearts. Absorbed in this delicate pastime, they were oblivious to all else in the round world.

The real cause of their disagreement was the shock to their nerves of this reckless adventure and the simple fact that being neither of them young they lacked the resilience to recover themselves.

Remorse in Richard made a bitter and poisonous background for new romance. Not for one single moment could he really obliterate his wife's figure – silent and upbraiding, ironical and mocking, beautiful with the beauty of youth, and bearing his child at her heart.

The very air of gallantry which the pleasure city exhaled, like the sea breath of Aphrodite, was bitter and vulgar in his nostrils. All this transitory woodwork, all these painted wooden shops and flaunted showhouses seemed thin, sad and insubstantial to his spirit. The immense waste of November waters, shot with pale white sunshine or desolately grey, seemed to reduce all these theatrical attempts at pleasure and passion to a sort of fantastic Maya or unreal illusion, a gaudy ripple upon a vast emptiness.

Too sick at heart, too cruelly torn between the two women, to enjoy the escape which now offered itself as they left the houses behind and began to breathe the unsullied breath of the Jersey coast, Richard had a strange sense, as he wrangled with his companion in one of those interminable lovers' quarrels which seem like elemental forces, that he and she were will-less automata, doomed to hurt each other for the amusement of unseen spectators.

Struggling to break loose from the exhausting logic of anger which poisoned the air about them, he stopped at last and began tracing patterns with his stick in the white sand.

He drew an ornamental _E_ and a deeply indented _A_ on that smooth surface. But no sooner had he done so than an angry contempt for his own sentiment made him erase both of them with a violent gesture. The dancer's face was pale and sardonic as she watched him; her red lips curved in a hard significant smile.

'You don't know what the word _love_ means,' she said suddenly.

'I wasn't writing _love_,' he retorted childishly.' Can't you read English? I was making your initials.'

'In sand,' she said.

'Well! they're gone now, anyhow.'

'It's the fact of your being English, I suppose,' she remarked, looking at him with a misery of indignation. 'I hate all you English. Your feelings are clotted up with clods of earth – gross, thick, heavy clods of earth! Not one of you can be clear and free and honest. You worship what _is_, just because it _is_. It's worse than materialism, it is absolute deadness! And what's more you're not content until everyone's as dead as you are. Dead words, dead sentiment, dead hearts! You've no real courage in you . . . without courage everything becomes initials written on sand!'

Richard's face assumed the bewildered expression of a child that is beaten for an unknown fault. His superficial cynicism was swallowed up in real trouble. He looked at her like a dumb flogged animal.

His bewilderment increased her anger.

'These three days with you have killed my love,' she said. 'You've done the unpardonable thing . . . and you've made it worse by your stupidity. It would have been far better if you'd *known* what you were doing. It has been like being tied to a corpse!'

'I thought we'd been so happy,' he murmured.

'That's just it,' she cried, 'it's always *happiness, happiness, happiness* with you! Have you *no* idea of great, beautiful, terrible things that have to be paid for by the loss of all that? Happiness? My God! It means *comfort* to you – a nice, easy, complacent English comfort.'

'It's you who are not honest,' he muttered. 'Why can't you confess the truth? You're angry with me for quite a different reason from the one you're talking about.'

She flashed at him a look of splendid fury, a look that made her so beautiful that he was completely disarmed.

'What reason?' she flung out.

'Oh you know . . .' He hesitated. 'What's the use of my saying it? It's you who drive me on till you force me to say these things.'

'Tell me what you were thinking. Tell me! Quick!'

'It was nothing,' he stammered. 'We both think all sorts of unfair malicious things.'

'You must tell me. I must know. What was it?'

'It was natural enough . . . I daresay it's not true. I meant that you're angry with me because I felt remorseful about Nelly.'

'Ah!' She drew in her breath and her eyes grew dark against the pallor of her skin. Of course you'd say that. Being the most ill-bred thing you could possibly say, it's characteristic of course. As it happens, it's untrue. But if it *were* true, would that let you out? Can't you see that such remorse with you is only fear for your own skin? Or are you really such a baby as to think that you can make your wife happy by holding her hand?'

'You are very unfair,' said Richard. 'I can't help hating to make a person suffer.'

'We all suffer,' retorted the dancer.'And the worst cause of our suffering is a man like you who thinks he can carry an ointment pot about with him to heal the wounds he makes. Haven't you even got the courage of your callousness? Haven't you even got the courage to face the fact that you are utterly and profoundly selfish? Must you go on slipping out of it and evading it and covering it up, to the very end?'

'I don't slip out of anything,' protested Richard. 'I wish I did!'

'It's because of this that your poetry is so bad,' she went on. 'It's only your ingrained conceit that makes you think it anything but thoroughly bad. You deceive yourself far more deeply than you deceive anyone else.'

Richard's face assumed the dogged obstinate look of a much persecuted mule, and this seemed to hound her on to further malicious stabs.

'You talk of bringing your philosophy into your poetry. My good man, you must realize once for all that your poetry is a fraud, a fake, a piece of rank charlatanism. You're the very last person to be a poet. The whole business is an elaborate edifice of humbug!'

'If my poetry isn't real,' said Richard, 'nothing in my existence is real.'

'Nonsense! Stuff and nonsense! You've got a sound critical faculty. You're receptive enough. You're capable of doing very good honest literary work. But you're so ridiculously proud that you pretend that all this is nothing. You must be the great poet of the age – or you will sulk in your tent and do nothing at all.'

'You are most frightfully unfair,' he began. 'No one can tell for certain where their power is until they—'

'Until they stop lying,' she interrupted. 'Don't you understand that art is a thing connected with character?'

'I thought it was a thing connected with imagination,' said Richard sulkily.

The great dancer fixed her eyes on a sailing ship far out to sea.

'God knows what it is, my dear,' and she sighed deeply. 'I only know it is a thing we seem unable to get into our life with each other. But it may be my fault quite as much as yours. I'm sorry, Richard. I'm sorry I've been bad. Shall we go back?'

He took her hand and kissed it and they began slowly retracing their steps. They were silent. With the splash of the long waves breaking beside them an infinite sadness gathered about their hearts, the kind of sadness which no argument can destroy and no hope can lift; the sadness which is of the very nature of life itself, when the distractions of desire and curiosity are for the moment in abeyance.

They had not moved far in the direction of the town when they heard themselves called by name from one of the high ridges of sand overgrown with grass that separated them from the marshes on the left. They stopped and turned. Two figures rose from a hollow place in the sand dunes and came running down the slope towards them.

Catharine's extravagant greeting of Elise was a reminder to Richard of how small a place in the great world he himself held in comparison with his companion. Elise had never met Karmakoff; and before she condescended to notice Richard at all, the enthusiastic girl eagerly introduced him to the dancer.

The encounter between Elise and Ivan was like the encounter between two feline animals of the same jungle. They watched each other furtively, measuring one another's strength and weighing in the balance one another's magnetism. Her accumulated anger against Richard made the imperious dancer ready for any kind of an emotional plunge; the womanish eyes of the cynical Russian, with their strange green lights, dilated in amorous reciprocity to the furtive challenge which she gave him.

Poor impassioned Catharine had already wearied him with her unsophisticated emotion. She had irritated him, too, by queer fits of deep depression in which she had returned to her childish scruples, and incidentally she had made the situation more strained by constant references to Roger Lamb.

When the four of them moved on together towards the town, it appeared inevitable that Karmakoff and the dancer should outstrip the others – vehemently and passionately absorbed, as it seemed, in what they had to say to one another.

'One day you'll be coming to Moscow,' Ivan remarked, among other things. 'Our people ought to have you. You're precisely what they *must* have. They'll give you authority over our whole art movement, which owes so much to your genius already.'

'There's nothing left now in the world except art,' sighed Elise.

'And the only way to get anything beautiful,' added Karmakoff, 'is to put an end to the economic struggle.'

'Can that really be done?'

'It can be tried.'

'By force?'

'Why not?'

'But force only breeds force.'

'Words! my dear lady. It's force when you prune a tree, but what *that* produces is fruit.'

'It does me good to talk to you. I don't know why.'

'I have waited long to make your acquaintance. We were destined to meet, sooner or later.'

'You've seen my work?'

'I've seen you nine times this season.'

'Do you like me better when I'm Greek or when I'm Christian?'

'You are never wholly either. You are a woman Dionysus.'

'When a woman Dionysus really does appear it will bring all our misery to an end.'

'By bewitching us into thinking it isn't misery?'

'By undermining misery with tragedy.'

'Ah! you separate those two; so do I. That's where Cathy and I quarrel. She enjoys the sentiment of misery and loathes its boredom. I am never miserable.'

'What are you, Ivan Karmakoff?'

'I am never happy. I know that. And I am never unhappy. I am a person who works and plays.'

'Is our dear Catharine part of the play?'

'You know the answer to that, or you wouldn't ask it! Catharine and I belong to two different worlds.'

'And *we* belong to the same world?'

'You will always be a symbol to me; of what I live for.'

'And that is?'

'To bring a little order into chaos.'

'I am the most chaotic person in creation.'

'You are the greatest artist in America.'

'What's the use of being that if no one understands me?'

'Doesn't Storm understand you?'

'I'm afraid my Richard lives in the same world as your Catharine. Poor darlings! They are both children.'

'Where and when have you and I talked like this before?'

'In Nineveh probably, or in Carthage.'

'Do you believe that kind of thing?'

'I didn't – an hour ago.'

'Don't bring me into your play, my friend. I belong to your work.'

'You belong to the object of my work.'

'Where did you get those woman's eyes from? I shall think of them when I dance next week.'

'Neither of us is pure woman or pure man. That's why we understand each other.'

'What are we?'

'We're messengers of the forgotten gods.'

'We ought to give the password, then – the secret sign.'

'We've given that already.'

'Have we? Without knowing it?'

'We are messengers. We know nothing.'

'I thought when I first saw you just now, that you were the most brutal materialist I'd ever met.'

'I thought you were the most unhappy woman I'd ever met.'

'Now we have been flung together we must say everything.'

'And prove our kinship?'

'And make the sign of the meeting of messengers.'

'And leave our play for a day and a night?'

'How can we do that, Ivan Karmakoff?'

'Dare you, if I dare? An interlude, a resting place.'

'I thought you were the most cynical realist I'd ever seen.'

'I thought your mouth had the look of a thing hunted by dogs; a torn mouth, a bleeding mouth, a mouth of suffering.'

'Did you try to imagine what it would be like to heal that hurt?'

'I imagined nothing. I knew that I had been sent for that.'

'Because of our both being messengers?'

'Because of our purpose. Because of the clearing up of chaos.'

'What nonsense we've been talking, Ivan Karmakoff! These seagulls must think us the biggest prigs they've ever listened to.'

'We have to get used to being thought prigs – by seagulls. The wild geese up there would understand us.'

'No doubt they would! But I'm afraid our dear pair of tame geese back there wouldn't! To come to a practical question. How are we to manage? How are we to see a little more of each other?'

'Your new programme doesn't begin until next week, does it?'

'No, my friend. It doesn't.'

'When has Richard to go back?'

'Tomorrow. But oh, dear me! let's have none of this manoeuvring, you green-eyed savage! I'm not married to Richard and you're not married to Catharine. Let's go straight to our hotels, get my things and your things and take the train back to New York.'

'And leave letters explaining everything?'

'And leave letters explaining *nothing*! What's the use of living in a modern city if you cannot live in a modern way? We'll treat it simply as a joke. We'll write humorously. It is a joke, you know. Why shouldn't we go back to New York together? Richard has been telegraphing his wife that he was with you and Catharine. Well! He *will* be with Catharine!'

'And he'll go back with her to Nelly?'

'Oh *you* know the lady too? I've just met her. She's as pretty as a picture. But oh dear me! *how* English the poor dear is!'

'I don't think our gods have given us any message to the English.'

'They've warned us to run away from them. And that's what we'll do.'

They both turned round at that, and surveyed the long line of sand and spindrift that lay behind them white and chilly, lit up by the November sun.

A darkly outlined breakwater, about a mile away, broke the line of their vision. Their companions had evidently not yet arrived at that point. The two reckless ones had walked so quickly during their strange dialogue that they were already out of reach of pursuit.

'You're sure you won't worry about Catharine?' remarked Elise as they made their way up from the sands to the board-walk above.

'Not if you don't worry about Storm,' retorted Karmakoff.

They exchanged a glance of intimate understanding and allowed their eyes, which certainly had a queer resemblance in colour and expression, to meet and hold each other's gaze.

'The world would say we were following a funny road to our purpose,' murmured the woman, as they threaded their way through the crowd.

'You're thinking of what I said about reducing chaos,' responded the man. 'But it's only when you've got that ingredient in your own veins and are using it with your brain that you can do anything. To bottle up chaos doesn't help. It has to be ridden on and bitted and bridled. Most people's minds are burial grounds of that kind of thing, sprinkled with dead flowers. We're not leaving our friends for the sake of pleasure. We're leaving them for the sake of our work. We need one another at this juncture, Elise. Perhaps, later, it will be different!'

Again their eyes met and clung together in a long mysterious questioning look. And after that they both were silent.

'Perhaps later it will be different!' the dancer repeated under her breath; and there awoke within her a sickening envy of that rare company of faithful souls who have the power of loving once and not again.

Then as the great fantastic hotel loomed above them, like the dream palace of some mad king of Thule, the old Dionysian mood surged up once more. 'I've found him at last!' she whispered to herself. 'The free spirit worthy of me. It will be easy enough if he loves me. But if I love him – let him beware!'

And in her heart she caught a strain of that southern music to which she was wont to dance when the northern harmonies grew too heavy for the fire within her.

A couple of hours later Richard stood in the hallway of the Hotel Ransom watching Catharine read Karmakoff's letter.

As he saw that tall willowy figure shiver from head to foot and bend and sway under the blow, he thought within himself quite suddenly – *We are all wrong, we irresponsible ones! Suffering goes deeper than joy and to save from suffering is better than to give pleasure.*

When the girl turned to him at last, mechanically crumpling up the wicked note in her hand, the look upon her face went to his heart as nothing in his whole life had ever done before. For Catharine had nothing of Nelly's pride, and to see her inarticulate suffering, nakedly exposed before him, made him hate the whole business of love and the whole system of the world in which such things were possible.

It was even worse when the girl tried to smile at him, tried to take the thing lightly. She was so smitten that not a tear came to her eyes. She just swayed backwards and forwards and smiled, her hands fumbling weakly, foolishly, meaninglessly, at the piece of paper which she held. She kept thrusting it into the envelope and taking it out again; and her words tripped over one another blunderingly, confusedly, like the words of a person in a fever.

Richard experienced such a pang of pity for her that he felt as though his whole philosophy of life would be different from that moment. 'Damn these cruelties!' he said to himself. 'This can't be endured!'

They had gone first to his own hotel, thinking to find them there. His feelings when he read Elise's letter had, even then, been swallowed up in his concern for Catharine.

The link between himself and the dancer had been already stretched to the breaking point. *I must get her back to New York at once*, he thought. *I must take her to Nelly.* His naïve dependence upon his wife's powers of comfort did not arouse any sense of humour in him, did not appear to him as singular under the circumstances.

He could be cynical and sardonic enough sometimes, but at other times he behaved with the innocent egoism of a spoilt child. Elise being disposed of, his natural instinct was to go straight back to Nelly. *She need never know, except in vague suspicion*, he thought, *how things worked out down here.*

Catharine was like wax in his hands during the rest of that day. She let him help her pack her things; she let him convey her to the station and place her by his side in the compartment, without a word.

He wondered, as he saw her lean sideways against the edge of the window, whether she wasn't half-asleep, whether indeed she hadn't swallowed some sort of drug. Once, however, when by a sudden movement forward he obtained a glimpse of her face he knew that she was only too completely in possession of her faculties. It was clear to him then that it was the blow to her heart which had deprived her body of all muscular resistance.

Chapter 20

It was about nine o'clock in the evening when Richard and Catharine mounted the steps of the Charlton Street house.

Richard left the girl leaning helplessly against the wall of the passage, as if she were an umbrella or a stick that he had been carrying and, quickly turning the handle of the door, he entered the room.

The place was dark except for the light of a lamp in the street opposite. *Nelly's gone to bed*, he thought. *But I must wake her, as Catharine's here.* He could not help experiencing a certain cowardly relief at the girl's presence, as it was an obvious raft of escape from immediate explanations. He struck a match and lit the gas. Then he went back into the passage. Leading in Catharine by the hand he placed her in that same big armchair where he had first made her acquaintance.

The girl looked at him out of hollow miserable eyes and murmured Nelly's name.

'Hush! my dear!' he whispered. 'It's all right. I'll wake her now and she'll look after you.'

He opened the door of the bedroom and went in. The bed was unoccupied, and the empty room, left in perfect order, mocked him with its neatness as if with a leer of derisive contempt.

He went up to the dressing-table, entirely bare now of Nelly's brush and comb and bottle of eau-de-cologne.

In the place of these things was a letter addressed to himself in Nelly's girlish hand.

He returned to the living-room where Catharine was sitting exactly where he had left her, her eyes fixed in vacancy.

Standing under the gas burner he opened the note and read it. It ran as follows: 'If you only hadn't lied to me it would have been different. Why did you do it, Richard? How *could* you do it? I should have thought – but what's the use of saying any more? If neither for my sake nor the child's you can't give up your pleasures, it's no use pretending that you care for us. By the time you read this I shall be on the sea. Robert is sailing on the same ship. He will take me to Mrs Shotover's. He wants me to divorce you, but I shall never do that. He is very angry with you and unhappy. I think I am myself too sad about everything to be angry ever again. Goodbye Richard. When you get tired of this person, as I know you will very soon, you will be sorry you forced me to leave you. I have to think of my child and I couldn't endure it any more. You will never be able to understand what a woman feels. Perhaps it isn't your fault altogether. I am afraid I must ask you to send me a *little* money, at regular intervals? I shall be happier when I see the Downs. Don't be afraid I shall do anything rash. I feel only too clear-headed. It is the Village Laundry, not Ebstein's, who come for our washing now. Goodbye. I am all right. The voyage won't hurt me.'

The letter was signed 'Nelly' and there was a postscript to it containing one sentence: 'Please keep in touch with Catharine, for the girl has no friends.'

Richard carefully folded up this letter and put it in his pocket. Then he took it out of his pocket and read it again very slowly. Then he carried it to the chimneypiece and placed it under a book.

He noticed casually as he did this that the elemental sprites, who accompany every human disaster with their satiric commentary, had arranged that the book under which he placed it should be the *Vita Nuova*. Well did he recall the romantic nonsense he had written for Nelly on the flyleaf of that book. But it served very well as a letter weight just then to keep that particular letter from blowing away!

He walked up and down the room several times trying to visualize Nelly on the ship. He felt no jealousy of Canyot at that moment. He felt only relief that his wife was not alone. But how he longed for her; for her voice, her look, her silent reproaches even! He had never longed so much for the presence of any human being.

At last he stopped in front of Catharine. What was to be done with the stricken girl?

'Nelly has gone away,' he said. 'I've treated her badly and she's gone away. She's sailed for England.'

Catharine stared at him with a puzzled uncomprehending look. 'Nelly's left you?' she murmured.

'Yes – devil that I am! She's treated me as I deserve and has gone off.'

'Not alone?'

'No, Robert Canyot's with her.'

The absence of anything in his tone except self-abasement seemed to rouse Catharine's pity.

'Poor Richard!' she murmured and stretched out one of her long arms towards him. That naïve gesture of sympathy from one so cruelly hit herself was too much for Richard's self-control. He found himself on his knees by the side of the girl's chair struggling with violent sobs that shook his whole frame. Still tearless herself Catharine smoothed his hair caressingly with her fingers. An on-looker would have been made aware at that moment of what an immense fund of passionate human feeling lay beneath that queer Greenwich Village smock-frock, coloured like a Matisse painting.

He rose to his feet in a little while, relieved by his outburst. One of the cynical demons that were always ready to whisper un-pardonable things in his ear commented with sardonic interest on the fact that somewhere within his consciousness there was an actual throb of self-congratulation that he was still able to shed tears.

The question now presented itself vividly to his mind: what was to be done with Catharine?

The girl had crossed her knees and clasped her hands round them, and now sat staring blankly in front of her.

It struck his inner consciousness how queer a thing it was, this pathology of wounded love! How it seemed to be something imper-sonal, like a madness that fell upon a person out of the air, quite independently of the value or worth or nature of the object for which it vexed itself.

He looked at his watch. It was already past ten. 'Shall I see you back to your flat?' he said, touching the girl's hand.

The idea of her room in Thirty-fifth Street, full of little objects associated with her friendship for Ivan, brought such a woebegone expression into Catharine's face that he wished he had not suggested such a thing. But what else was to be done? He hesitated for a moment, looking helplessly round the apartment. Then he said, 'All right. The best thing you can do is to stay right here, where you are. You shall sleep in Nelly's room and I'll pull my own bed into this room. Nobody will be any the wiser. And after all what does it matter? We're both past fussing about things of that sort!'

She seemed relieved at his suggestion; and he got a grim satisfaction from the thought of that postscript in Nelly's letter – *Look after Catharine. She has no friends.*

Having settled this matter he proceeded to drag the second of the two beds into the sitting room. Then he lit the gas under the stove so as to make them both some tea. He was touched by finding that Nelly had stocked their small cupboard with more provisions than he had ever seen there before.

He managed with difficulty to persuade the unhappy girl to swallow some oatmeal biscuits and a raw egg made palatable by the last drops of his brandy flask. These things and a cup of milkless tea formed their melancholy supper.

It was a curious situation, not likely to recur in either of their lives – sitting thus alone together beneath the same roof, while the man and the woman who had thrown them aside were no doubt drinking Olympian drinks in the sumptuous apartment so well known to Richard.

'I shall have to get another job,' said Catharine wearily. But Richard was relieved to hear her say even that; still more relieved when she didn't refuse the cigarette he proffered.

'How lucky Roger is to be safe out of the whole thing!' she remarked after a long silence.

'Well! we shall all be out of it before so very long!' responded Richard.

'I've got some morphia tablets in my room,' she added.

He laid his hand upon hers. 'You mustn't talk like that, Catharine,' he said sadly. 'You'll have to see it through, just as I shall. Sometimes I feel as if the whole mad business were a sort of dream and that when we wake up we shall be quite free from all this misery.'

'Do you mean death?'

'Yes. Death – but something else too. Anyway we should quite spoil what I mean by killing ourselves.'

The girl sighed. 'I wish I could understand better what is underneath it all. If there were any point in it, any purpose in it, it would be easier.' She added desperately, 'I would give my life for Ivan.'

'I have a sort of idea,' Richard went on, 'that after death all the people who care for each other come together without any of this wretched jealousy.'

'I shall never bear to see him again, or her either!' cried Catharine Gordon.

'Some day,' said Richard, 'it may be completely different with these complications. The human race may learn to disentangle itself from its flesh and blood. It may learn to love without wanting to possess.'

'Do you feel like that now?' she asked him suddenly.

'No, no, my dear; I'm far below such feelings. Don't talk about me. I sometimes wonder whether I've got a heart at all.'

She looked at him with a puzzled frown and he fancied that she had been hurt by his words as if by something clumsy and banal.

'You must never say a thing like that to anyone who loves you,' she said earnestly.

Richard smiled. 'Why not, my dear?'

Her answer was a surprise to him. 'Because it's unfair; because it's mean and cunning!'

There was a considerable flicker of annoyance at that moment flung across 'the lake of his mind'. Had the girl managed to pierce the core of a very subtle form of self-complacency and vanity? Her words certainly broke up Richard's mood of superior protective strength. In some profoundly recondite way they gave him the sensation of being exposed. The feeling he derived from this sensation was not a pleasant one; he experienced that kind of unharmonious shock from it which, as he had noted on other occasions, gave a severer prod to his life illusion than anything else.

'I expect you are right, Catharine,' he muttered, resuming his walk up and down the room. He made that time a genuine effort to break the crust of egoism which imprisoned his soul. Yes, the girl was undoubtedly right. That vague self-accusation 'I have no heart' was only too obvious an example of a mental trick he was always playing himself – an unctuous salve of moral evasion with which he covered up drastic issues!

His analysis of his real inmost reaction to all these events revealed to him that he had been all the while, secretly and without any self-forgetful suffering, dramatizing his situation. He had been making it all a part of one long stream of not wholly intolerable occurrences, in the flowing tide of which the figure of Nelly herself, the figures of Elise and Catharine and all the rest, were there to be exploited, were there to be contemplated subjectively, as scenes in the human play which after all remained his play – whereof he was not only an actor on the stage but an appreciative critic in the gallery!

His thoughts whirled confusedly through his brain now as he paced that little room, his guest's purple stockings and white sandshoes mingling with first one mental image and then another.

It cannot, he thought, be altogether selfish and contemptible to dramatize one's life and to detach one's self from it. Nelly never does that. Catharine never does. But surely Elise must do it, or she couldn't put so much art into her dancing. How is it then that I annoy Elise so much with the way my mind works? Why does she despise my poetry so? Poetry must, surely, be detached from a person's life and yet be the residuum of a person's life. Am I hopelessly inhuman and unnatural in all this?

Suddenly it occurred to him, as quite a new discovery, that it was queer that instead of being reduced to hopeless misery by his wife's departure he could occupy himself like this in cold-blooded abstract analysis!

Was it that, at the back of his mind, he felt confident that he had only to return to England, to receive Nelly's forgiveness and settle down happily with her as before? Or was it really that *nothing*, beyond extreme immediate physical pain, could break up the crust of his indurated egoism? Was he actually wanting in some normal human attribute; and did everything that occurred to him approach his consciousness through some vaporous veil like a thick sea mist? He began naïvely to wonder what the great artists of the world were like in these complicated human relations. It occurred to him that they must have the power of transfiguring the results of analysis and forcing the issue by the use of some sort of creative energy which the gods had completely denied to him.

Where was *his* place in the world then, he who was neither a normal human being nor a creative genius? Was he doomed for ever to live this wretched half-life, neither deeply happy nor deeply unhappy, cheated in some mysterious way of the prerogative of being born a man? He looked at the long tenuous figure of the young girl in the chair; and he felt, for one swift moment, as some fabulous *merman or neckan* might feel, as it craved for the human soul that had been denied it by destiny.

When Catharine was at last safely in bed in Nelly's room and he had kissed her goodnight and turned out her light, he felt amused to note how the mere fact of sleeping in the sitting room gave him a curious pleasure.

He lay for a long time before he went to sleep, smoking one cigarette after another, enjoying in spite of his conscience a certain primitive and heathen satisfaction at being alive at all in this mad complicated world; at being able to say still, with the royal villain in the famous drama – '*Richard is Richard – that is I am I.*'

His mind called up the image of Roger Lamb as he had last seen him. And with the thought of the dead boy he found himself re-calling an interview which he himself had had with a great Paris specialist, when his heart troubled him in earlier days. 'Any ex-treme physical strain may finish you off,' the great man had warned him. He had thought of that verdict during his fit of exhaus-tion at the stage-door of Elise's theatre; he thought of it again now as he began to grow drowsy. 'That would be a better way than morphia,' he said to himself.

Chapter 21

Richard slept long and heavily that night. Once he woke with a start, in complete bewilderment as to where he was and with a feeling that someone had called him by name. He sat up and listened; but if it had been a cry from Catharine she did not repeat it. He heard no sound from her room.

After that he fell into complete unconsciousness till Catharine herself aroused him with the news that breakfast would be ready in ten minutes.

The girl looked lamentably hollow-eyed as they sat down op-posite each other. He surmised from her appearance that she had hardly slept at all; and this, in his morning mood of malicious irritation, made him almost angry with her. What right had she to punish him with a miserable face like that, when he had turned out of his room to make her comfortable?

Just as he was leaving for the office she suddenly said, 'Would you like me to get your supper for you or shall I go away when I've washed up?'

The idea of coming back to a lonely room struck his mind at that moment as the one thing he couldn't endure. 'Will you do that?' he rejoined eagerly. 'Here's a couple of dollars.' And he placed the two notes on the table. 'Then we can manage again as we did last night,' he added. 'I don't suppose either of us cares for Greenwich Village gossip.'

So it was brought about that these two took up their queerly assorted and entirely chaste domicile together.

Catharine reverted to her former method of earning a little money by embroidering Russian smocks which she sold at one of the numerous little art shops which abounded in that vicinity. Richard sent off many passionate and penitent letters addressed to Furze Lodge and by every weekly mail received a brief acknowledgement from Nelly of the small sums he punctually dispatched to her.

He worked more assiduously at the office of *The Mitre* than he had ever done before, receiving sometimes a bonus from the editor for work done beyond his original contract.

But he was all the while anxiously looking out for some means of rehabilitating his literary fortunes. He had constantly in his mind the idea of sailing for England; but it was obviously impossible to do so until he had obtained some permanent income. He could not see himself arriving in Sussex without a cent. To present himself before his wife, not to speak of Mrs Shotover, penniless as well as disgraced, was more than he could contemplate.

The weeks and months dragged on and the innumerable circles of people in that cosmopolitan city began in their various ways to prepare to celebrate the far-off event which for a minority meant the birthday of a God, while for the majority it signified parties and presents and desperate attempts to defy Prohibition.

The afternoon of Christmas Eve found Catharine occupied in a pathetic effort to adorn their bachelor apartment with some sprigs of holly and mistletoe, purchased in Jefferson Market.

The girl had seen nothing of Karmakoff since that day at Atlantic

City, and as far as she knew Richard had seen nothing of Elise. Her receptive nature, passively docile to the will of fate, had slipped insensibly into a sort of trance-like domesticity, the seclusion and regularity of which had a healing effect upon her wounded spirit. It was the first time in her life that she had felt herself to be *necessary* to another human being. The naïve way in which the incompetent Richard clung to her ministrations was a profound solace to her self-respect. Nothing but the feverish activity of that whirlpool of human effort which seethed and eddied around them could have enabled their association to pass uncriticized.

They invited no one to the flat and they went to see no one together. The few separate encounters they did have with former acquaintances led to no sort of inconvenience to either of them; and if one Greenwich Village *habitué* remarked to another that Cathy Gordon had 'moved downtown', the worst commentary that resulted was some such remark as, 'They say she's having an affair with that fellow in Charlton Street whose wife ran away.'

Richard did not mention to Nelly in any of his passionate love letters that he and her friend were living under the same roof. The instinct that prevented him doing this at first was an entirely unconscious one. It was Catharine herself who converted it into a deliberate and conscious repression.

'I'd rather you didn't say anything to Nelly about my being with you. She wouldn't understand it. And why should we agitate her unnecessarily when we know that if she *did* understand it she would be quite satisfied?'

Richard, amused at this innocent piece of sophistry, had not worried further about the matter. Since his conscience was clear, let the affair go! He had grown accustomed to Catharine's companionship. He had got fond of the girl; and his renewed loyalty to Nelly did not seem in any way impinged upon by this relationship. If any sort of scruple did flicker for a moment across his mind it was constantly being quelled by Nelly's reiterated requests that he should look after Catharine. Well! Catharine was looking after him. So all was as it should be!

On this Christmas Eve, while the young girl was standing upon a chair, holding in her hand two large bunches of holly with the intention of fixing them behind a print after Watteau, she heard a sharp knock at the door.

She hurriedly jumped down and cried, 'Come in!'

To her amazement and indignation the door opened and admitted Elise Angel.

The dancer was wrapped in a black Spanish cloak which she promptly flung down upon a chair. She then quite calmly closed the door behind her and, folding her arms with a dramatic gesture, ejaculated the words, 'So it's as they told me! I didn't believe it. It seemed too funny to be true.'

'What seemed too funny to be true, Miss Angel?'

'That you and Richard should be living together.'

'We're *not* living together!'

'Well, that you should be here, then. It isn't for outsiders of course to inquire any further.'

'I'm expecting him back any moment; so unless you want to meet him I advise you to leave your message quickly.'

'*Mon dieu!* We *have* changed from our little devoted Cathy! Richard must have been telling you fine stories about me.'

'We've never spoken of you once. Not once. Will you sit down?'

The last words were uttered in a reluctantly softened voice. It was difficult in the presence of Elise Angel, even for a jilted rival, to keep up the role of moral indignation.

The dancer settled herself in the armchair and fixed upon Catharine a look so disarming that the young girl asked hurriedly, 'Can I get you anything, a glass of water?'

'No – no! child. I'm only a bit tired. Your friend has left me and sailed for Russia.'

Catharine Gordon turned pale and leant against the table. 'Sailed for Russia?' she gasped. 'When?'

'Oh several weeks ago. I ought to have come and told you before. We quarrelled before he went – of course.'

'He left you, too?'

Elise Angel smiled. 'Yes, my dear, he left me too! It seems that neither you nor I are very clever at keeping people. But you seem to have got Richard safely anyhow!'

'Have you come to take him away?'

'*Mon dieu!* little one, heaven forbid! But my impression is that our good Richard is pining for his wife. You know that pretty young person is going to have a child?'

'A child? He never told me!'

'I don't know why he *should* have told you, you funny thing, unless you're in love with *him* now.'

Catharine Gordon frowned at this and shook her head.

'Not yet?' repeated the dancer. 'You're just living – what shall I say – like brother and sister?'

The young girl coloured and nodded furiously.

There was a moment's pause during which the two women exchanged one of those indescribable glances which reveal without words so many things. Then the dancer stretched out her arms.

'Come and be friends again, you darling! We're both deserted now!'

The look which accompanied this gesture was too much for the generous-hearted Catharine. She slid down upon the arm of her rival's chair and hugged her impetuously.

'What you and I have to think about now,' said Elise Angel, 'is what we're going to do with our dear Richard. I caught a glimpse of him in the street the other day and he looked to me wretchedly thin.'

Catharine pouted like a child at this.

'I give him very good meals,' she said.

'I'm sure you do. But he's an Englishman, my dear, and English-men, whatever they may do in New York, pine for their rainy fields. We don't want to have to bury our Richard out here do we?'

'But he's got no money. He sends home nearly all he makes, as it is.'

'Well! We must get him the money. A thousand dollars would keep him going till he could get over to Paris. And once in Paris he'd soon pick up again. They know his value over there.'

'But – a thousand dollars!'

'It isn't so much as it sounds, you dear baby. Why, Pat Ryan lent me as much as that only two months ago! I mustn't go to him for this; but I could sell my pearl necklace.'

Catharine looked at her with tears in her eyes. A wave of vibrant sympathy flowed between the two.

'You dear!' cried the younger girl.

Elise smiled. 'You'd do the same for him. I'm not blind. You're one of those people, little Cathy, who put their genius into their heart, just as I put mine into my legs!'

Catharine looked at her thoughtfully. 'Yes, I *have* got fond of him. But that's because he's got so used to me, I expect. It's a new thing to me to be really *wanted*.'

The dancer put her arm around her waist. 'Well! now we're friends again, I may tell you that *I* want *you* most abominably. So you see my cunning design! I pack off our good Richard to his wife and have you all to myself again! For you *will* come back to me now, child, won't you? No! don't shake your head. You *must* – I can't be deserted by everyone.'

Catharine looked wonderingly into those mysterious eyes which were neither grey nor blue nor violet nor green, and yet were all those colours together.

'If you're very good and very nice, I *may* teach you to dance,' said Elise Angel.

Catharine leapt to her feet at those words and clapped her hands. 'Not really? Do you think I could? That would be simply heaven! I used to dream of that when I was a little girl. And to be taught by *you*!' She snatched at one of the dancer's hands and kissed it fervently.

'Meanwhile,' said Elise, 'I've got to go round and pick up a thousand dollars.' She rose slowly from the armchair and laid her hand on her Spanish cloak. 'Richard won't, I suppose, be too proud to take it when I've got it?' she said, as Catharine arranged the cloak round her shoulders.

Once more they exchanged that curious enigmatic glance with which women converse without the necessity for words.

'I don't think so,' responded the girl smiling. 'I don't think he is very proud – in *those* things.'

'Well! goodbye, you dear child. I'll bring the money round to you in a day or two. By the way, why don't you bring him to see me dance tonight? I'll tell them at the box office to keep you good seats. But just as you like of course. It won't matter if you don't come. Goodbye!' And she ran lightly down the narrow stairs and let herself into the street.

That last word of Elise's had a little clouded Catharine's pleasure.

Somehow she felt reluctant to sit with Richard in a prominent seat at that theatre.

She left her pieces of holly lying on the table and, sitting down with her hands around her knees, fell into deep meditation.

Just very faintly, across the most remote portion of her consciousness, there flickered a vague shadow of suspicion. It was scarcely articulate. It had no definite shape or form. But like a small cloud on the horizon it spoilt the complete harmony of her thoughts. Before Richard's return, however, she had recovered the balance of her normal generosity and had driven this little cloud altogether out of her mind. The pieces of holly with their red berries were now adorning the 'Watteau' print and the table was decorated with copper-coloured chrysanthemums, candied ginger, New England grapes and a bottle of California wine.

He arrived at half past six. He was already in better spirits than he had been in for some long while, and the sight of his 'young monk', as he called her, with this festive background gave him a thrill of pleasurable excitement.

They were halfway through their meal, drinking wine and tea in shameless propinquity, and laughing with most keen amusement over what Richard called 'crackers' and she called 'bon-bons', when Catharine broached the subject of Elise's visit and her offer of tickets for that night.

It was only her sense of honour that made her refer to this latter point, as she herself would have greatly preferred to continue, in the quiet of their own *ménage*, an evening so auspiciously commenced. But her hope was that Richard would, as she said to herself, 'turn the thing down'. Whether it was the California wine, however, or a sudden craving to see his ivory goddess dance her Dionysian dance on this 'night of all nights in the year', he leaped eagerly to meet the suggestion, and at once began to hurry through the rest of the meal.

Catharine was surprised at herself over the vexation which this interruption of their little feast caused her; but she fell in gallantly with his mood and while they were washing up the things together the effort she had been making, ever since Elise first appeared, to be 'good' in the whole affair was rewarded by one of those rare inspirations of disinterested happiness which selfish people never know and which are by no means as frequent in the experience of the unselfish as ideal justice would demand.

Thus it happened that when, an hour later, they found themselves seated side by side in the new Stuyvesant Theater there was hardly a more excited or more carefree pair among all that holiday-thrilled Bohemian audience.

The new Stuyvesant was in every respect worthy of the great artist. It had been designed by a young acquaintance of Roger Lamb; Richard and Catharine whispered to each other a mutual recognition, as they looked round them, of the passionate theories of their dead friend now realized for the first time. The decoration was not only simple; it was austere. It was rigid and reserved in a manner suggestive of Byzantine work. There was about it something of that kind of ritualistic imagination which, perhaps erroneously, the modern world has come to name 'archaic'.

Richard could not help becoming conscious that here, in the middle of this orgy of raw newness, there had been evoked something more suggestive of the passion of the human spirit ransacking the remote past and steering into the unborn future than anything in London or Paris. He recalled Karmakoff's casual remark about certain affinities between Russia and America; and he whispered to Catharine that Roger Lamb's idea of a revival of real *mythology*, of something that was both adventurous and religious, was actually present in what they looked at now.

The dancer's inevitable black curtains were there; but they were there for the first time as an organic portion of a setting that might have been designed for some ancient classic ritual, some real worship of the Platonic idea of beauty, envisaged as a palpable presence. What the new Stuyvesant represented was preeminently an achievement of youth, of youth coming sternly and resolutely into its own, after the deadly disillusionments of the recent war. The actual fabric of the building itself – its contours, its curves, its nobly designed blank spaces – was all part of a musical rhythm which only reached its consummation when Elise began to dance.

It seemed to both Richard and Catharine that Elise had acquired yet more subtle art since they had last seen her. Her first dance was one to a certain musical fantasy written by a little-known Russian composer who was at that moment coming into fame in Revolutionary Moscow. Richard recognized Karmakoff's influence over the dancer in this choice; and he recognized it without the least touch of jealousy.

There was indeed something about this whole Christmas Eve performance that lifted him as it evidently lifted the girl by his side into a region where personal and possessive instincts had no place. Richard felt ashamed of himself, of his own inadequate and chaotic work, in presence of this achievement. He felt ashamed of himself that he had allowed this thing, this great new creation, to be born without his knowledge. The quiet cynical Roger, the inscrutable Ivan, his own ivory goddess, had together produced something, through the medium of an American boy of whose very name he was ignorant, which put his whole life's intention to shame!

While he had been trying to detach himself from life's flood and to see the mystery in large and flowing outlines, these alien spirits had plunged into the stream and had moulded those evasive waters themselves into vast stern human shapes of exultation and grandeur.

What he recognized as he glanced over that audience of cosmopolitan enthusiasts was that here in this new world, in this turbulent city of youth, was an opportunity for the old human passion for beauty such as the earth had never before known. The crudity and rawness of the crushing materialism around that bold experiment gave it an angry and free power which the very mellowness of more civilized places tended to undermine. But what struck him most of all in that thrilling hour was the amazing *anonymity* of the whole thing achieved by some unknown boy out of the far west whose youthful receptiveness was that of a reed played upon by the undying spirit of dead generations.

As he watched Elise dancing to a rising crescendo of hidden music, it seemed to him as though the whole architecture of that place, with every curve and space and line and mass and colour which it contained, melted into the rhythm of her movements and became part of the Dionysian passion which she evoked. By a wonderful touch of genius, beyond all his expectations, it seemed as though the youthful architect had allowed for the very audience there, and had given *it* also a part to play in the resultant harmony.

He experienced the sensation, and he was certain that everyone in the theatre experienced the sensation, of taking an actual part in some passionate ritual, some ritual that was itself a very dithyramb of exultant protest against all that was base, gross, possessive and reactionary amid the forces of the world.

Thus he became more vividly conscious than ever of what he had always vaguely held; namely, that art is not something separate from life, but the premonition, reflected inhuman intelligence, of what nature is perpetually aiming at and never altogether reaching.

Elise danced a much larger variety of motifs than he had ever seen her bring together in one evening. She seemed bent on extracting something congruous to her spirit from the music of every race. Richard noted that there was one insistent mood running through the whole series on that night, a mood that was at once heathen and Christian, rebellious and sensual, yet full of a passionate faith.

In her grand finale the amazing woman certainly surpassed herself. Catharine was so wrought up that she clutched at Richard's hand and held it tightly in her own. An electric thrill of excitement passed like a spiritual vibration through the whole of the excited house.

Richard thought in his heart, *This is more than the work of Bernhardt or Eleanora Duse or Yvette Guilbert. This is on a level with Milton or Nietzsche!*

When it was all over and the great audience rose to its feet with one wild cry of applause Richard and Catharine raised their hands into the air and shouted, 'Elise!' in the same way no doubt as, at some similar festival, two platonic friends in ancient Hellas might have shouted '*Evoé!*' Their cry seemed perfectly natural to the ardent young persons about them, and it was caught up, and echoed from every quarter of the theatre.

At length the ovation was over and the two friends, in a state of tremendous excitement, were carried out with the rest of the crowd into the street. They both felt that they could not see Elise again that night. Even to touch her hand after what she had done for them would have seemed a profanation and banality.

They hardly spoke to each other as they made their way across the centre of New York to their own Seventh Avenue subway.

Before their train arrived at Houston Street, Richard, as was his wont when excited to such a pitch, mentally gathered up into one swift vision all the persons and events of his life's drama. He saw them, these events and these persons, all beautiful, all mysterious, all full of the magic of that Nameless One who, whether he were born child of Semele or child of Mary, had the power to turn the sordid tricks of chance into the music of an exultant rhythm that 'redeemed all sorrows'.

Richard followed the tall languorous figure of his companion up the narrow stairs to their room; and as soon as they stood alone facing one another there they seemed driven by the power of the impersonal emotion within them to gain relief for their feelings in each other's arms. Neither of them could be said to have been more responsible than the other for this disloyalty to Nelly. If anyone was to be held guilty it was the impassioned dancer who had put them both under so irresistible a spell that it seemed to bring with it its own plenary absolution.

The embrace they exchanged at that exalted moment was neither chaste nor unchaste. It was the genius of Elise as it had stirred the soul of the man – rushing to meet the same genius as it had stirred the soul of the woman!

Without any shame or remorse they drew back from one another and resumed their normal mood. And long before the clock in the Metropolitan Tower struck the dawn of Christmas Day the door was shut between them and they were monks again!

Chapter 22

It was early February. In the ditches on both sides of the narrow lane that led up from Selshurst to Furze Lodge the yellow celandines among their great cool leaves shone like stars seen through watery darkness.

In the smaller oak and hazel woods there were already a few early primroses out, throwing upon the moss-scented air of those shadowy places that faint, half-bitter sweetness which seems like the very spiritual body of the spring.

Richard had not wired from Southampton to tell his wife of his arrival, though he had written from New York to let her know the name of the ship. He only prayed that he might be lucky enough to find her alone; and it was this hope that led him to time his appearance to just that particular moment of after-lunch siesta, when it was the custom at Furze Lodge to retire to rest.

He had not been able to resist the temptation to snatch a moment *en route* in the nave of the familiar cathedral.

The sleeping crusader with the 'eternally praying hands' lay there unmoved and unchanged, his mailed feet upon the back of his marble hound.

Arriving straight from the piled-up snow of a great New York blizzard, the warm misty sunshine of the early English spring was like the breath of an amorous and beautiful god; as Richard came out from the cathedral and looked at the yellow and purple cro-cuses in the ancient gardens, that same indescribable sense of peace descended upon him which he had felt when, nearly a year ago, he had first set his eyes on Selshurst.

As soon as he left the secluded portion of that long West Hor-thing lane and emerged upon the open Downs he found the air as full of the singing of birds as it had been on the day when he discovered Littlegate. The songs of individual skylarks were lost in one ubiquitous chorus which seemed to descend upon the earth as if it were the voice of universal space, corresponding in the sphere of sound to infinite blueness in the sphere of colour.

His pulses were beating with a good deal more excitement than he had anticipated as he approached the lodge gates of Mrs Shotover's drive. But he felt confident of the result of his interview with his wife.

The flawless beauty of the day seemed an invincible omen of success; and he had in his notebook eight hundred and fifty dollars!

He rang the bell of the front door at precisely half past two o'clock – the hour of all hours when he deemed it most impossible for Mrs Shotover to be in a state of visibility.

He asked, in a purposely low voice, whether he might see Mrs Storm at once and he repeated his name in a whisper. The servant was apparently a stranger for she gave no particular sign of surprise and, ushering him straight into the well-known drawing room, closed the door discreetly behind her. Richard walked up and down in excited perturbation. His mind called up the image of Nelly. He thought of her child, and how it would be born before April was over, or at any rate in the beginning of May – exactly a year since he had first arrived in Sussex.

It would be wonderful to have a child of his own! If it were a girl he could call it after his mother; and if it were a boy, after his father. He was sure Nelly would be willing to leave the name in his hands! He supposed Canyot would have to be its godfather and Mrs Shotover its godmother. About those little matters he could afford to be generous!

How slow she was in coming! Had that confounded maid forgotten to announce him? Perhaps she too was resting, and they were reluctant to disturb her. Well! he could wait. She would probably be up and about before the lady of the house showed herself. He surveyed the teasing knickknacks and the incredible frippery of that early-Victorian shrine. Why was it that young English women in evening dress photographed so badly? He supposed they ought to be 'snapshotted' on the hunting field or in walking costume. They seemed to be all chin and forehead and shoulders and elbows when adorned for civilized intercourse!

Suddenly the door opened. He sprang forward with a cry of recognition on his lips, only to step back in cold dismay at the entrance of Mrs Shotover. The lady closed the door behind her and bowed stiffly.

'I can't think what your purpose can be,' she began, uttering the words very much as some pompous statesman of her youth might have addressed a recalcitrant delegacy, 'in forcing yourself into my house. You don't suppose for a moment, do you, that I can permit you to agitate my dear Eleanor by silly dramatic scenes? She has done with you, sir! Let me make that quite plain: she has done with you and your ill-bred vulgar behaviour.'

'But Mrs Shotover—'

'I won't argue with you. It is bad for me to get angry directly after lunch. Fortunately I had lunch late today because of that idiot of a vet, making such mistakes with Bobby, else I shouldn't have been able to tell you what I think of you.'

'I don't want to argue with you, Mrs Shotover. I want to see Nelly. I want to explain to Nelly that—'

'It's no use, my good man. I can see what you're after. You're after money. You're trying to blackmail us. But let me tell you at once that though I *have* made your wife my heir and left her everything, it's all tied up so that you cannot touch a penny of it! So there! The best thing you can do is to clear right off, before I am compelled to ring for Thomas.' And the lady with a grand toss of her head opened the door for him, making a vague movement with her hands as if she were about to drive off an intrusive fowl from a precious flowerbed.

Richard stepped out into the hall; but instead of meekly picking up his hat from the hall table he made a sudden bolt up the polished stairs and, arriving at the top where all the bedrooms were, called in loud violent tones the name of his wife.

One of the doors promptly opened and Nelly appeared. She had evidently just removed her dress, for she wore a long soft bedroom gown and her hair was loose about her shoulders.

She turned very white when she saw her husband and leaned against the side of the doorway uttering his name in a tremulous voice as if she had seen a ghost.

He rushed up to her and was about to embrace her when Mrs Shotover who had closely pursued him pushed her way in between them.

The old lady dragged the girl back into her room and held her tightly there with her thin arms, muttering all the while, 'The rascal! the bandit! the highwayman! the scoundrel! I'll have the law on him! Why doesn't Emma come? Where is Thomas?'

Richard, following them into the room, made a desperate appeal to Nelly. 'Send the woman away, sweetheart! Send her away! I must and will talk to you!'

Making a brave effort to gather up all her mental and physical energy, Nelly extricated herself from Mrs Shotover's clutches; turning sternly upon her, she said in a tone that the old lady seemed to recognize as not to be controverted, 'I must see him alone. You must leave us alone, please. You needn't be afraid. He is my husband. It will not be for long. Go now, dear, and leave us by ourselves.'

Like some eighteenth-century caricature of a defeated Juno, obedient to the commands of an irresistible daughter of Jove, the indignant old woman retreated, muttering vague threats. Nelly closed the door and turned the key in the lock. But she astonished Richard by waving him back when he tried to take her in his arms.

'My darling! my sweetheart!' he cried, making a second attempt to embrace her. Again she drew away from him and, wrapping herself closely in her dressing gown, clutched at it as if it had been protecting armour, her hands against her breast.

'Nelly!' he whispered with an intensity in his voice that betrayed an emotion which she had never noted in him before.

She looked straight into his eyes. 'Have you given up that woman?' she said, repeating the words as if in the presence of some formidable tribunal. 'Do you promise me that never, under any circumstances, you'll see her again?'

Richard murmured the word 'yes' and added hoarsely, 'I will never see her again without your consent.'

As soon as those words had been uttered Nelly's face changed and her whole body seemed to relax and unbend, as if relieved from an unbearable load.

She turned whiter still and, taking her hand away from his, clasped her fingers tightly together while her mouth also compressed itself into an almost hard expression.

'What do you mean?' she said.

'You needn't look so scared, my dearest one, it's all over now and thank God there are no complications!'

She bit her underlip; her eyebrows twitched; her fingers clasped one another so violently that they became white as her face.

If one of his demons had whispered into his ear some huge palpable lie at that juncture and had compelled him to utter it, the situation might still have been saved for both of them. But by a cruel irony in things the good in him – if such an instinct for confession *was* good – drove him so fast that no demon's help arrived.

'You know you told me to look after Catharine?' he said.

A tiny little red spot appeared on both her cheeks, but she only answered by a barely perceptible nod.

'Well, I did take care of her.' He gave a little uneasy laugh. 'And she took care of me. In fact we lived together in Charlton Street right up to the end. She slept in your room and I slept in the sitting room. We were always good – like two monks – and I left her much happier when I came away.

'Elise Angel is teaching her to dance; and I've no wish to see her again, any more than I want to see—'

The figure upon the bed sat up absolutely erect, like a lovely image of judgement. Her eyes were blazing with anger. She tried twice to speak, the indignation within her strangling the words. Then at last in a low cold frozen tone, 'I can't stand it. This is the end. I must ask you to go away at once please. You can write to me and I will answer your letters. But this is the end of everything between us. I can't live with you any more, Richard. Will you go quickly, please? No! No! Don't touch me! I can't bear it. I suppose you don't want to drive me insane, do you? No! No! I must ask you to go at once. Now – quickly! Before they come to answer this!'

And in a sort of panic terror lest he should touch her, she flung up her hand and pulled violently at the bell rope which hung above her bed.

But he did not attempt to touch her after that: he did not utter one single word. A kind of dizziness came over him and a dull knocking in his brain like the knocking of the hammer of fate. He heard the bell she had rung resound loudly in some room below. Like a man who has been shot through the heart but still retains his consciousness, he mechanically unlocked the door, opened it quickly, ran down the stairs and was out of the house and halfway down the drive before the shapes and figures of the external world renewed themselves in his brain.

Once clear of the Furze Lodge premises, his first mad flight, like the flight of Christian from the City of Destruction or like Adam from the gates of Paradise, subsided into a shambling and weary shuffle.

He became irritatingly aware of two little subordinate annoyances, which vexed him out of all proportion; vexed him as an exhausted patient after an operation might be vexed by a buzzing fly: he had left both his hat and his stick in Mrs Shotover's hall.

He missed his stick the worst of the two losses, as he never went out without it, and the absence of it gave him a most unpleasant feeling, as if he were disarmed, humiliated, not properly himself, and exposed to universal ridicule.

He missed his hat, because the sun was hot with that peculiar heavy relaxing heat of a warm day in February.

With slow, bewildered and drifting steps he made his way down the lane till it led across the open Downs. Other emotions began to succeed that first sense of blackness and the knocking of a great hammer inside his skull. He found himself making a kind of articulate appeal to his unborn child, crying upon it to intervene and soften its mother's harshness. He had the sensation of the child being actually conscious, and of its stretching out its arms to him, while Nelly sternly repressed it and forced it to be still.

Then out of the depths of his wretchedness his pride rose to the surface; and as he walked he pulled himself together and ceased shuffling and dragging his feet. He no longer held his mouth open like a panting dog. His eyes lost something of their hunted animal look.

Very gravely, knowing perfectly well what he did, he cursed the possessive instinct in women, their savage jealousy, their insatiable vindictiveness.

She can never have really loved me, he thought; *not as I have loved her. It must have been a kind of infatuation. Otherwise she couldn't treat me like this – after I told her everything; after I promised to give up everyone!*

It did not at that moment occur to him that compared with his own 'love', which was simple physical desire compounded with pure affection, *her* love was one of the vast terrible tragic forces quite beyond the balances of good and evil, which spring up out of the deepest levels of nature. It did not occur to him that if she had loved him *less*, she would have shown more generosity. He was in fact unconsciously comparing her primitive indignation not with his own masculine tenderness but with that 'love of the saints' which neither men nor women are often permitted to reach: the love that forgives – not out of a lower intensity of feeling but out of a deeper intensity. An emotion of that sort was as far beyond his own reach as it was beyond hers; thus when his pride began to rise to the surface, mingled with a bitter sensual memory of how beautiful she had looked in her anger, he found it possible to curse her as he strode forward.

I am alone again, he thought within his heart, *alone, alone, alone! I'll go straight back to Paris – Paris that is wise and indulgent, Paris that has always understood me . . . To be quite alone in the world, to fight for one's own hand, that is the only thing! I'll have a flat in the rue des Arts; and I'll know no living soul except gamins and grisettes. Damn these good women! They have hearts of marble. To be absolutely alone in the world, that is the thing! To love nothing but beauty! All these women, every one of them, are ready to destroy everything, to murder everything, in order to possess, to possess!*

But this first mood of his did not last long. His wife's fragile loveliness haunted him and the memory of how she had yielded to his kisses remained as a thing that troubled his blood. The image of her standing in that doorway, the familiar outlines of her figure changed by the presence of their child, came between him now and every curve and contour of the chalk hills around him.

As he grew weary with walking in that relaxing heat, his pride ebbed completely away. He had cursed her once; but he never cursed her after that. 'Nelly, my love, my darling, my true love!' he cried aloud.

More and more exhausted did he grow; there came a real humming and hammering in his brain and a sickening sense of dizziness. He had been too excited to do more than swallow a cup of tea that morning and he had eaten nothing. It was now well on in the afternoon.

By the time he reached the point where the open Downs lost themselves in the alluvial plain at their foot, he was so faint that it was with a deliberate and conscious effort that he took each individual step.

At length he stood still and looked hopelessly round. 'I can't do it,' he muttered. 'I can't do it.'

He sank down on the ground and rested for a few minutes. Then he got up again and tried once more; but the brief rest seemed to have made his legs weaker than ever and his head dizzier. 'Damn!' he muttered in a fit of childish irritation and tears of sheer physical exhaustion came into his eyes.

He looked back along the path by which he had come and forward towards the valley, hoping that some kind of cart or wagon might be in sight, which would help him to reach a farmhouse or a village.

The long white perspective of the empty chalk track offered no trace of any living or moving object.

He left the path then, and staggered across a ploughed field to where a high hedge of hawthorn and holly completely blocked his eastern view.

Reaching this hedge he sank down on the bank beneath it and gave himself up to a comatose acquiescence in whatever might befall.

Several hours passed over his head and the sun sank below a mass of clouds. It began to grow cold and damp; the inherent chilliness of the rain-soaked February earth making itself felt as soon as the heat of the sun was withdrawn.

Feeling very cold at last, for he had no overcoat, Richard managed to crawl through a hole in the thickset hedge into the field beyond.

The moment he tottered to his feet on the further side he knew where he was; the knowledge came to him with a sharp and bitter stab.

He was looking down into Nelly's Happy Valley, the very place where he had first made love to her!

He sat down again and with his arms round his knees gazed dreamily at the gorse bushes and the last year's bracken.

Another hour passed away while he sat there; staring patiently down upon the scene of that lovemaking of nearly a year ago.

Suddenly he saw a figure coming along the bottom of the valley, carrying some object in his hand.

Richard was roused at once to something like a flicker of hope. Well did he know that figure and what he carried! It was Robert Canyot with his easel frame and paint box returning after a day on the Downs. With a warm breath of reviving hope the thought crossed his mind – *Canyot will explain to her. She will listen to* him. It never occurred to his dizzy and exhausted brain that there was anything fantastic in thus begging his rival to act as his intermediary with his wife. There was something about Canyot that inspired this insane sort of confidence and Richard had always been careless and childish, if not blunt and insensitive, in matters of this kind.

He struggled to his feet and shouted wildly, waving his arms.

The young man's astonishment at the sound of his voice was obvious even at that distance but he saw him carefully put down the things he carried under a gorse bush and come striding up the hill towards him.

'How damnably faint I feel!' Richard said to himself. 'I pray I shan't collapse before I've sent him off to her!'

He sat down again to await the painter's arrival, drawing each breath with conscious deliberation, lest the dizziness which hovered over him should intervene before he made his appeal.

He remained seated when at last Canyot stood over him leaning on his stick.

'So you've come,' was the young man's laconic remark.

'Yes, I've come,' responded Richard. 'But I'm feeling damned ill at this moment. You haven't got any brandy on you, have you?'

Canyot shook his head.

'You look rather queer,' he muttered. 'You'd better come and stay the night with me. Do you think you can walk? You look awfully shaky.'

'Never mind how I look,' said Richard hurriedly. 'It's only want of food. I've been up there, Canyot. I've been up there and I've seen her. But I told her everything, you know, and she got very angry and sent me off. She sent me off, Robert, after I'd sworn that I wouldn't speak to Elise again.'

'What do you want me to do?' said Canyot suddenly.

Richard looked confused and miserable. A sort of hangdog expression of dilapidated helplessness came into his face.

'How did you know I wanted you to do anything?' he said with the ghost of a smile.

Canyot chuckled grimly. 'Pretty obvious!' he remarked. 'You don't shout to a fellow like that just for fun.'

'Yes, Robert,' Richard pleaded, fixing his eyes desperately upon him. 'I do want you to do something. I want you to go straight to Nelly – now, at once – and make her understand that I will be faithful to her, after this, for the rest of my life.'

'How can she trust you?' retorted the young man.

'I love no one else,' said Richard in a low voice.

Robert Canyot looked at him closely. 'It is an agreement between *us*?' he said. 'Between you and me?'

Richard nodded and held out his hand.

'Very well,' muttered the other after their hands had met. 'I'll go. I tried to get her to divorce you, but she wouldn't. She loves you, I suppose, God help her!' He gave a harsh little laugh. 'I'll go,' he added, 'but for heaven's sake, stay exactly where you are, so that I know where to find you! I'll be back in a couple of hours anyway. And look here, eat some of this.' Fumbling in his pocket he handed Richard a piece of cheese wrapped up in tissue paper. 'You look most confoundedly ill,' he said suddenly, as he prepared to force his way through the hedge; 'I hope you're not going to kick the bucket or anything, while I'm gone? Maybe after all I'd better get a cart for you from Littlegate before anything else. 'Richard's look of blank despair at this suggestion decided him, however, to do what he had promised.' After all,' he called back to him, as he forced a path through the hedge, 'West Horthing is as near as Littlegate and I can get a trap or something for you there! But you shall sleep with me tonight, whatever happens, and we'll have a talk. Don't move from where you are!'

Left to himself again Richard tried his best to eat the piece of cheese. The taste of it nauseated him. 'Oh, for just one drink of water,' he moaned aloud. As if in mocking answer to his prayer, the heavy clouds which had been working up with the growing darkness from where the sun had sunk, now burst over his head in torrents of rain.

He crept closer to the hedge for shelter; but the rain fell in such heavy floods that the hedge itself was soon penetrated through and through, and the continuous dripping from it became almost worse than facing the storm in the open. The man remained crouching there, his head whirling with strange wild thoughts, alternately full of hope and hopelessness.

At length, with a tremendous effort, he gulped down the cheese in three rapid mouthfuls. It nearly made him vomit, but his thirst was now partly quenched by the rain which drifted across his face and trickled down his cheeks. Although he found himself shivering with cold he began to feel stronger and less faint. His dizziness was as a matter of fact rapidly giving way to feverishness; and the more the fever grew upon him the more exalted and less wretched his mood became.

He must have remained under that hedge about half an hour when he became conscious of a melancholy bleating carried on the wind towards him from across the Downs.

Over and over again he heard it; and at last its reiteration got upon his nerves.

He rose up, stiff and shivering, from his huddled position, and listened intently. Yes – it came from the direction of West Horthing and it was quite different from the ordinary sound of a sheepfold. It was the cry of a solitary animal in great distress.

He crept through the hedge by the same hole he had come by, and when he rose to his feet on the other side he recognized that Canyot's bit of cheese had considerably restored to him his powers of movement. 'It was simply want of food,' he said to himself. 'What an idiot I was!'

It was almost completely dark. The driving rain, lashing against his face, was like the palpable force of some huge hostile elemental being.

He heard that pitiful bleating very clearly now, and he made his way across the ploughland, a little northward of where he had come, until he reached the turf of the Downs.

He could see no more than a few yards in front of him, but the bleating sound was so clear a guide that he had only, as it seemed to him, stumbled up the slope of the hill about a hundred yards when he came upon the cause of it.

He found himself in collision with some low wooden railings. Leaning over these he made out a shimmering whiteness below and then a grey level circle into which the rain hissed, water falling upon water. He had been long enough in Sussex to know exactly what he had found. It was one of those mysteriously constructed dew-ponds upon the secret of which whole books had been written, none of which really solved the problem of how the thing was made.

The books agreed upon one point, that whatever the secret of these places was, it had been totally lost.

There were no *new* dew-ponds. The circular basin upon which Richard now gazed through the darkness was about twenty feet in diameter. The whiteness which struck his eye was the slippery sloping surface of the pond's steep banks, made up of chalky mud.

In the summer such a place was the resort for all manner of Down birds, such as the wheatear and the whinchat, and at all seasons those banks were trodden into slippery mud by the great sheep flocks that came there to drink.

Richard remembered how Nelly's father had once brought him to one of these places, perhaps to the very one he was now scanning, and how the old naturalist had pointed out to him the great orange-bellied water lizards or newts, as they basked in the June heat at the top of the water.

Richard remembered lying once on his back below the circle of those banks, just a few days before they sailed for America, and how he had loved the effect of the white chalk against the blue sky.

He knew very well now, as he waited to make out exactly where that pitiful cry came from, what was the matter down there. It was some luckless sheep that had slipped down in the rain and darkness and was now imprisoned by those slippery banks.

It was some while before he could locate its exact position. When he did so he lost no time in sliding down the slope and in wading through the water until he got hold of the woolly derelict.

To get hold of it was one thing, however; to get it out of the pond was another matter.

Desperate were Richard's struggles to get the animal up those slippery banks. With the rain hissing into the pond below him and lashing his face in driving gusts as the wind whirled it round within that enclosed circle, he pulled and tugged and wrestled with that bleating mass of drenched wool until at last, with a superhuman effort, he got it safely over the brink.

He placed the thing on its feet, pushed it under the railings and clambered over them himself.

To his annoyance and surprise, instead of trotting off as he had expected, the animal fell over on its side, uttering once more a long-drawn pitiful bleat.

Now it became clear that either in its own struggles to escape, or in *his* struggles to help it, the unfortunate beast had broken or seriously injured one of its legs.

Richard sat down beside the bleating sheep and uttered a wild laugh. He lifted up his face to the sky and was met by the whirling downpour of merciless rain. He began to be alarmed lest Canyot's two hours should have passed and the young man, returning with some conveyance, should find him gone.

With this thought in his mind he took a few steps down the slope of the hill in the direction he fancied the ploughland to commence. But the miserable bleating of the wretched sheep, apparently realizing its desertion, brought him to a standstill. No! He could not leave it there – even to meet the messenger who brought the deciding of his fate.

Hurrying back to where the creature lay, he stood regarding it, uttering once more a wild chuckling laugh.

The fever in his veins was running high by this time, giving him an unnatural strength. His one instinct was to convey this animal to some sort of shelter, if it were only the inadequate shelter of that hawthorn hedge! Once there, if Canyot came with some kind of conveyance, both himself and the sheep could be rescued together.

If Canyot came!

On Canyot's appearance, with the message he brought, everything in the world at that moment seemed to depend.

'Nelly, my darling!' These words seemed to the man who uttered them aloud into the wind and rain, to issue from some other being than himself – some stronger, braver, nobler being at whose imperious bidding the shivering exhausted wretch who called himself Richard was now compelled to act.

He bent down, and after two or three hopeless struggles he succeeded in getting the sheep upon his back, its belly round his neck and its feet held tightly in both his hands.

Burdened thus, and swaying under the creature's weight, he staggered down the slope in the direction in which he supposed the hawthorn hedge to lie.

As he went, with the rain whirling round him as if the darkness itself were one great river of water, all manner of strange ideas passed through his mind. It seemed to him as though he were carrying on his back the burden of his great unfinished poem, the poem which he had so often changed in character – and which had now taken the form of a sheep!

Then it seemed to him as if he were arguing with Nelly's father about the existence of God. It seemed as though God too, like his poetry, had turned into a heavy woolly sheep that bleated pitifully into his ear.

Then he suddenly, thought of Karmakoff the Russian; and he imagined himself putting the question to him as to whether they would have slaughter houses in an ideal state!

And he thought of Elise dancing, dancing on the edge of a great grey sea swept by hurricanes of rain . . .

He knew he must be getting near the hedge, because of the feel of ploughed-up land under his feet. It was just then that he stumbled and bent low under the weight he carried and something seemed to snap in his heart.

After that he saw nothing at all – nothing but darkness, dense black rainy darkness, that seemed full of bleating cries, cries, that called upon him for help.

'All right! It's all right!' Was it he who uttered those words?

Something pricked his face. The hedge! The hedge!

He stumbled to the ground beneath its shelter, and fell heavily down with the animal above him.

The next thing he was conscious of was the sensation of something burning being poured down his throat and of a swinging lantern. With one last desperate effort he forced his eyelids to open against a weight like lead.

'I – can't – get – my breath,' he gasped. 'Does she forgive me?'

'She loves you,' said Robert Canyot.

The look of unutterable happiness that spread over Richard's face, as the lantern flickered upon it, remained to the end of the painter's life the best return he ever obtained for a love that had learned to be unpossessive.

The head of the dead man fell back upon the living body of the sheep. And so it was that the moment most unalloyed by critical self-consciousness in all the experience of the author of the Life of Verlaine was that moment which, in human speech, it is the custom to refer to as his last.

Canyot, using his one arm with well-calculated effect, lifted the man and the sheep upon the cart he had brought from Furze Lodge. The weight of both the living and the dead was heavy upon him as he drove towards Littlegate through the darkness. *She killed him because she loved him*, he thought. *Well! She will have his child; and I shall have – my work!*